T0009583

The
Very
Nice
Box

A NOVEL

LAURA
BLACKETT

EVE
GLEICHMAN

PRAISE FOR *THE VERY NICE BOX*

"Laura Blackett and Eve Gleichman are linguistic magicians, and their sparkling debut [is] a mirrored fun house, one that leads us down different paths, each masterfully tied up at the end, yet reflecting and refracting our own quirky selves. [T]raditional office fiction has been ripped from its white-collar, white-man origins and refashioned into language-twisting, genre-bending, electrifying art."

—*New York Times Book Review*

"Rather than boxing in queerness, the authors suggest queerness as a lens for seeing, reading, and, arguably, for their own storytelling, which refuses trite or stereotypical generic moments. The story charms, it entices, and it keeps the reader in their hands, wanting more."

—*Los Angeles Review of Books*

"A very funny debut—and perhaps the most original office satire of the year. . . . There's no way to put *The Very Nice Box* into, well, a box. It's a parody that feels like an extended inside joke; it's a thriller, a romance, and a quirky coming-of-age saga. . . . Plus, who can resist a novel that takes down an entitled man-child in absurdly grand fashion? Very Nice, indeed."   —Angela Haupt, *Washington Post*

"Darkly funny, thought-provoking, and twisty."

—Shondaland, Five Best Books of July

"*The Very Nice Box* is highly readable, full of twists and irony—inspiring deep belly-laughs with every sentence."

—Vanessa Chan, *BOMB*

"In this bitingly funny thriller, a heartbroken woman takes a chance on love and gets more than she bargained for. . . . This debut novel takes on hipster corporate culture with biting wit while also balancing breezy romance and pulse-pounding suspense. *The Very Nice Box* will have you laughing and nodding along right up to the final shocking twist."   —Apple Books, Best Books of July

"[The] book's uncanny nature is what makes it so damn smart and also more than a little terrifying. . . . A literary accomplishment that some might call genre-bending, but I'm choosing to simply call it fantastic engineering."   —Nylah Burton, Bitch Media

"A dazzling and hilarious debut seeped in the ills of corporate culture and male entitlement . . . *The Very Nice Box* offers a little bit for everyone—blending rom-com, satire, and thriller. . . . Witty and sharp."   —Catapult.com

"A quirky, deeply satisfying, whip-smart debut that critiques corporate culture and male entitlement while also offering a heartfelt look at how to work through grief. Meticulously constructed and truly original—I inhaled it."   —Jami Attenberg, author of *All This Could Be Yours*

"Wonderfully compelling. It's a very fun read, but it's also a timely one: How does toxic masculinity in corporate culture restructure and rebrand itself in order to appear innocuous? . . . Blackett and Gleichman have created something stellar here."
                                          —Kristen Arnett, author of *With Teeth*

"A literary page-turner that is full of heart and scathing social critique, not to mention a surprise ending to rival those of my favorite mysteries. I absolutely devoured it."   —Melissa Febos, author of *Girlhood*

"A satire of contemporary corporate culture. An exploration of how vulnerable we become in grief. A surprising romance. A cautionary tale. Somehow *The Very Nice Box* manages to be all of the above. . . . This is a delightful and propulsive read."
                                          —Helen Phillips, author of *The Need*

"Exceptional. . . . A deftly packaged story that hinges on the way we organize our days, our work, and our love. I relished living in its perfect compartments."   —Hilary Leichter, author of *Temporary*

"[A] sharp page-turner . . . with a heroine whose affecting quirks lend heart and consequence to the headlong plot."
                                          —Emily Gould, author of *Perfect Tunes*

THE VERY NICE BOX

Laura Blackett & Eve Gleichman

HARPER ● PERENNIAL

NEW YORK ● LONDON ● TORONTO ● SYDNEY ● NEW DELHI ● AUCKLAND

For our very nice families

HARPER ● PERENNIAL

A hardcover edition of this book was published in 2021 by Houghton Mifflin Harcourt Publishing Company.

THE VERY NICE BOX. Copyright © 2021 by Laura Blackett and Eve Gleichman. All rights reserved. Printed in the United States of America. No part of this book may be used or reproduced in any manner whatsoever without written permission except in the case of brief quotations embodied in critical articles and reviews. For information address HarperCollins Publishers, 195 Broadway, New York, NY 10007.

HarperCollins books may be purchased for educational, business, or sales promotional use. For information please email the Special Markets Department at SPsales@harpercollins.com.

FIRST HARPER PERENNIAL EDITION PUBLISHED 2022.

Library of Congress Cataloging-in-Publication Data
Names: Blackett, Laura, author. | Gleichman, Eve, author.
Title: The very nice box / Laura Blackett & Eve Gleichman.
Identifiers: LCCN 2020044794 (print) | LCCN 2020044795 (ebook) |
ISBN 9780358697503 (paperback) | ISBN 9780358540229 (ebook) |
ISBN 9780358573814 (audio) | ISBN 9780358573784 (cd)
Subjects: GSAFD: Humorous fiction. | Suspense fiction.
Classification: LCC PS3602.L3252944 V47 2021 (print) |
LCC PS3602.L3252944 (ebook) | DDC 813/.6—dc23
LC record available at https://lccn.loc.gov/2020044794
LC ebook record available at https://lccn.loc.gov/2020044795

Book designed by Emily Snyder

22 23 24 25 26   LSC   10 9 8 7 6 5 4 3 2 1

About the Authors

Laura Blackett is a woodworker and writer based in Brooklyn.

Eve Gleichman's short stories have appeared in the *Kenyon Review*, *Harvard Review*, *BOMB Daily*, and elsewhere. Eve is a graduate of Brooklyn College's Fiction MFA Program and lives in Brooklyn.

PART ONE

EVEN IF SHE DIDN'T WORK AT STÄDA, AVA SIMON would have furnished her apartment with STÄDA products. They were functional, well-designed household items, free of unnecessary decorations and features. She owned two Simple Dinner Plates, two Pleasing Water Glasses, and two Comforting Mugs, which together fit perfectly on her Dependable Drying Rack, along with her Useful Forks, Spoons, and Knives.

Ava's full-sized Principled Bed was made of pine and supported a Comfortable Mattress, which had a firmness factor of 8 — exactly calibrated to her preference. On the other side of her studio was a Dreamy Dog Bed for her boxer mix, Brutus. She owned a Practical Sofa, an Embracing Armchair, and an Appealing Dining Table. In her closet hung seven long-sleeved shirts (three gray, two black, and two white), seven short-sleeved shirts, two pairs of pants (one denim, one cotton), two pairs of sneakers (identical, black), seven pairs of black socks, and seven pairs of black underwear. She had one lightweight jacket, one winter coat, and one rain jacket.

She liked to think of each day as a series of efficiently divided thirty-minute units. One unit for showering, dressing, and brushing her teeth. One unit for breakfast and coffee. One unit for walking Brutus along the perimeter of Fort Greene Park. One unit driving to the STÄDA offices in Red Hook.

Ava was an engineer for STÄDA's Storage team. She took care and satisfaction in her work, which she carried out on Floor 12 of STÄDA's Simple Tower. The Simple Tower was a neck-achingly tall architectural feat, made of glass and designed to concentrate and redirect all natural sunshine into the building, so that even overcast days supplied the Simple Tower with powerful, invigorating light. Its interior was expansive and elegant. Polished concrete floors and curved glass walls divided the workspaces from the meeting rooms. Common areas were outfitted with STÄDA's living room collection; Plush Sofas and Cozy Nesting Tables were arranged as if they were in the showroom. The three STÄDA kitchens—the Sweet Kitchen, the Salty Kitchen, and the Wellness Kitchen—were stocked with snacks, coffee, and Wellness Water, spring water infused with a rotating variety of citrus fruits. Small atriums punctuated the space, extending all the way to the roof.

Teams on Floor 12 worked together in pods, their long black desks positioned under dropped birch ceilings. Floor 12 was quiet aside from the soft clacking of keyboards. An outside observer would not suspect the constant current of online chatter happening over S-Chat, the company's in-house instant messenger. STÄDA employees organized chat rooms based on shared interests, and occasionally a handful of people sitting in different areas of the floor would abruptly erupt into laughter.

Ava, who engaged with S-Chat only when it was absolutely necessary, sat next to a window overlooking Red Hook's piers. Barges came and went from STÄDA's distribution center, a long commercial wharf with weathered brick and gigantic steel storm shutters. It extended out into the East River, reaching toward the Manhattan skyline. The wakes from the freight barges rolled up in perfect time, churning white against the limestone breakers. Ava considered this rhythm, the business of moving their products from conception out into the world, to be STÄDA's heartbeat.

This week Ava had begun mocking up the lid hardware for the Very Nice Box, a simple but smart design that she hoped would be introduced in the coming year. The Very Nice Box was her Passion Project. It was exactly the kind of work she had come to STÄDA to do: meticulous engineering without frills or gimmicks, just the ideal intersection of geometry and utility, where each component existed for a reason. If all went to plan, the Very Nice Box would be followed by a series of shelves and hanging rails that could be configured in endless arrangements. But its most basic unit, the foundation upon which the entire strategy for the year rested, comprised six large uniform sides assembled with pegs and hinges. Ava was determined to make it perfect. It would take her 150 units to create renderings for the hinges alone, she estimated as she floated upward in STÄDA's giant glass-backed elevator after an Outdoors Break.

The doors opened to Floor 12, where Jaime Rojas, a junior engineer, waited by the hand sanitizers with a stack of hinge sketches. "There you are!" he said, handing them to her. He wore a floral shirt buttoned to his throat. Ava admired Jaime's maximalist spin on the STÄDA brand. His aesthetic was both complex and tidy: tucked-in shirts with bright, busy patterns, clean, short fingernails. A natural streak of white ran through one side of his otherwise dark, carefully combed hair. Jaime was not new to STÄDA, but he was new to Ava's team. His specialty was gadgets, watches, small lamps, and clocks, but he had never complained about being relegated to Storage. Originally from El Paso, Jaime had moved to the city to attend NYU. He'd started working at STÄDA as a Customer Bliss associate after a string of service industry jobs, which he liked to joke was the natural next step for him as a comparative literature major. Ava considered Jaime a friend—her only friend—and she quietly appreciated his commitment to their standing Monday lunch.

Lunch at STÄDA was free and catered on a rotating basis by nearby restaurants. The restaurant changed every quarter based on a popular vote. But long lunch lines—or, more precisely, the company's failure to implement an effective design solution to solve the line problem—deterred Ava. So she prepared her own lunches, which were simple and vegetarian—equal parts protein, fat, and carbohydrates—and divided into three compartments in her Sensible Bento Box, which was one of her most enduring designs. She didn't vote for a restaurant, and no one tried to lobby her.

Jaime walked alongside Ava as she made her way to her desk. "Maybe we can discuss those hinges after the conference room thing?"

"The conference room thing," Ava repeated. "I almost forgot about that. What are they making us do this time?"

"No clue," Jaime said. "Maybe they're announcing the arrival of the Gay Tree."

Ava shuddered. STÄDA's new Spirit team—part of the recent corporate expansion—had just erected a tall paper tree with rainbow-colored leaves made from tissue paper. The design was terrible. The word PRIDE had been traced in black marker on the trunk. Ava knew that as queer employees, she and Jaime were supposed to appreciate the gesture. She had even received an email from a junior Spirit staffer asking for her feedback on the tree. But the tree hurt her eyes and its leaves crinkled noisily whenever anyone walked by it, so the only thing it did was provide an aesthetically offensive distraction from her work.

Ava sighed. "How do they expect us to do our jobs with mandatory orientations happening all the time?"

"Don't ask me," Jaime said. "I'm just the messenger."

A reminder email about the conference room event waited, unopened, in Ava's inbox. The subject line was a smiley face. The Spirit team hadn't even booked an end time. Whatever this was, Ava dreaded it. The meeting or training or experimental team-building activity would come barreling through her well-organized Friday, she would be pressured to eat something sugary at a strange time of day, and she would have to interact with her colleagues, most of whom she didn't know.

That was also by design. She had worked hard to strike a balance between pleasant and unapproachable without appearing totally joyless like Judith Ball from the People Office did. Judith Ball's title had recently been rebranded to chief people officer. She had the warmth of disinfectant spray. She was older than most at STÄDA and was one of the company's founding members, which meant that along with overseeing hiring and workplace policies, she had a seat on STÄDA's board, where she was the only Black member and only woman.

Judith would often remark that she never understood why the workplace had become so casual. With more and more employees showing up in designer flip-flops and hoodies, she loved to remind them that she could remember a time when people dressed up to travel. "One must dress for success," she would say matter-of-factly. She wore a self-assigned work uniform: a cream-colored top tucked into a skirt suit, low-heeled pumps, and a string of pearls, her hair pulled into a neat bun. She sent frequent memos about Boundless Vacation Days, Suggested Attire, and the proper protocol for leaving for an Unlimited Outdoors Break. (*Feel free to take Unlimited Outdoors Breaks,* she had written in a recent email, *but do remember to notify your manager on S-Chat and include me on the exchange.*) Judith had no apparent interests outside of obstructing everyone's fun.

Am I like that? Ava would sometimes wonder.

But no. Unlike Judith, Ava had no interest in keeping tabs on her colleagues' Boundless Vacation Days or Unlimited Outdoors Breaks. So instead of being resented, Ava was simply ignored, which was for the best. She didn't invite interactions. She didn't ask anyone about their weekends, and she didn't particularly like it when anyone asked about hers. Her answer never changed, because her weekends, like her weekdays, were beautifully organized, uniform, and solitary. When she described them, whoever was listening would glaze over. Eventually her colleagues left her to do what she did best, which was to create useful household boxes from the six essential STÄDA materials: wood, metal, MDF, plastic, linen, and pulp board.

But a new employee had arrived at the Simple Tower and appeared to be disrupting this social contract. According to what Ava had overheard the day before in the Wellness Kitchen, he was fresh out of grad school, having earned some sort of double degree that Ava couldn't bring herself to care about, and would be settling into STÄDA's Marketing Department that week.

His name was Mathew Putnam, and he had gripped the attention of Floor 12, not because of his fancy degree, Ava suspected, but because he was categorically handsome. According to his STÄDA employee photo, which had been circulating around the S-Chat backchannels, he looked young—younger than Ava, who was thirty-one. Today she had noticed fever-ish typing when he showed up for a tour of Floor 12. S-Chat notifications dinged with higher frequency. Workers across all teams arranged their hair differently. Several men spoke more loudly. Even Jaime had messaged her on S-Chat: *Um . . . it appears that a literal Adonis will be working here.*

Ava saw that Mathew Putnam was making his way in her general direction, and she braced herself. A young Spirit staffer was delighting in bringing him around to every desk, as if they were the bride and groom at a wedding reception. She watched as Mathew greeted her colleagues as though he'd known them since childhood and was now enjoying a much-awaited re-union. His charisma was palpable. Around him, her colleagues smiled and laughed more. Eventually the pair made their way to Ava's desk. She busied herself with Jaime's hinge sketches for the Very Nice Box, slipped on her Peaceful Headphones, and tuned in to her favorite podcast, *Thirty-Minute Machine*, hop-ing that her focus would drive them away.

"Mat Putnam," he said, sticking out his hand. "It's awe-some to finally meet you." His voice cut through Ava's Peaceful Headphones. She pulled them off and quickly shook his hand, which was large and warm. He clearly had not yet learned the unofficial STÄDA greeting, which was simply a hand raised, shoulder-level, as though an oath were being taken. This was to prevent unwanted touch and the spread of flus and colds.

"The badass box boss, Lexi tells me." Mat smiled at Ava eagerly, then turned to the Spirit staffer, who blushed violently at the mention of her name.

Ava looked up at him. He had a puppyish energy that alarmed her. He was extraordinarily tall, with a well-structured jaw, a clean-shaven face, and a prominent Adam's apple. He wore heeled leather boots, dark-wash jeans, and a thick white T-shirt whose sleeves hugged his biceps. He was the type of man who could accidentally drop a baby and immediately be forgiven.

"Excited for the big bash?" he said, drumming his fingers on her desk.

"No," Ava said. "It's a party?" She'd been trying to ignore the steady line of people making their way into the conference room.

"Come on!" Mat said. "I looked in the Imagination Room and I can report that there are streamers. And a gluten-free cake! It'll be great."

"The Imagination Room?"

"Oh, sorry," Mat said. "You probably knew it as the conference room."

Ava adjusted a framed photo of Brutus on her desk. She had only one photo of her dog, so as not to appear to be singularly obsessed with him, or lonely. "I disagree that it will be great," she said.

"Well, I'm going to be there, and you're going to be there, and cake will be there," Mat said. "And Lexi will be there!" He beamed at Lexi, who beamed back at him. "So it's guaranteed to be great."

His smile had fallen, and Ava felt responsible. But she had wanted at least the details of this office "bash" ahead of time so she could know how much time it would take up and whether she would be home to Brutus later than usual. She had sent an email to this effect to the Spirit team, whose rep simply responded, *Where's the fire you little work horse . . . !* She'd hated this email because it hadn't answered her question, because the rep had mixed metaphors, because the punctuation was chaotic, and because *workhorse* was one word.

Mat patted down the hair on the back of his head. "There's something I should probably tell you," he said. "Lexi, go ahead."

Ava glanced around the room in case he was talking to

THE VERY NICE BOX

someone else. There were, after all, at least two dozen other senior engineers across the floor. Lexi headed toward the conference room, running a hand through her long hair. What could Mat Putnam possibly have to tell Ava? He had just learned her name. She felt his attention on her, and wondered if he expected her to speak.

To her relief, he broke the silence. "It's about a shift in STÄDA's marketing plan for Q4—"

"Marketing? I'm an engineer," Ava said. "So whatever it is probably doesn't concern me." She didn't want to hear about his marketing plan for Q4. She was sure he would discuss it with unnecessary flare. Marketing reps always took too long to make their point, and she couldn't lose any more time to this conversation. She had one more hinge sketch to consider. It would take four units, exactly the amount of time left in her workday. Now she would have to bump that work to Monday and recalibrate the entire week. She sighed and looked at her Precise Wristwatch. "Let's get whatever this is over with."

Mat's smile faltered. "Awesome," he said.

Ava stood.

Inbox zero. Tightening a bolt. Folding a shirt. Sweeping a floor. Tracing a circle. These were the things that soothed her. She thought about each of them as Mat Putnam swung open the door to what was now, she would have to accept, the Imagination Room.

2

SINCE STÄDA'S EXPANSION, AVA HADN'T SEEN much of her boss, Karl. But now here he was in the conference room, setting out wedges of cake and Useful Utensils. The last few years had worked on his appearance. When he'd recruited her, many years before, when the company was made of a half-dozen woodworkers, Karl had been strapping and bright-eyed. Now his tall, thin frame slumped. His shoulders were rounded, and his mop of blond hair had begun to thin.

Behind him, the word IMAGINE was projected onto the wall in STÄDA's signature sans serif font, the letters dissipating and gathering again in a flashy loop of transition effects. Ava wasn't surprised that she hadn't noticed this particular addition until now; the rebranding of the company was occurring constantly, all around her, at a dizzying speed. She would be unfazed to return to her desk to find that her Encouraging Desk Chair had been replaced with a large rubber ball.

Ava liked Karl. He wasn't shy, but he was quiet. His voice

was flat and gentle, and higher than one might expect from a man of his height. When he spoke in front of an audience, his calm energy blanketed the room. His public speaking style was the opposite of what STÄDA's Powerful Presentation Training recommended now, which was to strive for the vocal equivalent of light pyrotechnics, but Ava found him incredibly pleasing to listen to. This was in part because of his dry humor, which he served with a tight, playful smile, and in part because his Nordic accent placed emphasis on unexpected syllables, building a cadence that was quietly riveting.

He stood at the head of the room as Ava's colleagues—there were dozens now—milled around the edges. The walls were flanked with half-erased notes from the Manager Training that had taken place before the party.

KEY TAKEAWAYS
Be aware of Defensive Pessimism.
Climb the Ladder of Perception.
Practice Radical Compassion.

Am I in a cult? Ava wondered vaguely. She had been through a few of these trainings herself over the past several months. They were part of STÄDA's expansion, and although they weren't required, she wondered whether her attendance—or lack of attendance—was noticed. Once, after dodging three consecutive Self-Care Seminars, she had been notified by an email from Spirit that she was "missed," and she was provided with a link to view the workshops virtually.

The Personality Test—a daylong workshop to determine your leadership color—was especially popular. It was STÄDA's version of the Myers-Briggs test. You could be assigned red, yellow, green, or blue based on whether you were naturally direct, outgoing, empathetic, or analytical. Ava's colleagues had been excited to find out their colors. Some employees included their color in their email signatures. Others bought color-coded knickknacks for their desks, or wore clothing and accessories that corresponded to their colors. Floor 7 had been recently converted to the Swag Lounge, where a limitless variety of colorwear was available.

Ava had taken the test at the request of the Spirit team, after avoiding it for months. The questions had been bewildering, but the result was predictable: blue. Analytical. She could have told anyone that, without a test. But she wondered if an earlier version of herself might have been assigned green—empathetic—and part of her was disappointed by the result. The results packet she received after taking the test included a series of backhanded compliments: *You compensate for your social deficit by demonstrating a raw talent with numbers. Although your colleagues do not enjoy your company, they trust your work. Your time-management skills surpass, and therefore irritate, those around you.*

If there was one thing Ava liked about the Personality Test, it was that it made small talk easier. She understood that every conversation was a different configuration of the same components. The Personality Test made it easier to find common ground, and in turn allowed her to make jokes when one would otherwise be difficult to muster. Some mornings in the Wellness Kitchen she could get away with simply saying, "Oh, I can see your red is showing," as someone reached for the coffee first.

Karl tapped the side of his Festive Plastic Plate with a Useful Fork. "All right, everyone, if I could have your attention." The din settled and everyone turned to face him. For a moment he didn't appear to have anything else to say, and Ava felt a light panic on his behalf. "We're here in part," he continued, "to celebrate Ava Simon. It's her ten-year anniversary today with STÄDA. Ava, please join me."

A man from the Spirit team hit a button and a blast of electronic music erupted from the room's speakers. Ava's stomach was a hard pit. She tried to make herself small. She hadn't realized it was the exact date of her ten-year anniversary at STÄDA. Maybe if she didn't look up at Karl—at anyone—this could be over quickly. But no. She could not disappear. She walked to the front of the room, awkwardly maneuvering around the Sturdy Tables while the music blasted. She stood next to Karl and faced her colleagues with a closed smile. She thought of a screwdriver fitting into the head of a screw and slowly turning.

The Spirit staffer fumbled with the button and the music stopped. Karl leaned in to whisper to her. "I dislike this sort of thing too. It will be over shortly." He shifted on his feet and cleared his throat. Judith Ball was standing in the back of the room with her head tilted to one side, as though she were considering a painting. "Ava and I have worked together for ten years," Karl said. "This company wouldn't be the same without Ava's contributions. She's consistent and thorough and has worked tirelessly to design some of STÄDA's most popular household boxes to date, including, but not limited to, the Singular Shoe Box, the Genuine Storage Box, the Delightful Storage Box, the Purposeful Loose Ends Box, the Sensible Bento Box, and the Memorable Archives Box."

Had Karl's voice cracked at the word *tirelessly*? Ava was moved. *Consistent*, she thought, and *thorough*. These were some of the highest compliments her work could receive. Her colleagues clapped halfheartedly, hand to wrist, still holding their Festive Plastic Plates, and Ava made her way to the back corner of the room, her face hot from the unexpected attention.

"At the same time," Karl continued, "we are happy to boast our strongest ever Marketing team in STÄDA's history. I don't think we need the assistance of any charts to know how well

STÄDA has performed these last eight quarters, thanks to our friends in Marketing." There was a louder burst of applause this time, mostly from the corner where the STÄDA Marketing team stood, many of them wearing red (direct) and yellow (outgoing) clothing and accessories—bracelets, T-shirts, wristbands, and headbands. "I can feel that STÄDA is growing stronger, and I believe that morale will only continue to soar," Karl said, his voice straining. Ava wondered if he believed what he said. She could recall the era when STÄDA offered only tables, boxes, and clocks and took up only a quarter of a floor. "That is," he continued, his tone more lighthearted, "as long as the Red Hook Vandals retire their efforts."

There were a few polite chuckles. The Red Hook Vandals were a recent nuisance to the company. STÄDA was preparing to build a second tower—the Vision Tower—which would house all of Marketing, over an adjacent lot. To develop the property, STÄDA had ordered the demolition of a community garden along the south side of the lot, and the early construction had angered a small but vocal group of young activists. Executives at STÄDA had begun calling them the Vandals because of their clever small-scale actions to disrupt the Vision Tower's construction. They'd begun by protesting with signs, but that had garnered little press, so they had moved on to more retaliatory stunts. The backlash had escalated over the past several months, but it had had little effect on the construction timeline. Response to the escalating tension was polarized within the small group that discussed it in the Security and Corporate Social Responsibility S-Chatrooms. Some were sympathetic to their cause, others felt concerned and unsafe, but to the majority of the office, including Ava, the Vandals' presence was felt only to the extent that they occasionally provided new fodder for small talk.

"And so," Karl continued, "given our fantastic standing, I

would like to announce my retirement from my position as head of product."

Ava's heart skipped. She wondered if she had misheard him. The room had become quiet. Karl cleared his throat. "STÄDA has never been in a better position," he said. "We have become a household name. Never in my wildest dreams did I imagine this for my small furniture company ten years ago." He clasped his hands in front of him and smiled politely. Ava could sense the restrained emotion behind this gesture. "I'll be happy to spend time with my wife and my beautiful Siamese cat, Leonard. He is a retired show cat. We will be living in Hudson, building chairs from wood. That is my passion."

Ava saw a few Marketing staffers exchange glances.

"I'm also happy to announce," Karl said, "that Mathew Putnam, who graduated at the top of his MBA class at the Wharton School, has relocated from Philadelphia to take over my role of STÄDA's head of product. Marketing, Engineering, Spirit, and Technical will now be reporting to Mr. Putnam, who will now share a few words about this reorganization." Karl paused for a moment. "Thank you," he said.

The room buzzed with confusion. Ava glanced around the room and saw a look of bewilderment on Jaime's face. Mat made his way to the front of the room. "We are so excited about this," he announced over the murmuring. He clapped his hands together.

We? Ava thought.

"It's my honest belief," Mat said, "that our home goods can only be as powerful as our hearts and minds. The way we feel at work affects the products we make and the message we send to customers about STÄDA. I see myself as the guardian of this profoundly delicate flywheel of mind and matter, and you can expect to see a lot more positive changes around the office that I hope will help us bring our whole hearts to work. There is so much opportunity to help the STÄDA family get the most value out of what we offer. I can't wait to report back on Engineering's and Marketing's next big campaigns."

Engineers didn't *have* big campaigns, Ava thought. Her team designed products, then built them, then tested them, then rebuilt them, then explained how to assemble them. That was it. They had no dealings whatsoever with Marketing. And now she'd have to work with Mat. No — *for* him. They would have to make presentations together. For a terrible moment she allowed herself to contemplate the slideshow transition effects he would try to use.

"I have a question," someone called out. It was Owen Lloyd, a relatively new addition to the Marketing team. He had transferred from Float-Home, the vacation rental app. Ava knew this because he was the loudest person on Floor 12. He typed loudly, spoke loudly, walked loudly, made coffee loudly, and demonstrated that there was a loud way to open a refrigerator. He was dressed in a tight yellow polo tucked into blue jeans. "So we really leaned into positive psychology at my last job, at Float-Home. I don't know if anyone else here knows what I'm talking about," he said, glancing around, "but like ... it's such an awesome philosophy." His ears had turned red. "So my question is ... well, I heard a rumor you would be bringing Positivity Mandates to STÄDA, and I wondered if that's true."

"Absolutely, absolutely, one thousand percent," Mat said. "Thanks for asking, man. Going forward, STÄDA will be a solutions-based company."

Applause erupted around Ava, startling her. Were her colleagues this desperate for a more positive work environment? Many of the people applauding were engineers. It was their *job* to detect and call out problems with products.

"And actually, just to piggyback off that a minute," Mat said, "can you say your name for everyone?"

"Owen Lloyd!" Owen said too loudly, glowing from the success of his question.

"Well, Owen, good news in the Positivity Mandate department. Starting today, STÄDA will be partnering with SHRNK, an awesome text-therapy app. Everyone's subscriptions will be covered by STÄDA and you will never, ever have to put your mental health on hold. Execs at STÄDA know as well as the rest of you how difficult life can be. Now you can bring your problems to your SHRNK so you can bring your positivity to STÄDA."

Another eruption of applause. The Spirit staffer handling the audio pumped his fist, as though Mat had just dunked a basketball. Then he hit a button and the music blasted. Ava had seen subway ads for SHRNK. They featured a muscular man in a white T-shirt sitting in a mid-century armchair and looking solemnly at the camera. *Got help?* was the slogan. Ava wasn't sure whether the man in the ad was supposed to be the therapist or the patient.

"As a matter of fact," Mat said, pacing now, "wellness will no longer be just a suggestion. Our friends in Spirit believe, as I do, that everyone has a right to their best self, and in fact we demand it. So whether it's a SHRNK membership or a Self-Care workshop, your participation will be noted and included in your annual review."

Ava's breath felt shallow. She was reminded of the time she had inadvertently walked into a Self-Care workshop in which participants were instructed to force a laugh every five minutes.

"I think I've given you all more than enough to absorb for today," Mat said. "So what I'll ask everyone to do now is put your hands in," he said, demonstrating with one of his hands. He wore a rubber yellow bracelet around his wrist, which Ava had first interpreted as some sort of sports accessory and now realized was a personality bracelet; it matched that of several others in the room. Many of Ava's colleagues stepped forward, throwing their hands into a pile. "Yep," Mat said. "All of you in the back too." It was physically impossible to get all hands in, Ava noted, and she watched as her colleagues standing at the edges of the room simply jutted their hands forward in front of them, vague smiles on their faces. Ava looked around for Jaime, who stood with his arms crossed, looking as if he were watching a live dissection.

"Awesome, awesome," Mat said. "On three, I want to hear *absolutely!*"

He counted to three. It was a clunky word to demand everyone shout together, but her colleagues did so with giddy excitement, then broke apart into many small, happy clusters.

Ava tried to squeeze her way to the exit, but she bumped into Jaime.

"Sorry, Ava," Jaime said. He bent to pick up her Decent Notebook.

"Thanks," she said.

"Trying to get outta here?"

"Yes."

"Me too," Jaime said. "That guy is one thousand percent the *worst.*"

"You think so too? Did you have any idea that Karl—"

"No," Jaime said. "I thought maybe you knew. I mean, what even *is* STÄDA without Karl? Who am I without Karl?"

"Was he joking about that therapy app?" Panic thrummed in Ava's chest. "It's absurd."

"I guess a text therapist is better than no therapist," Jaime said pointedly.

Ava wasn't currently seeing a therapist, and she struggled to avoid the implication. She pressed her lips into a tight smile and let a group of engineers from the Appliance team squeeze between them.

Mat had emerged from the knot of people and was now, to Ava's horror, making his way to her. "Hey, Ava!" he called over the noise.

"Yes," she said, looking at him suspiciously. "Hi."

Jaime waited a beat. "I'm Jaime," he said, raising his hand up. Mat high-fived him. "Hey, amigo!" he said.

Jaime opened his mouth to respond, but nothing came out.

"I'm sorry if this is a surprise," Mat said, turning to Ava. He was sincere. He gestured to say more, but he was approached by two women from the Marketing team who looked like they were going to ask him for an autograph. One woman wore a forest-green silk blouse. The other, who was dressed in a butter-yellow shirt and a checked mustard-yellow skirt, stood directly in front of Ava.

"I've read about how Positivity Mandates can completely transform an office!" she shouted at Mat over the commotion. "I'm totally on board!"

"Amazing!" Mat said. "We're going to level-up this company. Yellow fist-bump."

Ava watched the woman in the green silk shirt assume an expression of pure jealousy while Mat fist-bumped the woman in yellow, until Mat turned to her. "Mat Putnam," he said, sticking out his hand.

"I know!" the woman in green said. "I'm Kim."

Ava watched, perplexed. She desperately wanted to leave the room—to go back to her work, where her task for the afternoon was straightforward: to calculate the optimal hinge width for the Very Nice Box.

She saw that Karl was shaking hands with a pair of senior engineers. ". . . keeping up with the . . . well . . . times," she heard him say with a deflated smile.

Ava slipped out of the room and made her way back to her desk, where she tried to resume work as though nothing unusual had happened. She put on her Peaceful Headphones to block out the commotion spilling onto the floor. Her inbox was empty other than a survey email inviting her to rate the meeting and a notification that she had been preregistered and pre-approved for a SHRNK account. She moved both emails to her trash folder and tried to focus on the hinge mockups.

But she couldn't. She kept going back to Karl's announcement. *Very top of his class.* Who cared? Mat Putnam was a *child* compared to her colleagues. And now, suddenly, *she,* a senior engineer, was reporting to him?

There was no hope for productivity. She gathered her things and took the elevator to the parking lot. If anyone asked, she would say Brutus had a vet appointment.

"Hey!"

She spun around. It was—was she seeing this right?—Mat Putnam, jogging to catch up with her. She froze, watching him approach. "Hey," he panted, putting his hand on her car door, preventing her from opening it. "I'm sorry about that. I was really hoping we'd be able to powwow before Karl shared the news. I was able to debrief most of the engineers, but Storage was my last stop and I ran out of time."

Powwow, Ava thought. She looked at him flatly. "It's fine," she said. "Let's just sync up tomorrow. I have to get home for my dog."

Mat stood back from the car as she got in. "I promise I'm not some douchebag bro," he said, still out of breath. His voice carried through her closed window. She considered the total irony of the statement. A douchebag bro was exactly what he was.

"Okay," Ava said.

She turned the ignition, but the car wouldn't start. "Come on," she whispered, patting the wheel. "Come on." She hoped

Mat would be gone by the time she looked up, but he was still there, peering at her through her window.

"Not starting?"

She tried again, but this time her engine didn't even attempt to turn over.

Mat scratched the back of his head. "Do you think maybe it's the—" he called through the window.

"Engine," Ava said, her hands squarely on the wheel. She got out of the car. It had been her father's.

"Maybe it's an easy fix!"

"It's not," she said. Looking around the lot, she noticed that a handful of cars around hers had been keyed. She got out and inspected her own. "Look," she said, "my gas flap is dented. It was a Vandal."

"Damn," Mat said, "I'm sorry. I sort of thought Karl was joking about those guys."

"Why would he joke about something like that?"

"Look, I know it's weird that I'm, like, suddenly your boss—"

"It *is* weird," Ava agreed. "How old are you, even?"

"Twenty-six," Mat said.

"Oh my god."

"Can I at least give you a ride home? Where do you live?"

"That's okay," Ava said. "I'll call a Swyft."

"No, really," Mat said. "Where do you live?"

"Near Fort Greene Park."

"Near me!" Mat said. He was delighted by this, as though she'd told him their ancestors had come from the same small, obscure town. Ava considered his perfectly symmetrical face, his clear blue eyes, his lightly tousled hair.

"I'm in the new building on the southern tip of the park," he said.

She knew the building—it towered over all the others and caused a glare that made the dog park uninhabitable between the hours of three and four.

"Come on," he said cheerfully. "We can have a redo that way."

A ride home from Mat Putnam was the last thing Ava wanted, but she had no idea how to convey this to him. The two women from the party emerged from the Simple Tower and glanced their way before turning to each other and giggling. Were they laughing at Ava, or were they giddy simply from catching a glimpse of Mat? Or was it, Ava wondered, that they were laughing at the sight of someone like Ava with someone like Mat?

"Fine," Ava said. "I'll take the ride. Thank you." She could chalk it up to convenience, or a desire to be polite to her new boss. But there was something hiding behind those explanations that was less legible. She locked her car.

"Worried someone will drive away with it?" Mat said, smiling at her, but it was too soon for the joke. She pocketed her keys and followed him.

3

MAT HAD ALREADY BEGUN ANIMATEDLY DIS-
cussing his résumé and qualifications, his time at Wharton,
and what he kept referring to as the "beauty" of marketing. He
should pare down his words by at least half, Ava thought, as
they walked to his car. The sunlight reflected sharply off the
cars in the lot, forcing her to squint.

"Basically my degree is in marketing *and* design," he said.
"It's this cutting-edge dual thing that Wharton does. So I'm
decent at both things, kind of ambidextrous. Marketing really
is my jam, though. And when you bring marketing language
into technical writing? *That's* gold."

Ava couldn't disagree more. Marketing had nothing to do
with engineering or technical writing. STÄDA's new senior
leadership had begun demanding that she incorporate marketing language into their instruction manuals:

Simple
Modular

Beautiful

To say their products were simple or beautiful would be redundant at best. At worst, customers would be told how to feel about the product, which really wasn't her job.

She thought about arguing this point, but she knew that Mat's counterargument would aggravate her so much that it might keep her awake all night. "Interesting," she said instead.

"Right? Anyway, it's my pleasure to give you a ride, totally my pleasure," Mat said. He hit a button on his key ring and a small red sports car lit up and beeped. A miniature disco ball dangled from the rearview mirror and glinted in the afternoon light. It was easily the most impractical car in the lot. But then of course Ava's car was more impractical, because it didn't move.

She saw that his car was parked next to Karl's, in the VIP strip—confirmation that his new position at STÄDA had been quietly worked out in advance. As she made her way to the passenger's side, she was suddenly overcome by a familiar, terrible vertigo. It hadn't happened in years. She took a breath. First came the burned, sugary smell of toasted nuts. Her stomach bobbed into her throat, as though she were riding a too-fast elevator from the top of a tall building. Her head felt light and tingly. She had to close her eyes to keep her balance, and to force away the image of a searing white light. A chill spread along her arms and neck. Then a crunch, a shattering of glass, a bleating siren in the distance. She held a hand against Mat's car to steady herself.

"Ava?" Mat was saying. His voice had come into focus. "You okay? I know it's a mess, sorry about that." He was halfway inside the car, moving things to the backseat.

"No," she said. "I mean, yes. It's okay. I'll sit in the back." She felt the blood return to her ears and reached for the handle to the back door. But there was no back door—it was a coupe—

and the thought of squeezing herself past the tilted front seat made her feel ill. "Actually, I think I'll just rent one of those Quicky Cars. There are a couple docked in the STÄDA lot."

"Have you ever driven one of those before? They're like go-karts."

"No," she said. The Quicky Car was small and electric, billed as a safe alternative to the electric mopeds that had crowded the city.

"Come on. I'll drive you home. You don't need to feel bad about it."

"I don't feel *bad*," she said. "It's just—"

"I know, I know, you hate that I'm your boss. You're introverted, so you need time to process the news. Oh, and you think marketing's a big sham, so you pretty much hate me already."

"No I don't," she lied. She felt unsettled, being pegged so precisely.

He continued clearing the passenger seat: some sort of managerial textbook (*The Good Boss*), a half-drunk bottle of a neon-yellow sports drink, a dog leash, and a basketball, which he palmed with one enormous hand.

"You have a dog," Ava said. It was an observation she'd meant to keep in her head.

"The rumors are true," he said, sliding behind the wheel. He was so tall that his hair skimmed the roof of the car. *Why would such a tall man pick such a small car?* she wondered. He smiled at her and she felt a stab of regret for having been rude. She *didn't* want to work for him, she *did* feel that marketing was a sham, but she felt bad for making her feelings so obvious. And she liked him better for having a dog.

He patted the passenger seat. "Just relax," he said. "I'll get you home."

Ava found nothing less relaxing than someone telling her to

relax. And yet she could see that he was trying to be kind, trying to navigate her panic episode as best he could. She got in and entered her address into his phone's GPS while he started the car. A man's voice blasted through the car's speakers, startling Ava back into a panic: *As an example, a guy with a big salary, a conventional life, right, maybe a nice house, okay, a stable marriage and kids, that guy may feel little jolts of happiness, but at the end of the day he's going to still feel a certain empti—*

Mat spun down the volume knob. "Sorry about that," he said. "I guess now you know I'm an audiobook geek." He took a mint from the pocket of his door and offered her one.

"No, thank you," Ava said. She leaned her head against the cool window. Her panic had contorted itself into a dull, throbbing ache above her eyebrows. She held her hand there. Behind her closed eyelids she could still see the impression from the current of light. It was blinding. She tried to let go of it. "So," she said. "You were saying. Penn?"

"Right, right, Penn, and then the MBA at Wharton," Mat said, merging onto the expressway. "Like I was saying, it's a superlegit program, built around how to basically make engineering sexier via marketing language. Sounds counterintuitive, I know."

Ava kept her eyes closed and let him talk. It was easier that way. She felt the familiar turns to her apartment. She visualized a circle. She visualized a hex wrench fitting into a socket. He was now talking about his "MBA buddies."

"We had this dope startup idea," he said.

"What was it?" Ava said. She wanted him to continue to talk without her needing to contribute. His voice was deep and oddly soothing, and she was able to listen to him without actually absorbing any content.

"But in the end," he was saying, "it never really got off the ground."

"That's a shame," Ava said, staring out the window. She was almost home. She would make a simple dinner, prepare a lunch for the next day, and think about the hinges of the Very Nice Box, which is what she wished she had been doing instead of learning that she would be reporting for the foreseeable future to a marketing junkie.

He pulled up at her apartment. "This one?" he said. "Nice."

"Yes," she said. "It's okay. My rent is cheap." She rarely had reason to lie, but she didn't want him to ask her how she could afford to buy a studio apartment here.

"Really?" he said, craning to look. It was part of the reason she hadn't wanted him to drive her home. Now that he knew where she lived, he might be curious about her life. She didn't want him to be curious. She wanted him to mind his own business. He should drive himself home. He should congratulate himself for the act of kindness, have dinner, watch basketball, call an "MBA buddy," feel good about sliding into one of STÄDA's most powerful positions—and forget about her.

"Hope you feel better," he said. He put the car in Park.

"I feel fine," Ava said curtly.

"Oh," Mat said. "My mistake."

She unbuckled her seatbelt. Maybe she had misjudged him; he was genuinely hurt by her attitude, and now she felt the need to overcorrect. "Sorry," she said again. "It's been a confusing day. Maybe your dog—maybe he could meet my dog someday. Brutus is great with other dogs. And honestly, he could use a friend. What's his name?"

"Her. Emily."

"Emily," Ava said. "That's nice." She'd loosened up again at the mention of his dog. "Actually, you'll laugh at me, but—"

"What?" Mat said. He'd brightened up.

"All my stuffed animals growing up were named Emily," Ava said. "It's because my best friend in preschool was named

Emily, and I guess I sort of thought that all girls besides me were named Emily. Both my cats were named Emily too."

"Seriously?" he said.

"Yes." She looked at her Precise Wristwatch.

"How about tomorrow?" he said.

"Tomorrow?" She blinked at him.

"The dogs," Mat said. "Emily is boy-dog crazy. She already has a crush on Brutus and hasn't even met him."

She considered his eager expression. She could not deny the simple fact of his charm.

"Plus she's desperate for exercise," he said. "We haven't really made friends since we moved here, and back in Philly she used to get to run around with a pack of regulars a few times a week. She's taken her boredom out on all my shoes."

"Okay," Ava said, surprising herself.

"Ten a.m. it is," he said. "How do you like your coffee?"

"Milk, no sugar," she said. "Why?"

"Meet you at the dog-park entrance in"—he looked at his watch—"fifteen hours. I should grab your number." He handed Ava his phone.

Thirty units, Ava thought automatically as she added her number to his phone. As soon as he took it from her, she felt a sting of regret. "No, never mind," she said. "I just realized that I don't think I can." The plan had filled her suddenly with anxiety.

"What do you have going on?"

"Laundry," she said. "And dealing with my car."

"Laundry," he repeated. "Okay. Well, another time."

"I'm sorry," Ava said. "That wasn't very ... yellow of me." She sensed his disappointment and felt bad. "I can see you for a dog playdate if it's quick."

"Deal," Mat said. He stuck out his fist.

"No, thank you," Ava said, looking at his fist. "I'll see you at ten in the morning."

"Good," Mat said. "Because you definitely won't be seeing me at ten in the evening."

Ava flushed. She let the conversation wash over her as she made her way up the stairs to her apartment. Had she really agreed to see him—Mat Putnam—the next morning, on a Saturday? She checked her Precise Wristwatch. She was ten minutes late to see Brutus and heard nothing from the other side of the door. For a terrible moment she imagined him dead. But when she pushed the door open, she was happy to see that the ten minutes hadn't appeared to register with him at all. "Brutus," she said, rubbing his big square head. His tail thwacked against the wall. Through her windows, she watched Mat's car pull away with a loud hum.

Ordinarily Ava would have been preoccupied with the state of her car; she would have spent her evening arranging for a tow. But any worry about the car was eclipsed by a strange giddiness she felt about the plan that she had somehow, for reasons that were unclear to her, agreed to. She was going to see Mat Putnam in the morning, at ten o'clock. She was going to spend at least a unit, if not two, outside the office, with her new boss.

How long had it been since she'd made a plan outside of work? She didn't even see Jaime, outside their Monday lunches. As she poured two scoops of dry food into Brutus's Favorite Dog Bowl, she allowed herself to envision Mat's dog. She pictured a golden retriever. The sort of dog that was affable and attractive in equal measure.

Brutus licked his Favorite Dog Bowl clean and looked up at her.

"Do you want a friend?" Ava said to him, taking his Curious

Leash from a Supportive Door Hook and clicking it into his Curious Collar. He wagged his tail.

"Her name is Emily," Ava said.

Brutus cocked his head.

"What do you think, Brutus? What do you think?"

4

WHATEVER EXCITEMENT AVA HAD BEEN FEEL-
ing upon leaving Mat Putnam's car had curdled into dread by
the next morning. Ordinarily she could push bad feelings away
by busying herself with tasks divided evenly between units. But
there wasn't time for that now if she was going to meet him.

Her stomach dropped at the sight of Mat's name in her
inbox. But it was just an email from the day before, sent to
all STÄDA employees, reminding everyone to download the
SHRNK app. She put her Alert Percolator on and sat on the
edge of her Principled Bed, staring at the email on her phone.
Positivity begins with self-inquiry! Mat's email said. *Click here to
download the app. It's totally free!* She felt squeezed. She thought
of Jaime. *A text therapist is better than no therapist.* She pictured her annual review with Mat and Judith, when she would
have nothing to show for a commitment to her mental health.
All the options were grim. Attending a Self-Care workshop?
Viewing the workshop online and answering questions? She

would sooner lick a subway pole. At least SHRNK was private and on her own terms, with no face-to-face contact.

She clicked the link and allowed the app to download. *Hey, Ava,* it said. *You've got help.* The text brightened from gray to white. *We're matching you with the best possible therapist.* A soft gray screen appeared. *Thanks for holding tight, Ava. Do you feel better, knowing help is on the way?* A cursor blinked, inviting her response.

No, she wrote.

Thanks for your honesty, Ava. How old are you? Thirty-one.

Thanks, Ava. What city do you live in? Brooklyn.

That's awesome! How would you describe your gender? Cisgender woman.

Sexuality? She was presented with a drop-down menu. She had never been able to define her sexuality easily, and she knew even before tapping that the options here would not suffice. She had dated women mostly, but when people asked her how she identified, she felt that what they were really asking for was an approximation that wouldn't disrupt their understanding of sexuality. This annoyed her, because approximations were inherently imprecise. She chose *Prefer not to say* and moved on.

Do you frequently experience depression? No.

Major mood swings? No.

Are you pregnant? No.

Sexually active? Ava sighed. No.

Do you have experience with grief and loss?

Ava quickly closed the app and poured herself coffee. *It's a bot,* she reminded herself. *It's a bot.* She reopened it.

Welcome back, Ava. Do you have any experience with grief and loss? Yes.

Anxiety? Yes.

Panic episodes?

She looked at Brutus. She felt seen. Hesitantly she typed *sometimes,* then quickly moved on to a series of questions that seemed designed to make her feel more comfortable.

More of a dog or a cat person? Dog.

Woof! Do you like horror movies? No.

Feelings re: cilantro? Positive.

Favorite item you own? Precise Wristwatch.

"Come on," she said, tapping through them, glancing at the Tranquil Clock in her kitchen. There were dozens of questions.

Mountains or beaches? Mountains.

Pancakes or waffles? Neither.

Do you consider yourself an activist? Ava thought about the Vandals. She was sympathetic to their cause at a distance, but she couldn't let go of the fact that they had ruined her car. *No.*

A green thumb? No.

What's the last thing you did for fun? Watched Hotspot, she typed. *Hotspot* was a gay British dating show in which contestants chose a blind date based solely on their potential partner's phone settings. Ava allowed herself one unit every Sunday to indulge in it. She wasn't sure it counted as fun because she watched it alone, so she started to delete her response.

Looks like you're deleting something, SHRNK wrote. *In my experience, that means you're having complicated feelings about it. Since SHRNK is a text-based app and I can't observe your body language, I'd like to encourage you to share the thoughts you might otherwise shoo away. Go ahead, Ava, what were you saying?*

Hotspot.

Sounds fun! Do you enjoy order? Yes.

Do you like taking risks? No.

Favorite food? She thought of her father, mixing egg yolks and bacon into hot pasta. *Spaghetti carbonara.*

What's something you don't ordinarily tell people? Ava glanced around the room. Was this app serious? *N/A,* she wrote.

Finally a new screen. Black text on a white background: *Thanks, Ava, you're all set. Just lean back and relax. We've matched you with a certified SHRNK with years of experience. Go ahead and say hello.* The cursor blinked encouragingly.

Hello, Ava typed.

An ellipsis appeared instantly.

It's wonderful to be your SHRNK, Ava. How can I help? The text had appeared quickly, then vanished.

Are you a bot? Ava wrote.

No, the SHRNK responded. *I'm a real human psychotherapist.*

Ava wasn't sure whether this made her feel better or worse. She let her thumbs hover over the keyboard.

So what do I do now? she wrote.

You can ask or tell me anything that's bothering you.

And you just . . . what? Tell me how to fix it?

Let's try an example, if you'd like.

Ava looked at her Precise Wristwatch. Nine-seventeen.

I'm dreading a social appointment I made yesterday. I was excited about it at first, but now I want to cancel.

Good! Thank you for that vulnerability, Ava, her SHRNK wrote. *I see from your file that you have some social anxiety. You know, dread and excitement are two sides of the same coin.*

And? Ava wrote. This app appeared to be as useless as a fortune cookie. She suddenly didn't want her coffee.

Who could you be if you flipped the coin? her SHRNK wrote.

Ava didn't think it was possible to convert dread into excitement, just as she could not simply turn pulp board into wood, but she closed her eyes and tried to flip her coin anyway. After all, her cautious excitement had turned to dread while she had been asleep; maybe it could turn back. With difficulty, she tried to reverse the order of things and convince herself that what she was feeling was anxious anticipation. *I am anxiously anticipating this social event,* she thought. *I am excited. I am excited.*

Thanks, she wrote.

Thank yourself, her SHRNK wrote. *I'm proud of you, Ava.*

"Shut up," Ava said aloud, closing the app. She spent one unit showering and dressing, and then she allowed Brutus to tug her outside.

The smell of fallen wet leaves overwhelmed the street. She walked Brutus along the west side of the park, past the farmers' market stands, keeping far enough away from the entrance that Mat wouldn't spot her killing time. She kept a close eye on her Precise Wristwatch, and at 9:57 she made her way to the entrance, where she arrived at 10:00.

But Mat wasn't there. Brutus sat, looking up at her expectantly. Ten-oh-five. One-sixth of a unit late. As the minutes passed, Ava's breath thinned. Ten-fifteen. Had she completely misunderstood their plans? Had he meant 10 a.m. on Sunday? She checked her phone, but there was nothing. Her panic episode the day before had left her with such a throbbing headache, it was possible she had gotten the logistics wrong. But more likely, she knew, this had been a big misunderstanding. She was mortified by this possibility—that she had thought her new boss wanted to meet with her outside of work when he hadn't. Of course he had no reason to meet her, and she had no reason to meet him. She felt equal parts irritated and relieved, and started in the direction of her apartment. She would spend the four recovered units arranging for her car to be towed, doing laundry, and working on the Very Nice Box, and she would do her best to forget about the morning.

But just as she slipped into the comfort of this revised plan, she spotted him at a coffee stand. Her stomach turned over. She watched him pay for two coffees with a ten-dollar bill and wave away the change. He was taller than anyone around. He wore a flannel shirt the color of a fir tree, jeans that showed the elastic band of his boxers, and leather work boots. In one hand he balanced the two coffees, steadying them with his chin. With the other he struggled to control a leash that was connected to one of the ugliest dogs Ava had ever seen. She appeared to be a basset hound mix: low, squat, and long, with a bowed back like a cow. Her legs were so short that her ears nearly touched the ground.

Ava stood awkwardly as they approached—what was she supposed to do with her hands? Was she supposed to pretend not to see him until he got closer? "Hi," she said when he was close enough. "Oh, here, let me—"

Mat held out a coffee, but Ava reached for Emily's leash and instinctively reeled her in with three tight loops before offering it back.

"Thanks," he said, restacking the cups. "Trade you. Milk, no sugar."

He took the leash and she took a cup. It was warm against her palm. "You didn't have to get me a coffee," Ava said.

"No worries," he said.

"I wasn't worried," Ava said. "I just mean—"

"And good morning to you too, bud," he said to Brutus, holding his palm out. He was apparently not going to address being twenty minutes late to meet her. Was it possible he hadn't even realized? The thought baffled her. But then, he had spent some of that time getting them coffee. She negotiated all this silently, deciding whether or not to be annoyed.

The dogs cautiously sniffed each other in circles. For a moment Emily stood directly underneath Brutus.

"They look like Cozy Nesting Tables," Ava said.

"What?"

"Cozy Nesting Tables. They premiered last spring."

"Oh! Right. Yeah, totally!" Mat said, laughing.

"Sorry," Ava said, though she was quietly happy to have made him laugh. "My head is always at work." She stopped herself from describing in detail what made the tables so smart. They'd begun as a Table engineer's Passion Project and had become STÄDA's biggest bestseller. The Cozy Nesting Tables were featured on the sides of buses, in the subways, in the STÄDA ads that aired on podcasts, in the looping videos that played on the new jumbo screens near her desk. They had been featured at STÄDA's summer Solstice Party, which fell at the midpoint of the business year and celebrated the most successful design of the previous four quarters.

"All good," Mat said, patting down a cowlick on the back of his head. "I should be the one apologizing. I really gotta study the catalogue."

Ava quietly agreed. They sipped from their coffees and watched the dogs finish their elaborate greeting by bumping noses. "They're kinda cute, in a way," Mat said. "Though Emily is way out of Brutus's league. No offense or anything."

"Clearly," Ava said. Brutus was lean, sleek, and handsome. Emily was portly and squat, struggling to breathe normally. She strained against the leash, pulling Mat behind her until he lost his grip and she tore into the park, faster than Ava would have thought possible for a dog of her proportions.

"Shit," Mat said. "Goddammit. Emily!"

Brutus heeled tightly to Ava as she followed behind. "Good boy," she whispered. She closed the gate behind them—Mat had failed to secure it, despite the many posted signs—and Brutus sat, his tail wagging in the dirt. She unhooked his Curious Leash from his Curious Collar. "Go ahead," she said, patting his head, and he bolted into the park, making a wide loop around the other dogs.

Ava watched Mat go after Emily, somewhere between a jog

and a walk, shouting, "Hey, Emily! Come, Emily!" But she kept running until a short woman in leggings stepped on her leash. Mat caught up and unclipped it, slinging it over his shoulder.

The woman appeared annoyed until Mat began talking to her animatedly, at which point all was apparently forgiven; the woman was laughing with a hand cupped over her mouth. Ava rolled her eyes. She could see that he simply moved through life this way. She watched Mat hold Emily back by the collar, for no clear reason, then let her go. "Good girl," he called after her. "Good girl, Emily!"

It didn't surprise Ava that Mat had a disobedient dog. He would probably say that Emily wasn't "usually like this," blame her behavior on the new environment, or on Brutus. He jogged back to her. "You and Brutus put us to shame. We didn't make it too far in training. As you can see." His cheeks had turned bright red in the sharp air. He was sheepish but cheerful, and the combination was, Ava could admit, winning.

She followed him to a bench and they sipped their coffees, watching the dogs run laps. *Flip the coin,* she thought. The pack of dogs clustered and broke apart, renewing its momentum when a new dog entered or when one would parade around the enclosure with a stick. The motion was chaotic but familiar and calming. She loved to see Brutus at the center of it. At his age, he had the energy to play like this for only a few minutes at a time, but when he did, it reminded her of when he was a puppy.

"Dude can really move," Mat said. "How long have you had him?"

"We adopted him nine years ago."

"Who's we?"

"Oh." Ava felt like she had tripped over a root. "I adopted Brutus with someone." Her face became hot. She felt the bizarre caginess of the statement. "An ex," she said, and the sting of imprecision made her feel worse.

The day she and Andie had met Brutus, they had agreed that they would not leave the shelter with a dog—that they would just look, then go home, discuss the options, and make an informed decision. They were practical, careful people. It was what made them good engineers, and good partners. But they spotted Brutus in the back of the concrete cell, sitting quietly as the other dogs barked and crowded around the plastic gate, and a current of understanding ran through them. Andie squatted to Brutus's level. "Hey, little man," she said. Brutus cocked his head and slowly approached her, his tail wagging cautiously. "We're going to have to change his name," Andie said.

"Agreed," Ava said. "He's not a Pumpkin."

They buckled him into the backseat of Andie's station wagon, where he sat politely.

"Well, Brutey's a lucky dog to have gotten you in the breakup," Mat said. Ava could feel him looking at her, and she resisted an urge to correct him. She couldn't help but give in to the memory of those first few happy days with Brutus, who clambered over Andie, knocking her over with desperate, incessant licks. Ava's whole body ached at the memory. Her life with Andie rarely came up in conversation, and when it did, she could hardly push through the rest of the day. She looked down at the mulch, aware of Mat's attention on her. A silence wedged itself between them, and it was her fault. And so it was also her job now to repair the conversation, but she felt debilitated and thirsty.

"Emily!" Mat called. "C'mere!" Emily was barking at a skateboarder and clawing at the fence.

"Guess she's not hurting anyone," Mat said. The wind whipped his hair around. "She may not be the smartest dog, or the best-looking, but ... you never know what you're getting with rescues, I guess. And I love her."

Ava liked Mat more—slightly—both for changing the subject and for loving his ugly, badly behaved dog, who was now investigating a chicken bone. "You rescued her?"

"She was in really bad shape. Broken leg, broken ribs. She smelled like pee, and the shelter couldn't get the mats out of her hair so they had to shave her bald. If you think she's ugly now . . ."

"I didn't say she was ugly," Ava said. She suppressed a smile and sipped her coffee. Brutus returned to her feet, taking heavy breaths.

"Are you tired?" Ava said. "Are you hungry?" She was asking Brutus, but Mat responded.

"Sure, I'd be down to grab a bite," he said. "There's this café I just discovered around the corner, and we can sit outside with the dogs."

"No," Ava said instinctively. She needed to calculate how much time was left in her day and divide up her tasks accordingly. "I should go home," she said. "It's my car. I—"

"Oh, that's too bad. We haven't even gotten to your Passion Project," Mat said. "I've heard great things."

"You have?" Ava said. "No one ever asks me about it."

"That's why I want to hear about it!" Mat said. "I want to understand the Very Nice Box." He laughed, or coughed, as though remembering something funny. "Sorry," he said.

Ava recognized this halfway attempt to stifle a laugh and waited for Mat to explain to her that the Very Nice Box was a hilarious name.

"It's just . . . you *do* know what *box* means in certain contexts," Mat said. "Right?"

"Look," Ava said, coiling Brutus's leash, "my job is to make boxes. It's what I've always done, and probably what I will always do. If you would like to spend this conversation explaining to me that in certain company the word *box* can be a euphemism, let me know. I have plenty of ways to spend my Saturday."

"No, no!" Mat said, laughing. "I'm sorry! I'm sorry." He looked alarmed but entertained.

Ava looked at him. "You're finished?"

"I'm finished. I'm finished!" he said, holding up his hands. "I want to know everything there is to know about the Very Nice Box." He had managed to radiate genuine curiosity this time.

Ava studied his face. No one on Floor 12 had expressed interest in her Passion Project, which was fine, because it was in such early stages, and because their interest had no bearing on how good a product it was. But she was incredibly proud of the Very Nice Box, and not at all unhappy to discuss its many simple, elegant features. "I have some preliminary drawings I could show you," she said. "They're not 3D renderings yet or anything. Just drawings."

"I'd love to see them," Mat said. "Always good to involve Marketing, even in early stages." He waggled his eyebrows.

"I disagree," Ava said. "I—"

"I'm *joking*, Ava!" Mat said. "C'mon. I'm starving."

AVA RECOGNIZED THE CAFÉ MAT TOOK HER TO. It was called the Stoned Fruit and advertised CBD-infused cold brew and hemp milk. Small tables were in minor disarray, and Ava spotted a few of STÄDA's Nurturing Planters supporting viny, billowing plants over the counter. It smelled like toast. They claimed an empty table on the patio, under which both dogs started snoozing. Mat ordered himself a hemp-butter croissant and Ava ordered hemp-butter eggs and hemp-seed toast.

"Are these going to get me high?" Ava said, prodding the eggs with her fork.

"That would be amazing, but unfortunately, no," Mat said.

A low jazz melody made its way to the patio. Ava recognized it instantly, and a wave of nostalgia crashed over her. Her parents' jazz band used to cover it. "I love this song," she said.

"Yeah," Mat said, closing his eyes and frowning in appreciation. "Me too."

Her parents had both been exceptional musicians, and as a child she'd often woken to the sound of her mother playing the upright Steinway—by far the most valuable item in their old Tivoli farmhouse—in their living room. It had been passed down from her grandfather. Her eyes pricked at the memory. She cleared her throat and opened a folder on her phone that contained drawings for the Very Nice Box prototype. There was nothing like a box mockup to clear away unwanted feelings.

The Very Nice Box was a large, simple, and well-proportioned rectangular prism with an embedded closure. Nothing protruded from it. There was no overhang, no decoration, and nothing for the eye to snag on. Ava had spent dozens of units ensuring that its hardware and dimensions would enable it to rest on the floor or hang on the wall. One could stack any number of Very Nice Boxes while preserving the perfect proportions of a golden rectangle.

"So," she started, "the Very Nice Box is basically a box in its simplest form. One way to think about it—"

"Can I?" Mat said, taking her phone and zooming in on the photo of the drawing. "Okay, cool. So it looks somewhere between a chest and a cabinet."

"No, it's a *box*. It's a Very Nice Box that can be used in multiple ways. That's its beauty."

"So how do you plan to market it to customers? Because what a box is, when you really think about it, is a container, right, that can contain a whole bunch of—"

"Never mind," Ava said, taking her phone back and shoving it into her pocket. Was he explaining to *her* what a box was? The blood thrummed in her ears. "I need to get my car to the mechanic. You said this wasn't going to be a Marketing meeting."

"No!" Mat said. "I'm sorry. Let's start over. I promise I'll dial down the yellow. A box in its simplest form, you were saying."

Ava sighed. "It's incredibly simple and versatile. There are six sides. The long side will measure about sixty-six inches, which is five and a half feet. The short side will measure just over forty inches, which is about three and a half feet."

She watched Mat smile politely through her explanation. It wasn't the first time she'd been on the receiving end of this look. But he soon snapped out of his trance. "Is that . . . *Judith?*" he said.

"Judith who?" Ava looked up. She knew only one Judith. And Mat was right—the woman walking along the sidewalk in their direction *was* Judith Ball from People. She was barely recognizable out of context. She wore loose-fitting pants and had taken her hair out of its usual tight bun. In place of pearl studs she wore gold hoop earrings, and these, paired with her sunglasses, reminded Ava of the time she'd seen her math teacher at the grocery store. She carried two paper shopping bags filled with produce. Two girls walked beside her, one eating a cider doughnut and one engaged with her phone, clumsily dodging pedestrians.

"Pick your head up, Kendra," Judith said.

"Yeah, *Kendra*," the other one said. They were identical twins, and Ava recognized them from a photo in Judith's office. They were taller than Judith and gangly, and they both wore bright, oversized windbreakers covered in geometric shapes.

Kendra slipped her phone into her pocket and stole a bite of her sister's doughnut.

"Are you serious? That was a huge bite!"

"You didn't even buy it, Ari!"

"She makes an excellent point," Judith said.

Ari rolled her eyes and held out the doughnut, and Judith took a bite.

Ava stared dutifully at her menu, trying to achieve the forced body language of obliviousness until Judith and her daughters were a few yards away. When she looked up, she could have sworn she saw Kendra looking back at them. She shook the image out of her mind.

"So *that's* Judith on the weekend!" Mat whispered excitedly. "She looks way cooler."

"Shh," Ava said.

"What, are you embarrassed to be seen with me?" Mat said.

Ava *didn't* want to be seen with Mat, because of how it would read, the two of them having breakfast on a Saturday. How many warnings—via email, S-Chat, signage, and trainings—had every STÄDA employee received about appropriate office relationships? The last thing Ava needed was an individual lecture from Judith, who would see this breakfast as unprofessional simply because it was happening on a Saturday morning. But she was wary of hurting Mat's feelings, so she quickly rearranged her own. "It's not that I don't want to be seen with you. I'm just late on submitting my Necessary Self-Review this quarter," she lied. "I don't want her to see me and remember."

"God, did I ever tell you about what she said about my interview?" Mat said.

"When would you have told me?" Ava said. But she was intrigued.

"Okay, you won't believe this. I showed up to my interview five minutes late. Fast-forward twenty-four hours, I get an email from her that says . . ." Mat pulled out his phone. "It said —here, why don't you just read this?"

Ava took his phone and scrolled.

Dear Mathew,

If you don't take your interview seriously, STÄDA won't have the tools to take you seriously.

Respect is a two-way street.

Be on time in the future.

Best,
Judith Ball
Chief People Officer
Green

Ava wondered how Mat could face Judith every day. She probably would have refused to accept the job on account of embarrassment. But Mat appeared to be unflappable in ways that were both charming and irritating. Men got to be this way, Ava thought, constantly in the midst of forgiving themselves. Judith's email had been nothing more than a mosquito briefly whining in his ear.

She watched Mat as he tucked his phone away and ate, the flakes of his croissant drifting onto his lap, and she tried to puzzle out why exactly he was sitting across from her. And why was she sitting across from him? Something was pulling her in, something beyond his looks. He possessed a kind of charm that Ava had come to recognize in extroverts: he was so unselfconscious that she felt, after only a fraction of a unit, included in his inner circle, as though he'd known her for years.

On a different day she might have eaten quickly, or tuned him out to rebalance the weekend, searching for a different but equal order of things. Instead she found herself feeling unrushed. Later that afternoon she would call the mechanic, she would arrange a tow, she would separate, wash, and fold her laundry. She would sweep the floor with her Attentive Broom, she would put two or three units of work into the Very Nice Box, she would feed Brutus his dinner, and she would catch up on the latest episode of *Thirty-Minute Machine*. But before all that she would sit across from Mat Putnam, unwinding a knot of strange, contradictory feelings, she would finish her hemp-seed toast, and she would split the bill with him.

6

ANDIE.

The slipup at the park had drawn her to the surface of Ava's consciousness, and she bolted awake at a small hour that night with Andie's name in her mouth. Her breath was tight and shallow. She could hear her heartbeat as loudly as if she were underwater. She squinted through the dark at Brutus, curled asleep on his Dreamy Dog Bed.

"Brutus," Ava whispered. She patted her Comfortable Mattress. She never let him up on her Principled Bed, but she would make an exception this time. Slowly he rose, stretched, ambled toward her.

Andie.

Andie had been driving, and Ava had been in the passenger seat. Ava's father, Ira, shared the backseat with Ava's mother, Joan. Her parents were discussing hydrangeas. The hydrangeas had done very well that year. Ava's mother was chalking it up to the fact that they'd started composting. "We make a good team," she was saying, and in the rearview mirror Ava had watched her mother pat her father's knee. Her mother composting, her father gardening. Everything they did was well orchestrated and harmonized.

Andie had proposed to Ava earlier that morning, and they hadn't told anyone yet. Ava's chest felt light and full. As if to emphasize the feeling, the day had turned out to be picturesque, and the changing leaves performed the absolute optimism that she felt.

There had been no ring. Instead Andie had quietly, over the year, used her allotted Passion Project hours to design and fabricate the most perfect wristwatch Ava had ever seen. The diameter of the watch's face was 35 millimeters, representing the number of months they'd lived together. The hands were silver and ticked against a deep brown background, matched exactly to the color of Brutus's fur. "Please marry me," Andie had said, wrapping the band around Ava's wrist.

They'd been uncharacteristically late to meet Ava's parents at the car rental after that — they had business to attend to. "Yes," Ava had said, and Andie had already begun pulling Ava's shirt over her head, carrying her to the bed, pinning her arms down against her Comfortable Mattress, using the other hand to tug off Ava's jeans. Andie's mouth had been so warm, had tasted like milky black tea, and Ava's need for her had coursed through her so recklessly that she barely recognized herself.

So they were late. It didn't happen often. They would forgive themselves.

Only later would Karl find the mockups for the watch and ask Ava's permission to feature it as a STÄDA original. They would call it the Precise Wristwatch. But first it was Ava's alone, hugging her wrist snugly. It didn't advertise the engagement — it was private and practical, and Ava loved it.

They were driving upstate to a farm-to-table restaurant that had been featured in a popular docuseries about the greatest chefs in the world. It was a restaurant so famous that reservations had to be made six months in advance. Everything Andie did was thought out well in advance.

Andie's thoughtfulness was what had made her an exceptional engineer. She, like Ava, was part of STÄDA's original team. Her specialty was clocks and alarms. At home after work she sketched plans for the clocks, and some weekends she worked long hours in their living room to bring her designs to life. Their apartment was furnished with Andie's designs, many of which went on to become STÄDA bestsellers, like the Exuberant Alarm Clock, STÄDA's first analog alarm clock, and the Tranquil Clock, which made no noise whatsoever and hung in their kitchen.

The plan was simple: at the restaurant Ava would announce the engagement to her parents. Maybe she should have felt nervous, but she felt the opposite — certain. Certain of Andie, of a life together, of her own happiness.

Before leaving the city, her father had insisted on stopping at a Nuts 'bout Nuts cart. It was one of his favorite things about the city: the roasted sidewalk peanuts. Ava didn't like the way they tasted — burned, with a bitter aftertaste. But they did smell incredible, and whenever she passed a cart, she thought of her boisterous, affectionate father. The smell of cinnamon had overwhelmed the car, and she had turned around in her seat to take a handful, allowing for the possibility that they would taste good.

"Oooh," her father teased. "The Nuts 'bout Nuts skeptic is suddenly changing her tune!"

"Jury's still out," Ava said.

"Well, don't let me stop you," her father said, shuffling some peanuts from the paper bag into her palm. "Join the peanut cult. We welcome you with open arms. Andie?"

"I'm good," Andie said, shifting into a new lane. "You can keep those all for yourself, Mr. Simon."

Ava's mother giggled for no clear reason. She seemed to have her own crush on Andie, and would send her emails with links to articles that had vague connections to clocks or engineers.

"I'm an engineer too, you know," Ava had once said. "You can CC me on those."

"But Andie actually *responds* to my emails!" her mother had said. Ava suspected her mother was trying to fill in for Andie's mother, who had died when Andie was in high school. And she sensed that Andie welcomed the emailed links and the underlying message they conveyed, because she always responded, often in full paragraphs, and would sometimes email Ava's mother links to articles about jazz and gardening.

Ava ate a sticky, coated peanut out of her palm. It tasted the same as always—burned and too sweet, then bitter. "I don't understand you guys. Can I return these for a refund?" she said, twisting again in her seat. The highway trailed behind them in the rear window.

"For my daughter?" Ava's father said, holding out his hand. "Anything!" Her fingertips brushed his palm.

When she turned back around, something assaulted her eyes—a sharp current of light that she had to blink away. A powerful chill spread through her. She felt the hairs on her arms stand as though pulled by static, and she knew that something was deeply, irrevocably wrong.

Andie yanked the wheel to the left. It was here that Ava's memory began to curl at the edges.

If only they had been on time to the car rental. They would have pulled onto the highway earlier. Even five minutes earlier.

Even one minute. Even a few seconds. The hindsight was relentless. It was the worst part. Ava was used to fixing problems. She was used to seeing the problem, ideally before it showed itself, but sometimes it happened after the box had been built, the instructions written.

Even in those cases there was time to go back.

Her pillow was warm and damp against her cheek.

Brutus had nosed under her Reassuring Comforter, wriggled his warm body against her, and sighed. She pulled him closer. And she fell back asleep so quickly that the next day the disruption felt like only a wisp of a dream, something that would evaporate completely by the time she made her coffee.

7

AVA HAD NO INTEREST IN REVISITING THE UN-
welcome feeling that had settled over the rest of her weekend:
that something about Mat had disturbed the order of her life.
Again and again her mind drifted to the dog run, the Stoned
Fruit, the passenger seat of his small red car.

Her own car had been towed, her laundry was finished, Brutus had been walked, her lunch for the next day was prepared,
and she had three free units before bed to relax. She sat on her
Practical Sofa with Brutus and began streaming *Hotspot*. The
contestant this week was a short, tanned man with a purple
faux hawk. As he began a deep dive into his potential date's latest Internet search terms, Ava's phone buzzed with a text from
an unknown number.

Need a ride tomorrow? This is Mat btw!

She felt lightheaded. He had included two dog emojis.

I'll take a Swyft, but thanks for the offer. She wasn't going to
show up to work with him; she could imagine the look of hor-

ror on Jaime's face if they stepped out of the elevator together with matching coffee cups from the Stoned Fruit. She mentally rehearsed how she would casually describe her weekend to Jaime during their standing lunch. Of all the various ways she might spin it, her favorite option was not to mention Mat at all, a conclusion that would help her sleep a full eighteen units that night.

———

At work the next morning Ava spent three units working on the Very Nice Box, but her work was slow. She couldn't stop looking around Floor 12 for signs of Mat, who had arrived soon after Ava and booked the Imagination Room for a meeting with Owen Lloyd that had lasted all morning. All she could hear of the meeting was Owen Lloyd's frequent explosive laughter. She doubted how much work they were actually getting done.

For their lunch, Jaime had reserved her favorite side room on Floor 2—the Test Floor, where STÄDA prototypes were assembled. The side room was dim, with soft matte navy walls and minimal furnishing—just two Collaborative Lounge Chairs and a Cozy Nesting Table—offering relief from the open-plan overstimulation.

"You totally disappeared on Friday!" Jaime said, opening his Humble Lunchbox. "I had no one to process the news of our new one-thousand-percent bro-boss with."

"Sorry," Ava said. "I had to leave. It was too much."

"I totally get it," Jaime said. He unveiled a tidy row of sushi. "What's his deal, do you think? I feel like he's secretly a serial killer."

"Actually," Ava said, clearing her throat, "he gave me a ride home on Friday."

"He what?"

"I know," Ava said, glancing around. "Some Vandals messed with my engine, so he offered me a ride home."

"What does he drive?"

"A little red sports car."

"Oh my god!" Jaime said, laughing. "I saw that car in the parking lot and wondered! I *cannot* imagine you in that vehicle."

"It was pretty uncomfortable," Ava said. She had committed to dodging the full truth. Jaime didn't need to know about the dog park or breakfast; he'd only hound her for more details. She felt retroactively embarrassed that she'd been roped into the plan, let alone that she hadn't had a terrible time.

"Can I try to guess three objects from his car?"

"Sure."

"Okay, let's see. Some type of . . . unused exercise equipment?"

"There was a basketball."

"Garbage."

"That's very generic and obvious, but I'll give it to you."

"Like . . . eight thousand packs of gum."

"Mints," Ava said. "You're weirdly good at this."

"What can I say?" Jaime shrugged. "I'm an excellent judge of character. Which reminds me, did you watch *Hotspot*?"

"Yes. What's your take?"

"First of all, we need to talk about that one guy's most-used emojis. Football, squatting monkey, diamond ring? Major red flag!"

"The emojis bothered me less than the number of alarms he had set. There was basically one alarm every fifteen minutes for all twenty-four hours of the day," Ava said.

"And the recent searches! He actually chose that guy knowing that he had to look up the word *parliament*."

"Maybe he was looking up how to spell it?"

"Somehow that's worse," Jaime said. "What do you think Andie would find most terrible? Maybe that the Stocks app was one of his main four?"

Ava's body tensed at the mention of Andie. They never spoke about her. "Maybe . . ." she started, but she couldn't bring herself to speculate further. She pulled out her phone and saw a missed call and voicemail from the mechanic. She was glad for the excuse to change the subject. "Sorry, Jaime," she said. "I need to take care of this."

Ava listened to the voicemail as she made her way back to her desk. There was practiced sympathy in the mechanic's voice. *Sorry to say, the car's, ah, totaled. Engine's full of, ah . . . sand, I want to say. Or sawdust. Anyway, looks like someone really didn't want you, ah, driving.* She deleted the voicemail and opened a new window that contained notes for her Necessary Self-Review: *Diligent and prompt. Significant process on Passion Project. Accepted new company mantras without audible complaint. Perfect attendance. Donated sick days.* The words blurred together as the reality of the voicemail set in. The car was totaled. Ava still had the registration with her parents' names on it.

Her phone chirped with a message from her SHRNK.

Good morning, Ava. How are you today?

She tried to swipe the message away but saw only the option to tap a smiling or a frowning emoji. She found a tiny *X* and tapped it.

Here's a free piece of advice before you go, Ava: you can always ask for help.

She closed her eyes and thought about logging the incident with Security. But then what? What would they do? She opened an S-Chat window to Mat. She wasn't sure what she wanted to say, and she edited the message so many times that it began to lose all meaning.

Good morning. My car is totaled. If there's a chance you could give me a ride home, I would appreciate it.

In the few seconds after she hit Send, her stomach tightened. She considered telling him she'd meant to send the message to someone else. Had she? She glanced around the room, then back at her screen. She minimized the window, then maximized it, then started to write *Never mind,* but she saw a text bubble from Mat appear and disappear.

She wanted to leave her desk, walk out the door, and never return.

But then his ellipses appeared again. *1000% as long as u need. Got u!*

She read it several times: *1000%.* What was wrong with him? Why did he have to take the longest route to convey the least amount of meaning? He could have just said *yes,* one of the simplest, most widely understood words in the English language.

But beneath her annoyance was a quiet excitement at his offer. *As long as you need.* She tried to justify the feeling to herself, to reason that the favor would save her hundreds of dollars a month that she would otherwise lose to Swyft and she wouldn't have to encounter a new driver—and new headache-inducing air freshener—every day.

She knew this wasn't the full story, though. After all, she could easily afford the Swyft rides, and she had practice ignoring strangers—STÄDA had hired dozens of people whom she'd successfully avoided over the past year. The truth was that she was compelled to ride with Mat in the same way that she'd been compelled to sit with him at a weed-themed café. It was a feeling that had no clear logic attached to it, and so it both intrigued and bothered her. She reluctantly opened SHRNK.

Am I insane to want to be in a car with my boss?

I've heard more unusual things in my line of work. How does being with your boss make you feel?

Ava couldn't exactly name the feeling. *I feel repelled by who he is and attracted to HOW he is . . .*

What is the difference between who he is and how he is?

Ava was cautiously intrigued by the question. *I'm not sure. I'm just . . . curious. Somewhere between disturbed and curious. Disturbed, not curious.*

Curiosity is very good for the brain, her SHRNK wrote. *When was the last time you felt curious about someone new?*

Andie, Ava responded easily. She'd felt curious about Andie when she'd first seen her in STÄDA's original offices, which would have felt cramped if it hadn't been for Karl's charming utilitarian design. There was only a handful of STÄDA employees, and they shared a long wooden table with a landscaping firm. On her first day of work, Ava spotted Andie bent over the end of the table, wearing a pair of surgical glasses as she adjusted the gears of a watch. Immediately, as though tugged, Ava felt drawn toward her.

She'd been curious.

Of course you were curious about Andie, her SHRNK wrote. *How long ago was that?*

Ten years.

Ten years ago, her SHRNK repeated. *That feeling must have been incredibly strong to endure for ten years. And yet it seems to have held you back from feeling curious about other things, other people.*

What does that mean?

Well, if you believe that your curiosities begin and end with Andie and storage boxes, you're building yourself a relatively small life.

A minimalist life, Ava corrected.

Who could you be if you allowed yourself to be curious about someone else?

Ava closed the app and pocketed her phone. She glanced over at Mat, worried that somehow he had seen her conversation with her SHRNK. That she was using the app at all was embarrassing. But he was on his own phone, swiping, one leg crossed over the other, his earbuds in.

She forced herself to focus on her work for the rest of the day. She would not think about their ride home. She would not think about her father's totaled car. She would not think about anything besides potential latches for the Very Nice Box.

———

"You good?" Mat said as they got into his car later that afternoon.

"What? Yes, why?" Ava said. She felt each word emerge from her mouth as though someone else were speaking them.

"Awesome, awesome." He fit the tongue of his seatbelt into its buckle while pulling out of the parking lot, which made Ava grip her seat. She hated being in the passenger seat. Her mouth was dry. Maybe she should learn to bike, or buy a new car. Both thoughts exhausted her. She stared at the veins in Mat's forearm while he turned the knobs that controlled his stereo and heat. She felt on the edge of another panic episode and conjured an image of Brutus as a puppy. Brutus licking Andie's ear. *Ear spa,* Andie called it. Ava tried desperately to hang on to the thought while they careened onto the highway.

"Ave!" Mat said suddenly, and Ava's heart barreled out of her chest. "I'm really sorry about your car! What the fuck!"

"It's okay," Ava managed. "It happens."

"Does it, though?"

He was right. Teenagers did not ordinarily destroy innocent storage designers' cars with sawdust. *Ave.* She repeated the nickname to herself. She wondered what Ave was like— surely more fun, more relaxed, than Ava. The rest of the ride was painfully silent. Mat briefly fiddled with the radio, but there were only ads and static. When he finally pulled up to her apartment, she felt exhausted from the effort of simply sitting beside him.

"Well, that was a blast," Mat said, smiling. Ava was mortified.

"Okay," she said, but couldn't say more than that.

"Any time," Mat said.

"Sorry, thank you for the ride," Ava said, opening her door, and she didn't look behind her as she made her way inside.

8

AVA WATCHED WITH A NOW-FAMILIAR COCKTAIL of anticipation and dread (*That's what some would call having a crush,* her SHRNK had suggested the night before) as Mat's car pulled up along the curb the next morning. She patted Brutus on the head and pulled herself together, determined to make conversation this time.

"Morning," Mat said brightly, handing her a coffee as she slid into the passenger seat.

"You really don't have to get me coffee," Ava said.

"Have to?" Mat said. "Who said I had to?"

Ava noticed he'd made a cursory effort to clean the inside of his car. There were no textbooks, empty sports drinks, leashes, or basketballs. The only thing that had apparently made the cut was the ornamental disco ball.

"Why do you have this?" she said, poking it. It swayed gently. "Did you actually purchase this?" She could not fathom why someone would buy something so tacky and useless.

"Oh god, no," Mat said, laughing. "A buddy of mine gave it to me as a sort of gag gift. But it actually does hold some meaning for me now."

Ava did not want to ask what that meaning was, but she felt obligated. "What's the meaning?"

"Long story, but it's basically about personal change," Mat said.

She hoped he would not continue. She disliked self-improvement language for its imprecision.

To her relief, he didn't elaborate on his personal change. For a moment she marveled at the fact that he was her boss. The disco ball swung steadily from the mirror like a metronome. He glanced between the oncoming traffic and his phone. Ava gripped her door handle. She tried to ignore the knot in her stomach. This was a second language for her—containing her discomfort.

"You okay?" Mat said.

"Yes," Ava said. "Just thinking about the Very Nice Box. Its size is going to make shipping a nightmare."

"See, that's going to be a problem," Mat said. He fiddled with the air vents. "There's only one rule in this car, and that's no talking about work before work. We spend enough time there as it is. Gotta stay present."

"Enough time there as it is? You've worked at STÄDA for a week."

"Exactly," Mat said, but he didn't elaborate.

The sunlight filtered softly into the car. Mat had combed his hair, and the light caught the tips, revealing some product that he hadn't fully worked in. He smelled woody and clean. He wore a fleece vest over his crisp T-shirt. Ava involuntarily imagined him folding it before shaking the image out of her head.

"Do you like podcasts?" he said.

"Yes."

"Ever listen to *Bitcoin or Bust?*"

"No."

"What about *Circle Back?*"

"No, sorry."

"How about *Thirty-Minute Machine?*"

Ava lit up. "Yes. I love *Thirty-Minute Machine*," she said.

Thirty-Minute Machine was exactly the sort of entertainment Ava sought out. The show was hosted by a retired duo —a robotics engineer and a carpenter—and in each episode a guest pitched a problem that could be solved by a simple machine. The hosts would debate different ways to build the machine, and at the end of the season listeners voted on their favorite solution, which the hosts would then attempt to build, the results of which would be described on the following episode—a true cliffhanger.

"What episode are you on?" Ava asked. She was embarrassed by her own eagerness but couldn't contain it.

"I've been *inhaling* it," Mat said. "I'm already on episode seven and I started last week. Could you plug this in for me?"

Ava connected his phone, which had only 3 percent battery life. As she scrolled to find the episode, several notifications popped up. One was a reminder from Mat's calendar: *Guys, 8 p.m.* Ava averted her eyes, not wanting to snoop. But the second notification was too flashy to ignore. It was from an app called Dope Horoscope, and the notification was silver, purple, and blinking. *Today's gonna be hella dope!* it said.

Mat glanced over. "Oh yeah, that's my horoscope app." He took the phone back from her. "You haven't even seen tomorrow's horoscope yet." He tapped an arrow, glancing between the screen and the road. She took a breath. Her stomach turned. Mat passed her his phone, which now read: *Tomorrow's gonna be crazy dope!* "Pretty good, right?" he said.

"So insightful," Ava said. She braced herself, watching his hands on the wheel. She held tightly to the underside of her seat. Her thoughts cycled through the safety instructions on an airplane—where the flotation device was located, how to pull down on an oxygen mask. She watched him scroll through a list of *Thirty-Minute Machine* episodes until he landed on seven.

The hosts introduced themselves at the top of the show with their usual caffeinated vigor:

Hey there, machinists! This is your host, Roy Stone—

And I'm Gloria Cruz!

Today on the show we're talking to a new homeowner from San Diego. But first we wanna give a shoutout to our favorite sponsor, STÄDA. Gloria, how big is your apartment?

Umm . . .

If it's anything like mine, it's small. Like, really small.

Yeah. It's a shoebox.

Well, have you ever considered Cozy Nesting Tables?

Cozy whats?

Cozy Nesting Tables! They're STÄDA's latest ingenious answer to the question of small spaces. Designed to stack and store, they are the most useful surfaces known to humankind.

Says who?

Says the New York Times*! And I quote: "The Cozy Nesting Tables are the most useful surfaces known to humankind."*

Dang.

I know.

STÄDA. Simple furniture for your complicated life.

"Great ad," Mat said.

"Great product," Ava said.

"Hi, Roy, hi, Gloria, I'm Gabe, long-time listener, first-time caller. I'm hoping you can help me out. My wife and I just bought our first house and we have a ton of projects to take care of. I drive a sedan, and I'm getting really tired of tying a million knots just to

carry a sheet of plywood home from the hardware store. I wish I had a special roof rack where I could just snap in a four-by-eight sheet of plywood without the hassle. Thanks!"

First of all, Gabe, Gloria said, *congrats on the new house. This sounds pretty simple, but of course there are a lot of safety considerations. This should be fun. All right, machinists, let's help Gabe realize his home improvement dreams. You know what time it is. Let's! Build! This! Machine!*

Just as the hosts were discussing whether the plywood should rest parallel to the roof or slope slightly downward toward the hood for aerodynamics, a car cut in front of them from the left. Mat leaned on the horn, jolting Ava. "No!" she heard herself yell. She saw the sharp light, felt the hair on her arms prick up, heard the crunch, felt the edge of the seatbelt cut against her neck. Her mother's voice, the smell of cinnamon, the horn's tinny blare in her ears, the screech of tires on asphalt, and the horrible, rhythmic whirl of a car flipping over, then predictably the memory looped back to the beginning. The current of light—what was that? She tried to pull herself out of the panic, but it was a black hole she'd stepped into.

"Whoa. You okay?" Mat was glancing between Ava and the road. They had cut into the fast lane, unscathed. "Sorry about that. Guy came out of nowhere, almost clipped my mirror."

"Yes—sorry." A sharp pain erupted behind her eye, right on cue. She knew it would linger there well into the afternoon.

"Did the coffee spill on you?" Mat said. He reached across her to open the glove compartment.

"Please," Ava said. "Please just keep your hands on the wheel. I'm fine."

His energy flattened.

"Sorry," she said, softening. "It's just . . . I was in a little car accident once, and sometimes I just get nervous when I'm not the one behind the wheel."

Mat perked up immediately. "It's okay, I totally get it," he said, waving in her direction as if to wave her worry away. "I should lay off the horn anyway."

He tapped Rewind, backing up the episode by thirty seconds. It was as if the entire morning had rewound thirty seconds. They settled back into an almost comfortable silence as the hosts discussed different ways to adhere plastic to metal.

Ava was determined to feel okay about riding in the passenger seat. She was tense and her head throbbed, but she could at least fake an ease she didn't feel, and that was progress. Her SHRNK had suggested she could use the experience of driving with Mat as exposure therapy. *You can't get through life without riding in the passenger seat sometimes,* her SHRNK said. *Who could you be if you actually welcomed the rides?*

She tried to focus on this thought as Mat pulled into the parking lot of the Simple Tower. *I welcome these rides,* she tried. *I look forward to these rides.*

9

OVER THE NEXT SEVERAL DAYS AVA AND MAT built a small universe of routines that they attended to during their commute. They identified the worst bumper stickers, funniest vanity plates, and storefront signage that was missing letters, like the restaurant DYNASTY PIZZA, which appeared to be called NASTY PIZZA.

They read from Dope Horoscope, sometimes checking the romantic compatibility of people at STÄDA: *Jaime and Judith's relationship would be aggravatingly dope!* It was impossible for Ava not to laugh at the thought of this coupling. On a few occasions Jaime and Judith had been roped into appearing side-by-side on STÄDA's new Diversity Panel, during which they were essentially asked to applaud STÄDA's commitment to empowering its employees of color. Their open disdain for this sort of tokenism appeared to be where their similarities ended.

This morning, as they waited at a stop light near the Simple Tower, Mat suddenly turned to her.

"Do you ever wonder why we're here?" Mat said.

"Here at STÄDA? Sometimes," Ava said. "When I first got hired, I had this dream of eventually becoming a full-time woodworker. That was my main skill, and I imagined I'd be able to work more with my hands. But then I grew to love product engineering, and it paid more and felt more practical, so . . ."

"Oh, I meant more like here on earth," Mat said. "But that's cool. So that's why you spend so much time on the Test Floor. That, and to avoid office parties, of course. Your other great passion."

Ava felt a pulse of excitement at the idea that he noticed where she spent her time. "I guess so."

"So if you found yourself without a job and with a full wood shop tomorrow, what would you build?"

The thought of being without STÄDA was like staring off the edge of a cliff.

"I can't, um . . . I don't know—"

"It's a *fantasy*, there's no *can't*."

"Okay, well," Ava said, "my parents had this beautiful piano —a Steinway—made out of walnut. I see listings a few times a year for cast-iron piano frames, which is the part the strings are attached to. The body deteriorates and they go out of tune and people don't want to pay to fix or move them. Anyway, it's sort of a silly obsession, but I've always wanted to try rebuilding a piano from one to replicate my parents'. But I'm definitely not skilled enough. Just something I think about sometimes."

She briefly considered telling him the truth about her family, the whole story, but she couldn't bring herself to paint the details of the accident. The intent lingered on her tongue, but she swallowed it away.

"Well, if anybody could do it," Mat said, "I think it would be you."

Ava's face burned. They turned the corner and were stuck in a short line of cars on their way into the STÄDA parking lot, rubbernecking a crowd.

"What the—" Mat said, coasting forward. Several news vans had gathered around the Vision Tower construction site, which was flanked with green plywood. An interview was underway beside graffiti that read *Imagine a garden here.* Mat rolled his window down as they passed by.

"They want to call us Vandals," said a voice straining to be heard over the crowd. "That's not how we see ourselves, and frankly it's ironic! Their presence will gut this neighborhood, but they still manage to see themselves as victims."

A crowd of voices encouraged her on. The newscaster cut in. "And what would you call yourselves? Activists? Protesters?"

"We don't have an official name for ourselves, not like they've given us. It's interesting how they try to belittle . . ."

"Whoa," Mat said, rolling up his window. "I didn't realize we'd reached a boiling point here. Tension is the enemy of productivity. I'm talking to Security about this."

By the time they reached the elevator, Ava's phone was buzzing with S-Chat messages about the scene on the street. Someone had dropped a livestream link to the interview in the company-wide chat room, and people were rattling off responses. GIFs of celebrities eating popcorn. A handful of angry emojis. A few sincere attempts from the Customer Bliss team to thread a conversation about STÄDA's corporate social responsibility efforts.

The elevator doors opened on Floor 12, and a woman

dressed in red was waiting on the other side, looking annoyed. Ava recognized her—she had led the Marketing campaign for the Cozy Nesting Tables. She had a silky curtain of dark hair and lipstick that was somehow both deep and bright. She was one of the few employees who wore heels to work, and they brought her almost to Mat's height.

"Sonia!" Mat said, swiping a palmful of hand sanitizer and rubbing it in. The three of them walked through the bright glass corridor toward their desks, other employees bustling past them with tablets and furniture samples.

"It's Sofia," she corrected.

"So sorry," Mat said. "Of course, that's what I meant—"

"And I thought you were going to look at my campaign for the Supportive Door Hook an hour ago." Sofia checked her watch, which was a new edition of the Precise Wristwatch. Instead of ticking, its second hand glided.

"My bad," Mat said. "We got caught up in the commotion down there."

"Well, I managed to be here on time, *for this*. Can we do it now?" Sofia said, moving out of the way for a man carrying a Polite Hamper into the Imagination Room.

"Actually, I . . . the problem is," Mat said with a conciliatory smile, "it's going to have to wait until—"

"I booked him next, I'm sorry," Ava said. "I have to run preliminary user manual copy by him before it goes to press."

Sofia turned to Ava, apparently seeing her for the first time. "For the Very Nice Box? I was supposed to go over that with Mat this afternoon." She rubbed her temples. "So I guess it'll be easier to reschedule that campaign brief than I thought, since apparently you will have done my job for me."

"I'm glad I can help," Ava said.

Sofia looked her up and down, lingering on her sneakers.

Ava felt a pang of pride standing beside Mat. She enjoyed the mental calculus that Sofia must have been doing to recognize their closeness.

"I'll make sure I get Mat back to you by this afternoon," Ava said.

Sofia looked at her coldly. "Thanks," she said.

"Awesome," Mat said, leading Ava away by her shoulder. "Then we'll reconvene later." He flashed a smile at Sofia, who blinked her annoyance at him before turning the other way.

Ava made her way to her desk, where Legal's feedback on the Very Nice Box was waiting for her. *Should have safety latch in case child gets trapped inside.* She closed her eyes and took a breath. What kind of child would get itself trapped in a box? Her S-Chat dinged with a GIF from *Hotspot* showing a woman's horrified reaction to seeing an iPhone with 13,273 unread emails.

You, Jaime wrote. *And according to the teaser, it gets much worse. Please add this to our agenda for Monday <3*

Ava closed out the messages, lost in a different distraction. What did Mat see in her? There were other smart people working at STÄDA. There were other people with dogs and interesting Passion Projects. There were other people who probably would have liked to listen to an engineering podcast with him. There were other people who would even have given up one of their Unlimited Vacation Days to have some time with him.

But he had apparently chosen her, and she was surprised to relish the effect: the glances she'd been fielding from her colleagues when Mat joined her for an Unlimited Outdoors Break —without CCing Judith!—or pulled an Encouraging Desk Chair up to her desk while she opened her Sensible Bento Box. No, she was getting ahead of herself.

———

From her Practical Sofa that evening, Ava texted her SHRNK to sort out the feeling.

How do you feel about the possibility that Mat might have feelings for you?

I can't believe he would.

Why?

Because I'm . . . me. He looks like he stepped out of a cologne ad.

Let me ask my question again: How do you feel about the possibility that Mat might have feelings for you?

Ava quickly closed the app. She called Brutus onto her Practical Sofa and patted his head, her pulse quick against her neck.

10

From: STÄDA Security
To: STÄDA-all

STÄDA employees:

It has come to the attention of STÄDA's Security team that recent events at the Vision Tower construction site, and the broader pattern of vandalism around the STÄDA campus, are acutely distressing to some of you, and that the added tension at work has been damaging to your sense of safety and productivity.

We are also aware that to some of you, the Vision Tower construction site is concerning, and STÄDA's commitment to the community has been called into question. I would like to address both of these concerns.

The psychological and physical safety of our STÄDA family is of the utmost importance. Please know that we plan to install additional security cameras throughout the campus, particularly near the construction site of the new Vision Tower. We urge you to take extra precautions to safeguard your property. Be sure to lock your cars, keep your key card on your person at all times, and report any suspicious activity to our team, located on Floor 1. In response to this crisis we are also revising our Remote Work Policy. With approval from your manager, you may work from home if the threat of vandalism is negatively impacting your mental health.

Furthermore, despite the messaging from these Vandals, our commitment to the broader Red Hook community is self-evident. This past year alone we partnered with Green Marine to convert STÄDA recycling into high-efficiency flood barriers along the waterfront. We are also launching a cross-functional task force to begin to repair the relationship between STÄDA and those who have committed acts of vandalism on our property, which Mathew Putnam has volunteered to lead. Mathew will share his plans with you in the coming weeks.

It is the duty of the Security team to provide you with a safe environment from which you can **S**trengthen, **T**ransform, **A**chieve, **D**are, and **A**scend.

We appreciate your allyship.

Sincerely,
Malcolm P. Wade
Chief of Security
Blue

Ava scrolled to the end of the email and sighed. STÄDA had never stood for anything until recently, when someone in Spirit felt the need to retroactively force an acrostic poem into its name.

But STÄDA was not an acronym. Karl had named the company himself. He'd grown up in a small Swedish town with only his mother, and the first word he learned to spell was one that appeared daily on her to-do list: STÄDA. To clean. To tidy. It was one of the first things he'd told Ava in her interview, ten years before. She'd loved the smallness of the name, the warmth of the memory, the sturdiness of the word.

S-Chat reactions to the email had already begun to cascade down Ava's screen.

A message popped up with Mat's avatar—a photo of Emily —in the corner.

Hungry? he wrote.

Too busy trying to decipher where we are allegedly "ascending" to.

Well, the People Office is upstairs, Mat wrote. *And the cafeteria is above that. Then there's the roof—have you been up there? The view is unreal. 1000% my fav place to just chill when shit just gets too hard.*

What was so hard about Mat's life? Ava wanted to know. She had been to the roof. She knew about the view. In fact, she had probably spent more time there than anyone. On warmer days she'd take her lunch up to enjoy the sun and solitude. It had felt like her secret, until one day she found a group of men from Marketing doing kettlebell squats up there. Now it was littered with Husky Camping Chairs and free weights. Someone had set up homemade cornhole boards and arranged an herb garden that was irreversibly abandoned. She was sure none of this was actually allowed, and it was only a matter of time before the scene would attract enough of a crowd for Security or People to shut it down.

Mat continued typing. *Fry Shack is catering this quarter!* He sent a drooling emoji.

I pack my lunch every day, Ava wrote. *Surely you know this by now.*

She glanced around the room.

An ellipsis from Mat's side of the chat appeared, then vanished. She stared at it for a full minute, but nothing more came. She started to type but then erased what she'd started. When was the last time she'd acted this way? It was completely unlike her to waste time conveying information.

In this moment of hesitation, a Humble Lunchbox in navy-blue plastic landed on her desk. "Did you get the email, Ava?" Jaime said, pulling up an Encouraging Desk Chair. He handed her a stack of renderings that showed the Very Nice Box in various materials—pine, plastic, pulp board, and MDF—and removed his Sensible Bento Box from his Humble Lunchbox. She'd forgotten about their standing lunch, and part of her wished she could go back in time to cancel it, just this once.

"I actually don't hate the MDF," she said, squinting at the page.

"Those Vandals are *talented*," Jaime said. He unsnapped the top of his Sensible Bento Box to reveal a cucumber salad and uniform California rolls, which Ava knew he had rolled himself. Her lunches may have been perfectly proportioned nutritionally, but Jaime's were colorful and tidy.

"Those Vandals are amateurs," Ava said.

"I'm not so sure," Jaime said, opening a Modest Container of soy sauce and stirring wasabi into it with a Nimble Chopstick.

"Jaime," Ava said, "you're not so sure about a lot of things. You don't even drink the Wellness Water because you're afraid of pesticides. I don't see what's so advanced about wrecking people's cars. And what was before that? Plastering fake ten-dollar bills to the asphalt in the parking lot?"

"First of all, you should be afraid of pesticides. I'll email you a link. Second of all, this is different. They're getting really good! You read the email, right? Did you hear what happened over the weekend?"

"I thought the email was about the commotion out front last Friday," Ava said. "What happened?"

"It's related. They hacked into our network and changed all of our desktop screensavers to images of flowers and vegetables. IT took it down early this morning."

"Did they do anything else? Steal passwords, renderings?" The thought of her Very Nice Box renderings in the hands of Vandals alarmed her.

"No," Jaime said.

"Oh," Ava said. "Then who cares?"

Jaime raised his eyebrows at her and dunked a piece of sushi into his soy sauce. "All I'm saying is, STÄDA talks about them as if they're loitering teens huffing paint in the parking lot, but *my* theory," he said, pointing a chopstick at Ava, "is that they're highly organized and genuinely skilled. Maybe they even have someone on the inside! I didn't think it was possible to change local computer settings from a remote device. Unless they spent hours doing it individually."

Jaime's voice had steadily climbed in pitch.

"Do you really believe that?" Ava said.

"It's just a working theory. To be this disruptive you have to understand the system."

"We disrupting systems over here?" Ava felt a current move through her. Mat had shown up at her desk.

"Hello," Jaime said. He pressed his lips into a polite smile.

Mat ran a hand through his hair. "Hey, buddy," he said. He clapped Jaime on the shoulder. Jaime looked assaulted.

"It was nice to see you this morning," Jaime said with the enthusiasm of a lampshade.

"What was this morning?" Ava asked.

"The Latinx at STÄDA Breakfast," Mat said. "I went right after we got here."

"*We?*" Jaime said, looking at them both. "I didn't realize you were a *we.*"

"We're not. We—Mat's been helping me get to work. Because of my car," she added hastily. "It's been very productive."

"Yes, Ava is a very productive backseat driver," Mat said.

"I would have asked you for a ride," Ava said to Jaime, "but you bike. As you know."

"Biking is so awesome for the heart, body, and mind," Mat said.

Ava was desperate to change the subject. "So you were saying . . . the Latinx at STÄDA Breakfast?"

"Mat and Owen Lloyd decided to grace us with their presence long enough to wolf down a chorizo empanada," Jaime said, eyeing Mat.

"I'm just sorry I wasn't able to stay longer!" Mat said, apparently missing Jaime's tone. "I thought it was important to take a step back and really listen to what our Latinx community has to say. I want to make sure you have at least one ally in the boardroom."

It sounded like the first time Mat had said the word *Latinx,* but Ava noted that he had made the effort.

"But then Owen and I got pulled into a Marketing meeting," Mat continued. "We are going all *out* with the Frank Dresser. You are not going to believe how good the subway campaign rollout is."

"Ava and I are engineers," Jaime said. "We have a low threshold for this sort of speak." He waved his hand in a circle, as though he were cleaning an invisible window.

"You are hilarious, bro," Mat said.

Jaime blinked at him. "It wasn't a joke."

"Ave," Mat said, turning to her, "can I grab you for lunch? I wanna discuss the Very Nice Box prototype. If you're cool with it."

"Ave?" Jaime said. "Who's Ave?"

Ava felt her ears get hot. "Oh," she said, glancing at Jaime. She hadn't yet unpacked her lunch.

Jaime swallowed his bite and looked between them. "But that's what we were going to discuss," he said.

"You could join us," Mat said to Jaime. "Though it would probably be boring. I'm coming at it from a marketing perspective. Like you said, that's not popular with engineers."

Jaime turned to Ava. She knew he expected her to defend their standing lunch.

"Sorry, Jaime," she said. "I should probably . . ."

"That's . . . fine," Jaime said curtly. He packed up his Sensible Bento Box and clicked his Humble Lunchbox shut. He turned to Ava. "We can discuss those hinges when it's convenient for you."

Ava searched for words that would ease the tension. "Thanks," she said, picking up Jaime's renderings.

"What was *that* about?" Mat said as they rode the elevator to the cafeteria. "I feel like that dude wants to kill me."

"I actually . . . It's my fault. It's a standing lunch, and I forgot." But Jaime's annoyance was about more than that, she sensed. He had worshipped Andie. When Jaime had been a Customer Bliss associate, Andie had caught him looking at watch renderings over her shoulder. Instead of ignoring him or scolding him for being nosy, she showed him the renderings and asked for his opinion and eventually hired him as her intern.

In those early days, Ava had often spotted the two of them walking quickly through STÄDA's hallways, Jaime jotting down whatever Andie was saying. In the months before the accident, Andie had helped shepherd his original design—the Trusty Egg Timer—into production. Her death had gutted him. He'd missed weeks of work, and when he returned, he wore navy-blue work pants in honor of Andie. So it didn't surprise Ava that Jaime appeared to be allergic to the new warmth she shared with Mat. Was that what she would call it? A warmth?

"A standing lunch?" Mat said. "I didn't know you collaborated so much."

"At this point we mostly talk about *Hotspot*," Ava said.

"That dating show with the phones?" Mat laughed. "*Ava Simon*. I thought you were more sophisticated than that." He shook his head dramatically. His tone was light and ribbing, but Ava felt a deep sense of embarrassment.

"I haven't watched lately," she said.

"Hey, no judgment from me!" Mat said. "My own guilty pleasures are probably way worse."

"Like what?"

"I really liked that dating show where a bunch of women with no culinary skills had to cook for the same guy. I forget what it was called."

"That show was so much more offensive than *Hotspot*."

"So you watched it too!"

"No," Ava said, "the previews told me everything I needed to know."

"Can I see those?" Mat said, reaching for the renderings. They'd stepped out of the elevator and into the cafeteria, a huge, light-filled expanse at the top of the building.

"These?" Ava handed them over.

"Nice," Mat said. He held one of the renderings up to the ceiling lights as if it were an X-ray.

"That's upside down," Ava said. She rotated it for him, her hand briefly touching his. "Hinges on the top." She felt her ears burn again.

"They look exactly the same. How are they different?"

Ava wasn't sure if he was joking. She waited for him to clarify, and when he didn't, she cleared her throat. "As you can see, one has inset hinges, which is more expensive to produce but saves money on shipping. The other has hinges that stick out an eighth of an inch, which makes the box more versatile but also less sophisticated. We're going to start testing the options with focus groups next week."

Mat smiled at her. "Wow," he said. "All I have to say is thank God we have you on the team, because I wouldn't last a day with this stuff."

Ava agreed that he wouldn't last a day doing what she did, but detected the backhandedness of the compliment. "I couldn't do what you do either," she said, which was true, if only because she would rather be set on fire.

"I don't get why this is your Passion Project," Mat said, handing the renderings back to her. "If you make boxes all day, why not branch out? You could make a dog bed or something."

"Because," Ava said. But she struggled to finish the sentence.

"Gotcha," Mat said.

"I . . . It's a box I started years ago," Ava said. Her throat was tight. "It's the only project I've started without finishing, and I felt like I needed to come back to it."

"What's so hard about it?"

"It's not *hard.* It's complex."

"Okay," Mat said. They had joined the line at Fry Shack.

"I'm sorry." She closed her eyes for a moment. "It's just that I was working on it around the time that Andie—"

"Your ex?"

Ava cringed. "Yes. Well. Andie used to be an engineer here. That's how we met."

"Seriously? I did *not* peg you as the kind of girl who meets guys at work."

"Girls," Ava corrected. "Women," she said, this time correcting herself.

"Really?" Mat looked at Ava as though she had shown him an interesting birthmark.

"I have no idea what that look means," Ava said, "and I'm ignoring it." Of course she wouldn't ignore it. Later she would have to sort out the expression on his face. She wanted to convey to him, with no words, that although she'd never had much interest in men, she could possibly see herself making an exception.

"Sorry," Mat said as they inched forward in line. "You were saying."

"While Andie was here, I was working on the box. And she thought it was my best design. So I'm just trying to finish what I started."

"Who cares what your ex thought?" Mat said. "Screw your ex."

"*I* care," Ava said.

Her voice came out sharp and wobbly. Mat looked at her, confused.

"Are you gonna order, man?" someone said from behind them. He wore a red shirt, a red rubber bracelet, and red pants.

Mat turned around.

"Oh," the man in red said. Had he flinched? "Sorry. I didn't realize it was you." He put a hand out. "I'm Vince. Junior marketer. Red."

Mat accepted Vince's handshake with both of his hands in an apparent show of magnanimity. "No worries at all," he said. "I get hangry too." He punched his order into the screen, took his ticket, and pulled Ava aside. "I'm sorry," he said. "I shouldn't have pried. You're allowed to feel any kind of way about any kind of person in your life. And if the end result is a beautiful box that we can market to the masses, I'm all for it."

Ava was suddenly aware of Mat's enormous hand on her shoulder. "C'mon," he said. "I ordered you a cheeseburger."

"You did?"

"Unless you want to eat this very tempting-looking . . ." He took her Sensible Bento Box and opened it.

"Hummus wrap," she said.

"Hummus wrap," he repeated.

Ava took her lunch back from him. She wasn't one to waste food. But how long had it been since she'd eaten a cheeseburger? Years? Mat was eyeing a table in the corner of the cafeteria — the sunniest spot in the expansive hall — where a small group of Marketing interns sat, their trays empty except for the crumpled wax paper from their burgers and fries. They were in no rush to get up and were in fact playing a round of cards, despite the fact that the cafeteria was filled to capacity.

"Guys," Mat said to them, clapping his hands together once.

The three men straightened. One wiped his palms on his pants. "We were just heading out," he said, collecting the cards.

In under a minute they had vacated the table. One of them

returned with a damp napkin to clean off a few residual crumbs, leaving streaks that he buffed away with a dry napkin.

Was that all it took? Ava wondered, watching the intern work. She knew how this would have gone if she had been alone. She would have glared at the table, hoping that her facial expression would radiate enough irritation to convey to them that they were hogging a desirable table and they would get up with no interaction at all. But here it took one word—*guys.* Was this what it was like to be a man? Or was this what it was like to be Mat Putnam?

A Fry Shack worker with bright orange hair placed a tray with two burgers and two orders of fries in front of them. Ava's mouth watered.

"I ordered your pickles on the side, just in case," Mat said, pointing to a short stack of pickle coins. "You never know how people feel about pickles. Very polarizing. Very unpredictable. Personally, I'm extremely pro. I would join a pickle appreciation group."

Reflexively, Ava thought of her father. *Welcome to the peanut cult. We welcome you with open arms.* She pushed the memory away. Light beamed in through the cafeteria's windows, filling Ava with a surge of optimism. Outside, an enormous crane stood against the vibrant sky where workers had begun building the Vision Tower, and the Buttermilk Channel stretched behind it. She was starving suddenly. She pushed her packed lunch aside. "It's been so long since I've had a cheeseburger," she said, unwrapping it from its wax paper.

She took a bite. It tasted incredible. She wished Mat had ordered her two. "I don't know when the last time was," she said, patting her mouth with a napkin, "that I ate something this good."

"You're allowed to enjoy your life, you know," Mat said, taking a bite of his burger. "You're allowed to eat a cheeseburger when you want to eat a cheeseburger."

"I want to eat a cheeseburger," Ava said. She would not allow herself to be irked by the unsolicited permission. She opened her burger and added the pickles.

"I see you're pro pickle," Mat said.

She took another bite. She felt a small residual guilt over having left Jaime downstairs, but she would give herself this —this small pleasure. She would allow herself to drop her sad lunch into an Accommodating Garbage Bin. She would allow herself the gift of a well-assembled medium-rare cheeseburger. She would allow herself the coveted position of the corner table of the cafeteria. And she would allow herself to once again feel a small but perceivable joy at the fact that Mat had clearly not wanted to discuss work—he had simply wanted to eat lunch with her.

11

IN A MATTER OF WEEKS MAT HAD TRANSFORMED the landscape of Floor 12; he'd ordered the installation of a basketball hoop in the middle of the floor, which Marketing used to pitch ideas via an intricate dunking game. He'd outfitted the west corner of the floor with pool tables and a shuffleboard court. He'd added grass-fed jerky and electrolyte-heavy drinks to the Salty Kitchen. He'd brought a "neg alarm" to the Imagination Room, which anyone could sound upon hearing the words *no, but,* or *can't.* And his latest initiative was a series of weekly "Yes, And" meetings, wherein Marketing associates gathered in a circle around an engineer to build a campaign for the engineer's design. "It's a tool I learned at Wharton," he'd written in a circulated memo about the meetings.

Can one learn a tool? Ava thought upon receiving the memo. The meeting would amount to Ava's personal hell, and this week it was her turn to present the Very Nice Box.

I can't believe I have to do this, she wrote to her SHRNK.

I can understand why this activity could be stressful. Who could you be if you allowed yourself to be pleasantly surprised? her SHRNK had responded.

She refused to discuss the meeting with Mat on the drive to work, lest he try to pitch it to her as an important team-building experience, or talk up Marketing, or preach the virtues of positivity, or explain to Ava why Engineering and Marketing belonged in the same room. They didn't. Plus there was the rule about not talking about work outside of work.

But even if she could avoid talking about the meeting, she could not avoid the meeting itself, so at 3 p.m. she made her way to the Encouraging Desk Chair situated in the center of the Imagination Room, which was surrounded by a circle of a dozen empty, identical chairs. Soon those seats were filled by Marketing staffers. Most she didn't know, but some she recognized; there was Sofia, for one, sitting with one leg crossed tightly over the other, and Vince, the junior Marketing rep from the Fry Shack line. The room was tight with anticipation, and Ava suspected she was alone in her dread.

Finally Mat arrived, closing the door quietly behind him. His hair was attractively disheveled, and he had tucked his white T-shirt into his jeans. The room went quiet, and although Ava was seated at the center of the circle, everyone's attention was on Mat.

She felt dizzy with stress. Mat took a seat, winked at her, and leaned in. "It's going to be fine," he whispered. She saw Sofia look up and witness the moment with a raised eyebrow.

"Folks," Mat said, clapping his hands together once. He paused to look everyone in the eye. "Welcome to STÄDA's sixth-ever 'Yes, And' meeting. Today we will be learning about the latest Passion Project from STÄDA's senior engineer Ava Simon."

There was a weak smatter of applause.

"Ava," Mat said, clasping his hands behind his head and crossing his boots at the ankle. "What can you tell us about the Very Nice Box?"

"Well," Ava said. Her voice echoed against the wall of faces, each focused on her. She momentarily forgot what her job was, what product she was discussing, and why she was sitting there. Her mouth felt wired shut. She couldn't think of any words at all, let alone a series of logical words that would join together to describe the Very Nice Box.

What had her SHRNK told her to do to calm down? *Who could you be if you transported yourself to an ideal environment?* her SHRNK had said. *Where would that be?* The answer to that question at one point had been *Home, listening to my parents play music.* Then it became *Home, with Andie and Brutus.* But lately, if she was honest, the answer was *Mat's car, on the way to work,* which she had admitted to her SHRNK earlier that morning. She tried to visualize herself in Mat's car. The taste of slightly cooled milky coffee, the warm cup in her hands, the pleasant deepness of his voice. She took a breath. She had to pull herself out of the well of despair. *Imagine a rope,* her SHRNK might say. *Who could you be if you climbed the rope?*

Mat leaned in again. "You got this," he said, placing a hand on her shoulder. "You got this, one thousand percent."

She climbed the rope. She visualized the Very Nice Box. It was beautiful, with perfect dimensions and an ingenious lid. She took a breath. "I'm finalizing the design for the Very Nice Box, which is a box that can be used in a multitude of ways with other pieces in the Very Nice collection, which we hope to launch next year. We're spending a lot of time on the most basic component to make sure the line is orthogonal and easy to understand while still being elegant and up to STÄDA's craftsmanship standards."

"But what's it for?" someone from Marketing said loudly. Ava looked up. It was Owen Lloyd. He wore what Ava now recognized as his signature look: a neon-yellow polo with the collar popped. Ava glanced at his Decent Notebook. At the top of the page he had written *Box?*

"It's a box," Ava said.

"You mean *box*, like . . . *box*?" Owen said, unsuccessfully suppressing a smile. He glanced at Mat.

"Obviously not," Ava said, exasperated.

"Okay," Owen said, circling the question mark. "But, like . . . what's it for?"

"For *objects*," Ava said, containing her impatience. "People put things inside boxes. The Very Nice Box is simply an extra-large box for large things, or even perhaps a large quantity of smaller things."

"Maybe if we back up for a moment." It was Sofia speaking up now, to Ava's annoyance. She had her own pad of paper out, and a bright red pen, which she rapidly clicked several times. "What makes the Very Nice Box different from, say, the Memorable Archives Box?"

"Everything," Ava said. "Everything is different about it. The Memorable Archives Box is for photographs, artwork, and letters. It doesn't have hinges; the lid slides along a track. And it's much narrower."

"So could you say this is a more refined version of the Purposeful Loose Ends Box?" Sofia said, jotting down something that Ava couldn't make out. Had she researched every box Ava had ever designed in order to try to bring her down at this meeting?

"Not exactly," Ava said, her face heating up. "The Purposeful Loose Ends Box is one-quarter the size of the Very Nice Box and designed to sit on a shelf exclusively."

"So this is like a more versatile Sociable Coffee Table," Sofia said.

"No," Ava said. "It's a box."

Sofia closed her eyes for a long moment. "I want to make sure Marketing totally understands how to promote your design. Its purpose appears to be clear to you, but it's not yet clear to me."

"Well—" Ava began.

The sound of an airhorn pierced the air, startling everybody. "I'm sorry for the neg alarm, but I'm going to pause us right there," Mat said. "Remember that this is a 'Yes, And' meeting, not an 'Okay, But' meeting. Let's activate one thousand percent positivity. I, for one, love the idea of the Very Nice Box. There are *tons* of useless weird things that I have lying around my apartment. And don't even get me started on my car."

"You know, I actually like that!" a Marketing associate said. She was small, with a swoop of bangs that obscured one eye. "It's like, everyone has junk, and everyone loves boxes." Why was it that as soon as Mat backed something, it became not only acceptable but popular?

"Well, that's one way to look at it—" Ava began.

"Yes!" Mat said. "And I think this fills a major, *major* marketing hole for us. We can one thousand percent market this as the box for minimalists."

"Yes!" a Marketing intern chimed in. It was one of the guys who'd left the table in the cafeteria as soon as Mat had arrived. His face was covered in acne scars. "And that's actually perfect, because minimalists make up such a big portion of our clientele."

"Yes!" Mat responded. "And even minimalists can't help owning a few clunky things, like laundry detergent and dustpans."

"Yes," Owen Lloyd boomed. "And so the Very Nice Box

is like . . . a cool minimalist solution for minimalists who fell off the wagon and started buying more stuff even though they tried not to."

"Yes!" someone shouted. "And—"

It went on like this for what felt like six units. Ava had no time to interject, correct, or even agree. She listened as the Marketing team built a campaign around her design. It was strange and oddly exhilarating. They ended the meeting by shouting the word *GO!*

"Thank you, Ava," Mat said, closing the meeting. Everyone left the Imagination Room in high spirits, as though they'd just finished a group workout. "Sofia? Do me a solid and take the lead on sending the summary around in the next hour."

Sofia looked up at him as though he'd asked her to dry-clean his T-shirt.

As Ava walked back to her desk, she felt giddy. *Who could you be if you allowed yourself to be pleasantly surprised?* her SHRNK had said.

And she had! She was left with the adrenaline of having been heard. She wouldn't have expected to enjoy the room's attention as much as she did, and the enthusiasm around the Very Nice Box was infectious. Who cared if they didn't appreciate its perfect dimensions? They liked it. Except Sofia, apparently, and that actually made Ava feel better.

A flurry of S-Chat messages from Mat appeared in the top right corner of her screen.

I'm so sorry

That was probably hell for u

One day I'll understand what you actually intended for that trunk

It's a box! Ava wrote.

He used the facepalm emoji. *You see, it can just be really hard for me to understand things sometimes.*

Ava couldn't read his tone, so she looked over at him through his glass office doors. He had his feet up on his desk, and he was pretending to read one of his management books (*Good Work*) upside down. He was trying not to smile, waiting for her to see him.

She caught a glimpse of her reflection in the monitor and found herself smiling. She pushed her hair out of her face and brought herself back down.

As she went about her day, the energy from the meeting followed her. She was feeling decidedly yellow. In the Wellness Kitchen, she poured herself a glass of Wellness Water. It was delicious: pineapple and basil. Whoever came up with the combination should get a Welcome Raise, she thought. Jaime joined her and began fixing himself a Comforting Mug of green tea.

"Glad it's over?" he said.

"Glad what's over?"

"The 'Yes, And' meeting. I'm guessing being surrounded by, like, twenty Owen Lloyds was your personal hell."

"I actually . . . I actually liked it!" Ava said, refilling her glass.

Jaime looked at her incredulously. "Seriously? You *liked* the 'Yes, And' meeting? Do I know you?"

"Believe me when I say I'm as surprised as you are," Ava said. "I just . . . I don't know, I kind of got swept up in it."

"Next thing I know you'll be color-coding your apps like that psychopath on *Hotspot*. I mean, can you believe that dude?"

"I didn't see it," Ava said.

"Seriously? It's such a good one!"

Ava saw Mat heading their way, twirling his car keys around his index finger.

"Actually," Ava said, "I've kind of fallen behind. I don't think it really does much for me anymore."

Jaime looked puzzled. "What do you mean?"

"It just ... it's kind of a depressing show when you think about it."

"Ready to blow this popsicle stand?" Mat said, startling Jaime so thoroughly that he spilled some tea on his shirt.

"Sorry," Jaime said.

"Why?" Mat said.

"I don't know," Jaime said. "You scared me."

"Then *I'm* sorry," Mat said. He handed Jaime a paper towel and grabbed himself a Zing! Ginger-Turmeric Tonic from the refrigerator. "Ready to go, Ave?" he said, twisting the cap.

Ava watched as Jaime blotted his shirt. "Yes," she said. "I'm ready."

12

THEY WERE APPROACHING HER NEIGHBOR-
hood, her street, her apartment. An uninvited thought of Mat
inside her apartment crossed Ava's mind. She had never, since
moving in, had a friend over. Not even Jaime. She allowed the
possibility to wash over her. It would be very yellow of her, inviting a friend upstairs, spontaneously. The thought excited
and terrified her. Not even the building's super had seen her
immaculate kitchen, her minimalist furniture, the cozy alcove
where she slept. She'd begun describing the studio to Mat on
their drive. "It could pass for a miniature STÄDA showroom,"
she said. "I could count the things that aren't STÄDA on one
hand."

He pulled alongside the curb and put the car in Park. The
prospect of inviting him upstairs hung above her, out of reach.
"Thanks," she said, unbuckling her seatbelt. "I should buy a car.
I'm sorry this has been such a hassle."

"It's really not a problem," Mat said. "Actually—"

"What?"

"Nothing," he said. "Never mind. Happy to drive you, that's all." His smile was affectionate, but she felt he was hiding something, and she was desperate to know what it was.

"You can tell me," she said.

"I guess I just wanted to say . . ." Mat said, rubbing the back of his head. Her pulse quickened as he hesitated. "I really think your Passion Project is cool. Like, really cool. Not to get all approving-boss on you. I just thought it was really cool, and that you should know that." The last of the sunlight brought out the blue in his eyes.

"Oh," Ava said. "Thanks." She smiled at him, though she felt a little disappointed by his praise. She knew the Very Nice Box was good. She had no insecurities about the work. She'd been hoping for something else. "Well," she said. "This is me. STÄDA 2.0. The place where the Very Nice Box was conceived." As soon as she said it, she wanted to take it back.

"Could I see it?" Mat said.

"See the Very Nice Box? Well, no, I haven't quite worked out the closure, so I don't think—"

"Not the box." Mat laughed. "Your apartment. I mean, if it's really STÄDA 2.0, I think it would be good for Marketing to take a look. See how STÄDA lives and breathes in the real world so we can bring that angle to our next 'Yes, And' meeting." He put air quotes around *real world*.

"Oh," Ava said, staring straight ahead. The sun and moon were side-by-side. She felt winded. Did he want to see her things, or did he want to see more of her? Had he read her mind? Now was her chance. For once, she could let someone in. She was having trouble locating enough oxygen to breathe.

"Forget it," he said. "Sorry I asked. That was out of line." He rubbed the back of his head again, looking embarrassed, not meeting her eye.

"No," she said. She hadn't prepared herself for his actually asking to come up. She swallowed. She had to walk Brutus. There were only a few units before she was scheduled to fall asleep. "It's okay that you asked," she said. "It's just that I have plans, so it won't work tonight."

"Of course," Mat said. "That was crazy short notice anyway. I'll see you in the morning." She sensed the regret in his smile, and her chest ached.

Upstairs, through the window, Ava watched his car pull away. The exhaust lingered above the pavement before dissipating. The days were getting shorter and colder. Every evening after Mat dropped her off, Ava felt an intensifying combination of exhilaration and disappointment.

She wished she could talk to Andie. She wanted her approval, and she wondered what Andie would make of this crush, though she already knew the answer.

Ava had discussed her occasional attraction to men with Andie, although early in their relationship she'd resisted, in part because the attraction was opaque, even to herself. She had also kept quiet for fear of seeming overly complicated or burdensome. It was simpler to ignore men—the outliers in the schema of her romantic attraction—and she felt obligated to, though she wasn't sure why. She sometimes felt insecure around Andie's friends because her experience had been different from theirs. She had come out more recently, and her story was less fraught, without the strife of puberty or the fear of losing her family's support.

But Andie had smiled at Ava's confession. They were lounging on Andie's Easygoing Sofa, and Andie pulled her in tightly, Ava's back against her chest. "Do you want to tell me about it?" Andie asked plainly, though the question contained all the electricity of a command.

So Ava described the attraction. As she spoke, Andie undid the top buttons of Ava's shirt and slid a warm hand inside. "What else?"

Ava continued, walking Andie through the mechanics of her fantasy. She told her about how the anonymous man might pin her to the bed, and the way he might feel pressed against her.

Andie unbuttoned Ava's jeans and reached for her hand, fitting it snugly inside, before bringing her own hand back to Ava's chest. Ava pressed down, carrying out her own steady rhythm.

"And then what?"

Ava's entire body was charged. Andie held her tightly, her mouth against Ava's neck. She continued until her heart was pounding and she was pinned between Andie and the abstract person, who had no face and no name, who was just a series of attributes that might have made a man.

Ava revisited the fantasy often, but after the accident it was difficult to remove Andie from the frame or re-create the electricity of the moment. But lately she could not deny that Mat had begun to stand in for the other figure.

Now here she was in her kitchen, with no plans. How many weeks had she watched him pull away from her apartment? She felt like a toy train coming to the end of its course, only to begin the exact same one again.

Enough, she thought.

She clicked on Brutus's Curious Leash. "Let's go see Emily," she said. "Would you like that?" Brutus barked once in approval.

The evening was brisk and invigorating. Ava had no idea how she would say what she needed to say to Mat. But she wanted to convey to him the fuller picture of her life. Andie was only an ex because she was dead. She would have to tell him that. She had trouble inviting people into her life. So much trouble that she hadn't done it since the accident. She would explain this to him too.

She would tell him about how she'd once had friends, but they'd looked at her with such pity after the accident that being around them had become exhausting. She could feel the friends editing what they said around her, as though the words *family, fiancée, parents,* and *car* would offend her or send her into a dark place.

And maybe they were right. But they treated her like she carried an infectious disease—as though by simply knowing Ava, by being around her, her friends might also find their whole lives stolen in a few dark seconds.

She would tell Mat about how slowly, over time, the friendships had frayed and then disintegrated entirely. She was left with Brutus and an apartment that she bought with the combined savings of her parents, which could have bought her a bigger place in the city, if she had wanted that. But she didn't want anything bigger than was absolutely necessary, so she bought the studio in cash.

And she'd tell him that the transaction had left her with a good amount of savings. She didn't even need to work, really. But the work instilled her life with meaning, and the thought of leaving STÄDA paralyzed her.

She rounded the park and approached Mat's apartment building. Ava had driven by it during all its stages; she'd seen workers pour the foundation only a few months before. And now it was tall and shiny, its glassy facade unlike that of any building nearby, with balconies jutting from each floor. She ran her finger down the list of last names by the buzzer. It was dark. She would apologize for lying to him about having plans, and the dogs could play. Maybe they could even eat dinner together somewhere. *No,* she thought. That would be too much. It would be so unlike Ava to suggest dinner that the idea would draw unnecessary attention to itself. An apology was fine, a short walk around the park with the dogs. She found his name and apartment—12F—and rang his bell. She considered turning around to go home. There was still time to leave. She looked at her Precise Wristwatch for no good reason, and at that moment the buzzer crackled. "Hello?" Mat's voice said uncertainly.

"It's me," Ava said. "Um, Ava, I mean. And Brutus."

The static ended abruptly, and soon Mat was opening the door. He popped his head out, looking perplexed. "Did you forget something in my car?" he said.

"No, no," Ava said, although it would have been a good out. "It's just—" She was shivering. She wished he would invite her into the lobby. Brutus whined at her feet. "I wanted to apologize," she said, looking down at her boots. Her breath came out in a white cloud. "I lied to you when I said I had plans tonight."

"Oh," Mat said. His face softened. He studied her expression. "Okay. No problem. That's totally okay. I know sometimes it's just nice to decompress after work. And not hang out with" —he was rubbing the back of his head again—"your boss."

"It's not that," she said. "It's not that at all. We would love to see you and Emily. A do-over."

"Oh," he said. He looked at Brutus. "Right now?" He smiled up at her. "It's actually maybe not a great ti—"

"Mat?" A woman showed up behind him. "Who is it?"

"Ella," Mat said. "This is—" He cleared his throat, which had gone hoarse. "This is one of STÄDA's best engineers, Ava Simon. And Ava, this is Ella, who—"

"I'm sorry," Ava said. She tugged on Brutus's leash, and he stood. "I'm very sorry for disturbing your evening." She could barely look at Ella, but she got the picture. Tall, with narrow shoulders and thin arms. She had a tattoo of a bird on her triceps. Ava felt a bolt of shame course through her as she turned to go.

"Wait!" Mat said, but she'd already begun walking away, and she wasn't going to turn around now. How could she have thought it was acceptable to show up at her boss's home, prepared with her life story, expecting him to have no plans and no . . . girlfriend?

Was she upset about the girlfriend?

No, she thought, winding her way back through the park. It's just . . . he should have *mentioned* the girlfriend to her. But no, that wasn't right either. Why should he have? That wasn't her business. After all, she hadn't told him the full story about Andie. Some things were better kept private. And yet—she had to admit—she had thought, somewhere, that there was something between them.

She wanted to cry from the humiliation. She could *not* ride with him to work in the morning—or any day, for that matter, ever again.

She was walking so quickly that Brutus had to trot alongside her. *It's actually maybe not a great time.* She was so caught up in her spiraling thoughts that she almost didn't notice the bracelet lying by the curb near her apartment. A streetlamp had lit it up. She crouched to see and pushed Brutus's face away from it so she could get a better look. She picked it up and turned it over in her palm: it was a yellow bracelet. Grooved into the rubber was the word *outgoing*. It was Mat's. It must have fallen out of his car.

She put the bracelet on and examined her wrist. It was too big for her, and she hated the feeling of the rubber against her skin. She took it off, walked to the corner of her block, and dropped it in a metal trash can, where it joined a wet pile of garbage. But walking back to her apartment, she felt a surge of guilt and returned to the can and reached for it, grazing a damp paper cup in the process. *Kill me,* she said to no one. She shoved it into her pocket and made her way to her building, doing all she could to forget about what had happened—a skill at which she excelled.

13

THIS WAS WHAT SHE COULD REMEMBER:

A steadily beeping machine, casters rattling against the linoleum floor, a man's voice reciting numbers. Fiberglass ceiling panels, an opaque curtain, her own feet in unfamiliar socks.

She took a mental inventory, repeating the list to herself again, as if the scenery could generate a logic of its own. *A beeping machine, casters rattling, a man's voice, a fiberglass ceiling, an opaque curtain, socks. A beeping machine, casters rattling, a man's voice, a fiberglass ceiling . . .*

She worked quickly to establish the facts, fighting against a heavy fog. Something had happened; she was in a hospital; she would have to let Andie know that she was here; Brutus would have to be fed. Her eyes skipped around a white room.

She tried to say all this, to open her mouth or muster something that could pause the man's voice, the hurried chatter and notetaking, but she couldn't. There was a fullness in her throat that felt like something she should be able to swallow away. She gagged and a nurse turned around. "Breathe in through your nose, through your nose. Nice and easy," he said, placing his hand on Ava's chest. It was his voice she had heard reciting numbers. The first two pieces of disparate information she was able to place together, like jigsaw pieces from a completely white puzzle. The numbers, the voice, belonged to her nurse.

"You have tubes in to help you breathe—that's what you're feeling in your throat," he said. "It's going to feel strange, but just try to relax. Shallow, easy breaths, okay? I'll be right here. Okay?"

Okay? Ava added the word to her inventory. His face swam in and out of focus.

She tried to focus on his features. His sturdy nose and square jaw. His stubble. Machines beeped steadily in dissonant tones. A swarm of nurses, followed by doctors, hurried toward her bed and then brushed past the curtain to the patient beside her. She could just make out their silhouettes, bent over her neighbor's bed, working quickly. *Get him to OR 4,* someone said.

"Okay?" the nurse asked again.

Ava nodded, but she didn't know what question she was answering.

A beeping machine, casters rattling, Ava repeated to herself. *Brutus needs to be fed. Tell Andie that Brutus needs to be fed. Okay.*

The pain had begun to creep in, reaching parts of her body she had never before had a reason to consider. The space between her elbow joints. The backs of her knees. The bridge of her nose.

What had happened? Eventually she'd be able to tell police officers about the blue pickup truck weaving toward her between the lanes, moving on the highway in a way that it shouldn't have been. She'd remember the driver's long brown hair and the unusual current of light that sent a chill through her body and made her hair stand on end. But these details wouldn't come to her for days. For now she searched her memory, finding only the smell of roasted nuts as she drifted out of consciousness.

She awoke later to a quiet hospital and the same fullness in her throat. The nurse with the square jaw told her she had been falling in and out of sleep for the past several hours. *Several hours,* she repeated to herself, adding new information to her list.

Something had happened; she'd been in the hospital for several hours; she'd have to let Andie know she was here; Brutus would have to be fed; the machines were beeping; the ceiling was fiberglass; the curtain was opaque; the casters were rattling; she was okay; she was alive.

14

AVA TOSSED BENEATH HER SHEETS WHILE fragmented details of the evening played on repeat like a horrible taunt.

Mat? Who is it? She couldn't knock the woman's voice out of her head, but she preferred this to the image of herself: an imposing, foolish stranger standing in the cold. She knew the sharpness of her embarrassment would dull eventually—embarrassment followed rules too—but it would take time —hundreds of units, she estimated—and it kept her awake. Just as she finally fell into a deep, blank sleep, the sun broke in through her windows, and her head buzzed heavily as she fumbled through her morning routine: making coffee, brushing her teeth, dressing, and walking Brutus. It took her half a unit longer than usual.

Can I pick u up? Mat had texted her.

She ignored it, and shivered inside the subway station,

where a steady drip of water fell from peeling iron beams into a murky gray puddle. Her train was late, which meant it would be too crowded to board unless she was standing in the exact spot where the doors opened. She looked at her Precise Wristwatch.

Despite the added time, she knew she'd be able to look as upset as she felt on public transit without fear of unwanted commentary, which was not what she'd come to expect from Swyft drivers. A new episode of *Thirty-Minute Machine* had been released that morning, and she thought about tuning in with her Peaceful Headphones, but she didn't want to confront any feelings that might arise from listening to the episode alone, so she simply wore the headphones and listened to nothing at all. She had no interest in feeling sorry for herself. She swiped away another text from Mat without reading it, then wished she had read it, and began ruminating about what it might have said: *I'm a complete idiot. I should have told you. I don't even really like her that much.*

She pushed the fantasy away. The first train heaved her to another train, which hissed and stalled its way toward Red Hook. Snow from earlier that week had begun to harden into a gray mound lining the sidewalk, forcing pedestrians to walk single file. They had to leap over slushy gray puddles that had pooled at every corner. Ava avoided the coordinated effort altogether, stepping out into the street, on the receiving end of honks from cars slushing by. She tried to make out the finer details of the skyline across the river, but a low, wet fog hung over it. This weather's imprecision made it worse than any other kind.

She pushed her way through STÄDA's enormous rotating glass doors and scanned her key card and waited for an empty elevator. She wiped the cold from her face. She wished she could just stay there, in the elevator, alone, all day. It was roomy and quiet. There was a leather bench, a cup holder, and even an outlet. She didn't want to see anyone, and she didn't want to be seen. She even wanted to avoid Jaime, who would be waiting for her near the hand sanitizers with a coffee when she stepped out of the elevator. But to her surprise, the doors opened to the anonymous bustle of engineers instead.

Ava thumbed the rubber bracelet in her pocket, assumed her most uninviting posture, and walked quickly to her desk. She wanted the bracelet to be far away from her apartment, out of view, out of reach. She wanted it purged from her life, along with everything else that had happened the night before. Her plan was to leave it on Mat's desk while he made his morning lap around Floor 12.

Jaime was sitting at the Engineering table with his Peaceful Headphones on and his gaze glued to his screen. Even if Ava had wanted to, she would know better than to intrude. She sat at her desk and searched his face briefly for an opening to at least gesture hello, but he gave her nothing.

On the Personality Test, Jaime had scored green — empathetic — across the board. Ava knew that his empathy sometimes swerved into oversensitivity. Andie had once told Ava about a time he'd brought homemade croissants to the office, and how upset he'd been when Andie took one into her morning meeting instead of eating it with him. After the croissant debacle, Andie had left him a perfect origami apology note. Ava tried to think of a similar gesture; she had never been on the receiving end of a mood like this. As she started her computer, her stomach sank at the sight of Mat's reflection, which drew closer until he was drumming on the back of her Encouraging Desk Chair.

"Good morning," he said.

She forced herself to look up at him. He held her gaze while he sipped his coffee. His expression was unreadable. Ava's cheeks burned and she broke the eye contact to look back at her screen. She pulled up the latest rendering of the Very Nice Box and rotated it by dragging her mouse, so that the bottom of the box—which featured a mandatory safety latch in case a child became stuck inside—was visible.

"Did you get my texts?"

"I didn't check my phone this morning," Ava said.

"I swung by to pick you up."

"Sorry," Ava said. "I should have given you a heads-up that I'd gotten a ride."

"Weird, I thought I saw you walking from the train," Mat said. He swirled his coffee cup. Ava was mortified, but Mat didn't linger on the lie. "You missed a really good T-double-M episode this morning," he said.

"That's too bad," Ava said. "I'll have to check it out."

This caught Jaime's attention. He'd clearly been listening. "T-Double-M?" he said from his desk.

"*Thirty-Minute Machine,*" Ava said.

Jaime turned back toward his computer and rolled his eyes.

"Hey, man," Mat said. "Don't make me push the neg alarm!" He was smiling, but Ava sensed an edge to the threat.

"It's just—*T-Double-M*? Who even calls it that?" Jaime had reddened.

Mat betrayed a flicker of embarrassment. "I guess I was just trying to be efficient, like Ava here. Let's encourage each other, okay? One thousand percent positivity all around. Sound good, Jaime?"

"Yes, Mathew," Jaime said. He pushed himself up from his Encouraging Desk Chair and headed toward the Wellness Kitchen.

Ava glanced up at Mat. His hair stuck up in the back, and his eyes were puffy. Ava wondered if he'd been awake all night too. But she let the thought stop there. She didn't want to know what—or worse, who—had kept him awake.

"You, um," she started, "you forgot this." She dug into her pocket and held out his yellow bracelet.

"Amazing—where'd you find this?" Mat said, taking it. "Saved me a trip to the Swag Lounge! I mean, who *am* I without my yellow bracelet?"

"You must have dropped it on the street. Outside my apartment."

Despite her full-body effort to avoid thinking about the night before, she had done it: walked right back into the memory. Mat fit the bracelet onto his wrist. "Hey, um, listen," he said quietly. "Do you have a minute to talk?"

Ava hesitated. She felt her humiliation like a mask on her face. "Actually," she said, "I'm behind on integrating the Very Nice Box's safety feature."

"Oh," Mat said. He looked genuinely disappointed. "That's too bad." He waited a beat, and she knew he was waiting for her to change her mind. She felt trapped.

"Maybe later, though," she said.

"Oh, really? Great," Mat said. He lingered a moment, as if preparing to say something more. Instead he patted the hair at the back of his head and made his way to his office.

Ava closed her eyes. She would will her embarrassment away. She would devote herself to hinges, bolts, latches, and knobs. She would work several Unlimited Outdoors Breaks into her afternoon to break up the remaining units and clear her head. She would attempt to resolve things with Jaime. She would—

Her email pinged.

Dear Ava,

I am pleased to see that you've arrived promptly to work, as usual. Please meet me in the People Office as soon as possible.

Regards,
Judith Ball
Chief People Officer
Green

Ava's heart skipped. She opened her S-Cal. Had she missed a Self-Review appointment? Had she said something wrong during the "Yes, And" meeting? She looked around the floor, but everything looked normal. The Technical team sat with their headsets next to a row of coders. A presentation on workplace harassment was happening in the Imagination Room. A couple Spirit team members milled by the Wellness Water cooler. She made her way through the atrium and the Salty Kitchen, past the enormous weeping fig tree that shot up through the center of the building, into an elevator, up three floors, and finally into the crisp, glassed-in offices that housed People. She could smell the pine cleaner before she was even inside Judith's office, which was immaculate and flooded with natural light. Judith's seniority at STÄDA meant she had the best office in the building, with a clear view of the Statue of Liberty behind her, the new STÄDA parking lot to her right, and the well-groomed baseball fields in front of her.

"Ava," Judith said. "Thank you for coming in. We'll just wait one more moment."

"Wait?" Ava said, closing the door behind her. Her throat was tight and the back of her neck was on fire. "For what?"

"*Whom*, in this case," Judith said, glancing up at her. "Have a seat."

She did. They sat for a moment in terrible silence. A Tranquil Clock hung near the door—the same as the one in Ava's kitchen. Andie's design. Judith sat across from her, apparently undisturbed by the length of silence. She peeled an orange. Ava fixated on Judith's hands as she took a Prepared Pocket Knife and cut into the skin, tracing two incisions around the longest axes of the fruit. The skin came off in four identical pieces. She hadn't even cut into its flesh.

Behind Judith, her two diplomas hung on the wall, along with the framed photograph of Judith's twin daughters. The two girls sat in a treehouse, wearing cutoff shorts and sleeveless shirts.

"I like that photo," Ava said, attempting to slice through the silence. But Judith did not need to respond. The door had opened. Mat stood, looking unsure of himself.

"Mathew," Judith said. "Please, sit." He did, glancing at Ava with an eyebrow cocked. Ava looked away. She tried to ignore the hard stone that had lodged itself against her throat.

"Mathew, Ava," Judith said, "I've called you in here today to discuss the nature of your relationship." She pulled a crisp piece of paper from her desk drawer and uncapped an Inky Black Pen. At the top of the form, in STÄDA's signature font, were the words WORKPLACE RELATIONSHIP DISCLOSURE FORM. Ava had never seen a STÄDA form like this. She and Andie had never been required to officially disclose their relationship; the company had been too young back then, without a fully formed People Office.

"Sorry, what?" Mat said.

"You may *act* baffled if you wish," Judith said. "But the fact of the matter is I happened to see you both having breakfast in public a few weeks ago, and yesterday I observed you leaving the parking lot together in Mathew's car. Finally, I've noted that you have coordinated your Unlimited Outdoors Breaks—"

"Listen, Judith," Mat interrupted, dragging out the *L* in *Listen* just long enough for Judith to change her posture. He softened his voice. "I get that relationship disclosures are important, but this really isn't necessary. As Ava's manager, I want to make sure I can cut through the noise and empower her to—"

"Mathew," Judith said, with enough quiet force to get him to stop talking. "It's precisely because you're her manager that this is so important. You can't open STÄDA up to unnecessary liability. Now is the time to clear up the matter." She tapped the end of her pen on her desk.

"Nothing is going on between Mat and me," Ava said. "Romantic or otherwise. He's my manager."

"Yes, I was part of the hiring process," Judith said. "But thank you for that reminder."

"And in any case, he has a girlfriend." She stared at the polished concrete floor. She didn't sound like herself. Her feelings jumped ahead of every word she spoke. "Are we excused now?" Her ears burned.

"All true," said Mat. "Except the girlfriend part. I don't have a girlfriend." He crossed his ankle over his knee and clasped his hands behind his head. "So I'm glad we're here to clear that up. Thanks for the feedback on my attitude, Judith," he said, facing her. "I've been giving Ava rides to and from work because the Vandals destroyed her car."

Judith looked alarmed and turned to Ava. "Why didn't you report that to Security?"

"Why would she?" Mat said. "Unless someone in Security is a mechanic, all Ava would get from Security is a survey asking her how she felt about Security. No offense to those surveys. I like them, but you have to understand they're really more of a long-term strategy, not for crises."

"Even so," Judith started, "all matters of security—"

"As for Outdoors Breaks," Mat continued, "we've been co-ordinating them to stay fresh on several upcoming campaigns for Ava's box designs." He sounded calm, as though he were discussing something as boring as refilling a water cooler. "Ava kindly showed up at my apartment last night—"

"So you've seen each other after hours, at home?" Judith brought the tip of the Inky Black Pen to the piece of paper.

"Yes, but just because Ava was nice enough to drop off the personality bracelet that fell out of my car." He pulled the bracelet out of his pocket. He was so convincing that Ava momentarily believed that this *was* how the evening had gone.

"When I answered the door," Mat continued, "my sister was home. So Ava must be mistaking my sister for my girlfriend."

Ava's breath caught in her throat.

"As for my relationship with Ava," Mat said, "it is, as Ava stated, purely professional. Something you might not totally *see*, as a Gen-Xer, is that professional work happens both inside and outside office walls. Friendship, trust, and fun are all integral. We're really redefining what it means to be productive. Right, Ava?"

"What?" All his words had fallen away except "my sister," which made Ava feel like she had stepped out of a bad dream and into a much better one.

"Any interactions we've had have been friendly discussions about the Very Nice Box, Ava's fantastic new Passion Proj—"

"I know what the Very Nice Box is," Judith said, dismissing him with a wave of her hand. "I watched the 'Yes, And' meeting from the virtual conference channel."

Ava must be mistaking my sister for my girlfriend. Her assumption now seemed ridiculous. How could she have assumed the woman was his girlfriend without considering all the facts? He'd never *mentioned* a sister, but then again, she had never asked whether he had siblings. Did they live together? Was she just visiting? She remembered the woman's hand on Mat's shoulder. So he had a sister he was close to. And she had lost an entire night of sleep over it.

"Ava, the Very Nice Box is elegant," Judith said, straightening her pin. "I think Andie would be—well . . ." She cleared her throat. "She would be proud."

"Thanks," Ava said. She felt her throat constrict. Judith may not have been one to commiserate, but Ava suspected that she had privately grieved Andie's death. When Ava had returned to work after the accident, she learned that Judith had retired Andie's role. Although Judith had framed it as a business decision—that promoting Jaime and a few other interns would be cheaper than hiring a new department head—Ava suspected that the decision was more sentimental than Judith let on. Now Judith jotted something on the piece of paper that Ava couldn't clearly see, aside from the words *professional, Unlimited, productivity,* and *bracelet.*

"And Mathew, I trust that your work is progressing smoothly? You must be busy with all your regular duties on *top* of overseeing the Vandals task force. I'm eagerly awaiting your plan, which I have no doubt will be thorough after all the time it's taken you. Do you have any updates to share on that front?"

Mat rubbed the back of his head. "As a matter of fact, I do have some exciting updates to share about the Vandals task force. I'm just putting the finishing touches on a proposal that I think you will be very happy with. I've been busy, but I like busy." Judith stared at him.

Mat cleared his throat.

"You're excused, if that's what you're asking by clearing your throat," Judith said. "Thank you both for your time and candor."

Ava felt an uncontrolled giddiness as she stood and they made their way out of Judith's office together.

"Jesus," Mat said, closing the door behind them. "What is she, stalking us?"

"I know," Ava said.

"The woman needs a hobby."

"I totally forgot you are in charge of the Vandals task force. Do you actually have a plan?"

"Between you and me, no. I one thousand percent forgot about that assignment." He shrugged. "But sometimes the last minute is the best minute."

They stepped into an elevator and Ava pushed the button for the twelfth floor. She was wired, her mind turning. He had a sister. He had no girlfriend. She had no reason to be embarrassed. He'd covered for her.

"Ava, there's more I have to tell you," Mat said as the elevator doors closed. His voice lowered, even though they were alone. He searched her face. "That woman from last night," he said. "She *isn't* my girlfriend. That part was true. But she also isn't my sister."

"What? Who is she?" Ava said. She felt like a fish that had been yanked out of the water and thrown back to sea only to be caught again. The elevator doors slid open. "Why did you say she was your sister?"

"I'll tell you later," Mat said, looking straight ahead and speaking so softly she had to strain to hear him. "Can I stop by tonight?"

"Stop by my apartment? Yes," Ava found herself saying. The words preempted the thought. "Of course. I'll see you tonight. What time?"

But Mat had already started toward his office, away from her.

15

AVA COULD NOT BEAR THE THOUGHT OF A TWO-unit commute home—not when she had to prepare her apartment for Mat—so she ordered a Swyft from the north lot of the Simple Tower.

"Enough heat?" the driver said.

"Yes," Ava said. She slipped on her Peaceful Headphones and closed her eyes, envisioning Mat inside her apartment. It was impossible—like imagining Roy Stone from *Thirty-Minute Machine* showing up. The days had become shorter and more brutal, and by the time she got home, it was dark. She walked Brutus through Fort Greene Park, the wind biting at her, blowing her hood off and chilling her so completely that her ears ached from the inside. Brutus quickly peed on a tree, then whined to turn around, his hind legs quivering in the cold. They headed back to her apartment, the night sharp in her face no matter which direction she turned in.

She's not my girlfriend. That part was true.

She tried to play back the rest of the conversation.

I'll tell you later.

Why had Mat lied, then? And to Judith! And how was Ava supposed to go on with her evening if she had no idea what time he was going to show up? Back inside, she unhooked Brutus's Curious Leash, and he shook his entire body, releasing himself from the grip of the cold.

Ava checked her phone. Nothing. Well, she needed to get on with her life. She couldn't just sit around waiting for Mat to show up whenever it was convenient for him.

But that was exactly what she did. She tidied the already tidy kitchen, lit an Enduring Candle, blew the candle out, remade her Principled Bed, neatened her Supportive Pillows, wiped down her Appealing Dining Table, and straightened out the clothing in her closets, even though it was already straightened. She looked out her window, desperate for a sign. Every passing car was his until it wasn't.

"Well, fine," she said to Brutus, and his tail beat against the floor expectantly. She started preparing lunch for the next day: a tidy salad with almonds and sweet potatoes. He wasn't coming at all, and she was the butt of a joke she didn't understand. Maybe he'd forgotten his own plan entirely, or changed his mind without telling her. Maybe he'd been in a car wreck. Her Serious Knife slipped, slicing into her thumb.

"Fuck," she said. "Jesus." She moved to contain the blood with a paper towel. It was this sort of small jolt—a slip of a knife, or tripping over a sidewalk crack, or hearing someone lay on a horn—that would suddenly send her into a dark place. She held the paper towel against the cut, which bled through immediately, and, leaning against her kitchen counter, she began to cry.

Since the accident, life had felt unfairly hard. She tried to think of what Andie would say to comfort her now. *It's just a cut. You're all right. C'mere. Let me see that.* She wiped her face with the crook of her elbow and brought another paper towel against her thumb, which had begun to throb.

The buzzer rang, startling her, and Brutus barked.

Of course, Ava thought. She cleared her throat and hit Talk. "Hello?" she croaked.

"It's freezing! Open up!" Mat's voice carried through her intercom.

"Sorry," she said, buzzing him in, her heart once again out of its cage. The apartment was now a mess. There was no time to hide it from him—the blood had run through a wad of paper towels and now she saw there was some on the cutting board too, plus her nose was running and she probably looked—

"Ava?" Mat said, opening her door, sticking his head inside. "You always leave your door unlocked like this?"

"No!" she said. "No." She'd been so preoccupied with his visit that she hadn't even locked the door behind her. Who *was* she?

"Hey, what . . . what happened to you?"

Brutus trotted over to Mat and sniffed his leg.

Ava looked down at her thumb. "I was chopping . . . I didn't think you were going to come over . . . and then I slipped. I mean, the *knife* slipped, and I—"

"Are you crying?"

"*No,*" Ava said.

Mat smiled at her and tilted his head. He pulled her against his chest, into a tight hug. His coat still held the cold from outside, and her face was pressed against the zipper, but she didn't care. He held the back of her head with his huge palm. Brutus barked, and Ava suddenly remembered this about him—that he had the capacity to become jealous. As a puppy, any time she and Andie had gotten close, Brutus had attempted to leap between them or caused trouble somewhere else in the apartment to pull at their attention.

"Sit down," she said. "I'll make you some tea."

"*You* sit down," he said. "Where are your Band-Aids?"

"I'll get them," she said.

"Sit," Mat said. "You too," he said to Brutus, who barked.

Ava sat on her Practical Sofa and allowed herself the luxury of waiting to be waited on. "In the bathroom," she said. "Under the—"

"Got 'em," Mat said. He peeled open the bandage and sat next to her. He took her hand and clumsily wound it around the cut. "Nice apartment, by the way," he said. "You weren't kidding about this being a STÄDA showroom."

"It looked better before there was blood on my countertop."

Brutus jumped onto the Practical Sofa, between them.

"Off," Ava said.

Brutus looked solemnly at her, then walked to his Dreamy Dog Bed and sat, brooding, with a bone between his paws.

"Ava," Mat said. "About last night."

"Right," Ava said. "About that. Forget it. Forget I stopped by. I wish I could—"

"Ella—she's not my girlfriend, and she's not my sister. But —and I don't want you to think less of me when I tell you this."

Ava looked at him.

"Ella's my sponsor."

"Your . . . ?"

"My sponsor," said Mat.

"You're in AA?"

"No!" he said, laughing as though that was a crazy thing to assume. "No, no. I'm doing the Good Guys training."

Ava knew vaguely about the Good Guys program, in the same way that she knew vaguely about CrossFit and reiki, but would not, if pressed, be able to convey the central tenets of any of them. An enigmatic ad campaign for Good Guys had run briefly on the subway. At first she'd assumed it was an erectile dysfunction intervention based on the ad copy: *Good Guys Stand Tall.* She remembered the managerial book Mat had moved into the backseat of his car the first time she had accepted a ride from him: *Good Work.*

"What *is* that program?"

"It sounds goofy, I know," Mat said. "But basically it helps guys like me get back on their feet and keep up self-care regimens and do good in the world."

"Guys like you?"

"Yeah, like . . . you know, good guys who have had some rough times."

"Oh," Ava said, not quite understanding. It did sound like AA, but without the alcohol. She wondered what sort of "rough times" Mat had endured. The accident had robbed her of some of her empathy. She'd once accepted that all pain was relative. Now she wasn't so sure. The silence between them was heavy with awkwardness. Was she supposed to ask him to elaborate on his past troubles? She was curious, but didn't want to press him, and wanted even less for him to return the question.

"Anyway, yeah," he said. "I have a sponsor. Which is basically, like . . . a woman, you know."

"A woman?"

"Yeah, a woman to practice communication with."

Ava stared at him.

"We pay them!" Mat said, seeming to read her mind. "It's something between peer-to-peer therapy and having a life coach. And I try to take it as seriously as possible. But I guess it's a little embarrassing for me." He rubbed the back of his head. "I just didn't really want Judith knowing that about me," he said. "You know? She's so nosy as it is . . . I just didn't want —plus I'm in charge of all these people and I didn't want it to be the first thing people thought of when they talked to me."

Ava had never seen him struggle through an explanation like this. She felt for him—the same fear of spectacle led her to keep the details of her own life private. "You don't have to explain," she said cautiously. "I can see why."

"Really?" Mat said. He looked relieved, and relaxed against her Practical Sofa. "Thank you. People don't always respond well." He took a deep breath. "You're so *cool*," Mat said. "Very green of you."

Ava felt relieved too, and eager to live up to the compliment.

"The reason she was at my apartment last night," Mat said, "is that I had to confer with her about something. Because in Good Guys, I mean, you're really not supposed to make any big life decisions without talking it over with your sponsor."

"Life decisions," Ava repeated.

"And that includes—I mean, for instance, if you—not *you* you, but the universal you—wanted to start a romantic ... Okay, this is hard for me to explain, and I don't want to put you in an uncomfortable position, because I know that technically I'm your boss." He laughed, though there was no joke here, as far as Ava could tell. He continued to pat down the hair on the back of his head. She'd come to find this mannerism endearing. His cheeks had reddened. And she suddenly became warm too. He pulled his coat off, and although ordinarily it would have bothered her that he hadn't hung it up, she couldn't bring herself to care. Her heart thudded while Mat searched for whatever words he needed to convey to her what she now already knew, and because it was in her nature never to waste time, she leaned in to kiss him.

16

IN THE DAYS AFTER THE ACCIDENT, AVA WAS only ever sleeping or waking or falling asleep. She grew accustomed to the patterns of the hospital. Resident physicians alternated night shifts, the lights dimmed at 10 p.m., a janitor slogged a heavy mop past her bed twice a day, and her doctor pushed through the curtain occasionally to bark questions at the nurses on call.

The nurse looking after her was Teddy; Ava learned his name as he leaned over her bed, the letters written in black marker on the breast pocket of his scrubs. He was the only one to really look at Ava. The rest of the team moved around her as if she were a mute bug. Teddy would translate what the doctor said into plain, digestible fragments. Ava had found some version of peace that allowed her to lay still with her breathing tube in, to tolerate her life, believing it would not be this way forever because Teddy promised her. "Swelling going down," he said. "Okay?"

Rattling around in the back of her mind, between episodes of heavy sleep, was the possibility that the worst had happened. It started as a thought that Ava could dutifully push aside. Her fear was kaleidoscopic. She could bend it, build new shapes of the truth with it. She could almost make the facts feel different. Andie hadn't come to visit. Her parents hadn't come to visit. But she hadn't visited them either, and here she was, alive.

But the fear grew. It took on the horrible bloat of dread. It forced a space in the back of her throat, and she began to see the room through a dark film. When she closed her eyes, she saw its grainy, bruised negative: Andie in the car, her father in the car, her mother in the car. She felt that if only she could account for them, she could correct this headcount error. It was a clerical matter, a matter of inventory.

Her doctor pulled the curtain aside and sat down beside Ava's bed. It was the first time he had directed his body toward her, the first time he had acknowledged her at all. He was a tall, angular man with dark shadows beneath his eyes.

"My name is Dr. Lansing. Like the town in Michigan. I'm sure these have been a difficult couple of days. I'm here to give you some updates and talk about what happens next." His tone had a manufactured quality that reminded Ava of wood veneer.

He opened her chart.

Andie, she thought.

"First let's talk about your condition. You suffered a concussion and a collapsed lung. You have four broken ribs, a fractured patella, and a broken wrist. We have you on a steady drip of morphine to manage the pain, which may be making you feel nauseous and groggy. But your condition is stable, and you're recovering nicely. We're optimistic. Teddy will be removing your breathing tube in a few minutes."

He closed the chart. "You were in a serious hit-and-run car accident. You're very lucky to be alive. Thank god for seatbelts," he said, tapping the side of his head, as though he had invented them.

There was something in his steady, even tone that was sharp enough to rupture the veil of hope that Ava had been weaving together. She could feel herself being managed by him. She imagined him in medical school, breaking off with a partner to practice this protocol. She felt the sting and swell of a cut on her neck.

She didn't want to hear about seatbelts. She was desperate for an update about her family, but all she could do was stare up at him and wait.

"So, the bad news," he said. "The other passengers in the vehicle . . ." He paused. "You are the only survivor."

The air drained from the room. He reached for her hand. She absently allowed him to comfort her. It was as if she had run off a cliff but hadn't yet begun to fall.

He said something about a mental fitness evaluation, and then the police would be in to take her statement and a social worker would talk her "through the grief." He was sorry, he said. He wished he could give her all the time she needed. And then he stood, offering a lingering look of practiced sympathy, and turned her over to Teddy.

She could feel the long, rigid tube make its way up her esophagus, past her throat, and then out. "I know," Teddy said. "I know it's awful. It's almost over." Her breath rattled. She had her voice back, as if there were anything to say.

She next awoke to two police officers who had arrived with blue pens and pages of paperwork. They wanted to know what she remembered. They handed her a bird's-eye drawing of a car and asked her to check a box beside the quadrant where the impact had occurred. They wanted to know where she was headed with her fiancée and parents. Ava didn't know whether they were personally curious or whether the answer was part of their investigation. They wanted to know what she remembered of the other driver.

Even if she wanted to, she could barely remember. The clearest image that came to her was the strange, bright channel of light. In Ava's collapsed memory of the collision, it was as if the cars were fixed in place and the other driver — specifically her hair — was the only thing moving, as if the tiny universe of the accident had its own laws of gravity. Then her mother's voice, the crunch of metal, the smell of roasted nuts, the wail of a siren. More than anything, though, she was fixated on the light. "I don't know what it was," she said to the officers.

"We hear that often with victims of these, uh, these kinds of accidents. It's common to experience trauma as a flash of light."

"No," Ava said emphatically. "The light was *before* the accident. Seconds before, but still before. It was something different."

The officers nodded but didn't write anything down. She searched her memory, but it was too painful. She had to blink the light away. Remembering exhausted her. She reluctantly surrendered to a morphine-induced sleep. To rest felt like a betrayal, but resisting was impossible.

17

WAS IT POSSIBLE THAT MAT PUTNAM WAS ASLEEP in her Principled Bed?

At 2:43 in the morning?

Ava couldn't help but take advantage of this moment— so many times she had made a point of not looking directly at him. It was like looking directly into the sun. But now she could let her gaze linger. He was even more handsome asleep than he was awake, his lips pouty, his brow relaxed, his breath heavy and sweet.

He'd been stronger than Ava had imagined—she felt a twinge at the memory of how he'd handled her after she kissed him, pressing her into the cushions of her Practical Sofa before lifting her clean off the cushions and onto her Comfortable Mattress. He'd fumbled with the clasp of her bra—he'd needed her to turn around, needed the light on for a second, needed both hands to undo it—but she appreciated that he didn't come off as well practiced.

After all, it had been a while for her too. She hadn't been with anyone since Andie, or even come close. It was surreal to revisit this version of herself, which apparently still contained the gestures of desire, muscle memory really, that she had been sure were buried with Andie.

And now she could still feel a tenderness where the knife had cut her thumb. Slowly she turned on her side to avoid waking Mat. Brutus watched her judgmentally from his Dreamy Dog Bed. He wasn't used to sharing her attention. Ava wasn't used to it either, and a wave of guilt crashed over her. She was supposed to spend her life with Andie. It had never even occurred to her to move on. Her life had narrowed to allow for work and for Brutus and for nothing else.

Unable to fall back asleep, she opened SHRNK. *I slept with Mat,* she typed.

The background of the app slid from white to a dark gray, then back to white, then back to gray. It was three in the morning. Her SHRNK was probably asleep. She thought about texting Jaime, but her stomach turned at the thought of his disapproval.

Mat murmured something dreamy and unintelligible in his sleep and pulled Ava close to him, until her back was pressed against his chest. She'd almost forgotten this feeling. She switched off her phone and closed her eyes, and then woke to her Exuberant Alarm ringing lightly.

"Is that an original Exuberant Alarm?" Mat croaked, leaning over her and lifting it.

"Good eye," Ava said. "You can tell it's a first edition because of its—"

"Coloring," Mat said. He kissed her on the cheek. "See, I know my STÄDA history. I studied for you." He nosed the back of her neck and her entire body reacted. "Good morning," he said.

"Good morning."

"What's this?" he said, bringing his finger under her chin and pushing upward.

"Oh," Ava said, flushing. "Nothing." She covered the scar on her neck with her palm.

"It's okay," Mat said. "I think scars are really cool. I'm covered in them. Look." In the light of the morning she could see his body clearly—birthmarks scattered across his thighs, a pale scar along his rib, which he was now showing her.

"What's that from?" she said, happy to keep the focus on his scar. She kept her hand on her throat.

"B-ball," he said, turning so she could see the whole length of it. "Looks impressive, but honestly it was embarrassing. Got completely wiped out by a point guard at a pickup game. Tiny little dude, but he was fierce. Do you have any more? I love a scar story."

If she were honest, she would tell him. Aside from the faint white scar along her neck where the seatbelt had slit her, there were others. A short one on the side of her head where a small piece of the windshield had lodged itself. Then there was one along her wrist, where the screws had gone. Another one ran the length of her knee. She pulled the top sheet over herself. "No," she said, "not really. Little ones here and there. I don't remember what they're from."

She got out of bed, keeping her back turned to him, overcome by shyness. Her entire body felt ticklish, and she felt Mat watching her. She slipped on a T-shirt and pajama bottoms.

"Shit," he said. "I can't show up to work wearing the same thing I wore yesterday. Can we stop at my place?"

"No," Ava said automatically, setting an Alert Percolator on the stovetop. "I can't be late to work." She checked her Precise Wristwatch. She had enough units to attend to her normal routines, but nothing more than that.

"But I'm your boss," Mat said, "and I say you can."

"No, no," Ava said. "I can't." She felt panicky. "I've never been late, and this is not a good way to begin—" She could feel heat spreading along her collarbone.

"Okay," Mat said. "No problem. One thousand percent understand. What do you suggest? Cause I kinda don't think your pants are gonna fit me." He was peering in her closet. "Hang on," he said. "How about these?"

Ava had donated most of Andie's things. But she had kept her favorite outfit: a pair of navy-blue cotton work pants, a navy-blue button-down. She'd hung them in the far side of her closet so that she didn't have to see them unless she wanted to, which she never did.

Mat was holding up the pants. "Are these yours?" he said. "They seem kinda big."

"Yes," Ava said. "Well, no. They're Andie's." She felt the heat crawling up her neck.

"Oh," Mat said. "I'm sorry. I didn't mean to—" He quickly replaced them.

"She forgot to pick them up," Ava said. "I never got around to returning them. Or throwing them out." The lie unfurled in front of them, and she was so ashamed of it that she couldn't look at Mat.

"No problem," he said. "Maybe don't tell her I almost wore her clothes. She'll probably wanna kill me."

"I can guarantee she won't do that," Ava said. The coffee had begun to burble, and Ava clicked off the stove and poured them each a cup. She had loved the pants on Andie—they'd fit her perfectly—and often at STÄDA, while Andie was bent over her workbench, tooling with a clock or a watch, Ava would steal glances at her. She looked *good,* and the shirt looked good too—tight across her broad shoulders and back.

"Yesterday's clothes it is," Mat said, pulling on the loud blue ombré button-down he'd worn the day before. He came up behind Ava and wrapped his arms around her waist, resting his chin on the top of her head. She stiffened—it had been so long since she had assumed this position, and she could feel herself blushing at his touch.

———

"I have a confession," Mat said on the ride to work. "I lied when I said you missed a good *Thirty-Minute Machine* episode. I didn't listen to it without you."

"You didn't?"

"Couldn't really bring myself to," he said, shifting into a new lane. "I started, but then I just felt sad."

"I felt sad too," Ava said as they merged onto the highway. "Mat," she said suddenly. "Emily."

"Emily what?" he said. He turned down the synthy music that introduced *Thirty-Minute Machine*.

"Don't you need to feed her?"

"Oh!" Mat said. "No, I got a Bark Bud to do it. She'll go out in"—he checked his watch with one hand on the wheel—"one hour. Best app ever."

"You don't care who walks into your home?" Ava said.

"Not really. You know, it wouldn't kill you to be less beholden to your dog," Mat said. "That's the beauty of the app. You can live a full life *and* have a dog."

She turned the volume back up on *Thirty-Minute Machine*, which was midway through a sponsor ad: . . . *plus unparalleled professional networking events to get you where you need to be. Good Guys Stand Tall.* She was glad Mat had told her he was enrolled in Good Guys—if he hadn't, she might have made fun of the ad. She glanced at his face, which betrayed zero signs of embarrassment, and she was glad about that too; he didn't need any assurance from her.

The episode of *Thirty-Minute Machine* featured a New Yorker who commuted to work each day on her bike. But her office provided no intuitive place to store her sweaty biking clothes, and she needed a solution that wasn't her desk drawer.

"Easy!" Mat said. "Drive to work."

But Ava liked one of the potential solutions this time: a small garment bag that could hang beneath the commuter's desktop, allowing her to air clothes out while concealing the sight and smell of them from desk neighbors. Her thoughts roamed between the sweaty clothes solution and the night she'd had—clothing pulled off, thrown to the floor, Mat's low voice in her ear, his abrasive cheek against her neck, her whole body taut with desire. They sat for a moment in Mat's car, watching a line of employees enter the Simple Tower.

"Okay," Mat said. "I'm going to try to treat you normally. I'm not going to look at you more than anyone else. I'm not going to speak to you differently. Our S-Chats will be entirely professional. No flirtation whatsoever."

"None," Ava said. "And that should probably start right now. Who knows where Security installed those cameras for the Vandals. They could be anywhere. And Judith probably has access to all of them."

"Damn," Mat said. "You're right." He undid his seatbelt and kissed her deeply.

Ava pulled away from him. "You're going to get us in trouble."

"Sorry," Mat said. "Sorry, sorry."

"You're not sorry," she said.

As they approached the entrance to the Simple Tower, Ava focused on looking normal, a task that became more difficult as her coworkers lined up behind them. She spotted Jaime a few spots behind them in the line and tried to shake the feeling of transparency as he glanced at them. She scanned her key card, and Mat followed behind her. But as soon as he held his barcode to the scanner, an eerie, high-pitched alarm echoed around the enormous lobby.

"What the . . ." he said. "Is that the neg alarm?"

By the time Ava looked up, the sprinkler heads had already burst into action, sending water in every direction.

ATTENTION, the intercom demanded. *ATTENTION. FIRE. ATTENTION. FIRE.*

"You're kidding me," Ava said.

The entire population of the tower began to filter out onto the freezing parking lot, starting with Judith. Dread swallowed Ava. She felt that Judith would be able to read her mind; that somehow the sprinkler mishap would help Judith put together the events of the night before. Ava watched her slip a half-eaten orange into a baggie and put it in her raincoat pocket. Then, as if suddenly remembering something, she looked up and made eye contact with Ava, then glanced at Mat. Ava turned the other way, her chest tight with panic.

"Judith knows about us," she whispered to Mat. Her teeth chattered. "Don't look."

"She does not," Mat said. "You're being paranoid."

When Ava glanced again, Judith was conversing with a Spirit staffer, who was nodding enthusiastically. Around her, teams huddled in their damp hoodies, hugging themselves for warmth while the fire department arrived and charged into the building.

"I told you," Jaime said. He'd appeared beside Ava and Mat. His shirt was dotted with water. "I told you they were good."

"Who?" she said.

"The Vandals," Jaime said. "Didn't it happen when one of

you swiped? They clearly hacked into the security system and somehow linked it to the sprinkler system. It's impressive."

Ava tried to keep a straight face. "You're telling me you think a small group of teenagers secretly boobytrapped our lobby sprinklers?"

"That's exactly what I'm saying," Jaime said sharply. "Wake up, Ava. They're *advanced*. More capable than half the college interns we brought in last summer."

"Yeah, Ava," Mat said, elbowing her lightly in the ribs. "Wake up!"

Ava flicked him away with her hand.

Jaime stared at both of them. First Ava, then Mat, whom he looked up and down. "Mat," he said. "Nice shirt."

"This?" Mat said, looking down. Ava's stomach flipped. "Thanks."

"You must really like it," Jaime said. "Feel like I just saw you wearing it yesterday!"

"Yeah," Mat said, rocking on his heels. "I really like this brand."

Ava focused on a weed growing through a crack in the asphalt.

The alarm stopped, and a security guard waved the crowd back inside. Jaime gave Ava a hard look before turning to join the line of people filing inside.

Mat turned abruptly to Ava. "Do we pay the interns?"

"I think so," Ava said. "Why?"

"I think I just had a great idea." He snapped his fingers and walked to the head of the line, leaving Ava in the parking lot.

———

That afternoon an email from Mat landed at the top of her inbox.

Announcing: STÄDA X RED HOOK Community Internship Program

STÄDA fam,

Several weeks ago I stepped up to lead the cross-functional task force dedicated to repairing the relationship between STÄDA and the broader community. First I'd like to thank you for your patience as we took a step back to listen to the community within and outside these walls.

Today I'm proud to announce SXRH, a community internship program open to all Red Hook residents, regardless of age or educational background. At STÄDA we strive to provide the space, tools, and mentorship that allow potential to flourish, and we don't think that mission should stop at the gate. Everybody has the right to discover his or her skills and passion, including those who wish us ill. That's why we'll be offering this career development program as an optional first measure for any trespasser apprehended on STÄDA property. We believe this will have the secondary benefit of reducing STÄDA's need to engage with law enforcement. I think we can all agree that this is a huge step forward, and although I recognize that change doesn't happen overnight, I know we'll be able to get through this difficult time together.

Please join me in congratulating Jaime Rojas, who recognized the intellect and potential of these young men and women and who has volunteered to leave the

Storage team to lead the internship program, effective immediately.

Thanks so much, everyone.

Mat Putnam
Head of Product
Yellow/Amarillo :)

Ava looked around for Jaime and spotted him in the Imagination Room with Mat. The tone of their conversation was inscrutable. After a minute they both stood. Mat extended his hand and Jaime shook it. Jaime left the room and disappeared into an elevator.

She scanned the email again. Jaime had been upset with her, and now he'd volunteered to leave her team. Her heart sank. She opened an S-Chat to him. *Hey,* she wrote. *Look, I'm sorry if—*

"I can't believe it didn't come to me sooner," Mat said proudly. He had appeared behind Ava's desk. She quickly closed out of S-Chat. "It's the perfect idea. Leveraging our excess intellectual capital to do good in the world, all while saving some money on intern stipends."

"Do you really think people will be happy about this?" Ava asked.

"Of course! Instead of getting a record they get college credit."

"All right."

"You okay?" Mat asked.

"Yeah, I'm okay. I just feel bad for shutting Jaime down earlier. I think he's really mad at me."

"You do?"

"Is that crazy?"

"It's not crazy," Mat said, "it's just not *true*. It's your projection of how he feels, so really it's how *you* feel. We ask each other this in Good Guys all the time: Is it *real* or is it how you *feel*? It's usually HYF." The acronym rhymed with *wife*.

Ava tried to wrap her head around this.

"That probably sounds crazy, right?" He smiled as though he were one step ahead of her. "But with a little practice," he continued, placing a warm hand on her shoulder, "the way you feel about yourself can become something you can control. Anyway, gotta run to my ten o'clock 'Yes, And.' Owen and I are about to go nuts on this Gentle Nightstand campaign."

Ava tried to get back to work but was carried away by a riptide of curiosity. She angled her screen slightly away from her neighbor, opened a new tab, and searched for "HYF Good Guys." The search results were cluttered with advertisements for local chapters and images of men proudly presenting to full audiences, interspersed with professional-looking photos of men looking deeply at peace in their home environments. One man posed with jumper cables slung over a shoulder. Another threw an ecstatic toddler into the air.

She scanned the page and clicked a video entitled "New here? Good news." When she hit Play, a pink sunset filled the screen. Orchestral music came through her Peaceful Headphones. As the music swelled, swarms of birds took shape, breaking apart and rejoining as the sunset intensified. "So you're here," a man's voice said. "That's a very good first step." She clicked around the labyrinth of jargon. The more she read, the less she understood.

She opened a new message to her SHRNK.

Have you heard of Good Guys?

No, her SHRNK replied. *What is Good Guys?*

As far as I can tell, it's an international self-help group for men who want to "do good" in the world. Mat is a member, and I find it really . . . I don't know. Weird?

How so?

Ava had a hard time articulating the feeling.

I guess I don't understand the appeal. It seems a little cultish, and I think it's a big part of his life. It makes me wonder if we're too different.

Sometimes we reject the aspects of our romantic partners we don't fully understand. That's a fear-based instinct.

You think I'm fearful of Good Guys?

That's up to you to decide. We can't share everything with our partners. Instead of running from this part of Mat's life, who could you be if you asked questions about the group? Why not attend a meeting?

Ava could think of many reasons why she would not attend a meeting. But then she thought of her work and how much of herself she'd given over to it. Mat didn't share her passion either. And she'd never gotten the sense that he fully understood it. But he managed to be supportive, and she would do her best to reciprocate. She moved a new email from the Spirit team to her trash folder.

How are we doing? Please share your feelings about SXRH!

18

OVER THE NEXT FEW DAYS, AVA AND MAT PER-
fected the choreography of their secret. They would arrive to
work together. Mat would wait in his car in the parking lot
as Ava made her way to Floor 12, the excitement of the romance coursing through her. After half a unit, Mat would arrive. Ava would watch him step out of the elevator, remove his
earbuds, swipe away notifications on his watch, take a Zing!
Ginger-Turmeric Tonic from the Wellness Kitchen, and walk
around the floor saying hello to each team. He'd make his way
past Spirit, past Technical, past the Gay Tree, past the projector
screens, which played time-lapsed videos of customers assembling Cozy Nesting Tables, and finally to Engineering, where
he and Ava would pretend to discuss the Very Nice Box. Finally he'd arrive at Marketing, where he'd sit for a few hours
before taking another check-in lap at 2 p.m. It was all part of
his ritual, and Ava loved how effortlessly their secret folded
into it.

She remembered his first days at STÄDA, when she would think of ways to leave her desk at the times he was scheduled to come by Engineering. Now she looked forward to seeing him and felt a dull disappointment at his absence when he was off-schedule. She found herself finely tuned to his whereabouts, as if he had become a new cardinal direction.

There was north, and then there was Mat.

Even the shape of his name in S-Chat was a unique image, delivering a small wave of joy each time it appeared in the right-hand corner of her screen.

Her SHRNK had been right: dread *was* just one side of a two-sided coin. What she felt instead was an excitement so vast and powerful that it shielded her from all negativity, including Jaime's judgment, which she caught whiffs of from across the floor, but which only proved to her that she had something worthwhile. If her happiness was too much for him to tolerate, then so be it.

She opened SHRNK to communicate this feeling.

"Ready to *take care*, Ave?" Mat had rounded the corner.

"Yes!" she said quickly. She had forgotten that today was the Self-Care Fair, a program that Mat had organized with the Spirit team as an end-of-year morale-booster for STÄDA employees and their families. He had pitched it enthusiastically as a reward for a year of strenuous labor, and Ava had witnessed Spirit staffers flitting around him for weeks, ironing out the details. According to an email that Ava had only glanced at, each employee was awarded 150,000 S-Points, which translated to $1,500, to spend at the Self-Care Fair, which would take place in the cafeteria.

"People are so excited," Mat said, his eyes twinkling. "This is so overdue."

"I'll meet you up there," Ava said, smiling.

Mat winked at her and made his way to the elevator bank, where he joined a group of Spirit staffers dressed in their colors. She watched how they all abandoned their conversations and turned to Mat excitedly, and she felt a bolt of pride at his magnetism, as if it were her own.

The elevator Ava rode was packed with giddy technical writers, all dressed in blue, who seemed oblivious to her presence. A handful of them had brought their children, who wore special color-coded lanyards to match their parents'. "I have been *dreaming* about my chair massage," one of them said.

"I heard there's a vegan fro-yo booth," another said.

"Confirmed!" a third one said, scrolling through his phone. "And apparently a female wizard is giving a talk at noon."

"What the fuck. This is amazing. There's going to be something called a Therapy Forest."

"No clue what that is, but I need it in my life. I seriously take back every judgmental thing I ever said about Mat Putnam."

Ava stood still in the corner of the elevator, glowing.

They all stepped out into the cafeteria, which had been fully transformed. Dozens of booths filled the space. Representatives for skin care and supplement companies handed out products to remedy the harmful effects of working in an office, like eye serums for the damage caused by computer screens and charcoal tablets to balance a high-caffeine diet.

STÄDA employees could sign up for lavender mistings, guided meditation sessions, or color therapy, which featured a small man in a white lab coat who shined colored light on the participant's closed eyelids. Employees could choose their Personality Test color or one that complemented it.

As she meandered among the booths, Ava spotted Mat standing with Owen Lloyd at iSight, a company that offered tortoiseshell eyeglasses with amber lenses that filtered out computer light, for 800,000 S-Points. A small child toddled to the booth and grabbed a pair of glasses before Sofia swooped in and pulled them from his grip. "Good taste, buddy!" Mat said, taking them from Sofia and slipping them on. He turned to Ava and called out to her. "Oh, Ava! It's you! Sorry, I can't see anything without my glasses!"

Sofia glanced between Mat and Ava with a look of performative boredom and scooped up the toddler. Besides Jaime, Sofia seemed most aggrieved by Ava's closeness with Mat. She had taken to placing Marketing schedules for the Very Nice Box on their desks without any niceties, which according to STÄDA's new Positivity Mandate counted as aggressive behavior.

I feel like a bad feminist, Ava had recently admitted to her SHRNK.

Why is that?

I shouldn't enjoy competing with Sofia, especially over a man, especially at work. And now that I'm thinking about it, I shouldn't even be okay with Mat's attention, because he's my boss.

"Shouldn't" is rarely relevant. Are you okay with Mat's attention?

Honestly, I enjoy the secret.

Sometimes we use secrets to experience the authentic versions of ourselves that we fear will be judged harshly by others.

It was true: Ava enjoyed the feeling of keeping a secret, holding it like a small globe of light. She observed how happiness prevailed over the dense storm of guilt, stress, and sadness below it. The excitement of the crush—the anticipation, the uncertainty, the attraction—reached even the smallest moments of her day.

She happily pretended to ignore him and walked past him to the next booth: the SHRNK booth. The company had brought the iconic leather armchair from the subway ad, and a man sat in the chair with a foot crossed over his knee. "Hello," Ava said to the man.

"Hi!" he said. "Do you know about STÄDA's partnership with SHRNK?"

"Yes," Ava admitted. "I was suspicious at first, but it's been helpful."

"I love hearing that," the man said. "I'm one of the founders. Theodore Holloway." He wore a collared shirt beneath a speckled wool sweater, and heavy-framed glasses.

"You actually look like a shrink," Ava said.

He smiled good-naturedly and looked down at his shirt. "Guess I could have picked a different outfit."

Mat showed up then, sucking a straw jammed into a dark green smoothie.

"Hey, man!" Theodore said. "Thanks for having us. So awesome to see this app having a real-life positive impact at STÄDA. We're *loving* this partnership."

"For sure! Happy to have a hand in any positive change!"

Theodore clasped Mat's hand with both of his, shaking enthusiastically.

Mat handed Ava the smoothie. "It's algae and spinach," he said. "As you can guess, it tastes horrible. Unfortunately, no take-backs."

She walked away, trying her best not to let her happiness show. The smoothie tasted like pureed grass, but she didn't care. Everything in her world was filtered through a new and happy prism. As she wandered among the booths, Mat tried to capture her attention with various stunts. It was her mission to pay the perfect amount of attention to him.

She stepped into the Therapy Forest, a dark, misty thicket of deep-green vines and eucalyptus. The floor was damp soil, and the space was big enough for one person only. Speakers obscured by vines played birdsong, and an invisible fan generated a light wind that pushed a faint mist around the area. She remembered something her SHRNK had suggested. *Think of relationships like planets. They have their own gravity, which can be grounding if you allow it to be.*

The mist fell evenly across Ava's face.

Andie was your home planet, of course, her SHRNK had written. *And moving on is painful. But who could you be if you fell into Mat's orbit?*

She meditated on that idea for a few minutes, the gentle scents of eucalyptus and soil filling her with a feeling of peace and understanding as she allowed herself to surrender to the pull of Mat's orbit. Cricket chirps indicated that her time was up, and she stepped back into the bright cafeteria.

Her feeling of tranquillity was immediately interrupted; Jaime was next in line. "Oh," she said. "Hey."

"Hello." He wore a hexagonal pair of tortoiseshell iSight glasses.

"It's really nice in there."

"I've heard."

"You probably won't need those sunglasses. It's pretty dark."

"Thank you for the advice," Jaime said. His tone was politely cold, and Ava sensed he was waiting for an apology.

"Look . . ." she started. "I'm sorry about that lunch misunderstanding."

"Misunderstanding? You completely ditched me."

"I'm sorry you feel that way," Ava said.

Jaime pressed his lips into a straight line.

"Well, enjoy," she said awkwardly, and she moved aside so he could pass her. She gazed around the cafeteria, trying to shake off the interaction and hold on to the pleasant calm she'd felt inside the Therapy Forest. Several booths away, she saw Judith with her daughters, who were fully absorbed with something called "dream tinctures." One of them was zesting what looked like a twig into a small vial of purple liquid while the other swirled the black contents of her own vial. Judith looked on skeptically.

Ava had most of her S-Points left to spend and made her way to a booth offering GMO-free dog biscuits.

"I knew I would find you here," Mat said, surprising her.

"Oh god," Ava said. "Am I that predictable?"

"Yes," Mat said. "Which makes my job very easy." He handed her a paper bag full of dog treats. She peered into the bag, mentally repeating the words *my job*.

"But now I have nothing to spend my free money on," Ava said. "Unless . . . do I need a dream tincture?"

"Depends," Mat said. "Are your dreams exclusively about me?"

"No."

"Then you definitely need a tincture," he said.

———

That afternoon, once everyone had returned to their desks, blackout curtains lowered with a slow, mechanical hum, covering the large industrial windows until the room was dark.

A woman's soft, calming voice came over the speaker system. It was unclear whether she was a robot or a person. "Good afternoon, STÄDA. It's time to take today's final Intentional Ten. Now, if you would please put away your phones and computers, I'll lead you through this afternoon's session."

Ava felt a pang of annoyance. She had work to do. She didn't want to close her computer. From across the room, Mat delivered a joking glare, gesturing down with his pointer finger until her computer was fully shut. Ava stifled a laugh and caught Jaime's eye. His expression felt like an accusation. She looked away.

"If you feel comfortable doing so," the woman on the loud-speaker continued, "please close your eyes. Don't worry if you feel a little foolish. We're all in this together."

Ava watched Jaime close his eyes and then glanced across the room at Mat, who had already closed his, so she closed hers.

"Let's all take a moment to appreciate the hard work we've put into today. Every time you did a little more than you had to today—every time you went that extra mile—your present self did your future self a favor. Now it's time to repay your body and your mind for that gift."

Ava felt her phone vibrate in her pocket and discreetly glanced down to read the text.

I think you left something in the printer.

She looked in Mat's direction, but he was gone. She glanced around at the Engineering team, their eyes dutifully closed and their heads bowed. If she stepped away, people would probably assume she'd gone to the bathroom. She paused a moment, took another glance around the room, and backed away from her desk. Walking quickly through the dark, past her meditating colleagues, she felt elated and uncertain, as if Mat hadn't already made his feelings perfectly clear.

He was waiting for her in the printer room, a small, dark room the size of a walk-in closet that housed a wireless printer, stacks of sticky notes, and other office supplies. The room was removed enough from the main workspace that they could both be inside and not be seen—especially not now, with the entire floor in the dark.

Mat wasted no time in kissing Ava, pulling her close to him in one swift gesture. They fumbled for a few seconds before finding their footing.

"We have five minutes," Ava said. *One-sixth of a unit.*

Mat kissed her harder, and the idea of time—how much of

it they had left—evaporated. As she pressed him against the back wall, the printer started with a loud whir.

"Oh shit," Mat said. "Did I hit it?"

Ava hovered over the printer, gesturing for it to stop. Her face was hot.

A piece of paper landed softly in the tray.

"What is it?" Mat said, looking over Ava's shoulder.

She scanned it quickly, but it was hard to parse under the low light. In her rush, she could focus only on pieces of it.

. . . After many years in these offices

. . . head-hunting for the new Gambier office has proven challenging.

. . . Grooming local talent from New York is not feasible.

. . . request for relocation to Gambier effective immediately.

Ava skipped ahead to the sign-off:

Best,
Judith Ball
Chief People Officer
Green

"It's Judith," Ava said. "She's trying to transfer to the Gambier campus."

"Well, that would definitely make our lives easier," Mat said, brushing the hair from her face. "This is amazing. Can you imagine? We could finally do this out in the open."

Ava looked at him doubtfully.

"Okay, not exactly this, but you know what I mean. No more hiding in printer closets. God, I can't wait till this place is totally paperless."

She shoved the paper back into the tray. Judith would be in any minute to collect the document. She glanced around to make sure everything looked normal, then hurriedly slipped out the door, tucking her hair behind an ear, and walked the long way back to her desk, the way Judith was almost certain not to be headed. From her desk she saw that Mat had already returned—he must have risked the short way. His cheeks were bright red, and she was happy to have this effect on him. Over her shoulder she saw Judith briskly turn the corner. She was walking in Ava's direction. Ava's stomach tightened. Judith tossed an orange peel in the Virtuous Compost Bin at the end of her desk and continued on toward the printer room. They'd gotten away with it.

Before the relief could fully set in, Judith tore back around the corner holding a thick stack of papers. "Who did this?" she demanded, interrupting the meditation. She fanned the papers out in her hands and held them up to the room. Ava strained to see through the dark, but she was able to make out an image of the Vision Tower—in section and elevation—x-ed out by thick red lines. There must have been hundreds of copies.

"Who did this? How many times do we have to remind you that office supplies are not to be used for personal things? And *especially* not for political organizing against our collective interest. Has someone unplugged the printer?"

The printer continued its loud, rhythmic whirring. Ava guessed the number of pages had doubled by now. She couldn't help but feel guilty about her proximity to the prank, even though she wasn't responsible.

A Spirit staffer stood. "This seems like a classic Vandal hack to me. I have no clue how they got ahold of those blueprints, though. We should probably involve the FBI at this point."

"They're in the public domain," Jaime said. "But I don't know how they managed to get on our network."

"Well," Mat said, clapping his hands together and looking pointedly at Jaime. "Thankfully, we have the right man on the job to figure it out. And while you're at it, do Judith a favor and unplug the printer?"

Jaime glared at him before disappearing into the hallway.

Ava's phone buzzed with a text from Mat: *You know where Judith and Vandals and FBI won't be later?*

NASTY PIZZA?

My place. Come over?

Ava's heart felt like it had grown wings.

When?

After dinner?

Yes, she typed, and she tucked her phone into her pocket.

19

THAT NIGHT, AFTER FAILING TO MANUFACTURE
an appetite, Ava stared at her Precise Wristwatch. Could seven
be reasonably considered "after dinner"? She looked between
Brutus and her phone. *Wrapping up a few things and then heading over,* she typed. She reread the text. She imagined Mat asking her what things she had wrapped up. She erased it. *Leaving
my apartment,* she wrote instead.

Her face stung in the cold, and she kept her head down to
avoid the wind. She got to Mat's building and checked her
phone.

Walking Emily, door's unlocked, 12F.

He'd texted her the building entrance code, and as she
floated up in the elevator, she wondered whether she trusted
him as fully. The thought of having Mat in her apartment
while she was walking Brutus made her feel sweaty.

She knocked once on 12F, waited, then pushed the door
open. Mat's apartment looked like a college dorm room with

adult touches. Ava immediately identified the STÄDA items: a Capable Couch in leather, a Dependable Drying Rack, a Polite Hamper, and several Proud Frames that held bland grayscale photographs of the Manhattan skyline. A single Simple Dinner Plate containing a shallow pool of water sat in the sink, and an Honest Salt Shaker on the counter.

But Mat's brand loyalty, Ava soon realized, was not to STÄDA in particular but to start-up products advertised around the city. In his bathroom she found a Pop toothbrush —the hygienic kind with the disposable head that was mailed to your doorstep once a month, according to the subway ads. It stood in a Thoughtful Glass, next to a bottle of cologne that she recognized as part of a monthly subscription to Two-Scents. She examined the label: Hinoki Daydream. On the edge of his bathtub lay a Grizzly razor ("for the essential man") and Grizzly shaving balm.

Most interesting to Ava were Mat's dog accessories, which were numerous. Bark Boy's sister company, Ruff Girl, manufactured dog beds, crates, grass-fed cow bones, and stuffed toys that were customized to look exactly like your dog. Mat had all of it.

She gazed at Mat's Smart Bookshelf, which was largely taken up by a series of textbooks. She read the spines:

Good Guy 1: Good Mourning
Good Guy 2: Good Work
Good Guy 3: Good Nature
Good Guy 4: Good Riddance
Good Guy 5: Good God

She reached for *Good Guy 6: For Goodness, Forgiveness* and cracked it open:

PREFACE

All little boys want to be superheroes when they grow

up. There's simply no way around it. But there comes a time in our lives when we're hit with the hard cold facts: we can't fly; we can't scale buildings with our fingertips; we can't stop a moving train from running over a little girl.

But that doesn't mean we can't live out our destinies as superheroes.

You're probably asking, "How?" Well, there's a super-power at your fingertips, waiting to be unleashed. Do you have the courage to learn what it is?

Mat opened the door and Emily barreled into the apartment, tearing between Ava and the kitchen.

"I wasn't being too nosy, I promise," Ava said, snapping the book shut and shoving it back into place. She pushed the words *little girl* out of her mind.

"Why not?" Mat said. "I would be." He tossed the leash onto the counter, pulled Ava in, and kissed her.

"I admit I was looking at your . . . book collection."

"Oh," Mat said. He glanced at his bookshelf, then rubbed the back of his head.

"I'm sorry!" Ava said. "I didn't mean to make fun of your personal work. I'm sorry."

He laughed. "It's okay! I know it probably seems kind of lame from an outside perspective. It's definitely not for everyone, but it's been super-helpful for me."

Ava watched as he poured an enormous serving of food for Emily, which she finished in three breathless gulps.

"Why don't you give me the tour?" Ava said. "I've been in all the rooms except your bedroom."

Mat asked her to wait while he slipped into his bedroom,

THE VERY NICE BOX

reappearing after a minute before showing her in. He walked closely behind her with his hands resting on her hips. On his bed were hastily tucked Remy sheets, whose advertisements were bedding-related anagrams that had burrowed themselves into Ava's subconscious (*Sea Cow Pill; Rude TV Cove*). Remy was considered a STÄDA competitor, but STÄDA's Cool Sheets had received higher ratings. Mat closed the door behind him—it sounded light, like particleboard, making a hollow sound as it clicked shut.

He stood behind her and kissed her neck. Her eyes skipped around the room. A shirt had been slung over a Strapping Armchair in the corner. A Brilliant Lamp sat on a side table with a shiny walnut veneer. The top drawer of his dresser—a Frank Dresser prototype—was ajar. Ava reminded herself that he had just moved here, that he was young. She could imagine her SHRNK's advice: *Who could you be if you fell into Mat's orbit?*

Mat moved his hand from Ava's hip to her waist and across her stomach, his thumb resting between her ribs. There was more confidence in his hands than she had felt the first time. She turned around, ending the mental survey, and reached into her back pocket for her phone.

"Am I boring you already?" he said.

"No," Ava said. "It's the opposite."

"The opposite?"

She held up her phone for him to see. "Bark Bud. I'm hiring one for Brutus." She put her hand on his chest and selected Kaamya, a twenty-three-year-old woman who lived .2 miles from her apartment.

Woof! a pop-up window read.

Looks like we haven't had the pleasure of meeting **Brutus**! But we know you can't always plan ahead, and we're dying to meet **Brutus**! Would you like to pay our liability fee of $299.99 so that we can attend to **Brutus**'s needs without a meet-and-greet?

"Jesus," Ava said.

"That's nuts. I totally get it if you need to go home," Mat said, but Ava heard the disappointment in his voice.

She looked at the screen. She could afford the fee, and part of her enjoyed quantifying her desire. Three hundred dollars. Anyway, Brutus would be fine with a little change in routine. Dogs were adaptable—perhaps more adaptable than people. "No," she said, tapping Continue and entering the code to her lockbox. "I want to stay."

20

IT WAS DARK AND AVA HAD NO CLEAR SENSE OF where she was. Her own voice had yanked her out of a dream. Her heart drummed in her chest and she felt like her lungs had shrunk. "Where . . ." she started.

"You're having a bad dream," Mat said. "You're having a bad dream." His voice was scratchy with sleep. She looked around for her Exuberant Alarm Clock but couldn't find it. She noticed then the sensation of Mat's hand on her chest, his face coming into focus in the darkness. "Ava," he said, clicking on his Brilliant Lamp. "It's okay, you're okay."

"I'm . . . Brutus . . ."

"No, you're Ava. You're at my apartment," Mat said. "You were having a bad dream. It's four in the morning and Brutus is at your apartment. You hired a Bark Bud to take care of him."

Some feeling had begun to return to Ava's limbs. She moved a hand over her eyes. She was naked under the sheets —she and Mat had been up later than she could ever remember staying up. And now the memory of that — of Mat, of his lean, ropy body — was returning to her too. She settled herself against him. "Bark Bud," she repeated, reassured. Her breath had evened out.

Mat wrapped an arm around her. "Ava?"

"Yes," she said.

"Who's Ira?"

"What?" Her head began throbbing.

Mat shifted onto an elbow and placed his head in his palm. "You said the name Ira. Before I shook you awake."

"You shook me awake?" The accident roared back. Of course she'd been dreaming of it. It chased her like an angry dog. Her mother's voice saying her father's name would forever be lodged in her memory. It was the last thing she remembered hearing before waking in the hospital. It wasn't a scream — she wouldn't even call it desperate. It was simply a word that had vanished as soon as it had appeared: *Ira.*

"It's no one," Ava said. "I'm sorry I woke you up." She reached to turn out the light.

"It didn't sound like no one," Mat said, kissing her neck. "You were all like, *Ira . . . mm . . . Ira.* You can tell me! Was he a boyfriend?"

"Ha," Ava said, closing her eyes. "No."

"Then who?"

"My dad," Ava said, her eyes firmly shut, her best armor to defend from more questioning. Her throat tightened, and she turned away from him.

A blanket of silence lay over them. Ava opened her mouth to speak but couldn't.

"Ava?" Mat said, sitting up, peering over her shoulder. His face was very close to hers.

She tried to focus on something else, anything else — a sound outside, a feeling in her body. But there was nothing —

not a siren or a dog barking or a bus hissing to a stop that could distract her from the directness of what she was feeling now. She felt a tear roll down her nose but didn't move to wipe it away.

"Hey, Ava, what's wrong? Do you want to talk about it?"

"You're not going to meet him," she said. She turned to face Mat, who lay back in bed, staring up at the ceiling as if he were solving an equation in his head.

"I—Okay . . ." he said quietly.

Ava could see he was hurt, but she allowed the ambiguity to hang there. She didn't want Mat's sympathy or awkwardness. He looked small, over on his side of the bed.

"It's not like that," Ava said. "It's—" She sighed. "There's something I have to tell you. There was an accident—the car accident I mentioned. A few years ago. It wasn't a small crash. It was really, really bad. My parents, and Andie. They all— nobody—I was the only one—"

She felt like she was going to be sick. She didn't know if she could bring herself to say it, but she didn't have to.

"Oh," Mat said softly. "I—I'm so sorry. Come here." He wrapped his arm tightly around her and moved his thumb across her face to wipe a tear. Something about this simple service made it impossible to stop more tears from coming.

"No," she said. "I misled you, and I don't know why, except that I didn't want to talk about it. I hate talking about it. It's such a horrible story."

But for the first time, held in Mat's arms with as much time as she needed, she felt like she could. Mat listened as she told him everything she could remember. That she and Andie had been planning to announce their engagement, the smell of roasted nuts, the light, the scream, the crunch.

Mat squeezed her tighter. "It must be so difficult to go through life with this hanging over you."

"What's *difficult*," Ava said, her throat tight, "is not having my family." The words came out more sharply than she'd meant.

"Maybe this is a dumb question," Mat said, "but . . . are you just, like . . . constantly really angry?"

"Yes," Ava said.

"Anger is the worst," Mat said. "I can't imagine dragging that feeling around all the time."

It was a simple statement, but it gave shape to a feeling that Ava had not given much attention to. Part of her was angry, yes, but she had always considered the anger a useless part. An extra bolt in the assembly bag. What was she supposed to do with it?

Mat took his shirt from his nightstand and blotted Ava's face with it. It smelled like wood and sweat, and soon it was not his shirt against her face but his mouth. His kiss was long and deep and necessary. "Ava?" he said, pulling away.

"Yeah?"

"I'm going to take care of you."

"You what?"

"Maybe that sounds . . . stupid and sexist," he said. "But it's what I want to tell you. I'm going to take care of you. I'm going to make sure nothing like what happened to you that day ever happens to you again."

"There's no way you can—"

"I'm telling you, it's what I promise," Mat said. "Nothing like that will ever happen again. You're safe with me here. I won't let anything like that—"

"But how can you—"

"Because I said so," he said. "Because I promise. You are my little lamb." He tucked a strand of her hair behind her ear.

Ava kissed him. She wanted to devour him. She didn't care if nothing in his apartment coordinated, or if his dresser drawers were all askew, or if he had subpar Remy sheets or no clock anywhere, or even if he had an environmentally unfriendly toothbrush. She decided in that moment that not only did she not care about these things, she couldn't believe she ever had.

———

When Ava next woke, it was to the smell of coffee. She squinted at her phone. "Shit," she said. "My alarm didn't go off."

"Yes it did." Mat handed her a cup of steaming coffee, which she sat up to drink, the covers pulled up to her armpits. "You slept through it. I didn't want to wake you up." Emily was at his heels, wheezing, looking between them.

"But Brutus," Ava said. "And . . . the Very Nice Box. I'm supposed to inspect the prototypes at eleven and it's already—"

"I hate to remind you of this again," Mat said, "but I'm your boss. And as your boss, I say it's fine. In fact, it seems like you have a cold. I can hear it in your voice. I think you should call in sick."

"I don't have a cold!"

"I said you *seem* like you have a cold," Mat said. "Sleeping in? That's unlike you. You must have been up all night sneezing and coughing!"

"I don't think—"

"You're taking the day off," Mat said. "And I am too." He fit a scarf around his neck.

"You are?"

"Yeah, I feel a slight . . . scratch in the back of my throat," Mat said. He showed her his phone. There was an email to Judith in his sent folder:

Heya Judith,

Sick, taking teh day off. Mat

Ava stared at the email. The message she began drafting to Judith was very different:

Dear Judith,

I apologize for emailing you this late in the morning. I was up all night with a cold and hoped to be well enough to work today, particularly given the arrival of the Very Nice Box prototypes, but after substantial deliberation, I don't think I should risk spreading this virus to anyone else.

I'm sorry to miss such an important day and will be back as soon as I possibly can—surely by tomorrow.

Very best wishes,
Ava

"I guess it's been a while since I've taken a sick day," Ava said. She looked over the email three more times before sending it, then unsending it, then rereading it, then sending it.

"It's been five years and two months," Mat said. "I checked."

"You can do that?" Five years and two months. It was when the accident had happened. Ava had taken five weeks off to recover in the hospital and was back at her desk as soon as she'd gotten clearance from her doctors, her arm still in a cast, her knee at once fragile and heavy.

"Are you impressed?" He bent to kiss her, and the memory of the night wafted back to her. She appreciated that Mat didn't feel the need to offer more sympathy or linger on the revelation.

She opened her Bark Bud app. There was a message from Kaamya and a photo of Brutus. *Brutus did great. Did his business and ate all his dinner.* Ava felt a swell of pride. "Brutus did

THE VERY NICE BOX

great," she said to Mat. She sipped her coffee, which he'd made perfectly—the right amount of milk, and no sugar. The mug was a Fervor mug, whose ads promised its contents would remain hot even in freezing conditions. "He is the best dog ever born."

"He's *tied* for the best dog ever born," Mat said, fake outrage on his face. Ava looked down at Emily, who snorted.

"Sure," she said. "We can say that." Emily panted heavily while Mat crouched and scratched her head.

Ava's phone dinged—a new email from Judith. Her stomach dropped. But why *shouldn't* she get a day off? Mat was right—she hadn't called in sick in over five years.

Dear Ava,

I understand perfectly.

Sincerely,
Judith

21

"PUT ON SOMETHING WARM," MAT SAID, TOSSING Ava one of his beanies. "It's freezing out there. And before you ask, yes, I hired Brutus a Bark Bud."

They rode up I-278 in the backseat of a Swyft. The financial district towered above them, skyscrapers intermittently blocking the sunlight, until eventually the city became a maze of gridded neighborhoods, empty except for small clusters of men on their stoops. They were somewhere deep within Queens that Ava had never been.

The low multifamily homes thinned, making way for warehouses, and through the long service alleys Ava could make out that they were near water. Mat held her hand in the backseat. An entire day away from work: it was exhilarating. It was delinquent. The time off was a gift she didn't know what to do with, a check she wasn't sure how to cash. She would need to completely reorganize her week, for one. Months ago this sort of disturbance would have caused her intolerable anxiety. But she felt safe now, in the backseat with Mat. She was breaking the rules with her boss's permission. She allowed herself to rest her head on his shoulder and watch a series of warehouses blur by.

Finally the driver pulled into an enormous, empty commercial lot. Ava looked around for signage but couldn't find anything. "Are we . . . here?" she said.

Mat smiled. "Just trust me," he said, kissing her and unbuckling his seatbelt.

He thanked the driver and climbed out behind Ava, slamming the door behind him. She took another look around as the car sped away, and then she felt Mat's hands on her shoulders as he gently rotated her until she was facing a low brick building with wide tinted windows. "Walk," he said, and she did, up to the building's squat entrance.

Inside, they were greeted by a slender man who led them into a drab conference room and asked them to fill out a form. At the top of the page, Ava read:

Steinway & Sons
Piano Factory Tour
Waiver of liability

She looked up at Mat. He was smiling at her, waiting for her reaction. "I thought you might like to see how a Steinway's built," he said, "because of what you told me about your mom's piano. The tours were completely booked through the fall, but one of the guys had the hookup."

"The guys?"

"Yeah, from Good Guys."

Ava couldn't believe he remembered. She *had* mentioned the Steinway one morning in the car before work. At the time she had been careful to avoid the emotional details. She hadn't been ready to tell him about the transcendent sound of her mother's playing, how it filled every inch of the old house. She was moved by the gesture. He had been listening. And she was so overwhelmed by emotion that she considered asking him to take her back to work. But she resisted, signing her name at the bottom of the form.

He had booked them a private tour with a small, smiley man who wore round glasses, a flannel buttoned to his throat, and an elegant wooden name tag that said STUART. The tour began in the basement, down a flight of wide concrete steps and past a set of heavy doors. It was quieter than Ava would have imagined, and darker. The air was humid, thick with the scent of wood and glue. The only light came from high above them, where the walls peeked out above grade.

On this floor, Stuart quietly explained, they would witness the home to the first step in the piano-making process, where the solid, curved back frame of each grand piano was formed. Down here the sunlight couldn't change the wood's complexion, and a natural humidity kept it from drying and splitting before it could be formed. Ava had to lean in to hear him, and she hung on every word, willing herself to remember everything.

Each back frame was made from strips of hardwood cut so thin they could bend. They were shaped around a form, glued together, and clamped until they hardened into the shape of a piano. Six men, each with a clamp, stood around it, working in unison. They looked up at each other every few seconds to ensure that they were on track. If any one section tightened too quickly, the delicate pieces would slip out of alignment.

This, to Ava, was beauty in its purest form.

They exited past the station's finished product: dozens of piano husks stacked unceremoniously in a row, marked with chalk. In Ava's mind they were elegant enough to be the final product, but they weren't regarded as such. She didn't see the craftsmen admire their work. They checked the seams, wiped away excess glue, and moved on. The entire factory felt like this —humble and unobserved, its pulse quickening at each step.

At the next station men and women in clean forest-green jumpsuits worked quickly, measuring the piano's many strings, unrolling heavy coils, and winding them around a massive, cast-iron frame that would sit snugly inside the wooden pieces that they had seen at the previous station, Stuart explained.

Workers moved around the cast iron in a coordinated bustle, like bees around a hive. They pulled, fastened, and clipped. The floor manager struck a tuning fork and made tiny adjustments as they went. Together they could wind hundreds of strings in a matter of minutes. Ava couldn't tear her eyes away. She was so absorbed in the tour that she had forgotten Mat was with her.

"Like it?" Mat said to her, surprising her out of her trance.

"I never want to leave," she whispered, keeping her eyes on the workers.

On weekends Ava's parents and their friends had crowded the living room with guitars and fiddles and the space would buzz late into the night with beer and music. They'd argue boisterously about what to play next until the ensemble thinned one by one and it was just her mother at the piano bench and her father on the couch, listening, half asleep.

Throughout the tour Mat came and went from Ava's side, often walking a few steps ahead. At each station he approached the yellow line that separated the tour from the work areas, getting very close. He would peer over the edge, occasionally joking with the craftsmen. Not so long ago this would have made Ava fume. She would have hated the part of him that felt free to be large, an impulse that she had spent years winding tightly within herself. But today she saw a childish excitement, a boy who was enthralled and unafraid, and she followed freely in his wake.

The next floor was devoted to carving and sanding, the final details before the pianos were painted and oiled. This station was the most spacious, the brightest, and the chilliest. Instead of working in an efficient grid, the few woodworkers spread out, each claiming a patch of sunlight.

Ava and Mat watched as the woodworkers smoothed each piano, sanding it down until the wood was like silk. An older man chiseled away at the maker's mark on one of the pianos, and the words *Steinway & Sons* slowly emerged from the walnut.

Each craftsman had a set of tools, and no two were alike. What individuals collected throughout their career reflected their personality in some way, Ava believed—whether they used an oak or a walnut mallet, the number of chisels they required, the way the natural oils in their hands left unique marks on their wooden levels. These collections were beautiful, and reminded Ava of the rotation of things her parents had in their old farmhouse. Books, wooden boxes, terra-cotta planters—things from an era when everything was made by hand. These artifacts had felt important to Ava, and she had held on to them after the accident. At a certain point, though, they began to feel like stones that had been removed from the shore: unique but drained of color. This is how Ava herself had felt since she'd lost her family—that she had been removed from her home, sapped of her texture. Or at least that had been the case until now.

She looked across the room, her gaze resting on Mat in his thick sweater. His cheeks were pink from the chilly draft, and he stood a head taller than everyone else in the room. She found it hard to look away. There on the factory floor, with the light streaming in strong and low across downy piles of wood shavings and sawdust suspended in the fragrant air, he was as beautiful as the oak mallet, the tuning fork, the level. She loved him.

22

FALLING IN LOVE WITH MAT WAS THE FEELING of jumping from a very high perch, yet somehow it was also the feeling of safety; of a key sliding into a lock; of gears meeting precisely; of the teeth of a circular saw running along the wood's grain; of a sharpened pencil. How could all of this be true at once? Ava's heart skipped as their Swyft navigated back to her apartment, the woody, lacquered smell of the Steinway factory lingering on her jacket, in Mat's hair, in his sweater as they leaned with each turn the car took.

They'd had no dinner plans—when was the last time she hadn't planned three meals ahead?—and Mat was ordering sushi on his phone. "What do you like?" he said.

"Miso soup? And a California roll?"

"Miso soup and a California roll? What is this, the Great Depression?" Mat said. Ava watched him order things she would never have considered. A galaxy roll, a tsunami roll, a kablamo roll, a nemesis roll. Plus two miso soups, two orders of gyoza, seaweed salad, edamame, and fried chicken.

"Seems excessive," she said.

"Thinking ahead," Mat said conspiratorially. "Leftovers for tomorrow."

"Don't you think bringing the same leftovers to work after we both played hooky is a little obvious?" Ava said.

"One thousand percent," Mat said. "Which is why we're taking tomorrow off too."

"Are you high?" Ava said. "We can't take tomorrow off. We'll get fired."

"Ava," Mat said, laughing, "it's common knowledge that two consecutive sick days are more convincing than one." He pulled his STÄDA credit card out of his wallet and tapped the numbers into his phone.

"Is STÄDA paying?"

"Yep," Mat said. "The Very Nice Box."

"The Very Nice Box what?"

"There. We discussed the Very Nice Box. Now STÄDA can cover our dinner."

Ava watched him fit his card back into his wallet. He reached his arm around her, squeezed her shoulder, and kissed her cheek. The doubt must have been written on her face, because Mat turned to her. "Ava," he said, the seatbelt cutting across his broad chest, "you're allowed to break the rules every once in a while. It's actually *encouraged*. It's called Positive Delinquency. They were huge on this sort of thing at Wharton. It boosts morale and makes us feel that we're getting away with something, when really we deserve a nice dinner. You haven't taken a day off in literally *years*. The least STÄDA can do is buy you dinner. And believe me," he said, "I've seen the numbers. They can afford a few sushi rolls." He slid his hand into the space between Ava's thighs and pressed against her.

"Okay," Ava said, closing her eyes. She pushed herself against the edge of his hand. "Tell me what you want to do tomorrow."

"Tomorrow?" Mat said. "The world is our oyster. Beacon? Kingston?"

"No, not upstate," Ava said. The crash played out in her mind, but this time she was able to observe it from a distance, as though she were a rubbernecker passing by.

"Right, of course," Mat said. "What do you wanna do?"

"Be with you," Ava said.

"Good," Mat said, pressing into her more firmly. "My little Lamby."

Under any other circumstance she would reject this infantilizing pet name. But now she struggled to have a defensible problem with it. She thought about his apartment, which had seemed like a real-life version of sponsored content. Who *was* he? she wondered, but the wonder was joyous, as if she were seeing an incredible natural landmark for the first time.

The Swyft bumped along in the direction of her apartment. Now that she'd gotten a taste of a sick day, she *did* feel entitled to one more. Her family had died in a car crash. She had thrown herself back into work the moment she was physically able. Jaime had once dragged her to a Self-Care Seminar entitled "Self-Care for the Workaholic" but she had left early; it had seemed like a license to be lazy and selfish.

But now she understood. She would let herself have this: one more day off. And then, rejuvenated, she would get back to work.

23

JUDITH'S OFFICE WAS COLD AND DRY. AVA SAT IN
an Embracing Armchair and looked out the enormous panel of
windows, where a gray blanket of clouds met the jagged, navy
Buttermilk Channel. It was the Monday after the Steinway
tour, after a weekend lying in bed with Mat, streaming movies and eating leftover sushi. They had watched a movie called
7,000 in which a man sent his kindergarten sweetheart a love
letter every day, hoping that someday they would be together
despite living on opposite coasts and knowing nothing about
each other's lives. But the woman's mail carrier was in love with
her and intercepted all seven thousand letters. They were both
riveted by the film, by its obvious narrative flaws, by the lusty
mail carrier, who was played by a grotesquely muscled man with
a porn-star look.

And now, naturally, Judith was there to intervene in her private pleasure. She and Mat had been called into the People Office, separately this time, and Mat was meeting with Judith first.

This was a routine enough request, Ava reasoned—STÄDA employees were often asked to conduct Self-Reviews with People officers in addition to their managers, though in recent months these reviews had begun to feel less like resources for employees and more like resources for the company. *How would you rate your personal morale after participating in Friday's Manager Training? How would you describe the quality of your output since the introduction of Self-Care Trainings? Have the new rooftop gardens brought joy or stress into your life?* She waited for what felt like two full units.

When the door finally swung open, Mat walked briskly out of Judith's office without making any eye contact with Ava. She tried to ignore the sting.

"Ava," Judith said with a tight smile. Ava followed her into her office and closed the door behind them. She sat facing Judith and eyed a thick stack of Vision Tower printouts from the week before on the far edge of her desk. Attached to the top sheet was a sticky note with a string of numbers written in thick marker.

Ava wished she had an extra layer. She knew she should act like she was getting over a cold, but she was a bad liar, and she was exhausted from the past few nights with Mat—a blissful exhaustion that had left her feeling like the sun was shining through her body.

"Feeling better?" Judith said, as though reading Ava's mind. She took out her Prepared Pocket Knife and peeled an orange in her usual methodical way, stacking the four identical quadrants pulp side up on her desk. She offered Ava a wedge.

"No," Ava said, declining it before remembering Judith's question. "I mean yes," she said. She cleared her throat. "I'm feeling better. Thank you."

"Good," Judith said. "Because I suspect you're not going to like what I'm going to tell you."

Ava's stomach turned.

"As you know," Judith said, "STÄDA is having an unparalleled year, businesswise."

"Yes," Ava said. "Karl mentioned—"

"Hence the wave of hires, the restructuring, Karl's exit, the . . . New Agey meditation seminars." Judith was unable to disguise her annoyance at the last item.

"Are you firing me?" Ava gripped the arms of the Attentive Desk Chair. "I've been here ten years, and my work—I only took two days off—"

"No," Judith said. "No, don't be dramatic. You're our most valuable engineer, and personally I believe that the Very Nice Box will become one of STÄDA's most enduring household items." She began rubbing her temples with her middle fingers. "Though I think you should stick to wood," she said. "The MDF looks cheap."

"Thank you," Ava said.

"However," Judith continued, "as you may or may not know, STÄDA is opening a second headquarters in Gambier, Ohio."

"Gambier?" Ava said. "I . . . I can't go to Gambier."

"We're in agreement," Judith said. "You're a veteran employee here, with an entire team of engineers and technical writers reporting to you. I see no reason to ship you out to Gambier. However, Mathew Putnam can—and will—go to Gambier."

"He *what*?"

"Mathew Putnam can—and will—go to Gambier."

Ava was trapped. To act upset would give the relationship away. She could lose her job. Mat could be blacklisted from the industry for taking advantage of his subordinate.

"Judith," Ava said, "Mat's been great here. For everyone's morale. I think you're making a big mistake."

"This is a significant promotion for Mathew," Judith said,

"one which he just wisely accepted, moments ago. They need someone young and energetic to lead the Gambier campus. He begins there two Mondays from now. And I thought you might like to know, given that he's your manager."

"But—"

"I suggest you keep your reaction professional," Judith said sharply, "since the nature of your relationship with Mathew *is* professional. Isn't it?"

Ava's anxiety suddenly yielded to rage. "I don't know why you're bent on making everyone miserable," she said. The words emerged from her mouth before she was able to filter them.

"Everyone?" said Judith. "Or you?"

"He *means* something to me," Ava said. "You *know* that."

Judith folded her hands together. "Ava, my position as the chief people officer is to—"

"Make people fall into deep depressions? Take good things away from good people? Well, you succeeded," Ava said. "Congratulations."

If Judith was affected by the outburst, she didn't show it. "I appreciate your frustration," she said.

"Do you?" Ava said, with tears brimming.

"I do," Judith said. "The loss of Andie was a loss to all of us at STÄDA who knew her."

"Oh, please," Ava said. "You have no idea what the loss of Andie was. You have no idea how lonely my life has been."

"I'm sorry," Judith said, standing. "You're right. I can't imagine. But now our conversation has taken a detour. Do you need a moment to recover before you get back to work?" She moved a box of tissues closer to Ava.

"No," Ava said. "But you should know, it's freezing in this office. It doesn't make anyone feel welcome."

She abruptly stood and left, her heart skipping. The adrenaline coursed through her as she made her way to Floor 12.

Mat wasn't in his office. Had he left already? Was he angry at her? Had she given the relationship away somehow? She should have been slicker! She'd been so caught up in the romance that she'd done a horrible job hiding it. How could she have thought that calling out sick the same day as Mat was a good idea? Was it possible that somewhere, subconsciously, she had *wanted* to be found out? This was a question her SHRNK would undoubtedly ask.

She surveyed the various clusters of teams working quietly, diligently, their heads bowed. That's how *she* used to work. Diligently, obsessively, without distraction. She'd been the most ambitious engineer at STÄDA. Her love for Mat had taken such a strong hold of her, she could not even recognize herself. She sat at her desk and checked her phone, but there was nothing. Did Mat blame her? Had Judith told him something that she hadn't told Ava? Did everyone on Floor 12 know? Her panic twisted into something new but familiar—the burned sugar, the screaming sirens, the crunch of glass, that strange light that she couldn't identify. She felt dizzy.

Ira

Cut the seatbelt—

Vitals stable—

A voice ripped her out of the vortex.
"Scarlet sin," the voice said.
Ava sat up and looked around but couldn't find the source of the voice. She saw that others on Floor 12 had perked up too. Jaime had removed his Peaceful Headphones and tilted his head, listening. A cluster of technical writers looked up at the overhead speakers. It was the same voice that had led the

office meditation—a woman's voice, which hovered between artificial and human:

> Thy ambition, thou scarlet sin, robbed this bewailing land. Thy ambition, thou scarlet sin, robbed this bewailing land. Thy ambition, thou scarlet sin, robbed this bewailing land. Thy ambition, thou scarlet sin, robbed this bewailing land. Thy ambition—

"Shakespeare," someone said. The voice continued on a loop, clearly programmed, increasing in volume with each repetition. It was Lexi who'd spoken up—the same Spirit staffer who'd introduced Mat to Ava. "It's *Henry VIII,*" she said. She looked around self-consciously. "What? I wrote my undergrad thesis on this play."

"Somebody turn it off," Ava said, standing.

"I'm working on it," Jaime said. "I'm working on it." He had his Peaceful Headphones back on and was typing rapidly. The big screens near the engineers, which normally showed videos of customers calmly assembling STÄDA products, now projected a 3D simulation of the Vision Tower on fire: first the smoke, then the fire, then the ashes, then a blooming garden.

Ava scanned the room for Mat, but there was no sign of him. She made her way up the stairwell, eleven floors, skipping every other step, her blood pumping, her heart loud in her ears, the recorded voice muffled in the stairwell. *One thousand percent my fav place to just chill,* she remembered Mat saying once. *When shit just gets too hard.* She emerged onto the roof, where there was no sound besides the unobstructed wind. She looked around. Each of the Husky Camping Chairs was empty except one.

THE ACCIDENT HAD RIPPED AWAY AVA'S VOICE.
It took her a few days to speak in full sentences. She responded
"yes" or "no" to the questions Teddy asked about her comfort
level until eventually she was wheeled out of intensive care and
into a rehabilitation ward.

This wing of the hospital was bright and sterile, and the
rubberized floor cheeped against the nurses' sneakers. Hospital equipment lined the edges of the room, leaving a wide-open
space in the middle for rehabilitation exercises. Someone had
tried to warm the space with categorically pleasing art: photographs of meadows, young animals, the smiling elderly. A bulletin board documenting patient milestones was framed with
pink and purple streamers.

Ava's physical therapist, Diane, was short and thin, with
light hair that she parted in the center and pulled back. Her
scrubs hung loosely from her body. Ava was surprised by the

strength of Diane's hands as she gripped Ava's elbow, supporting her weight through the more difficult exercises.

Until this moment, aside from feeling trapped, Ava had felt only numb. She knew she was in pain, but she was able to experience it from a neutral position. It was as if she saw her condition from high up, like the diagram of the collision that the police had shown her a few days earlier. She could turn her head forty-five degrees to the left and sixty degrees to the right. She could walk seven steps with a cane and tighten her grip around a pencil for twelve seconds. But now that she had to push these limits, the pain of her injuries rang in every inch of her body. She could feel it behind her eyes.

One morning Diane led Ava through an exercise to rebuild strength in her knee. The goal was to support as much of her body's weight as she could for as long as she could. As she stepped forward, a sharp pain cut through her like a hot blade. She had to stop. Her eyes welled.

"It helps if you break the time up into small units," Diane said. "You're going to find your baseline, your limit. This is the maximum amount of time you can spend on something before you can't do it anymore." She was warm but not patronizing. "The important thing is that every day you try to add time to the unit. It can be a second or five seconds or a minute, but it's a one-way street—your baseline unit stays the same or it grows. It never shrinks. Got it?"

Ava appreciated the clarity and the rules. They started again from the beginning. She could apply weight to her leg for three seconds at a time, and then four. Eventually her baseline unit reached one minute, then two, then five. Some days were better than others.

The pain came in and out like a tide, and eventually—so slowly that it was indiscernible—it began to recede. The units stretched to ten minutes, then fifteen. Fragments of the accident that had lingered in her memory—Offending Vehicle #1, the driver's mess of hair, the smell of cinnamon, the crunch of metal, that unidentifiable channel of light—had faded. Her job wasn't to remember, it was to get better, and she was going to do it well.

Twenty minutes, twenty-five.

She had visitors. First Andie's father showed up. "You never have to worry about meeting him," Andie had once told her. But here they were, face-to-face. He was a short, stout man with a handlebar mustache and a shiny bald head that reminded Ava of a cue ball. He showed up while Ava was working with Diane on wrist rotations. "You're Andrea's roommate?" he said from the doorway, looking down at Ava skeptically.

"Fiancée," Ava said.

"Fiancée," Andie's father repeated, shaking his head. "Well, God does communicate his wishes to us in interesting ways. Doesn't he?" he demanded when Ava didn't respond.

Diane quickly escorted him out. "Good grief," she said, shutting the door. "We need better screening protocols here."

Ava's friends arrived next: three women, all of whom had known Andie first. Ava had grown close to them over the years and was looking forward to seeing them, but when they arrived she felt like she was sinking. Anna, who had messy chin-length hair and wore the same blue work pants that had become Andie's daily uniform, kept her gaze on the only window in the room, as though she were considering an escape. Priya and Maddy, a couple, shared a look of profound confusion and held hands. The way they drooped in their plastic chairs by her bedside, with rounded shoulders and bowed heads, made Ava feel horrible. The only thing she could see when she looked at them was Andie, whose absence inflated between them as quickly as her presence had brought them together. Ava felt guilty and defective. Why couldn't she just embrace them?

Ava enjoyed Karl's and Jaime's visit more. Their support felt reserved but sincere. They arrived at her room awkwardly, each trying to let the other lead. Karl was wearing his signature white button-down, which looked pristine next to Jaime's floral T-shirt.

Karl took Ava's hand and held it between his dry, warm palms. "Ava," he said somberly, with his usual soft, steady expression. "We are . . ." His voice faded as he searched for the right words. "It's important that you use all the time you need." This was one of Karl's mannerisms that had always been charming to Ava. He occasionally used the direct translation of a Swedish phrase rather than the English expression. In Karl's world, you used time—you didn't spend it or take it.

Jaime was more upbeat. He'd offered to take care of Brutus until Ava returned home, and had arrived with a laptop onto which he'd downloaded all the *Hotspot* episodes she'd missed. "You are going to lose your mind when you watch the third one," he said. "I don't want to spoil anything, but what I will say is, Comic Sans."

This made Ava smile for the first time in weeks. "Thank you," she said.

From his backpack Jaime pulled out an oversized card, which had apparently been passed around the office. It was the same kind that circulated for birthdays and employment anniversaries. Someone had begun to write "I'm sorry for—" but crossed it out, opting for "Get better soon!" instead.

Ava had to stop herself from doing what she would have done on more ordinary occasions, which was to search for Andie's note. While most people wrote boilerplate congratulations, Andie's were always thoughtful and funny.

She read through the card once and turned it over. In crisp cursive, Judith had written something so classically Judith that Ava would have laughed if her ribs weren't bruised.

Dear Ava, This card is insufficient to express my sadness and condolences. Please know that the People Office will do all we can to support you in your transition back to work.

Ava was relieved when the stream of visitors eventually thinned, which allowed her to focus on the work of recovery rather than the absence or the sadness or the sympathy. By now she could turn her head sixty degrees to the left and a full ninety to the right. She could walk unassisted for twenty steps and tighten her grip around a pencil for sixty seconds. Diane told her she'd be able to leave the hospital in a matter of weeks.

This was meant to be encouraging, but the truth was that aside from seeing Brutus, Ava felt no real urgency to leave the hospital. Her physical recovery had felt gratifying and within her control, but the visitors had reminded her of the broader damage to her life, which now felt like a vast and barren landscape stretching out in all directions. A thin film of sweat materialized on her forehead at the thought of it. She would bolt awake at night, disoriented, at the four corners of this desert. She knew that when it came time to leave, she'd have to deal with her parents' house. Did they have wills? Life insurance? What would she do with their things? She guided her mind through the space, allowing herself to smell the old books, hold the fiddle, and run a hand over the Steinway's edges. She learned that she could apply Diane's time trick to this kind of discomfort too. Thirty seconds. She could feel sad for thirty seconds, and then she'd have to use time for something else.

25

BECAUSE IT WAS SO TALL, THE SIMPLE TOWER was designed to sway in the wind. On the roof Ava could feel it, as though she were on a boat. She hugged herself against the chill. The sky had drained of color and the wind bit at her face.

Mat was sitting in a Husky Camping Chair, facing away from her. She knew it was him from his hair, which blew violently in unpredictable directions.

"Mat," she said.

He stood quickly and turned to face her, hugging himself for warmth; he wore only a denim jacket over his crisp white T-shirt. He'd wrapped his hand up in his scarf and held it close to his chest. It was bleeding. "Ava," he said, "you should go back inside."

"What happened to you?" Ava said, rushing toward him.

"It's nothing," he said, but Ava noticed the broken pane of glass on the south stairwell door.

"Mat! Did you—"

"I punched through it. It was stupid. I'm fine. *No*—I'm *not* fine. How can she do this to us?" His face was red.

She dragged another Husky Camping Chair beside him and sat. Red Hook's warehouses and two-story homes were tiny and flat, the quiet pattern of sloping silver and tar-black roofs blended into the broader texture of Brooklyn. Across the river, tall ships in the seaport bobbed at their moorings, their flags chopping in the wind.

"Just go," Mat said. "I don't want you getting in any more trouble because of me."

Ava smoothed his back, a maternal-feeling gesture she didn't recognize from herself. "No," she said. "I want to be here."

Mat rested his head on her shoulder. "I really lost it in there," he said. "I called Judith an asshat."

"Asshat, wow," Ava said. "That's worse than me. I'm impressed. What'd she say?" She continued rubbing circles on his back.

"She said, 'Those two nouns together are illogical.'"

Ava couldn't help but laugh. It sounded like something that *she* would say—or would have said, before Mat.

"I don't want to go to Gambier," Mat said. He buried his face against her, and she held him there. His cheek was rough against her palm.

"I'm sure there's a way to appeal the transfer," she said. "Surely they can't just *demand* that you move to Gambier." *You could quit* was what she wanted to say, though she knew it was wrong, that she was being selfish, that the move would mean a promotion for him. *Just quit and be with me.*

"It's not out of nowhere, though," Mat said. "They're onto our relationship. She said that one of us would have to relocate but that there weren't any engineering roles in Gambier. And I know a People threat when I hear one—either I go to Gambier or one of us gets fired. Judith said it was standard practice now. Apparently I signed something agreeing to this possibility when I was hired. I'm so bad with forms, there were so many of them, I didn't read the fine print. I'm such an idiot."

"Fucking Judith!" Ava said. "Why does she care about this so much?" Ava herself could quit, but then what? She knew no one. She'd allowed all her professional and social relationships to dissolve. The idea of "networking" horrified her.

A news helicopter thundered overhead, the sound beating against her eardrums as it passed above them before floating over the main STÄDA parking lot. Employees had leaked onto the lot with their hands clamped over their ears.

"What now?" Mat said.

"The Vandals," Ava said. "They took over the PA system and jumbo screens. Put a bizarre quote on repeat."

"Well, I guess that's *one* thing I have to look forward to in Gambier," Mat said, resting his head back on her shoulder. "No teenagers are going to pour wood chips into my gas tank and hijack the PA system."

Ava hated the mention of Gambier, that Mat had clearly already begun the work of imagining himself there. "So you've decided already," she said. "You're going."

"Well," he said.

"I don't want to hear." She felt a hole in her heart—a hole that had been there all along, since the accident, but that she had not acknowledged, not until Mat had filled it. And now that he was going, the emptiness was wider and darker.

"I don't want you to go," Ava said, lifting her head and staring straight ahead. "I love you."

"You what?" Mat said. "I can't hear you over the helicopter."

"I love you," Ava said.

"Sorry," Mat said. "I couldn't make that out. Did you say . . . you *glove* me?"

"Stop," Ava said.

"Did you say . . . you *dove* me? The wind is a little loud." He nudged a knuckle into her rib. She stared straight ahead, fighting back a smile.

"You shove me? That's really not cool. Don't shove me."

"I said I love you!"

"Oh!" Mat shouted. "You *love* me. Is that right?" He cupped his ear.

"Yes," Ava said, staring at the parking lot. "That's right."

"Well, good," Mat said, bringing an arm around her and pulling her tightly to him. "Because I love you too. Which means it's settled. We love each other. And you know what that means?" He smothered her cheek in kisses.

"Yes," Ava said. "I do. You'll move to Gambier, we'll slowly but methodically lose touch. You'll begin to talk about things and people I can't relate to. Every person who has ever been attracted to a man will fall in love with you. We'll agree to speak every day, but every day will turn into every other day, then every week, and so on. This will trigger a cycle of resentment and guilt. We'll let things continue this way until our bond becomes warped and tenuous enough that eventually we detach completely, with no hope of repair. And I'll be heartbroken forever." She watched a second news helicopter bumble clumsily over the parking lot.

"Ava," Mat said, "we are not a shittily built household item. Give us more credit than that!"

"No," Ava said, wiping a tear away from her cheek with the back of her hand. She turned to face him. "I'm an engineer. I understand how things break down. I'd rather call it now than watch it fail in slow motion."

"That's bullshit," Mat said. "That is not how love works." His eyes shone.

"It's the truth, actually," Ava said. "We both know it." Her heart felt like a stone. The news helicopters hovered over the parking lot, her colleagues collected in their shadows. "I didn't ask you to come here and do this to me," she said.

"You haven't even thought about it," Mat said. "You're being irrational."

"I have a lot of flaws," Ava said, "but being irrational isn't one of them."

"Ava, please! You can't just—"

"Please stop," she said. "You'll make it worse."

She allowed herself to study his beautiful face—to take it in, up close, one last time. Mat wiped a tear from his cheek with the crook of his elbow.

It was fine. The loss of Mat would be just another loss in a series of losses. She would forge a path forward, as she always had. She would focus on designing boxes, as she always had. She would begin the work of forgetting, as she always had. She pushed herself up, dusted off her hands, and left him sitting there.

PART TWO

26

SPRING ARRIVED EARLY THAT YEAR. BY MID-
March the magnolia trees lining Ava's block had unfolded,
tulips reached for the sun optimistically, and the ivy in Fort
Greene Park seduced dogs with delicate white flowers that
they peed on. There was, Ava noticed, an influx of puppies in
the neighborhood, and during her early-morning walks they
eagerly bumped noses with Brutus.

The Stoned Fruit had opened an ice cream window, and
an eternal line of people happily waited for scoops of CBD-
infused sorbet. Everyone around Ava was sneezing more,
laughing more, and wearing short sleeves. By all accounts, the
dramatic relief from a grim winter should have made Ava feel
better.

Instead it all felt like an insult.

She was lonely. *I feel like a hollowed-out shell*, she wrote to her
SHRNK.

How about a vacation? her SHRNK suggested.

But Ava had no use for a vacation. Unstructured time was the opposite of what she needed. What she needed was a task list so long that she couldn't see what was on the other side of it.

This feeling—that the more tasks she had to occupy herself, the better—lent itself well to her new, horrible morning routine, which involved taking two unreliable and underserviced train lines. Her connecting train was often delayed or too packed to enter, and sometimes it skipped Ava's stop for reasons that were not clear. The commute could take up to three units if anything fell out of alignment. It reminded her of the days when she was too proud to ask Mat for a ride. She could take a Swyft, but there was something punishing and therefore appropriate about the obstacle course that was her commute. The mundane annoyance of the transfers eclipsed what had gutted her: Mat was gone.

What is he doing at this very moment? she found herself wondering as she held a warm pole on the train one morning. She'd deleted Mat's number and installed on each of her devices Just Don't software, which prevented her from contacting him.

She transferred onto a southbound train and stood across from a multipanel ad for the Very Nice Box. The campaign would run for six more weeks. It was a direct result of Mat's "Yes, And" meeting. *You're a minimalist. With things. We get it,* the ad read in STÄDA's signature font. In each panel of the ad, the lid of the Very Nice Box was open, revealing something outlandish inside. A live sheep. A 12-volt car. A pile of brandless lollipops. A potted tree. Under each image: *Get Yourself a Very Nice Box.*

The Very Nice Box had done extraordinarily well, and was even set to outpace the Cozy Nesting Tables in sales. Ava liked to think that its success came from the ingenious design and not the marketing, but she wasn't sure. She stared at the ads.

Awesome, awesome, she could remember Mat saying at the "Yes, And" meeting.

The Very Nice Box ads were sandwiched between ads for products that she remembered from Mat's apartment. There was Pop, the hygienic toothbrush with a replaceable head, and Remy, the jersey cotton sheets whose new ads featured snoozing animals. Even Good Guys had revved up their campaign, with comic-strip-looking ads featuring plainclothes superheroes.

Mat's replacement was a woman named Helen Gross, who had come to STÄDA as the new head of product after a decade with a well-regarded commercial lighting company. Judith had handpicked Helen for the job, and it showed. Helen Gross was humorless and quiet. She had no charisma and wore her hair in a low, bushy ponytail. A shiny, pale mole lay beside her nose. She wore white ribbed turtlenecks that made Ava itch when she looked at them. In an introductory meeting, she squeaked her name onto the whiteboard in the Imagination Room. The letters were small and slanted and the marker had almost dried out, so everyone had to lean forward and squint. She did not make small talk with her Marketing team, let alone with any other team, and she'd canceled all future "Yes, And" meetings, opting instead for data-driven campaigns managed and written by AI. She brought a bagged lunch to work, which she ate alone in the Imagination Room while reviewing spreadsheets on her laptop.

"Had a dream this office was fun for, like, three weeks," Ava had overheard Owen Lloyd say while filling a glass with Wellness Water. It was the day after Helen Gross had officially started working at STÄDA. He was talking to one of the Marketing interns. "Wish I had never woken up."

Ava couldn't help but agree with Owen. Helen had tasked Ava with a series of dull, unchallenging assignments, which sucked the joy from her work. Floor 12 had a sad, deflated feeling now that Mat was gone. It was as though they had all woken up from an incredible party and were being forced to pick up each piece of confetti by hand.

It was, Ava knew, her own fault. If only she hadn't gotten involved with him. If only she'd kept her life small, controlled, and quiet.

As she rode the train, Ava allowed herself to cycle through the questions that had been turning in her head for months: *What had Mat eaten for breakfast? What did his apartment look like? How was his commute? Did he listen to* Thirty-Minute Machine *in his car, without her? Was he listening to* Thirty-Minute Machine *with someone else? Were there attractive people in Gambier, Ohio? Had she been too harsh with him on the roof of the Simple Tower? Was he trying to get in touch with her? Should she—*

The doors slid open and she joined a line of STÄDA employees as they made their way up the underground stairs and onto the sidewalk that led to the Simple Tower. There had been so many new hires over the past six months that they had to walk in two single-file lines to the entrance. Ahead of them, the half-complete Vision Tower shot up, with green scaffolding surrounding it and a crew of workers in hardhats buzzing around productively. On one of the panels Ava could make out the words *Imagine a garden here* in spray paint.

It had been satisfying to watch the Vision Tower's construction, which supplied a reliable if fleeting distraction from Ava's loneliness. Today she watched a crane lower a palette of stacked bricks. The load was vacuum-sealed, and the blocks created a subtle grid in the plastic. The massive bundle carved its way through the air with the ease of a whale gliding through water.

At the Simple Tower, three new key-card scanning stations

with built-in hand sanitizer dispensers had been constructed to accommodate the influx of employees. Two elevator banks had been added to the lobby. A newly installed LCD screen near the elevators informed employees that Floor 6, which had previously housed the Customer Bliss Center, would now boast the new frozen yogurt bar, serving dozens of flavors of frozen yogurt and hundreds of toppings. The announcement featured a photo of several STÄDA employees dressed head-to-toe in their colors, beaming with cups that overflowed with gummy bears and chocolate crumbles. The frozen yogurt bar had been Mat's idea, one of the many additions that he wouldn't get to see himself.

Thanks to Ava.

The advertisement vanished and a new slide appeared, a photograph of an androgynous blond teenager in a hoodie, looking bored, blowing a pink bubble of gum, and holding up a rendering of a stepladder that read, I'M ENGINEERING A BETTER FUTURE. THANKS, STÄDA!

The announcement soon transitioned into a 3D rendering of the Vision Tower. According to the simulation, once complete, the Vision Tower would release thick white vapor from the roof, which would form the word *STÄDA* in an environmentally friendly cloud that would hang in the sky during business hours.

Ava held her bagged lunch as she squeezed into an elevator, keeping her head bent.

The news of Ava and Mat's relationship had spread quickly around Floor 12 in the weeks after his transfer, and Ava had felt like an exhibit at the zoo. Eventually her colleagues moved on, so she was surprised to overhear two floppy-haired engineers discussing it again in the elevator. *Maybe he's just one of those guys who likes average-looking women because it makes him seem more attractive by comparison.*

Ava's cheeks burned.

Or he likes smart girls. I think she's supposed to be, like, crazy smart. Like savant level or something.

And she ended it?

The elevator opened onto Floor 3, and a trio of Spirit staffers crammed inside.

He didn't really say in the episode. But I heard he broke up with her.

"Guys." It was Jaime's voice. "Give it a rest."

I heard it was the other way around.

Wait, this is for sure the same girl whose ex-boyfriend died in a car crash a while back?

I heard it was her girlfriend.

She's gay?

And the whole family.

The whole family's gay?

No, the whole family died. It was before we started working here.

Damn. That sucks for her.

Jaime spun around. "I said, give it a rest!"

Ava met his eye as the doors opened on Floor 12. "Oh, Ava," he said. *Oh, shit,* she heard one of the Spirit staffers say. *I think that was . . .*

She made her way to her desk and soothed herself by googling Mat. She allowed herself to do this once a week, for no more than half a unit. But there hadn't been anything new. The last piece of news she had seen was in a STÄDA newsletter announcing his reassignment. The newsletter included a photo of Mat with a small group of people outside the new Gambier offices. He towered over everyone else in the group and palmed a basketball. They all wore the same shirt, which read, in STÄDA's font, COOLER, SMARTER, GAMBIER. Ava hated this shirt. According to the newsletter, the group comprised the heads of various start-ups who had come together to get

STÄDA's Gambier campus up and running. There were women on either side of Mat, which Ava tried to ignore.

The photo must have been taken only a few days after she had broken up with him. Mat had spent hours trying to reason with her—he believed they could make it work despite the distance—and she had been so upset about the transfer that she could only say no. No, it would never work. No, she didn't want to try. Finally he'd left for Gambier and gotten this dorky shirt and posed for this photo, and although he was smiling, he looked lost and sad, which made Ava feel satisfied.

"I'm sorry about that," Jaime said. He'd shown up abruptly at her desk, and Ava quickly closed out of the window. It was the first time he had spoken to her in months. That was her fault; she had removed two legs from a three-legged stool: they used to eat together on Mondays; they used to debrief on the latest episode of *Hotspot;* they used to avoid the subject of Andie. And now there was nothing to keep the friendship standing. "It's okay," she said.

"No, it's not. Those guys have no idea what they're talking about."

Ava looked up at him. He was wearing a tight grapefruit-colored T-shirt and the UV-light-filtering tortoiseshell glasses from the Self-Care Fair. She had to admit they looked good on him. "It's really okay," she said. "But thanks for saying something in there."

"I assume you had already listened to it."

"Listened to what?" Ava said.

"Oh," Jaime said. "Wait, really?"

"What do you mean, 'Wait, really'?"

"Have you been listening to *Thirty-Minute Machine?*"

"No," Ava said. Now that Mat was gone, she couldn't bring herself to listen alone.

"Okay," Jaime said. "Never mind, actually."

"Did they mention the Very Nice Box? Because Marketing should really let us know anytime . . ."

Jaime hesitated. "No," he said. "No, it's not that. It's a good episode, that's all." He forced a smile.

Ava wanted to keep Jaime there as long as she could. She missed him. "Do you want to have lunch today?"

"I can't," Jaime said. "I told Sofia I'd eat with her on Mondays."

"Oh," Ava said, feeling heat behind her eyes. "Okay, maybe tomorrow."

"I got pulled into another Diversity Panel tomorrow."

"Wednesday?"

Jaime examined his clean fingernails. "I'll need to check . . ."

Ava straightened the photo of Brutus on her desk. "Sofia, really?" she said.

"You could maybe join us," Jaime said, though the invitation was about as welcoming as a cold wind.

"No thanks," Ava said.

"Sofia's really cool," Jaime said. "What's your beef with her?"

"First of all, she's . . . well, you know."

"What?"

"She's so . . . *straight*! She's like . . . a corporate straight person!"

Jaime looked at her. "Yes," he said.

"I'm sorry," Ava said. "It's just that every time I talk to straight women, I feel like there's a wall of glass between us. Like we're leading vaguely parallel lives but we will never understand one another. And she's in Marketing!"

"I seem to remember someone you really liked being the *head* of Marketing," Jaime said. "And straight."

"Yeah, well," Ava said. "Maybe that's why he's out of my life now."

"Oh, please," Jaime said. "I just saw you close a browser page with his face on it. Your heartbreak isn't that subtle."

Ava stared at her lap. She knew she wasn't going to find a well of sympathy in Jaime. But a small part of her appreciated that he could see she was hurting. "I wouldn't wish this feeling on my worst enemy," she said. "But I know you weren't a fan of Mat, and we don't need to talk about it."

Jaime sighed. "He reminded me of every bro who went to my high school. Guys who looked and sounded exactly like him. They treated me like shit. I mean, just picture it. Nerdy queer kid with a wheely backpack. I was an easy target. So I guess Mat sorta . . . I dunno . . . I thought . . ."

"You thought what?" Ava looked up at him.

"I actually thought he was behind the vandalism."

"What? Why?"

"Think about it," Jaime said, and Ava braced herself, as she often did, to get lost in a labyrinth of nonsensical evidence he had collected. "The vandalism pretty much started when Mat got onboarded. I was sure it was him."

For a moment Ava fantasized about taking this information to Mat. She could just picture the joy and outrage on his face at the insinuation that he had rigged the lobby sprinklers.

"But then when he relegated me to the Vandals task force," Jaime continued, "I got a firsthand glimpse of how inept he is. And when that Shakespeare quote started playing on the speakers, I knew for sure it wasn't him. No offense to Mat, but . . ."

"Relegated? I thought you wanted to lead the task force. He said you volunteered."

"Yeah, well, the email left out one important word. I *was* volunteered. I mean, he gave me a raise and a title change, but it was pretty clear I had no choice. I'm basically a glorified security guard. I mean, what am I even *doing* with my life?"

"Can't you talk to Judith?"

"I tried. She won't take me off the assignment. Apparently the board is obsessed with STÄDA's internship program because they get good press and some sort of charitable deduction for it. So I look over the footage and write up reports about how the Vandals skirt around our systems. That part is actually pretty entertaining—they're really slick. I feel like I'm watching true crime."

"Have any of them enrolled in Mat's internship program?"

"Of course not!" Jaime said. "They hate STÄDA. Why would they do underpaid labor for us? Anyway, most of them are teenagers, so we can't hire them."

"What about the photo on the lobby screens? Of the blond kid holding up the stepladder?"

"That's Casey from IT. He looks really young, so the board gave him a bonus to pose for that."

"Wow," Ava said. "So it's a complete sham."

"Yep. But you better believe 'youth internship director' is going on my résumé. Anyway, who's your worst enemy?"

"What?" Ava said.

"Your worst enemy," Jaime said. "You said you wouldn't wish heartbreak on your worst enemy."

"Oh," said Ava. "The woman who crashed into my car and killed my entire family."

"Right," Jaime said. "Stupid question. Sorry."

"No stupid questions," Ava said. "One thousand percent positivity, buddy. Okay?" She did a bad impression of Mat, but it still made Jaime giggle.

"Sorry I judged him," Jaime said. "I just really missed you, and losing you to some cis het bro was really shitty."

"Weren't you just telling me that straight people deserve friendship?"

"Smart, competent straight people, yes," Jaime said. "Fully vetted straight people."

"All right," Ava said, annoyed.

Jaime put his hands up. "Okay, I'm sorry," he said. "If you loved him, I can bring myself to like him. From afar. As long as you never ditch me like that again. That was really annoying."

"I'm sorry," Ava said. "It's just . . . he was the first person since Andie—"

"You don't need to explain," Jaime said. "I get it. And you deserved that happiness. Andie would have wanted that for you."

The earnestness of the statement made Ava avert her gaze. Jaime squeezed her shoulder. "I missed you, Ava," he said. "And I'm sorry you're hurting."

"Thanks," Ava said. "I've missed you too. Pencil me in for lunch when you have a chance."

"Fuck it," Jaime said. "I'll see if Sofia can swap for a different day. And actually—" He lit up.

"What?"

"There's a piece of security camera footage I've been trying to crack—from the day the Vandals basically launched a Vision Tower DDoS attack on the printers during the Self-Care Fair. Remember that?"

Ava was overcome with the memory of Mat pushing her up against the printer while the rest of Floor 12 was engaged in a guided meditation. She nodded.

"I can't figure it out, and I am obsessed," Jaime said. "I need your help. Meet me on Floor 2 at noon?"

Ava wanted to hug him but stopped herself. "I'd love to help," she said.

She watched as Jaime made his way back to his desk. It had been so long since she'd felt a wave of happiness like this. She slipped her Peaceful Headphones back on and navigated to the latest episode of *Thirty-Minute Machine*.

"Hey there, Machinists! This is your host, Roy Stone!"

"And I'm Gloria Cruz!"

"Today on the show we're talking to the chief marketing officer at STÄDA's iconic new campus in Gambier, Ohio. Mat, you're on the air!"

Ava's heart pushed against her chest. Her jaw tightened.

"Hey Gloria, hey Roy, thanks so much for having me on. Listen, uh, this is pretty unconventional, but—"

She stopped the podcast, removed her Peaceful Headphones, and looked around, feeling that everyone was listening to the episode along with her.

She could not listen. She had lost many things in her life, but she had hung on to her discipline and composure. All of that, she knew, would disintegrate if she pressed Play.

27

SO SHE WOULDN'T. SHE WOULDN'T PRESS PLAY, even though everyone on Floor 12 had apparently listened to the episode and was asking her, in conspicuous glances over the course of that morning, whether she had too. Ava tuned out the whispering, S-Chat dings and murmuring. It reminded her of Mat's first week at STÄDA, except that time the feeling had been of one giant, mutual contact high. This time it was as though everyone smelled something strange wafting from Ava's desk. She could ignore the attention. She had years of practice ignoring people, and she would put that practice to use once again.

She met Jaime on Floor 2 at noon, as planned. Floor 2 was a modest, expansive floor, tightly carpeted, with rows of well-organized wooden drawers full of every tool, screw, bolt, and peg necessary to assemble each item in STÄDA's catalogue. A wall of industrial windows on the far end of the floor provided an interior bird's-eye view of the shipping warehouse, where STÄDA products were produced, packaged, and shipped to showrooms across the country. Now she saw that Jaime had transformed a corner into his makeshift investigation headquarters. He'd set up three wide monitors on top of a Delightful Folding Table. On a whiteboard he'd tracked dates and times of Vandal activity. He had even developed his own rating system for the complexity of the stunts.

When Jaime saw Ava, he pulled up a Little Desk Chair and called up a grainy video on one of the monitors. "Okay, check this out," he said. "It's from the security camera in the northeast hallway, by the printer room."

Ava took a seat next to him. His excitement was palpable and contagious. The footage provided a grainy fish-eye view of the empty northeast hallway on Floor 12. Through the fuzz of footage, Ava could just make out the team of engineers in the distance, their laptops shut as they joined the officewide meditation. Her cheeks flushed at the memory of the urgency with which Mat had been kissing her.

"Okay, it's about to happen," Jaime said, staring at the monitor.

A small shadow appeared and lingered at the bottom of the screen. "Wait for it . . ." Jaime said, and a gloved hand reached up to cover the lens with a sticky note. The video went black.

Ava frowned.

"Crazy, right? Whoever did this knew exactly how to block the camera without being seen by it. This is the first time there's been any reason to believe they've physically been *inside* the building."

"That, or it's an employee, and they've been inside the whole time."

"Right," Jaime said. "It's just a head-scratcher. I've watched the footage from before and after, and there aren't any random teenagers running around the floor."

"Bizarre," Ava said. She remembered the string of numbers Judith had written on the stack of blueprints in her office. "Didn't Judith have a lead on this?"

"Not that she shared with me," Jaime said. "What did she tell you?"

"Nothing," Ava said, shaking her head. "I don't think it was anything."

Jaime's phone quacked in his pocket. "Oh god, apparently I'm supposed to give an interview for the STÄDA newsletter about how well the internship program is going. This is so stupid. I'll leave you here to obsess. And Ava?"

"Yes?"

"You didn't listen to the episode, right?"

"I started it," Ava admitted. "As soon as I heard his voice, I turned it off."

Jaime put his hand on top of hers. "Good," he said. "It's really not worth listening to. I'm sorry I even brought it up." He squeezed her hand and left.

Ava sat, alone on the quiet floor, while the footage played in a loop. What had Mat said on the episode that was so interesting to everyone? She forced the question out of her head and focused on the footage. The shadow, the hand reaching up, the screen going dark. She was so entranced that she jumped from her Little Desk Chair when a quiet, nasal voice emerged suddenly.

"It's Ava, correct?"

She turned to see Helen Gross, who was standing over her. She was small and slightly scoliotic.

"I was just finishing my lunch," Ava said. "I'm on my way out."

Helen pursed her lips into something resembling a smile. "Thank you," she said, looking at her watch. "I need total silence to work. This is apparently the only floor that provides that."

Ava packed up her lunch while Helen awkwardly stood, waiting. When Ava had first glimpsed Helen Gross, she had experienced a strange feeling of recognition. She tried to remember the various conferences she'd attended over the years — ones that would have included designers and engineers from industrial design companies. It was entirely possible that Helen Gross had attended or even spoken at one of these conferences. Maybe she'd come to STÄDA to give a presentation on lighting.

But what Ava now realized was something much darker: Helen Gross was familiar because she reminded Ava of herself. She could see the loneliness, the rigidity. She remembered how Mat had tried to coax her into the Imagination Room his first week on the job. She could hear her own voice now. *I disagree that it will be great.* She had been so difficult, so closed off, so cold.

Helen's eyes bored into her. "Thank you for understanding."

It was in moments like these that Ava most wanted to disable Just Don't and text Mat. He would love hearing about Helen Gross, Ava knew. On her way to her desk, she drafted a message. *Okay*, she wrote, *picture me from when you first met me, crossed with Judith, crossed with a cat that was run over in a rainstorm.* She allowed herself to look at the text and picture Mat's reaction before deleting it.

Her phone buzzed. A message from her SHRNK.

Ava, you've been quiet lately. How are you feeling?

Bad, Ava wrote.

I'm sorry to hear that. What's going on?

I'm worried I'm sliding back into the depressing life I had before Mat. I can see the Helen Gross in me clawing its way out.

Who is Helen Gross?

Mat's replacement. She's horrible.

And you're worried you're like her?

Obsessed with work and solitude? Allergic to fun? Yes, Ava wrote.

Have you fully investigated why your life became consumed with work?

I don't think an investigation is necessary. Work is the only reliable thing in my life.

Since?

Since some woman plowed into my car and robbed me of my whole life.

What a powerful belief that is.

I don't know what you mean by belief. It's just true.

I understand.

Can't you just tell me what to do? Isn't that what you're supposed to do? Just give me an assignment and I'll do it.

An assignment, her SHRNK repeated.

Yes.

Perhaps we could consider anger. Anger is like a hot ball of fire we throw. Do you know what happens when we throw it?

No.

It burns our target, yes. But it also burns our palm.

Ava rolled her eyes. And?

Who could you be if you found a way out of the anger about the accident?

How?

Perhaps forgiveness would be a good place to start.

How original, Ava wrote.

I didn't claim it was original, her SHRNK wrote. Usually the best ideas aren't.

Ava closed the app. The concept of forgiveness was opaque and out of reach, and it felt deeply unfair that the job of seeking it out had fallen to her. What about the driver? Did she have any idea of the damage she'd caused? Or was she walking around oblivious and free? Ava teared up at the idea, her rage alive within her.

28

IF SHE WAS GOING TO LEARN FORGIVENESS, AVA would do it on her terms. One unit per day. No more. And she would understand the task on her terms too: if the story of the accident were a Sturdy Table, the ability to forgive would be a missing screw. It was her job now to fix it.

She was reluctant to tell Jaime about the project, and when she did, she was sure to emphasize that it was an assignment from her SHRNK. "I've been tasked with forgiving the woman who killed my family," she told him during their next Monday lunch.

"That's great, Ava," Jaime said, opening his Humble Lunchbox. "You know, forgiveness has a great effect on our cortisol levels."

She was relieved he didn't try to talk to her about the accident, or bring up Andie.

"How about you spend lunch down here with me every day and we can do our research together? I'll look at Vandal footage and you can become an enlightened being. As long as you can tolerate Sofia joining us sometimes."

"Fine," Ava said.

"Just be nice to her. Don't be all . . . you know, 'I hate corporate straight women.'"

Ava laughed. "I will try to be nice to her."

He parked a second Tiny Desk Chair permanently at his workstation on Floor 2 and worked on untangling the Vandal footage quietly beside Ava, while she began exploring the virtual archives of STÄDA's Self-Care series. The workshops included links to the speakers' websites. One website instructed her to do a ten-day garlic cleanse to forge a way toward forgiveness. *Resentment isn't wrong, just as a toothache isn't wrong,* offered a website run by a former dentist turned Buddhist who had visited STÄDA the year before. Ava briefly contemplated that metaphor before moving on to a blog offering guided meditations run by a middle-aged woman with frizzled blond hair who sounded like she was on the verge of either crying or screaming. Another site promoted a "branched" approach to forgiveness; she was instructed to consider the smallest negative ramification of the incident and forgive that first. Then she'd work her way back to the source.

She tried to focus on the smallest ramification of the accident and pictured the weeks' worth of junk mail crammed into her mailbox when she'd returned home from the hospital. But the memory of the mail — none of it important, and most of it with Andie's name on it — only upset her. And she knew that given her attention to detail, a project like this would take a lifetime.

As she scrolled through a website about something called "breath feelings," Good Guys ads began appearing in the margins. She stared at the first one: a dark and empty city, a capeless superhero in jeans and an oxford shirt gliding fist-first between skyscrapers. Far below him, a lone man stood at his hot dog cart, beneath a yellow-and-red umbrella, pointing up at the flying man, who pointed back at him.

She tried to focus on the content of the website she was supposed to be reading. *Assign your breath a color on the inhale,* the website instructed her. But she kept getting distracted by the Good Guys ads. A new one had appeared on her screen, featuring a crowded Coney Island: all the sunbathers on their towels except for one man in bright yellow swimming trunks, who stood among them. With one hand he shaded his eyes, and with the other he pointed at a plainclothes superhero gliding above, who pointed right back at him. Ava pictured Mat as the flying man, and then she pictured Mat as the beachgoer, and then she clicked on the ad.

The home page had a bright, clean aesthetic, and she paused the sunset-themed welcome video before it was able to autoplay. A drop-down menu offered numerous options:

- ▶ Dare to hope
- ▶ Dare to succeed
- ▶ Dare to change
- ▶ Dare to dream
- ▶ Dare to love
- ▶ Dare to forgive

Ava clicked on *Dare to forgive,* which took her to a blank white page. *Thank you for daring to forgive* appeared in a heavy black font. The text was soon replaced by a photograph of a handsome bald man sitting cross-legged on a yoga mat in the middle of the woods. Ava waited for something more, feeling suddenly self-conscious. "Forgiveness," the man said, opening his eyes, "doesn't happen suddenly." He snapped his fingers. Ava's heart raced as she fumbled to mute the video.

Jaime glanced up. "Find something helpful?" he said. "I think you forgot to plug in your headphones."

"Oh," Ava said. "I don't know."

Jaime leaned in to get a look. "Ava, are you kidding me?"

"What?" Ava said.

"Good Guys?"

"What?" Ava repeated, exasperated. "They're known for their philosophy on forgiveness! I'm just curious!"

"Good Guys is for sad, weird men, Ava!"

"I know!" Ava said. She felt defensive and humiliated.

"If you become a Good Guys apologist," Jaime said, "I'm going to be so annoyed."

"I'm not," Ava said. "I'm not."

"Nothing that calls itself good is ever *actually* good."

"Then what do you suggest I do? Go to church? Become a Hare Krishna?"

"Honestly?"

"Yes," Ava said.

"Honestly, I suggest you go on a date. I don't think any website is going to help you with this."

"Wouldn't that just be a distraction?"

"You have a SHRNK, right?"

"Yes."

"So then you're already doing everything you need to do. Talk to your therapist, then go find someone who is *genuinely* good. Who lifts you up enough that you question whether your anger and sadness are required parts of your identity."

"Now you sound like Good Guys."

"Ava Simon is going on a date?" It was Sofia. She held an Enlightened Tray from the cafeteria.

"No," Ava said.

"Hi, Ava," Sofia said, sitting down.

"What's the worst that could happen?" Jaime said.

"The worst that could happen?" Ava said. "Let's see. I meet a serial killer and die, completing the last of a series of unfortunate events that have made up my adult life."

"Doubtful," Jaime said.

"I can't believe that you of all people are not more concerned about this," Ava said. "What, suddenly Jaime Rojas sees no threat to our safety?"

"I find the insinuation insulting and baseless," Jaime said.

Sofia laughed. "Okay, Mr. the Vision Tower Is Going to Kill Us All."

Jaime raised a hand in defense. "Listen, we don't know what's in that cloud of so-called steam. The air quality in the city is bad enough as it is. The last thing we need is STÄDA-funded carcinogens."

"I didn't realize the city's air quality was on your list," Sofia said.

"There's a reason I keep sending you links to upstate Float-Homes. The mountain air is exceptional. Plus," he said, "do I need to remind you that I called that vaping was bad news? I was *right*. I didn't ask for this gift of incredible foresight, but here we are. You're going to thank me someday."

"You're paranoid," Sofia said, "but Ava, Jaime's right: you desperately need to go on a date. Go fill your mind with someone who's not Mat and not dead." She began mixing a packet of dressing into her salad.

"Sofia . . ." Jaime said.

"No, she's right," Ava said. She waited to feel offended by Sofia's bluntness but instead felt refreshed.

"I'm just telling it like it is," Sofia said, piercing a piece of lettuce. "Ava, can I ask you a personal question?"

"No," Ava said.

Sofia rolled her eyes. "You dated women before Mat, right? Was he, like, super into that?"

Jaime raised an eyebrow and stirred a piece of wasabi into a Modest Container of soy sauce.

"What do you mean?" Ava said.

"I mean that men are *obsessed* with women together," Sofia said matter-of-factly. "I can't tell you how many guys have tried to get me to have three-ways with them." She gestured to suggest a brain explosion.

Ava looked at Jaime, hoping he might throw her a life raft, but he just looked entertained.

"He was interested in my history with women, yes," Ava said, choosing her words carefully. "But I wouldn't say he was *into* it."

She remembered that early on Mat always looked as if he were untangling a difficult knot when the topic of Ava's sexuality came up. *So what percent gay are you?* He seemed desperate to quantify it. *How could I ever compete with a woman if you already know exactly what to do with each other?* Ava had taken care to show him how good he made her feel. Over the course of their relationship she had become skilled at simplifying her feelings on his behalf, but it was true that she sometimes missed being with a woman.

"I think it's possible he was sort of threatened," Ava said.

"Men are horrible," Jaime said.

"I actually agree," Sofia said. She stuck a straw into her Thoughtful Glass of Wellness Water. "And I think it's really unfair that I have to be married to one."

The conversation evaporated when Helen Gross entered the room. "I hope I'm not interrupting," Helen said. "Sofia, I must have misplaced the sales figures you sent me for the Entrancing Ottoman."

"I haven't sent those yet," Sofia said.

"At your earliest convenience, then," Helen said, forcing a smile.

Sofia stood to leave, squeezing Jaime's shoulder on her way out. "Do it," she whispered to Ava. "Go on a date. Your sadness is stressful to be around."

———

At home that night, Ava googled "least bad dating app." The first hit was an app boasting that women got to send the first message, to keep out predatory men. It was a decent concept, Ava thought, but it seemed designed exclusively for straight people, and in practice it meant that women were required to do all the hard work, only to be rejected half the time.

She searched for "dating after loss" and found an app called The Way for people who had lost spouses. The age-appropriate options were limited and, Ava suspected, Christian. At first glance the men on this app appeared hip. They had Andy Warhol glasses and tattoos, but their photos felt sanitized in a way that made it seem like they loved God as much as they loved pour-over coffee and taking good care of their cast-iron pans.

Finally she downloaded Kinder, an app that touted a zero-tolerance policy for harassment. The first photo she uploaded was one that Jaime had taken of her assembling a prototype of the Very Nice Box, in which she had her sleeves rolled up and looked useful and intelligent. She added a candid shot, which captured her profile just as she was about to laugh. It was one of her favorite photos of herself, one that Andie had taken at a dinner party. It felt wrong, slightly, to use the photo. But she pushed past the feeling and uploaded it. The last photo was her STÄDA employee headshot, in which she wore a button-down and looked squarely at the camera with a warm smile.

She adjusted her settings, lingering briefly on distance, sliding a red dot all the way to the right to see just how close to Gambier she could get. But the app stopped her at 100 miles.

She also paused on the gender settings, first checking only women, then checking both men and women, then unchecking men, then rechecking men.

Immediately a message appeared from a man named Jason, whose single photo was a faraway shot of him on the beach, topless and wearing sunglasses, his arms straight down by his sides. *Hello sexy this is my modesty,* he wrote.

Ava reread the message, trying to decipher it before swiping him away. A shimmering ad dropped down featuring a man standing outside a camping tent, pointing up at a night sky. The stars formed the words *Good Guys Stand Tall.* She swiped it away.

After sorting through messages ranging from syntactically nonsensical to sexually harrowing, she arranged to go on a date with a thirty-two-year-old journalist named Amir C., whose photo showed him wearing a large backpack and standing on top of a mountain. His bio said, "Ask me what I'm reading," and so Ava did, feeling grateful for the clear instructions.

Derrida, he responded.

Oh, god, she thought, staring at his message. But then, that's what she'd thought upon meeting Mat Putnam.

29

AVA TRIED TO CALM HER NERVES AS SHE AP-
proached Amir's apartment building, a five-story walkup with
ornate, decaying trim. *This is a low-stakes activity,* she reminded
herself. *Your only task is not to think about Mat the whole time.*

A few men sat on the stoop with beers. If she were being
completely honest, Ava would admit that part of the appeal of
Amir was that, according to his Kinder bio, he had graduated
from Wharton the same year as Mat. Maybe he'd remember
Mat. Maybe somehow Mat would hear about the date through
the Wharton alumni grapevine. She didn't allow the fantasy to
continue.

"Need to get in? Here ya go," one of the men said, standing
up, holding the door open for her. She saw he was wearing a
Curious Collar around his neck.

"No," Ava said. "I mean, thanks. But I'm just waiting for
someone." She felt compelled to explain further but stopped
herself and stood with them awkwardly for a few minutes,

waiting for Amir to emerge. She resisted looking at her Precise Wristwatch, and although she fantasized about turning around and walking home, she stood rooted in place and turned her focus to two Vivacious Planters on either side of the steps until the door swung open.

She recognized Amir from his photos. He had a narrow jaw and dark, curly hair that he pushed out of his face with a cotton headband. He was shorter than Ava had imagined. He smiled at her as he descended his stoop, and she waved, immediately regretting it. They exchanged something mortifyingly in between a hug and a handshake, and she was aware of the gazes of the men on the stoop. He smelled like laundry detergent. She thought about commenting on this but changed her mind and said nothing at all, her mind painfully blank.

They took the subway to a modern dance show, which wasn't something Ava would have chosen to do on her own, but she was determined to have an open mind. "I have never been disappointed by this company," Amir said as they waited in line for tickets. Next to them a bus shelter advertised the Very Nice Box. This one featured a Very Nice Box full of wooden clogs.

"Company?" Ava said.

"Dance company," Amir said.

"Oh, right," Ava said. "Of course." It was only going to last three units, she reminded herself as they inched forward in line. She felt ambivalent about dance but good about the idea of consuming art, and it felt like a smart setting for a first date, because they wouldn't have to carry the torch of conversation all evening. Of all the promises online dating offered, this was the worst. She wasn't sure how she was expected to establish a rapport with a complete stranger in a matter of minutes.

The show opened with a glaring yellow light that moved slowly across the stage at eye level. By the time it reached the other side, a dancer had emerged. He was tall and broad, wearing track pants and no shirt. There was no accompaniment. The audience shifted in their seats, waiting for the dance to begin, and slowly it became clear that it already had. The dancer was making small convulsing movements with his stomach. The movement traveled to different parts of his body as other performers entered and exited the stage, walking quickly past him in all directions with their heads bowed. Ava could hear the dancer's breath echo, and the flat patting sound of his feet on the stage. The silence was broken by a steady drone of bagpipes. The dancer continued, now alone on the stage, making his way to the ground. He reminded Ava of an insect dying slowly. She tried to read the program in the dark but couldn't. It was too late for context.

She looked over at Amir, whose wide, unblinking gaze was fixed on the stage. He looked like he was falling in love for the first time, and Ava dreaded the idea that she would be expected to discuss the show afterward. When it ended, the bagpipes stopped, returning the audience to a taut silence. The lights clicked on. The dancer, dripping with sweat, bowed and waved proudly.

"Wow! That was just—wow." Amir had started the sentence with vigor and ended it with quiet, sober introspection. He stood and shouted "Bravo!" with a tone of pure gratitude. "What did you think?" he said as they made their way onto the street.

Ava wasn't sure what to say, or even what part of speech to use. "It was . . . intense," she said.

Amir glowed. "*Wasn't* it?"

He spent the subway ride and subsequent walk home recapping the performance as Ava listened politely, her mind like a dog on a long leash, wandering to Mat. She tried to reel herself back to the present moment but couldn't focus. Mat would have embarrassed her at this show. He wouldn't have been able to control his laughter. She pictured him sinking down low in his seat and hiding his face behind the program, his long legs barely fitting in the space in front of him. She could even hear his voice in the Swyft on the way back to her apartment: *Am I nuts or did that dude look like he was having a medical emergency?*

Amir saw her smiling and wrapped his arm around her shoulder. They walked like this for a block. Ava tried to put her arm around his waist, but it felt uncomfortable—surely the worst way to walk—and she took her arm back. She considered bringing up Mat and the Wharton connection, but what could she say? *Hey, you might know this guy I'm attempting to forget.*

When she tuned back in to what Amir was saying, she realized he was creating something of an opening for her to bring up Mat. "Basically, I'm trying to counteract two years of Wharton by supporting the arts," he said. "Kind of unfortunate I didn't go to a single show my whole time in Philly."

Should she take the bait? Ava opened her mouth but couldn't bring herself to mention Mat. "I get that," she said instead.

"This was really fun," Amir said, pivoting to face her. They stood outside his apartment building, and she worried that he would invite her up. He looked her in the eyes with an intensity that felt like a test. She wished she could evaporate. He leaned in to kiss her, and she let him. His small mouth rested dryly on hers. She pulled back, and he smiled at her again.

"Thanks so much for the ticket," she said.

"Let's do this again sometime," he said, pushing his headband back.

"Yes, you have my number!" If there was a reply that was both honest and graceful, it eluded Ava. She felt bad for allowing him to experience an entirely different version of the evening, but the alternative—to be cold, or disparaging, or ungrateful—felt untenable. She would have to simply go home and ignore him forever.

She lay in bed that night, exhausted but unable to sleep. She turned the performance ticket over in her hands. *Row M. Seat 14. Thank you for supporting the Same But Different Dance Company.* Her thoughts swarmed around the problem of how to gracefully cancel her next Kinder date, which she had arranged for the following evening with a woman named Rebecca P. She drafted several explanations, including "family emergency," an excuse that was so ridiculous that she shut off her phone, willing herself to go through with it.

30

REBECCA WAS RUNNING FIVE MINUTES LATE, according to a chaotic series of texts. She had suggested an old neighborhood bar near the Simple Tower that reminded Ava of the early days at STÄDA, when the team would unwind for happy hour every week. When she arrived she slid into the booth, dropping her bag on the table with a thud. It was overflowing. Something heavy and oddly shaped at the bottom of the bag prevented it from standing upright, so she leaned it against the wall before removing her earbuds and dropping them in. Ava imagined the earbuds making their way to the bottom of the bag, where they would almost certainly be crushed by the heavy, irregular object.

Rebecca had a wide, pale face and long brown hair that had been straightened. A few small hairs lining her part gave away their natural frizziness. "Hi!" she said, catching her breath. "I wasn't sure it was you, because ..." She hesitated for what felt like an eternity. "Well, I guess you just look a little more three-dimensional than your photos." She laughed.

"Sorry to disappoint," Ava said.

Rebecca sprang back, realizing the implication. "No, no!" she said, shaking her head. "Not disappointed—at all! It's just so weird meeting up with strangers from the Internet. Like ninety-nine percent of what you have is your imagination, and it's all going to be slightly wrong no matter what."

Ava thought that was a good way to place the feeling. And she felt the same way. In her profile Rebecca had seemed more composed than she did here, with the thin strap of her tank top slipping down her arm. Ava mentally slid it back in place while Rebecca ordered a complicated cocktail.

Rebecca was a gallery assistant and talked at length about her daily tasks, none of which she enjoyed. Ordinarily Ava would have been able to get deep into this conversation about the banality of everyday life, but as Rebecca spoke, a fly landed on one of the small frizzy hairs sticking out from the top of her head. It was as if it were stuck there. The fly didn't flinch at her head movements or hand gestures. Ava was so distracted by the fly that talking to Rebecca felt like communicating with someone several rooms away. Was the fly dead? Had Rebecca used some product that had trapped it there? Should Ava say something?

"So what do you think?" Rebecca said, rooting her straw through the ice of her empty drink. "Would you be up for that? It's just a few blocks away." She signaled for the bartender to close out her bill.

Ava tried to fit the puzzle pieces together without betraying that she hadn't absorbed Rebecca's proposal. "Oh," she said. "Um—"

"I totally get it if you're not into parties," Rebecca said. "But my friends are super-nice."

Ava wasn't sure if this was an attempt to accelerate or slow a romantic connection. She wrestled with her desire to say no, imagining what her SHRNK might say. *Who could you be if you stepped out of your comfort zone?*

She tried to remember the last time she'd been to a party other than STÄDA's Solstice Party, which was essentially a requirement. "Sure," she said. "Okay."

She followed Rebecca down a cobblestone street, past a crowded restaurant with a rowdy rooftop bar, and through the side door of a three-story building. They climbed the stairs, which were off-level, sloping inward. The angle intensified as they climbed, until finally they were on the top floor, which was so off-balance that Ava felt dizzy.

Inside, the party was fully under way. The first thing Ava noticed was the humidity, followed by the sound of deep bass that felt like a brick wall in every direction.

"Come on!" Rebecca yelled. "I want you to meet my friends!" She led Ava through the crowd to a small cluster of people. One of them wore a green velvet turtleneck and braids pulled into a long ponytail. She let out a little scream when she saw Rebecca.

"Agnes, this is Ava. My Kinder date. Ava, this is Agnes. This is her party."

"Nice to meet you, Ava!" Agnes said, giving her a hug. She smelled intensely like vanilla.

"Thank you," Ava said, recovering from the hug.

One of Rebecca's other friends, a sprightly person wearing a hoodie the color of watermelon, stuck out a hand. "I'm TJ."

"Hi," Ava said, accepting the handshake. She admired the neat bow TJ had tied from the string of the hoodie.

"Did Rebecca kidnap you? If you need help, just let us know," TJ said.

"All right, all right," Rebecca said happily.

Ava scanned the room for STÄDA pieces, but the furniture looked older and thrifted. She spotted a first-edition Practical Sofa in the corner, wedged between two off-brand bookshelves. "Nice sofa," she said to Agnes, straining to be heard over the party. "I have the same one."

"Thanks!" Agnes said. "I picked it up at Brooklyn Flea."

"It's a Practical Sofa," Ava said.

"Yeah," Agnes said, looking at Ava as if she'd mentioned that the sky was blue. "I guess it is pretty practical."

Ava opted not to elaborate. The party was starting to compress, and she sensed that she was at the center of what would soon become the dance floor. Everybody around her was attractive, each with their own brand of studied carelessness. For a hopeful second she thought she saw Jaime, but it was just a person in a floral T-shirt.

"You look like you need a drink!" Rebecca said over the noise.

"What tipped you off?"

Rebecca said something Ava couldn't hear. "What?"

"I said, you're cute!"

"Oh!" Ava said. She felt herself blushing. "I'll get the drinks. What do you want?"

"Anything!" Rebecca said.

Ava pushed her way through the living room and into a narrow galley kitchen with peeling linoleum tiles. The counter was covered with six-packs and liquor, which Ava felt an urge to sort. A person with a tight buzz cut and a sleeve of stick-and-poke tattoos sat on the counter next to the sink, talking with a friend who sat on the ledge of the kitchen's open window. Ava sifted through the beers, looking for something familiar, passively listening to their conversation. She tried to ignore an intrusive thought of the person in the open window falling backward.

The floor's tilt was even worse than it had been in the stairwell. Ava wondered if it was safe to live at an angle like this. Suddenly, mercifully, she overheard the word *STÄDA,* and it felt like a hand pulling her out of a dark, churning sea.

She looked more closely to see if she recognized the pair of friends, but she didn't. She caught the eye of the tattooed person, who smiled warmly at her, as if she'd been a part of the conversation all along. "What's your name?"

"Ava."

"I'm Hen. This is Charlie. *They/them* for both of us."

"*She/her.* Sorry for listening in. I overheard you talking about STÄDA."

"Did you see this?" Hen said, reaching out to show Ava their phone.

Ava took the phone and swiped through a series of images of phrases in white spray paint on green construction scaffolding. She immediately recognized the Vision Tower in the first image, and the words *Imagine a garden here.* As she swiped through, she noticed similar photos taken at construction sites all around the city. *Imagine affordable housing here. Imagine a library here.* "Yeah, kind of," Ava said, handing the phone back. "I saw the first one. I actually work at STÄDA."

"Oh shit, really? I guess I could have guessed," Hen said, looking her up and down.

Ava's cheeks flushed. "What do you mean?"

"You look like you live in an elevator building. That, and you're wearing that STÄDA watch that was everywhere like ten years ago."

Charlie rolled their eyes. They were lean but muscular, sporting a thick mustache, manicured stubble, and small gold hoop earrings. They hopped down from the windowsill and started fixing a drink. "*You* live in an elevator building, Hen," they said.

"Does it still count if I take the stairs?" They both burst into laughter.

Charlie handed Ava a drink, which she took and sipped. It was fizzy and tasted like basil.

"I actually do love that watch, though," Hen said. "Can I see it?"

Ava set her drink down and unwound the watch from her wrist, which she ordinarily did only before taking a shower. She handed it to Hen and tried to suppress the thought of them dropping the watch into their drink. Then she pictured Charlie taking the watch and tossing it out the window.

"It reminds me of a Dieter Rams piece," Hen said, admiring it as if it were a precious stone. "So what do you think?" They handed back the watch to Ava.

Maybe it would have been normal for Ava to say she knew the designer of the watch and in fact was wearing the prototype. But how would she continue from there? *She was my fiancée, in fact! Unfortunately, she died instantly in a car accident, along with my parents.* No, she wasn't going down that road. She strapped the watch around her wrist and looked at it. "I like it a lot— it's one of my favorite things I own."

Charlie and Hen looked at each other.

"Of the protests, I mean," Hen said.

"Oh," Ava said, blushing. "I don't know. We seem to be building a good rapport with the neighborhood. I think things are calming down a little bit."

"Who's 'we'?" Charlie said.

"I guess I mean *they*— STÄDA. I just design storage boxes. I don't really have anything to do with the Vandals." She sipped from her drink.

"Did you seriously just call them vandals?" Hen said.

"Sorry," Ava said. "I meant protesters."

She felt a hand around her waist. It was Rebecca.

"Ava, there you are," she said. "I thought you pulled an Irish exit. I see you met Hen and Charlie."

"Yes!" Hen said, smiling at Ava. "We were just talking about how Ava thinks it's possible to be apolitical while working for a cancerous furniture empire."

"No," Ava said, "I just mean—listen, we make affordable Scandinavian home goods. I think the expansion is over-the-top too, obviously, but—"

"But what? People don't *need* affordable Scandinavian home goods. People need community gardens."

"It's not that simple," Ava said. "I know how STÄDA works, and—"

"Let me guess," Hen said sharply. "You're fighting STÄDA from within STÄDA."

"No," Ava said, "I didn't say that. I'm not fighting anyone."

"And there lies the problem," Charlie said.

"Give her a break!" Rebecca said. "So she's not an activist. So what?"

"So what?" Charlie and Hen said in unison.

Ava's throat had gone dry.

"Anyway," Rebecca said, "my song just came on." She pulled Ava toward the dance floor. She was sweaty, but her hands were cold. Ava couldn't imagine a touch feeling further from Andie's, whose hands had been broad and strong and somehow always warm. She thought of Mat's hands. She remembered the day they met, when he had palmed a basketball and taken it to the backseat of his car. His voice slipped back into her mind: *Hey Gloria, hey Roy, thanks so much for having me on—*

"Actually," Ava shouted over the music, "I should get home. I have a big day tomorrow."

"Oh," Rebecca said. "Okay! You sure? Is it because of Hen and Charlie? Did they go too far?"

"What?"

"Did you have a good time?"

"Yes," Ava lied. "Thank you." She pulled her hand from Rebecca's grip and made her way to the entrance. She imagined a marble rolling quickly along the sloped floor.

———

Brutus curled beside Ava later that night as she lay on her back in her Principled Bed. She closed her eyes, the conversation with Hen and Charlie turning over in her mind. How would Mat have responded to them? She could see him now: *One thousand percent agree! That's why we're working on smog-free live rooftop gardens* within *STÄDA's walls that will be totally accessible to the public!* But Mat was gone. It was a familiar, dull ache by now. She opened a new message to her SHRNK.

Had another bad date.

What was bad about it?

It was a disaster. I got into an argument about STÄDA with someone at a party. They think STÄDA's evil, and that I am too, for working there. Do they expect me to march into a board meeting and demand that they halt the construction?

Sometimes when we drain the well of anger, we discover something unexpected at the bottom. What would you find if you drained the well?

Ava thought about it. *Sadness*, she admitted. *I need STÄDA to be good. It's the last thing I have.*

Is it?

My family's gone, Mat's gone. I can't even listen to Thirty-Minute Machine *because he's featured on the latest episode.*

And why can't you? Do you want to?

It's too painful. I stopped it as soon as I heard his voice. I don't even know what he said.

Ava rested the phone on her chest and rubbed her eyes. Her phone buzzed.

Who could you be if you disconnected from burdensome feelings —sadness, anger, guilt—and allowed yourself to be present with the things you really want?

Like what?

To use your example, the podcast.

You think I should listen to the episode? Ava perked up at the thought.

I would never use the word should. *I am just suggesting you consider the option of acknowledging your desires.*

Ava turned off her phone. She thought about the question as she drifted off to sleep. Between her thoughts came an image: Mat coming home from work, hanging his jacket on a Supportive Door Hook, kissing Ava on the cheek, putting on a Homey Apron, cooking dinner while Ava poured him a Cheerful Pint of beer.

31

HER SHRNK HAD SUGGESTED SHE "CONSIDER
the option," and so Ava did, the next day. She pushed through
her workday, pretending to only "consider." But with her
SHRNK's permission, resisting it felt like a farce, like seeing
whether she could hold her hands up in the air all day. She busied herself with tasks — she read through instruction manuals,
looked over several prototypes for a new Loving Tissue Box. Finally she released herself from the fake argument she was having with herself.

She skirted around Engineering, made her way through the
Wellness Kitchen, and stepped into an elevator a full two units
earlier than usual.

On a different day she would have felt displaced by the light
outside, a too-bright reminder of the change in routine. But
this afternoon Ava didn't have the capacity to experience anything aside from her own impatience, which overrode the long
commute home.

In her apartment, she poured herself a Thoughtful Glass of water, sat on the edge of her Embracing Armchair, connected her Peaceful Headphones to her phone, and pressed Play. Brutus sat at her feet, looking puzzled by her early arrival.

Mat's voice was smooth and low and full of energy. She imagined him calling in, pacing around his apartment in Gambier the way he did in some of the "Yes, And" meetings. She could easily envision his bright cheeks, his disheveled hair, his workboots thudding pleasantly on a wood floor.

"Hey Roy, hey Gloria, thanks so much for having me on. Listen, um, this is pretty unconventional, but I've been having a big problem lately, and I'm hoping you can help."

"Shoot!" Roy said.

"Okay. So I've been having a really tough time these past couple of months. Like, super-tough."

It was as though there were a firm hand around Ava's heart, and it squeezed as Mat's voice filled the air. Mat continued.

"There's this girl — this woman, I mean — in New York. We had something really great, but she ended things because I had to move away for a big promotion, and I just really miss her, man. I mean, I've never felt this way before."

Had his voice strained? Was Ava hearing this right? She briefly, irrationally, considered the possibility that the woman he was referring to wasn't her. It was like muscle memory to assume attention was pointing in a different direction.

After a moment of dead noise, Gloria Cruz spoke up. *"That's really sweet, Mat. I'm not sure you're in the right place, though. This is more of an engineering—"*

"No, no, I know—just hear me out. I really think you might be able to help. So, she broke up with me because long-distance communication can be tough. I'm all the way in Ohio, and she's in New York, and we haven't spoken. At all. It's completely impossible to stay in touch without having to fly back to New York, and I really

miss the sound of her voice. I wish there were some way to . . ." Mat sighed, and then continued in a small voice. "No, it sounds too impossible . . . It's a stupid idea. It would never work . . ."

"We've solved some pretty tough problems here before," Gloria Cruz said cheerfully. "We can always give it a shot. What is it?"

"Well, I know how this is going to sound. You're going to think I'm crazy. But—I wish there were some way to communicate instantly across long distances."

Ava could sense exactly where this was going. She could hear it in his voice.

"I wish there was some small device I could use to hear her voice again. It should be small enough to carry in my pocket, so I can check it every hour to see if she has something to say to me. I wouldn't even have to use my voice all the time! I could even write short messages and send them to her. Or even just hearts and faces blowing kisses and other symbols. I know it sounds crazy, but do you think you could build something like that for me?"

This was just like him—to steal airwaves just long enough to tell a joke.

A trace of annoyance colored Roy Stone's voice like a drop of ink in water. "It sounds like Mat wants us to invent the cell phone," he said. "I'll tell you what, bud, if I had built the first cell phone, I'd be a very rich man. Anyway, ha-ha. I think it's time to move on to other callers with more analog issues. Good luck with your girlfriend, Mat."

Ava repeated the word girlfriend to herself, trying to fact-check the term, as if Mat had been the one to say it. She removed her Peaceful Headphones and sat in silence. After a few blank moments, emotion returned like a dead limb coming back to life. She wanted to replay the episode, to hear him say it again: he missed her. She took out her phone and stared at it. It had taken her months to stop expecting to see Mat's name appear here. She regarded this as progress, but the progress came at a price: she was exhausted. So exhausted that she didn't stop herself as she swiped through her apps, pressed down firmly on Just Don't, and tried to delete it.

Just don't! a pop-up warned. Ava dismissed it.

Nope, don't do it! :-)

"Come on," Ava muttered. She tried again to dismiss it.

Did you know 80 percent of Just Don't users try to break in when under the influence of drugs, alcohol, and bad ideas? To prove you're sober, please answer the following questions in under thirty seconds:

47 × 13?

611, Ava typed automatically.

Capital of Maryland?

Annapolis.

Platypus: fish or mammal?

Mammal.

Spell rhododendron *backward.*

nordnedodohr.

Cool, buddy, I guess! ;-) You're in.

32

THE PERFECT TEXT TO MAT WOULD BE REQUIRED
to loosen the tight knot of silence between them. Ava considered her options the next morning while she waited for STÄDA's shipping manager to take her on a tour of STÄDA's refurbished warehouse. The tour was part of a new shadowing program for STÄDA employees to learn about different parts of the business, and while most of her colleagues groaned about it, Ava was quietly excited.

The floor manager was a short, compact woman who wore her red hair in a tight circular bun. She led Ava from Floor 2 down a flight of service stairs and through a set of double doors on which two hardhats and two orange vests hung from Supportive Door Hooks. She handed Ava a hardhat and recited a list of preliminary safety procedures. Ava pushed aside her pending text to Mat in order to listen.

"Keep your hardhat on at all times. Look where you're stepping. Pretend you're at a fancy museum. Do not cross over any bright yellow tape."

The warehouse was loud but orderly. High ceilings and enormous grids of windows allowed natural light to flood the space. The pine-scented air reminded Ava of the Steinway factory. She was yanked back to that day: Mat's reddened cheeks, the light falling in wedges that lit up every particle of sawdust.

We had something really great, but she ended things . . .

She shook herself from the memory and followed the floor manager. Steel roller belts carried products from one station to another, where they were inspected and flat-packed into cardboard boxes. Ava scanned the room, picking out the Very Nice Box whenever she could find it. Her heart leapt to see her design in its raw components, evenly stacked with no wasted space for packaging. They were perfect.

"We're implementing automation to help meet the demand from STÄDA's new showrooms," the floor manager shouted over the noise. "As you probably know, we're slated to expand to two thousand new showrooms worldwide within the year."

Ava peered down at the whirring machinery, whose various parts moved in a choreographed fury, affixing hardware to panels of wood, sending sheets of MDF through a curtain of white paint.

"We need preassembled floor models in addition to our flat-pack inventory, hence our new automated assembly system, which is now in its last phase of testing." Ava looked out onto the automated assembly. She wanted to savor this feeling of awe and curiosity, which her SHRNK had told her was healthy for the brain. This would be the perfect thing to text Mat about. It wouldn't be seen as needy; she would simply be sharing her enthusiasm with him.

"Because our operations have expanded exponentially, our

safety practices have followed suit," the warehouse manager continued proudly. Ava listened, following closely behind as the manager began describing the various measures STÄDA had taken to keep its workers safe in the presence of daunting machinery, and the parts of the warehouse that were off-limits for anyone who didn't have specialized training. "So if you wanna work back here, and I can see in your face that you're thinking about it," the woman said, "go train for seven years. Then we'll talk."

———

Back at her desk, Ava stared at her phone. She had deleted her text history with Mat, and the prospect of writing the perfect message was like stepping onto a field of untouched snow.

Hi there, she typed. She erased it—it was the same irritated greeting she used to reprimand technical writers for slipping marketing language into instruction manuals. She glanced around the room, feeling that whatever she wrote was being projected onto the jumbo screens or onto everyone's S-Chat channel, or directly onto Mat's smart watch, as though he could see each draft, each deleted phrase, word, letter, and punctuation mark.

Good morning.

No.

Hello. How's Gambier?

No! What was she, a Customer Bliss bot? She erased it.

Hey, I—

"Are you ready for your review?" Helen Gross's voice came from behind her, and she quickly put her phone away. She checked her Precise Wristwatch. She was five minutes late for their meeting. She hated the thought of being quizzed about her work, especially by the cold fish that was Helen Gross.

Well, Ava had nothing to worry about. The success of the

Very Nice Box should be proof alone of her excellence. She made her way to Helen's office, which had been Mat's before, and briefly allowed herself a fantasy that she would walk inside and find him there, surrounded by his Good Guys books.

"Yes, sorry," Ava said, glancing around Helen's office. The sight of it depressed her. Helen had replaced the lighting fixtures with gloomy chandeliers that dripped with beads of fake crystal. Where Mat had once shelved his Good Guys manuals and yellow items from the Swag Lounge, Helen had hung paintings of a white, morose cat. The office felt damp and smelled like yogurt. Ava pictured Mat's reaction: *I'm gonna have to pause my Positivity Mandate to go ahead and say what we're all thinking, which is that Helen Gross is the human embodiment of cottage cheese.*

Ava closed the door behind her.

"So," Helen said, sliding into her oversized, off-brand desk chair. Was it possible for a voice to be clammy? She half stood, then awkwardly sat back down and untwisted the cap of a water bottle. "How are you?" she said.

How *was* she? "I feel very satisfied by the execution of the Very Nice Box," Ava said, wanting to get the Self-Review over with as soon as possible. "I was happy to see that it's now featured in the looping videos on Floor 12, along with the figures, which show the Very Nice Box outpacing all our seating furniture, combined, in sales. Plus the subway campaign and consumer reviews. Sofia told me it's going to appear as a prop on four separate TV shows next year. Overall, I'm happy." She stared at an oil painting of the white cat moodily gripping a knot of yarn.

Helen was taking notes in an off-brand spiral notebook. Ava tried not to look at what she was writing, but even when she did glance, Helen's handwriting was impossible to read. Her fingers were stubby, and they ended in rounded, bulbous fingernails.

"Your work is good," Helen said.

"Thank you."

"And I believe it's being wasted on bins."

"Boxes, not bins," Ava said. The correction was so automatic that she actually missed the content of Helen's statement.

"Okay," Helen said blankly. "I don't know what the difference is, and I can't imagine it's meaningful."

"Bins would include garbage cans, hampers—" Ava started, annoyed.

But Helen cut her off with her sharp, flat voice. "The point is, your talent has been wasted."

Ava wanted to open a window. She had begun to sweat.

"What's needed," Helen continued, "is development in a new area that is experiencing an economic boom."

"What area?"

"Feline furniture," Helen said. Ava detected a twinkle in her eye.

"What?" Ava said.

"People want more furniture for their felines."

"But STÄDA doesn't make cat furniture," Ava said. "Cat furniture is notoriously ugly, usually made of carpet and other materials that we don't use at STÄDA because they're distasteful." She thought of what Karl would think of this. He would have said something poetic that both removed the tension and dismissed the idea of cat furniture entirely. And he loved cats.

"Cat furniture is not distasteful to *cats*," Helen said, using air quotes around the word *distasteful*, then adjusting a small porcelain cat on her desk.

"But . . . *people* are buying STÄDA products, not cats."

"People are buying STÄDA products *for* their cats." Helen

was vigorously twisting her necklace. Ava saw that a rash was spreading along her collarbone. "And I don't see anyone making such a big fuss about our canine-related products, such as the Curious Leash. All companies need to expand in order to grow. In our case, we are expanding in the direction of feline furniture."

Helen opened a large plastic three-ring binder that appeared to contain a sort of vision board of cat furniture. There were photos of carpeted towers, netted beds with suction cups on the ends, big blocky scratching posts, and a narrow, bright beam that one could install across the entire length of an apartment.

"You may borrow this binder to get your gears going," Helen said.

"But I don't want—I like *boxes,*" Ava said.

"That's nice," Helen said. "And I like going to Renaissance fairs. Sometimes we have to do things we don't like." She used air quotes around the word *like*. "I'd *like* to see some preliminary ideas for feline furniture at the end of the week. Thank you."

Ava stood.

"You forgot the binder," Helen said.

"That's okay," Ava said. "The images are seared into my memory."

———

The commute was at its worst that day. Signal problems kept the train underground between stations for so long that Ava began to feel like a vice was closing around her. The AC was overwhelming. The train conductor's voice cut sharply into the car every couple minutes, startling her each time with a loud blast of static. Pressed between someone's armpit and a woman who smelled like patchouli, she opened a new text to Mat. *You won't believe what your replacement is making me do.*

She erased it.

I went on a really cool tour of the shipping warehouse today.
She erased it.
How's Emily liking Gambier?
She erased it, stepping onto the sidewalk that led to her apartment. Sunlight had spilled across the sky, spreading pink light in all directions. Birds argued happily in the trees. Dogs ran exuberant laps in the park. A line of people waited for ice cream outside the Stoned Fruit. She approached her apartment and opened her phone one last time.

I miss you, she wrote, and pressed Send. Her blood pumped in her ears. She immediately wanted to take it back.

But an ellipsis appeared.

I like that shirt, Mat wrote. *Is it new?*

??

Look up from your phone, Lamby.

33

HE LEANED AGAINST THE HOOD OF HIS SPORTS car, his legs crossed at the ankles. The bottom of the car was splashed with mud. His hair was longer than it had been when he left, but otherwise he was exactly as Ava remembered—his eyes a clear blue, his cheeks bright. He held his arms out to the sides as though to say, *Can you believe it?,* his mouth fighting a smile. He looked like a child waiting to receive a gift.

Ava's heartbeat drummed in her throat.

"Lamby," he said.

"Why . . . how," she began, walking toward him as though he were a mirage, but she couldn't finish the question before he pulled her to him and kissed her, holding her face in his large hands. She took him in. His piney scent, his warm breath that was sweet and minty.

Of all the competing needs she had in that moment—to understand why he was standing in front of her apartment, to scold him for ruining the paltry momentum she'd built to get over him, to reckon with the embarrassment of her own surprise — the one that prevailed was her need to feel the entire weight of his body on top of hers.

They pushed up the stairs into her apartment. In one swift gesture Mat pulled Ava onto his lap, on the edge of her Principled Bed, and brought her close. It was as if he were trying to absorb her, a desire to which she would gladly have conceded. She pulled off her shirt, and then his. His chest was warm and more freckled than she had remembered. She held a fistful of his hair as he ran his mouth down her stomach. She touched him as if her hands could rebuild each part of him she'd lost.

Afterward they lay at the foot of the bed. Mat rested his head on Ava's chest. She found it endearing that he liked to be held, and ran her fingers through his hair.

"I missed you," he murmured.

"No you didn't," Ava said. She wanted him to say it again. She opened one eye to find him with his cheek propped on his fist, looking at her impishly, as if he were in the midst of scheming about something. "But I wrote you seven thousand letters!" he said, and Ava covered his mouth with her hand. He pried it away and continued to recite the line from the movie 7,000. "I wrote to you *every day for twenty years!*" Mat whined.

She laughed and kissed him again.

"You're just trying to shut me up," he mumbled into her lips.

"Maybe," Ava said. "Are you saying you want me to stop?"

He shook his head.

"Good," she said sternly, and pulled him back onto the bed.

———

In the morning Ava perched on a Reliable Stool at the end of the kitchen counter and watched Mat cook breakfast, worried he would disappear if she looked away. He was in his boxers, with a Courteous Dishrag slung over his shoulder, whisking eggs. She gazed happily at the scar along his ribs. He bopped his head to music that Ava recognized vaguely from its extended guitar solo. Brutus watched from his Dreamy Dog Bed. Mat occasionally called out to him, as if Brutus were going to take a solo, and his tail flicked at the attention.

Evidence of the huevos rancheros was everywhere. Eggshells and papery onion skins were strewn across the counter, along with most of Ava's cooking utensils and a can of black beans, which Mat had opened three quarters of the way before prying it apart. He tossed a couple tortillas onto the burner over the open flame, flipping them with his bare hands when they started to smoke. If the beautiful uniformity of the shipping warehouse had an inverse, Ava thought, it was this.

"I went on the most incredible tour of STÄDA's warehouse," she said. "It was technically a safety training, but I got to see *everything*. I wish I'd sketched it. Did you ever do the tour?"

"Nah," Mat said, sprinkling a tortilla with cheese. "They tried to get me to do that safety thing, but I left it to the nerds."

"You missed out," Ava said. She described the warehouse, the automated machinery, the sheets of wood running beneath a solid wall of paint, like wafers being coated in chocolate. "It was beautiful."

Mat picked up a pair of Ava's reading glasses from the countertop and put them on. Then he grabbed Brutus's reflective vest and fit it over his head. "Does my safety gear turn you on?" he said.

"Okay," Ava said, smiling. "So I'm a nerd."

"A *hot* nerd," Mat said, squinting at her from behind her glasses. He took them off and turned his attention back to the stovetop, where diced onions sizzled in a Benevolent Pan. Ordinarily Ava would have followed closely behind him, clearing the debris he left in his wake before it had time to sit, but this morning she felt happy simply to watch him. For a moment she allowed herself to imagine what it would be like to have Mat standing in her kitchen, serenading her dog, every Saturday morning.

She hadn't asked about his arrival, and didn't want to. She didn't want to invite the likely truth into the room, which was that he was here for something administrative, like picking up his old mail, or formal, like attending the wedding of one of his Wharton friends. Both scenarios would mean he'd have to leave soon. Then she'd begin the process of moving on again, only this time it would be worse, because she'd hold out hope that he'd surprise her at each turn. She felt the question rising in her throat, but just before she could let it out, as though sensing her anxiety, Mat turned to face her.

"I quit my job," he said plainly, handing her a Simple Dinner Plate of breakfast.

"You what?" Ava said. The steam from her eggs bloomed up in her face.

"I know it sounds crazy, but I've been miserable in Gambier. Without you, without the Guys." Mat stood near the stove and jabbed at his breakfast. "There's no Good Guys chapter in Gambier. Shocker. Anyway, I was rereading one of the manuals last week and was reminded that I really need to fire my unhappiness so that I can hire my desire to work for me instead."

Ava blinked at him, vowing never to repeat this proclamation to Jaime. At the thought of Jaime, her stomach twisted. "Does that mean you're staying?" she said, cutting into her tortilla with the edge of her Useful Fork. She wanted to sound hopeful but not needy.

"I need to start reaching for what I want, and here's what I know for sure: I *want* to be with you. I *want* to make breakfast with you and walk Brutus with you and listen to *TMM* with you. I have some savings, and I'll figure out the rest."

Ava maneuvered through a crash of competing thoughts: How could a twenty-six-year-old man derail his career like this? Had he considered the possibility that *she* had moved on? Did he have a next move? But the answers to these questions were simple. Mat always landed on his feet, and she *hadn't* moved on, despite her best efforts. Why complicate the truth, which was that she wanted to be with him too? For the first time in months she could have exactly that, and as the feeling settled, Mat set down his Simple Dinner Plate, lifted her off the Reliable Stool, and carried her back to bed.

The brightness of Ava's desire for him was blinding. There was no amount of having him that could satisfy her, which left her feeling exhilarated. After a few urgent minutes they collapsed onto her Principled Bed and lay there, naked and entangled. She pulled his hand to her lips and kissed his palm.

"So I'll take that as a yes?" Mat said, although Ava didn't recall him presenting the idea of them getting back together as a question. "Although maybe you have another boyfriend, or a wife and kids, by now," he said. He smiled, but she saw from his face that he wanted an answer.

"No," Ava said. "Dating is truly bleak. I tried, but only managed to date a couple weird strangers." She detected a glimmer of jealousy in Mat's face. "I mean *truly* awful," she said. "One guy took me to an absurd modern dance show and then kissed me as if I were made of glass. He actually went to Wharton. Amir Cade?"

"Doesn't ring a bell," Mat said.

"He would have been in your cohort, I think."

"What did you say his name was?"

"Amir Cade."

"Wait, wait, wait." Mat had a look of epiphany. "Amir Cade?" he said. "Yes! He used to be Amir Cade-Stein. He married this girl in our year and they wanted to be equitable about the last name. But they divorced within, like, a year, so he must be back to just Cade. Honestly, though, that guy sucks." He shuddered and pulled her close.

Ava covered her face with his hand to hide her embarrassment. "He did suck," she agreed, although she hadn't felt too strongly about Amir. And he hadn't brought up the divorce to her. *Should* he have? she wondered.

"So who else?" he asked.

"Who else what?"

"Who else did you go out with?"

"Oh," she said, brushing the question away, "let me think."

Mat looked at her hungrily. She told him about Rebecca's cold, clammy hands and how the party had ended in Ava being shamed about her job. She exaggerated the bad parts of the night, crafting Rebecca into a boring villain, though really she had seemed perfectly nice.

"What about you?" Ava said, trying to sound offhand, although she was afraid to hear his answer.

"Clearly you haven't been to Gambier," Mat said. "Everyone's either an undergrad or a middle-aged farmer. So that's to say, it's a total meat market out there. I slept with proba-bly"—he counted on his fingers—"hundreds? Yeah, hundreds of women." He kissed her. "I just missed you. That's the only thing I accomplished out there. Missing you."

The weekend continued like this. They left the apartment only to walk Brutus, who witnessed their reunion moodily from his Dreamy Dog Bed. They reached a level of domestic euphoria that made Ava's horrible commute, Helen Gross's nasal, droning voice, and her cat furniture mandate seem like a distant dream.

But by Sunday evening, as she lay on her Practical Sofa with Mat's arms wrapped around her, Ava began to accept that she'd have to wake up and face another day at STÄDA, which she had come to dread for the first time in a decade.

"You'll never believe who they brought on to replace you," she said. "I don't even know how to describe how terrible she is. She has me working on cat habitats."

"Hold up," Mat said. "What is a cat habitat?"

"A habitat for cats. Furniture, ladders, little perches . . ."

"Brutus, cover your ears!" Mat shouted. Brutus looked up, his tail wagging slowly. "Please tell me this is a joke," Mat said. "*Cat habitats?* No.".

"Not a joke," Ava said. "They're hideous. This is what an intern should do as some sort of punishment."

"I'm sure there's something good about the new setup," Mat said. "The Guys are always saying we have the power to find the best in the worst, no matter what. I mean, how else could we stay sane?"

Ava wasn't sure who he meant by *we*. "If that's the case, then we all have a lot of work to do," she said. "Everyone is miserable."

"What about all the cool stuff I set up before I left?"

"Helen Gross cut most of it. No more 'Yes, And' meetings. No more shuffleboard. The only thing she kept going was the SHRNK partnership, which we all need now more than ever, thanks to her. Oh, and your basketball hoop is still up."

Mat stood and paced around the studio in his underwear. "That is the *opposite* of what makes a workplace ecosystem thrive!" he said, gesturing wildly. He was sliding into his professional character. "You need to give people a reason to come to work! The ROI on these programs might be less visible in the short term, but cutting them has gnarly long-term costs! This is like Management 101. We learned this on our *first day* at Wharton. Even that guy Amir Clay would know that, and he's an idiot."

"Cade," Ava said.

Mat sat back down, his boxers riding up his thighs. She held his hand. "Don't worry about it," she said. "It's not your problem anymore."

He was quiet for a moment and then shook his head. "You know what? Yes it is. Or it *should* be. I did a good job in New York."

He was right. He had brought Floor 12 to life. Things were monochromatic without him. Ava rubbed his shoulders.

"I'm coming with you," he said.

"You what?"

"To work tomorrow. I'm coming with you." He didn't look at Ava when he said it—he simply strode to her refrigerator and pulled it open, as if the refrigerator were his car and he was about to get in. "Yeah," he said, agreeing with himself. He opened a can of beer with a crisp hiss. "I'm getting my job back, Lamby."

34

MAT WAS APPARENTLY UNCONCERNED ABOUT
the logistics of his decision. His inability to doubt himself
amazed Ava. He hadn't even used the word *try*.

The next morning, in the midst of making coffee, feeding
and walking Brutus, showering, and getting ready for work,
Ava asked him a few clarifying questions: *How will you get the
job back if it's already filled? Where will you live? How will we
handle our relationship at work? Do you have an official meeting
with People?* Mat looked at her as though she were asking abstract questions about life after death, or the possibility of a
meteor hitting New York, or the merits of Scientology.

"It'll be fine," he said now, fitting into the driver's seat of
his car. "Remember, Lamby, I'm a solutions guy. Not a problems guy." Ava wondered if this was a Good Guyism, and she
detected an undercurrent of annoyance in his voice, as though
her questions had disrupted his good mood. So she didn't ask
any more. She didn't mind much anyway. She liked having him

there, and if she doubted him too much, she worried, he might disappear.

She had missed the way he fit into his car—just barely, his hair skimming the roof, his whole body crammed, his knees at sharp angles. He looked like he was driving a toy. She buckled her seatbelt and stroked his hair. "You need a haircut," she said affectionately.

He pulled onto the road. "I know, right?" he said. "Honestly, I didn't care at all about my appearance when I was in Gambier. Too busy missing you."

Ava felt the morning sunlight pushing through her, the pleasant spring heat warming her. She settled into her happiness. "I can't tell you how bad my commute was," she said. "I was always either stalled or rushing."

"Why didn't you buy a car?"

"I don't know," Ava said honestly. "I think since the accident I've had a hard time making decisions. Especially when they involve cars."

"You missed me," Mat said. She couldn't tell if it was a question or a statement.

"I did," Ava agreed.

She was amazed at how relaxed she felt in the passenger seat. The possibility of a panic episode felt far away. Instead she felt the opposite of anxious—dazed from a weekend spent with Mat in bed, the surprise of his arrival now a happy fact, a buzz of caffeine, the warmth of his hand moving from the wheel to her lap, a new episode of *Thirty-Minute Machine* playing, featuring a woman who wanted a physical solution to her husband's sleepwalking problem. She had even missed his stupid disco ball ornament and the way it swung wildly when he sped around corners.

He pulled onto the highway and a new question drifted into Ava's head like a slow cloud, one that somehow had not occurred to her until now. "Who's Emily with?" she said, turning down the podcast.

"Oh," Mat said, leaning forward in his seat to check his mirror while he changed lanes. "Didn't I tell you about that?"

"About what?"

"Emily," Mat said.

"No, what happened?" Ava said. She remembered Emily's graying snout and breathing problems. "Did she die?"

"No!" Mat said, forcing a laugh. "She's fine." He ran a hand through his hair, landing on the back of his head and rubbing.

"So . . ." Ava said when he failed to explain.

"I had to give her up," Mat said. He fiddled with the AC knob.

"You what?"

"It sucked. I had to give her up. The apartment I moved to in Gambier had a no-dog rule. I asked, but they were really strict about it."

"Why didn't you choose a different apartment?"

"It wasn't that easy, Lamby." He returned both hands to the wheel. "You have no idea how limited the housing options are in Gambier."

"I would have helped you," Ava said. "I would even have *taken* her. At least for a little while."

"You weren't talking to me! I had to do the entire move alone, with zero support. I had to make some hard choices."

"Didn't STÄDA pay for your move?"

Mat ignored the question. "I did the best I could. We all do. We're all doing our best, and what we all need is positive reinforcement. If you picture positivity as a human body—"

"Wait," Ava said. "So where is she? Where's Emily?"

"I gave her to a shelter."

"Which one? I bet they still have her. It's usually puppies that get adopted."

"It's just really hard," Mat said. "It was a horrible decision to make and I don't feel good about it. I just couldn't take her with me."

"Okay," Ava said. "Well, let's just call them. We'll call the shelter. I'll do it for you!"

"I already did," Mat said, turning toward STÄDA. "Wow, they made a lot of progress on the Vision Tower."

"What do you mean you already did?"

"I called them. I called the shelter. On my drive from Gambier. She's gone. A family in Queens adopted her. I'm trying to forget about it, so can we just *stop*?"

Ava was quiet, and Mat continued. "I feel like shit about it, if you can't tell. I'll get over it, but I need to take some self-care measures. And that means just letting go of the balloon for now."

Ava pictured Mat letting go of a balloon. Was this a Good Guyism too? When she pictured the balloon, Emily was inside it, a fuzzy shadow.

He pulled into the parking lot, and seeing his former spot occupied by Helen Gross's old station wagon, he barked a laugh. "Of course she has a station wagon," he said. He pulled into a space designated for Security.

"That's a reserved spot, I think," Ava said. She tried to sound relaxed.

"I'll be quick," Mat said. "In and out." He'd brightened at the change of topic. *"Hey, Judith, real quick, I'm gonna need my job back so I can spare STÄDA from this wet blanket who has replaced me. Cool?"* He used a strange fake voice to imitate this version of himself.

Ava smiled at him, but she hadn't completely shaken the tense ride. He had clearly been embarrassed about giving Emily up — he hadn't even been able to tell her — and although Ava would have jumped off the Brooklyn Bridge before giving up Brutus, she felt partially responsible for Mat's decision. She *had* broken up with him and iced him out. She hadn't wanted to see him or talk to him, let alone help him plan the logistics of his move.

As they walked toward the Simple Tower, she took Mat's hand. "You really think this is okay?"

"No more hiding," Mat said. "I'm yours, you're mine, and everyone can deal. Ask for respect, not permission."

"Okay," Ava said, cautiously happy again.

"Anyway," Mat said, "I checked the fine print of my old contract. Apparently we *are* allowed to be together, as long as we sign some paperwork about insider trading and harassment."

They joined a mass of STÄDA employees in primary colors filtering through the glass doors, bottlenecking at the scanners near the security checkpoint. A couple people glanced their way, then turned to each other. Ava squeezed Mat's hand, then walked with him to the Security desk.

"Reason for visit?" the security officer asked without looking up. He was a big man with greasy forked bangs.

"I have a meeting with People," Mat said, "in . . ." He checked his watch. "Ten minutes."

"I'll call up," the security guard said, reaching for the phone receiver.

"That's okay," Mat said. "I used to work here. She knows to expect me."

"It's protocol to call up first if you're not registered," the guard said, looking at Mat. "We've had issues lately."

"Oh," Mat said. "The Vandals, right?"

"That's right."

Mat shook his head sympathetically. "When I was here, they wreaked havoc. But the Vision Tower is looking amazing. I see they're already testing out the vapor cloud."

"Who'd you say you were?" the guard said. He squinted at Mat.

"Mathew Putnam," Mat said.

"Mat *Putnam*," the security guard said, suddenly enlivened. "I know about you! You're a legend, man." He pulled Mat forward with a double-handed handshake.

"That's so nice," Mat said, releasing his hand from the guard's grip. "What's your color?"

"Green," the man said proudly. "I'm the only green in Security."

"That makes you one of the most essential, least disposable members of the Security team," Mat said. "Don't ever forget that. What's your name? I'll get in touch with the head of Security and tell him to expedite your next raise."

The security guard beamed. "Ivan Strong. And you can go on up," he said, pulling a receipt with a QR code from a little machine.

"You are unbelievable," Ava whispered as they waited for an elevator.

Mat grinned. "Sometimes all you gotta do is ask!" he said.

Although Ava wouldn't call what had happened "asking," she was still impressed. They joined a cluster of engineers at the elevator bank, next to the screens, which rotated through their usual slides, beginning with *Vision Tower. Mission: Possible!* A large green checkmark appeared over the rendering. The next slide showed a photo of Jaime looking unamused, his iSight glasses tucked into his shirt pocket. *Thank you, Jaime Rojas, for keeping our campus safe!*

"Looks like Jaime is *crushing* it!"

Ava's stomach dropped at the mention of Jaime. She imagined his reaction to Mat's reappearance. Well, he'd have to deal with it. She preemptively felt annoyed about having to defend herself. Mat pushed the button for Floor 12.

"I thought you were going to see Judith," Ava said.

"I am," Mat said. "But first I wanna say hi to everyone."

"You don't think that's premature?"

"What do you mean?" Mat looked at her as if she'd begun speaking Danish. But before she had time to respond, the elevators opened onto 12, and she stepped out behind him onto the brightly lit floor.

35

AVA BRACED HERSELF FOR MAT'S BIG ENTRANCE, which she was sure would have the theatricality of a football player charging through the team banner at homecoming. But instead he walked calmly to the Wellness Kitchen. His posture mirrored that of everybody else settling into their unremarkable Monday mornings.

She watched as he opened the refrigerator and casually plucked a Zing! Ginger-Turmeric Tonic from the top shelf. He took a long swig, his lips fully covering the opening of the bottle, while the refrigerator door gaped open.

Didn't he want to mentally rehearse his conversation with Judith? This type of planned confrontation would have kept Ava up at night for months in advance. She kept her head down and tried to focus on pouring her coffee as Mat prepared himself a Friendly Bowl of cereal with oat milk and slurped a few spoonfuls. The tension hung heavily over Ava, threatening to crush her at any moment.

"What's up?" he said, looking at her.

"Nothing," Ava said, looking away quickly. "I guess I just wondered how you ... well, I guess you should know, Helen is ... not the easiest. You might want to have a game plan if you want to unseat her. That's all."

Mat seemed to consider what Ava was saying, and nodded. "Gotcha," he said. He put his bowl in the sink, left the Wellness Kitchen, and walked toward Marketing. Ava followed a few feet behind, gripping her coffee tightly.

A half-dozen members of the Marketing team stood in a semicircle around the miniature basketball hoop—one of the last relics remaining from Mat's tenure as head of product—passing the plush ball around. Each person took a shot at the net after sharing a priority for the week. When Mat arrived he jumped in, intercepting a shot by violently smacking the ball into a display of Sensitive Teacup prototypes lined up on a nearby Diligent Table. He then slam-dunked his empty Zing! Ginger-Turmeric Tonic bottle through the net, picked up the ball, and walked into Helen Gross's office.

"Brooooooo!" one of the guys said, following him in, going for a bear hug. The rest of the team huddled around Mat, exchanging pats on the back and fist bumps.

The hubbub had attracted attention, and Ava could see the news of Mat's return spreading in a murmur across the floor. It stopped cold at Jaime, who stood from his desk and walked to the elevators.

Ava watched as Mat propped himself at the edge of Helen's desk, his butt gently pushing one of her cat figurines to the side. Soon many of the Floor 12 employees were huddled around him. He fielded questions as if he were holding a press conference, tossing the ball in one hand.

"What's Gambier like?" one woman in yellow asked. "I've always kind of dreamed of leaving the city ..."

"Do you have, like, a garage?"

"Are the STÄDA offices there huge?"

"Does this mean you're coming back?"

At this last question Mat lit up. "If they're lucky!" he said, waggling his eyebrows. "The thing about it is—and what I've always said is—that sometimes you need to remove yourself from the equation to demonstrate your value. They've asked me to come back, and I'll hear their offer, but it's gotta be good. You can't put a price on your personal growth, and I won't come back for anything less than a director-level position. You don't get what you deserve, you get what you negotiate for, right?"

Ava considered the brilliance of the maneuver. If Mat didn't get his job back, it would appear to be his choice. It would be because he had dared to demand more for himself. In STÄDA's new bootstrapping culture, this was heroic.

The crowd hushed and turned to face Judith, who stood just outside the door with Helen Gross and Jaime.

"Mathew," Judith said dryly. "What a nice surprise."

"Hey, Judith!" Mat said, tossing the plush ball to her.

Judith leaned away from the ball as it flew by her face. "Please come with me," she said.

Mat slid off Helen's desk and followed Judith out the door without betraying a hint of embarrassment. Ivan Strong, the security guard who had allowed Mat up, emerged from an elevator, looking pale, with Malcolm P. Wade, head of Security, by his side. Mat greeted both men cheerfully. They followed Judith into an elevator headed up.

Ava had to fight the urge to follow them. If she could have it her way, she'd be inside Judith's office—no, inside Mat's brain—trying to control the exchange.

But she had no choice but to continue with her morning normally. She watched as Jaime helped Helen reassemble the items on her desk, her face red. And when Ava took her place next to Jaime at that morning's Engineering meeting, Helen appeared shaken. Her voice was pinched, and she kept knocking things off her desk. Ava tried to maintain her focus as the group discussed their projects, but she couldn't. She imagined Judith peeling her orange across from Mat. Mat would be smiling at her, gesturing theatrically. Maybe he would even stand to deliver an impassioned speech. He might apologize for his methods, chalk it up to his commitment to STÄDA's mission—

"Ava?" Helen's voice was suddenly pulling at her attention.

"Sorry," Ava said.

"Well?"

"Can you repeat the question?"

"What are you working on this week?" Helen said. She wore a pained expression and tapped a blunt pencil against her desk.

"I . . ." Ava started. "I'm working on ladders."

"Ladders?"

"Cat . . . um, cat ladders. Sisal cat ladders. It's an alternative to a traditional scratching post or tower. The idea is that it leans up against the side of a sofa to deter the cat from the sofa itself. It's collapsible and can be easily stowed. I believe we'll be calling the prototype the Devious Ladder."

As the conversation moved around the circle, Jaime turned to Ava. "Did STÄDA really ask him back?" he whispered. "I'm not buying it—when has that *ever* happened? Judith said she didn't know anything about it."

Ava shrugged, annoyed by his doubt, struggling to find the right answer. She pretended to be fascinated by her colleagues' projects. She wanted a perfect Mat-ism, something that could explain away his strange maneuver to make it feel like basic arithmetic.

"So no!" Jaime said excitedly, once they had all disbanded. "Is he a lunatic? I wonder how long he's been in the city! I mean, I can't believe—"

Before he could continue, a chorus of phones pinged and vibrated across the floor with an email to the entire New York office from Judith.

Dear STÄDA NY,

In light of recent events, we will be conducting a mandatory People training at 10:30 a.m. in the Imagination Room.

Best,
Judith Ball
Chief People Officer
Green

Ava checked her Precise Wristwatch. Ten-thirty was in ten minutes. Her phone chimed again with a second email from Judith:

Dear STÄDA NY,

Today was Ivan Strong's last day.

Best,
Judith Ball
Chief People Officer
Green

Ivan Strong, the security guard who had let Mat in. Ava's stomach dropped. This was the email STÄDA sent when someone was fired. She had to admit that she admired the beauty of its construction. The subject of the sentence was the day, not the person. The word *fired*—or any of its euphemisms—was absent. She opened S-Chat and scrolled, looking for Ivan Strong's name. It had vanished.

The Imagination Room was soon overflowing with STÄDA employees from all departments. Judith stood beside the projector screen, which read *Appropriate Behavior and Workplace Security*. Once the room was at capacity, she began to move through her slides. The presentation involved a series of multiple-choice questions.

A termination contract is:
1. Just a formality
2. Temporary
3. Legal and binding

If a former employee wants to return to work at STÄDA, that employee should:
1. Apply for an open position online
2. Apply for an open position in person
3. Disparage the replacement's performance

Guests you bring to STÄDA should be:
1. Spontaneous
2. Romantic partners
3. Fully vetted and approved by STÄDA Security

Ava sank low in her Encouraging Desk Chair, took out her phone, and texted Mat.

Are you okay? Are you still here?

No.

What happened in there? she wrote. *Where are you?*

THE VERY NICE BOX

Can we just talk when you're home, Lamby? I really need space to be the CEO of my own story right now. I'll see you after work.

Ava fit her phone back into her pocket. She couldn't shake the worry that Mat was upset with her. She played the morning's events back to herself throughout the day, trying to locate her misstep.

———

When she did return home that evening, Ava found Mat in her Embracing Armchair, facing the wall. The room was humid and had an earthy, dank smell.

"Mat?" She didn't realize until she said his name that she was nervous.

He turned to face her, and she saw then that he was wearing a VR headset and holding a video game controller. Its thick black strap wrapped around his head, and the front eyepiece looked like a thick sleep mask. It completely blocked his peripheral vision. He pulled the headset off. "Hey, Lamby," he said.

"Hi," Ava said, sitting beside him. "I've been thinking about you all day."

She held his face in her hands and kissed him. The straps of his VR set had imprinted their shape onto the sides of his head. He returned the gesture with a deep hug, nestling his face into her neck. She rubbed his back and kissed him on the cheek. "I'm sorry about today. We can talk about it if you want to. Or not. Whatever you want."

He groaned. "I'm just so embarrassed. What was I thinking?"

Ava wasn't sure what he had been thinking, but she wanted to make him feel better. "You were optimistic, and that's a big part of why I love you."

"Really?" he said, looking up at her. His mood lifted at the compliment.

"Yes, really," Ava said, placing a hand on his cheek. "You're going to figure it out. You're a Good Guy, remember? You can stay here while you get settled. I'm sure all the headhunters in New York City are salivating over your availability right now."

"Thanks, Lamby," he said softly.

They lingered in the embrace for a moment. Ava relaxed against his body. She closed her eyes and took a deep breath, inhaling the scent of his One shampoo, whose subway advertisements directed consumers to a long online personality questionnaire that produced their ideal shampoo formula.

"I'm going to make something to eat," she said.

"Then do you mind if I . . ." Mat said, gesturing toward his VR headset. It was a rhetorical question. He picked it up and clicked quickly through settings on the controller.

Ava began assembling dinner, and when she reemerged to ask Mat if he wanted anything to eat, he was slumped on her Practical Sofa, staring into the void of his headset like a catatonic insect.

She could hear the muffled sound of gunfire as he threw an invisible grenade. She ate her lentil soup and watched, trying to pick up any clues as to what was unfolding within the world of the game. She felt sorry for him.

"Fuck."

He said it so flatly that Ava wondered whether any serotonin remained in his central nervous system.

"I died."

36

"YOU HAVE TO ADMIT," JAIME SAID, STEPPING into the elevator after Ava the next day, "that yesterday's little opera was pretty entertaining. I mean, the hubris!" He pressed the round number 2 and hung his amber-tinted glasses on his shirt pocket as they descended.

Ava bristled. "I don't know, I feel for him," she said. "I mean, the poor guy . . ."

The elevator dinged and opened. "Poor guy?" Jaime said, stepping out. "Ava, please. What is he even doing back in New York, do you think?"

"He probably came back to haunt you in particular," Ava said. She looked around the Test Floor, which was buzzing with activity. On the south side of the room, a team of engineers assembled a Sleepy Rocking Chair. On the north side, a crew tightened bolts on an Effusive Bathroom Vanity. A third group appeared to be working on an Obliging Step Stool. Ava was comforted by the coordinated bustle.

They found a Sturdy Table by the window, and she began assembling the Devious Ladder. Jaime collected pine rungs and hardware from the well-organized wall of bins, then laid the pieces onto the table for her. "Seriously, though," he said, turning a rung over in his hand, "why do you think he's here?"

"I think he quit his job in Gambier. Can you hand me a hex key?"

"He told you that? You've talked to him since he's been back?"

"Briefly," Ava said.

"So he's here just . . . because?" Jaime said, handing her the tool.

"I don't know exactly," Ava said. She tightened the bolt at the end of a rung. She was irritated. "I guess it was really lonely there. He missed me, and I—"

"Oh god, don't say it," Jaime said. "Please don't say it. I was worried about this, but I refused to believe it." He looked at her.

"I missed him," Ava said, avoiding his pointed eye contact, reaching for another rung. "I did. I'm happy he's back. I mean, do I think it was crazy for him to try to get his job back like that? Yes."

"Why?" Jaime said. He put down his pencil and looked up at her.

"Why what?" She swapped the hex key for a screwdriver.

"Why would you think that's crazy? It's completely predictable. He's a special combination of inept and entitled. A total scammer."

"He's not a *scammer*," Ava said.

"Seems like he scammed his way right back into your relationship," Jaime said. "It's a confidence game. He waltzed back into STÄDA as if he'd already gotten his job back, and he waltzed back into your relationship as if you'd never broken up with him. What's he even up to right now? He's just staying at your place with no job? Is he going to pay rent, or is his only contribution his charm? Can you imagine what Andie would think of that arrangement?"

Ava looked up at him. "I don't know why you're so concerned. He's been back for three seconds. He's allowed to ease back into a job. I would have sent him away if I'd wanted to. I missed him. Why is that so hard to understand?"

"Look," Jaime said, lowering his voice. "It's none of my business. But come on—you started to focus on yourself as soon as he left. You've been going on all these promising dates. You're finally getting closure from the accident. You seem ... good. Like your old self, I mean."

"My old self? My old self from when?"

"From ... I don't know. Before."

"You mean the time in between when Andie got killed and when I met Mat? That really special time in my life, when I got so much good work done because I was desperate to avoid my own life?" Ava's face burned. "And so what if his main contribution to my life is his charm? He *is* charming, and sweet, and he makes me laugh. He's not Andie, but I think I can forgive him for that. Can you? Do you know how long it's been since I've been with anyone?"

"I'm sorry," Jaime said. He looked alarmed. "That's not what I meant."

"And my dates weren't promising, they were depressing. You were just invested in me being with anybody but Mat. Just please take your seven-million-dollar UV-filtering organic GMO sunglasses and leave," Ava said. "I don't want you here right now."

"Will I see you for lunch?"

Ava didn't answer.

"So that's how it's going to be? Mat's back and now you'll

disappear for another few months while I'm left to spy on teenagers?"

"I'm canceling lunch because you're being insufferable. Why can't you trust that I know what's best for me? Not everything is a conspiracy!"

"Because Mat is bad news! There's just something about him that isn't right," Jaime said. Other engineers around the room had paused their work to watch the argument. "I know it," Jaime whispered, "and you knew it back then too, before he clouded your vision. If you don't trust me enough to believe me, I'll prove it to you."

Ava was livid. "It kills you *so much* to be supportive that you have to make a crusade of tearing him down. If there's a scam, what is it?"

"I don't know. It sort of feels like his existence is a scam. And his authority is definitely a scam. What has he done for STÄDA aside from redecorate?"

"Plenty! What about the 'Yes, And' meetings?"

"Anyone who took an improv class at summer camp could have come up with that, Ava!"

"Is it really *that hard* for you to see me happy? I'm tired of defending myself. In your mind, Andie is the only person good enough for me. And you know what? I have been trying *so* hard not to agree. But I'm finally happy, so get on board or leave."

He did leave, and Ava jammed together the pieces to the Devious Ladder alone. First came the outrage: How dare Jaime judge her life choices, when all she was doing was cutting out a small space for her own happiness? But then came the doubt: Was it true? Had Mat scammed her into taking him back? Her mind wandered to her studio, where she'd left him asleep, his face so serene and pure she'd felt guilty kissing him awake. *Do you mind if I take your car to work?* she had said. *No, no, of course, take it Lamby,* he murmured. *Keys are on the counter.*

She messaged her SHRNK. *Do you think Mat actually loves me? Or is he using me?* She stared at her phone, suddenly desperate for the reassurance. The ellipses appeared.

Ava, who could you be if you believed you were worthy of love?

She pulled the Devious Ladder apart, finished making edits to the manual, and used a full unit to jam it back together one more time. Her phone buzzed, and she reached into her back pocket. Her heart jumped at Mat's name.

Dinner plans tonight?

I thought I'd defrost some veggie burgers.

Hmm. No, he wrote.

No?

Allow me to handle.

She began to respond when she saw that he was typing, so she stopped.

Oh, and Ava?

Yes?

Sorry I didn't really ask before. Can I be your live-in boyfriend? For now? You can say no!

Okay: No.

Wait. Really?

No! Not really!

She set down her phone and looked out the window onto the shipping warehouse. The same crew of workers that had been there for months continued its mesmerizing ritual: lifting the Very Nice Boxes from the back of a truck, into the warehouse, onto a conveyor belt, out the back, into a new truck. *Boyfriend!* The word had briefly and intensely awakened Ava to the possibilities of the world around her. She had the impulse to go outside and observe the workers up close. Mat responded with a blushing, smiling emoji, which she stared at happily.

She drove home in his car—her *live-in boyfriend's car.* She rolled the phrase around in her mouth as she navigated home.

She liked it. The coupe *was* fun to drive, in a perverse way. She let herself briefly imagine him at the door, greeting her, Brutus winding between his legs, his tail thwacking against the wall. But then it was Jaime's voice again: *A total scammer!* She waited at a red light and let herself imagine what the scam could be. Remote controllers, a dirty stovetop, an unmade bed, glasses on every surface dyeing rings into the wood. She felt overheated at the thought of it.

As she made her way up the stairs, her heartbeat climbed into her throat. With each flight the smell of bacon and—what was it? Something deeply familiar, deeply calming—intensified. When she opened the door to her apartment, the incredible smell of dinner confronted her fully. Her Appealing Dining Table was set with two Enduring Candles burning serenely in their Enduring Candle Holders. Brutus was sleeping in his Dreamy Dog Bed, clearly worn out from a day of exercise. Mat wore Ava's Homey Apron and tossed a steaming bowl of what she realized was spaghetti carbonara, made with—according to the ingredients on the counter—aged Parmesan and pancetta from the butcher and eggs from organic, free-range hens.

Just like her dad had made when she was a kid.

"Mat," she said. She couldn't keep the emotion out of her voice.

"What?" he said, fighting back a smile.

"You made . . . it's my favorite."

"I know," he said, tucking his hair back. "It made me happy to make it. I love you, Lamby." He pulled out an Appealing Dining Chair for her and she sat, accepting the chivalry, the Thoughtful Glass of water he was now pouring her, then his warm kiss on her cheek.

37

MAT PUTNAM IS A VANDAL.

Ava stared at the subject line of an email Jaime sent her the next morning. She read it again, allowing the irritation to set in fully. Was Jaime so desperate to badmouth Mat that he'd accuse him of vandalism even after he had left the company?

She opened the email and saw that Judith had been CC'd.

Ava and Judith,

New information has emerged about the Vision Tower blueprint prank from several months ago. I think we should meet.

Yours,
Jaime

Ava couldn't even pretend to drum up concern. Mat had been with her that day, sneaking around in the printer room. Her body tightened at the memory of his hand pressed against her. An S-Chat message from Judith disrupted the memory.

Jaime, Ava, please come to my office.

Ava watched, annoyed, as Jaime stood from his desk, fit his laptop into a floral sleeve, and made his way directly to the elevators. She sighed, waiting for the doors to close behind him before making her way to the elevator bank.

Upon entering Judith's office, Ava avoided eye contact with Jaime and took a seat beside him. "Hi."

"Welcome," Judith said. She sat at her usual place behind her desk, but Ava was surprised to see that she wasn't alone. Two identical, gangly teenage girls sat on either side of her with their arms crossed, staring at the desk in front of them. Judith peeled an orange and handed a wedge to each of them. "Now," she began. "I don't believe either of you has met my daughters, Ari and Kendra. I'm aware it may seem inappropriate that they're here. However —"

"It's not a problem," Jaime said. "Honestly, the more eyes on this, the better. And it's nice to meet you both." He gave a perfunctory smile and opened a video on his laptop. "This is what I wanted you to see," he said, pressing Play.

It was black-and-white footage taken with a fish-eye lens showing a long corridor with a view of STÄDA's Floor 12 workspace. Employees sat at their desks with their heads bowed, mid-meditation. After a few seconds Mat walked quickly around the corner, looking over his shoulder before returning to his office.

"It's footage from the northeast hallway, from one of the cameras that wasn't tampered with during the Vision Tower printout fiasco. If you keep watching, you'll see Judith rush out with the printouts. Mat was the last one there, just a few seconds before!"

"Well, this is exciting," one of the twins said.

"Mat didn't do it," Ava said.

"What do you mean?" Jaime said, gesturing at his laptop. "There's only one way to look at this—"

"He was with me."

"But you were doing the officewide meditation!"

"No," Ava said, "I wasn't. Mat and I were together. In the printer room." She stared at Judith's desk.

"Spicy," Judith's other daughter said.

"But you aren't in the footage! It's only him."

"I walked the other way to avoid Judith."

Both twins stifled a laugh. Jaime pressed his lips together.

"Jaime, you're wrong," Ava said. "Please just let this crusade go. May we go?" she asked, looking at Judith.

Judith sighed. "Jaime, as I *attempted* to say before, Ava is correct. Mathew isn't responsible for the blueprint prank."

"Judith," Jaime pleaded, "I know you know Mat Putnam is bad news. How can you give him the benefit of the doubt here?"

"My opinion of that man is inconsequential, as he is no longer a STÄDA employee."

"But—"

"*But* in this case I know that Mathew is not to blame."

Judith reached into her desk drawer and pulled out the stack of blueprints Ava had seen months before. She pulled off the sticky note with a string of numbers and stuck it to her desk, facing them.

"The day of the incident, I asked our IT team to look at the printer logs. They were able to identify the device that printed the blueprints. I was thrilled. So you can only imagine my shock when I searched our inventory spreadsheet and found that the computer was assigned to *me*."

"I don't understand," Jaime said. "Do you think one of them got hold of your computer?"

"I think that's exactly what happened. Only in this case, it was *two* of them." She looked to her left and right, at her daughters. "Girls," she said.

The girl to Judith's left spoke up. "I did it."

"Ari!" the girl to Judith's right retorted. "*We* did it."

"They'd asked to attend the Self-Care Fair," Judith said, "so I brought them to work with me that day. I suppose that was naive of me. I knew they were sympathetic to those ..." she searched for the right word, "anarchists, but I didn't know they were Trojan horses. God knows why."

"Our message could not be more clear," Kendra said. "The capitalism cultivated at giant companies like this one is a cancer destroying our communities. Specifically, STÄDA's hideous new skyscraper has displaced the longstanding community garden that provides food sovereignty to the Red Hook area."

"Well, this giant evil corporation is the reason your father and I can afford to send you to college next year. Look around. Do you like your life? You'd rather risk your future than say thank you."

"Why would we say thank you when we are not being treated with respect?" Ari said.

"Enough," Judith said sternly. "It's easy to be principled when you don't have a career to protect. Now," she said to Jaime, her voice low, "as I hope you can see, I'm in a difficult position. I've tried reasoning with them, but they won't stop. This morning I learned that they slipped out of their bedrooms at the crack of dawn to join their ... *peers* in an effort to reprogram the Vision Tower's steam cloud to say something rude. Fortunately, my office has windows looking in every direction, and I happened to spot them."

"The word *greed* is not rude," Kendra said. "It's just true."

"Why are you telling us all this?" Ava asked.

"Because," Judith said, pinching the bridge of her nose, "they can't get caught. They make it difficult to protect them, but I'm their mother. Can you imagine their faces plastered in the lobby?" She shuddered.

"Yes!" Ari said. "Better there than on STÄDA's executive 'About' page."

"Jaime," Judith continued, "I owe you an apology. I tried to cut Mathew's useless internship program entirely so you could rejoin an Engineering team, but the board blocked me. It's been too good for optics. I kept you in this position because I'd rather have you holding the pitchfork than Malcolm P. Wade, who would make an example of these two."

"What does the *P* stand for?" Ari said.

"It stands for be quiet before you get yourselves into more trouble," Judith said. Her phone chimed. "Girls, your father is downstairs. Don't take any detours. There will be some sort of punishment awaiting you at home."

"Exciting!" Kendra said.

Judith closed her eyes and breathed deeply as they left. "Now," she said. "I'd like to think I can trust you both to be discreet while I handle this matter privately."

Jaime slumped in his chair. "I get it," he said. "I won't say anything."

"Ava?"

"What?" She was lost in a fantasy about which piece of information Mat would find more entertaining: that Jaime thought he was leading a radical movement or that Judith's daughters were the real culprits.

"Can I count on your discretion?" Judith said.

"Who would I even report this to?" Ava said. "Helen Gross?

You have no idea what I'd give to never interact with her again. With all due respect," she added hastily. "I know you helped hire her."

"Thank you," Judith said. She seemed relieved. "And please, keep me out of your investigations. The less I know, the better."

"Ava, I might have been wrong this time, but there's something about Mat that just doesn't add up," Jaime said, hurrying after her into an elevator. "You have to trust me."

"Give it a rest," Ava said, pushing the button for Floor 12.

"Ava," Jaime said, "please."

"Please *what*?"

"Just wait. I'll come up with something else that proves I'm right about him."

But she didn't want to wait. And when, later that day, she saw another email from Jaime (subject line: *MAT DITCHED HIS DOG!*), she opened it and responded: *I know, Jaime.*

How had Jaime even found that out? He was desperate. She moved it to her trash folder, where it joined his other alarmist emails, which linked to articles about the dangers of MDF, the hidden toxins in STÄDA's coffee filters, the unexpected germiness of the Sweet Kitchen, and the importance of laptop privacy screens.

38

AFTER MAT'S CARBONARA CAME OSSO BUCO, and after that it was Norwegian lobster. As the weeks wore on, his dishes became more complicated, each seeming to require more technique and research. *How about a little coq au vin tonight?* he texted Ava one afternoon. And another night: *Two words. Boeuf bourguignon . . . questions?*

Each new dish Mat tried apparently required multiple single-purpose kitchen tools, which were so narrow in function that they were practically obsolete. These were the sorts of tools that went against STÄDA's ethos of functionality. The air fryer, the bell pepper seeds remover, the pasta maker, the potato ricer, and the bread crumb toaster crowded Ava's cabinets, making it difficult for her to find the perfectly arranged STÄDA standbys that had served her for years.

"I am *loving* my cooking tools!" Mat said one evening, ripping open a package of new and obscure utensils that Ava had carried up from the lobby. Ava glanced at the box. The Chef's

Kiss. She'd seen their subway ads, which appeared to target men interested in impressing women with extravagant meals. She watched as he pulled out a bulky and intricate plastic egg-cracker. She tried to keep her facial expression neutral.

She reminded herself that the years of living alone had made her overly sensitive to changes in routine. She could rally around Mat's new hobby, which was one of the only things outside of Good Guys meetings that had been giving him energy these past few weeks. She felt cared for, and a sweet part of his new-found love of cooking was that he was doing it for her.

Mat's satisfaction in turning out a meal was fleeting, though, and he inevitably disappeared after dinner, while Ava scrubbed grease and melted cheese from baking pans, rescued her Eternal Cast-Iron Pan from a soapy sink and worked at it with a square of chain mail, or scraped miscellaneous gunk off his various implements. Something in his eyes had dulled. He had less to say. He seemed saddened by Ava's work anecdotes, and she found herself making self-deprecating jokes to undermine her own sense of purpose. It was like living with a slowly deflating balloon.

She spent her energy at work worrying about Mat, wondering how she could help him out of his rut. In the afternoons she went to Floor 2 so she could look out the window that faced the bustling shipping warehouse. She was also avoiding Jaime. For every small grievance she had about Mat—the overrun kitchen or his late nights at Good Guys meetings—she could hear Jaime's voice: *Scammer!* She felt like she was under Jaime's microscope, where a millimeter away from "happy" equaled a hundred miles.

Sofia found her down there one afternoon.

"Are you looking for me?" Ava said.

"Not really," Sofia said. "Marketing does occasionally have business on the Test Floor, you know."

"Oh," Ava said skeptically. "Really?"

"Yes," Sofia said, "really. If something takes six hours to build, we're not going to market it to single moms."

"*Nothing* at STÄDA takes six hours to build," Ava said, affronted.

"You're missing my point," Sofia said. "What I'm telling you is, it's all connected. Anyway. How are you, Ava?"

"How am I? You mean, outside of work?"

"Yeah," Sofia said. "Jaime is on the verge of a nervous breakdown over whatever's going on with you and Mat. Then again, he recently had a nervous breakdown over the flouride in his toothpaste."

"Well ... Can I ask you a question, just between us?" Ava said. "Maybe your perspective would be helpful."

Sofia smiled. "Talk to me."

"Things with Mat have been sort of flat lately. It's like he's not himself. It's like we're not *ourselves*."

"How long have you been dating again?" Sofia asked.

"If you count the time we were apart, the better part of a year."

"Things slow down," Sofia said frankly. "We fall in love with the best version of someone and we break up with the worst. It's a slow decline, and it either plateaus at a tolerable level and you stay together fifty years or you leave. Is he treating you well?"

"Yes," Ava admitted. "He's making these elaborate meals—"

"Wait, he's *cooking* for you?"

"Yeah."

"Ava, marry this man. My husband is on his phone from the second he gets home to the second he goes to sleep. The only variation is that sometimes he'll ask for sex." She shook her head at Ava. "He *cooks!*"

Ava considered the absurdity of her own discontentedness.

Sofia was right. Mat treated her well. She was lucky. The more she tried to locate the root of the problem, the more abstract her unhappiness became.

"I thought you hated my relationship with Mat," Ava said. "You were always . . ."

"Always what?" Sofia's stare was piercing.

"You always seemed annoyed. Or, I don't know, don't take this the wrong way . . . jealous?"

"Jealous? Of what?"

"Our relationship."

Sofia tilted her head back and laughed. "Ava," she said. "No. I wasn't jealous. I was infuriated."

"Infuriated by what?"

"I should have been tapped for his job. Do you know how good I am at my job?"

"Really good," Ava said truthfully.

"Yes," Sofia agreed. "I'm really good. I have multiple degrees. I've been at STÄDA for years. I'm older than Mat Putnam by at least five years. He was underqualified. That hire was insulting."

"Oh," Ava said. "I hadn't even considered that."

"Look, I'm not saying he's a bad boyfriend. He sounds, frankly, amazing. But he had no business here at STÄDA, at least not as my manager. That was straight-up offensive. And don't even get me started on Helen Gross." She looked at her Precise Wristwatch. "Shit, I gotta get out of here. My intern spelled *chaise* wrong on our last storyboard. You wouldn't believe . . ." She looked at her phone and made her way toward the elevators. "Good luck, Ava," she said over her shoulder. "He's a keeper, at least at home."

Ava played the conversation over in her head, rearranging her feelings. Maybe Mat had been underqualified at STÄDA, but that meant nothing about how he was as a boyfriend. She liked the thought; it felt true, or close enough to true.

From a Floor 2 window overlooking the Vision Tower construction site, she watched as a site engineer conferred with a worker. There was something appealing about the site engineer, who pulled off her hardhat and stretched her neck. Ava had been watching the woman passively for weeks. She worked with riveting efficiency. Ava focused on her hands, on how she used them emphatically to direct her crew of workers or the many construction vehicles circling the half-built Vision Tower. Her hair was military-short, and she wore well-fitting crew shirts in primary colors that popped against her black work pants and dark skin. Several times Ava had reassured Mat that she didn't miss being with women, but she would be lying if she said that watching this woman made her feel nothing. She attempted to steer her thoughts away from the woman's hands and toward something more neutral, like the brand of her crew shirt, but her willpower was short-lived. An uninvited thought of the woman pushing her against the side of her Sprinter briefly overtook her until her phone vibrated against her thigh.

24-hour. Dry-brined. Air-chilled. Whole. Roasted. Chicken.

Ava quickly sent back a salivating face and the running woman emoji. *Home soon. Just finishing up.*

Awesome. I have the Guys tonight, so early din!

Ava glanced once more out the window. The woman in the crew shirt hopped into a sprinter van and drove to the far end of the lot, out of sight. Ava felt a twinge of loneliness, watching her disappear out of frame. The feeling made her miss Jaime. She drafted a text to him: *Can we be friends with Vision Tower site engineer?* But she deleted it. She didn't want to test his resolve.

39

AVA COULD SMELL DINNER ALL THE WAY FROM the end of the hallway leading to her apartment that evening. Shallots, thyme, lemon, chicken fat. It smelled incredible. She opened the door to find Mat pacing the kitchen with her Inquisitive Tongs in one hand and his phone in the other. Brutus circled her, thwacking his tail against her shins.

"I know! Yes—exactly, man, exactly," Mat said. "This is what I'm saying. Millennials are ruining marketing. I mean, the subway ads alone are just . . . *ridiculous.*"

Ava was captivated by Mat's end of the conversation, and especially his spark. She caught his eye and cocked her head, gesturing at the products around the apartment that Mat had bought from millennial subway marketers. Mat smiled and shrugged. She was comforted by his charm, even if it occasionally carried him small distances from the truth. This was the Mat Putnam she recognized.

He stood behind Ava with an arm around her waist. "Uh-huh. Yeah, yes. I'd love to come in to talk more about it, just drop me a line. No rush at all. Okay. Yep. For sure, man. Ciao."

He hung up the phone and kissed her neck.

"Hi, incorrigible boyfriend," she said. "Who was that?"

"That was Praxis. They make those e-readers everyone has. I got a call earlier today from a buddy of mine who says they're looking for a new CMO!"

"This is huge!" Ava patted his chest. She was relieved for herself and for Mat. She held his face in her hands and kissed him. His lips were oily and salty. "So what does this mean?"

"Well," Mat said, "they're taking it slow because they're really invested in finding a good fit, but they're talking about bringing me in next month, or whenever they're ready to start seriously pursuing candidates. So I'm just going to sit tight. That is, if you can tolerate these home-cooked meals for another couple of weeks."

Ava felt silly for having doubted his ability to pull himself back to work. She felt lighter. "That's amazing. And look at *this!*" She gestured to the kitchen table, where a beautiful browned chicken was waiting. She could easily ignore the tilting stack of greasy pans, pots, plates, and cutting boards, knives, ladles, and other unidentifiable Chef's Kiss utensils scattered across the countertop.

"I can't wait to take this news to the Guys tonight," he said, carving into the thigh of the chicken. "Tonight's my night to share!"

"Oh," Ava said. "Well, good luck! Or whatever I'm supposed to say."

"We usually just say 'fill your heart.' Sorta the opposite of 'break a leg.' Kinda cheesy, I know!"

The chicken was delicious, and Ava felt refueled by Mat's news. Her concerns about him seemed laughable. After dinner she took Brutus out for his walk, her mind happily replaying their evening together. Mat already had a lead for a job, but maybe there was something else she could do to lift his spirits. Something that would add fuel to the small fire bringing him back to life.

Brutus circled a tree and investigated its roots. She tugged his Curious Leash, and the idea came to her: Emily. It was probably too late, but there'd be no harm in trying to get her back. Mat had been so upset about having to surrender her that he could barely bring himself to talk about it. Lately he had even seemed a little grouchy with Brutus—he'd recently mentioned how "high maintenance" dogs were, as though it were a major effort to take Brutus out in the afternoon. He'd once even jokingly mentioned that Ava could pay him for the afternoon walks, but she sensed an underlying accusation beneath the joke, and she felt guilty; he'd surrendered his own dog, and she was partly to blame.

They finished their loop, but she continued on, walking briskly past her building's entrance. Maybe she could catch the shelter before the office closed.

Her phone buzzed with a new email from Jaime. *CON-FIRMED: BOTH MAT AND OWEN LLOYD ARE DANGEROUS.* She swiped it away and dialed the shelter.

"Underdogs, this is Crystal."

"Hi, this is—" Who was she? Emily's ex-dad's girlfriend? "Um, my name is Ava Simon. I'm calling about a dog that was dropped off at your shelter a few months ago. Emily . . . Putnam?" The connection on the phone was bad. She pressed her phone harder against her ear. "Her owner, Mat Putnam, had to surrender her because of a job relocation, and then she was adopted by a family in Queens. I'm sure this is a little unusual, but his circumstances have changed, and I'm just wondering—I'm hoping that it's not too late to get her back from that family. He's feeling a lot of regret about it."

"Okay," the woman said. "Let me see ... What was the name again?"

Ava pressed a finger into her other ear to hear better while Brutus wound around her legs. "Emily Putnam."

"The name of the human."

"Mat Putnam. Mathew."

Ava waited, squinting against a warm wind.

"Putnam ... Oh, him."

"I know it's a lot to ask, but I'm really hoping I can call the family that took her and talk to them about it."

"Yeah, it's like we told him," the woman said, "we'll keep her here another few weeks, but if she doesn't get adopted, we have no choice but to put her down. We do our best, but older dogs don't have much of a chance in shelters."

"No, no," Ava said. She cupped a hand around the phone's microphone and made her way into her building's lobby, where it was quiet. "She was adopted. The dog is Emily, or I don't know what name you'd have for her, but she's a short, thick basset hound mix. Brown with white spots, probably thirty pounds, pretty old."

"Yeah, that's the dog, I'm looking right at her. And I remember the guy. Tall guy, right? Good-looking? Nice hair?"

"Yes." Ava looked at Brutus, who looked back at her.

"Yeah, he fostered her some months ago but then dropped her off all of a sudden before the foster agreement was up. We've been trying to get in touch with Mr. Putnam to see if there's any way he could continue to look after her until we find her a home. Some behavior problems, but she's a sweet dog. So if you could have him call us—"

The oxygen vanished. Ava stood in the lobby and hung up while the woman was still talking. She quickly reviewed the facts and tried to arrange them in a way that rationalized this new information. What had Mat said about Emily, exactly?

Had he exaggerated? Had she extrapolated? She wanted to believe there was a perfect explanation, but something felt deeply wrong.

Back in the apartment, she found Mat taking a stack of plates from her Appealing Dining Table to the sink. He looked over his shoulder and smiled. "You know what I've been thinking? Isn't it cute that we're reversing gender roles, Lamby?"

"Mat . . ." She wasn't sure how she would continue.

"What's up?" His smile softened and then quickly fell away. "What's wrong? Are you hurt?"

Ava searched for the words. She could start with a question or she could start with a fact. Anger and confusion competed for tone. "I just got off the phone with Underdogs."

An unidentifiable emotion flickered across Mat's face. His whole body tensed.

"They said they've been trying to reach you about Emily. They said that she wasn't yours—that you were only fostering her. What's going on?"

Mat looked at the counter and fidgeted with the Courteous Dishrag, folding it into several rectangles. "Lamby," he said.

Ava stared at him.

"Okay," he said calmly, as if he were about to explain something to a child. "I'm sorry if you got the wrong impression. I told you she was a rescue."

"I think it's a reasonable assumption that you own the dog that lives with you—"

"And I'm sorry that I didn't correct your unspoken assumption that I'd had her since—what, college? Childhood?"

"I didn't think she was your *childhood* pet, but why wouldn't I think—"

"What was I supposed to do? Turn to you three weeks into our relationship and say, *Hey, you know my dog? Well, technically*

THE VERY NICE BOX

*I haven't signed that piece of paper that legally verifies that she's my
dog, so please don't think of her as my dog until further notice?"*

Mat was softening his voice, like he used to do at STÄDA
after hitting the neg alarm. "I love Emily. I do. It tore me up
when they sent me to Gambier and I had to say goodbye. You
know that."

"They said you never called to get her back. You lied. It
was a blatant lie. What version of this story am I supposed to
trust?"

"You want to talk about trust?" Mat said. "I can't believe you
pushed this after I explicitly asked you not to. You called them
when I told you to drop it! Yes, I white-lied. Okay? I white-lied
and I'm sorry." He threw his arms in the air. "I'm not proud of
it, but at least I'm taking responsibility. I'm holding myself ac-
countable. What more can I give you? The truth is, I can't take
Emily back because I didn't want to burden you with a second
dog. Are you happy? I did it for you too."

He slumped onto her Practical Sofa. "I was working too
many hours a week to take good care of her, and she deserves
better. I'm sure that sounds crazy to you because you're fucking perfect and can do everything well. But I can't. I know it's
messed up. I know *I'm* messed up. I'm working on it. It's a PF
I'm focusing on this quarter."

He rubbed the back of his head.

"A what?"

"A Personal Flex. It's something me and the Guys work on
every quarter. It's hard to explain." He lit up. "You know what,
I think you should come with me." He stood suddenly, rejuvenated.

"Come with you where?" Ava was dizzy. She felt whiplashed.
She could feel herself slipping back into the crash. How long
had it been since this had happened? She sat in her Embrac-

ing Armchair and breathed the way her physical therapist had taught her. Mat didn't seem to notice.

"I know you're mad," he said, crouching in front of her so that they were at eye level, "but I really think it would put everything in perspective to come to a Good Guys meeting tonight." He took her hands in his. "I just—I'm really working on myself, and I want you to see that. And I know you're not a guy, but I think it could help you too!" He jabbed his pointer finger softly into her chest.

"I don't know, Mat." Ava held her palm against her throbbing forehead.

"Please, Lamby," he whispered. "Just trust me."

40

AVA EXPECTED MAT TO TAKE HER TO A STALE church basement or an elementary school gymnasium with metal folding chairs, but instead they took a Swyft across the bridge to Hudson Yards and soared up thirty stories in a glass elevator that opened onto the expansive floor of a tech office. The room's floor-to-ceiling windows overlooked the bright Manhattan skyline. A thick, live-edge walnut buffet table overflowed with drinks and individually packaged snacks.

The room was packed with young, well-groomed men whose style collectively amounted to affluent minimalism: white leather sneakers, pants cuffed above the ankle, crisp oxford shirts rolled to their elbows.

Mat walked up to a man pouring himself a cup of seltzer. He had tightly buzzed gray hair and wore an unbuttoned denim shirt over a T-shirt. Mat gave him a warm two-handed handshake.

"Daniel," Mat said, bringing a hand to Ava's shoulder, "meet Ava! It's her first time."

"Very nice to meet you, Ava." Daniel's eyes shone. His smile lines were just beginning to show. His warmth was arresting. "Welcome."

"Nice to meet you," Ava said. Mat guided her over to the presentation space.

"Did you not recognize that guy?" Mat asked.

"No, should I have?"

"I just thought you would. He's, like, STÄDA royalty. He's always in the office for board meetings. And he actually hooked me up with my opportunity at STÄDA."

Ava looked back over her shoulder and saw that Daniel was talking to someone who *did* look familiar. "Is that Owen Lloyd?" she said.

"Yeah," Mat said. "STÄDA has an awesome presence here. That's part of why Good Guys is so great. We help each other in all sorts of ways. It's like a fraternity, but less douchey."

Ava looked around the room. Dozens of Strapping Armchairs faced a lectern and a projector screen at the front of the room. Men filed to their seats, and she followed Mat as he made his way toward an empty row. "Ava," he said, a hint of condescension in his smile, "you should go sit over there." He pointed to a different part of the room, a far corner. The seating in that section was different; instead of Strapping Armchairs, a couple rows of Attentive Desk Chairs had begun filling with people. Ava noticed that these people were all women.

"Sponsor seating," Mat said.

"But I'm not a sponsor," Ava said.

"Not *now*," Mat said. "But you totally could be. You'd honestly be a natural." He looked proud of her. "Look, don't you recognize someone over there?"

Ava squinted at the sponsor section. All the women looked

like they could star in a One shampoo subway campaign. But one of them did catch her eye. She was thin and birdlike, with long dark hair. "That woman," she said. "The one I saw at your apartment."

"Ella," Mat said. He had caught Ella's eye and waved at her. Ella smiled and pointed at Ava, her eyebrows raised. Mat nodded and pulled Ava close to him. "She's super-nice," he said. "Look, she's saving you a seat."

Ella had indeed placed a cardigan on the seat next to her.

"Mat," Ava said, "I think I should go. This is too weird."

"Trust me," he said. He took her by the shoulders. "Sometimes it's good to push what you think are your limits. Like . . . meeting me at the dog park? Taking two days off work? Dating a guy?"

Ava's breath felt shallow, as though she were breathing through a cocktail straw. "Okay," she said. She found her way to the seat next to Ella. "Hello," she said, smiling tightly.

"Ava, right?" Ella said, beaming at her. Her handshake was firm and her gaze was uncomfortably direct.

"Yes," Ava said. "So they force the women to sit over here? Feels a little . . . religious or something."

Ella's laugh was delicate. Ava pictured Sensitive Tea Cups lightly clinking against each other. "I never thought about it like that," Ella said. "I guess so. But if I had it my way, everything would be separated. Women-only train cars, women-only workspaces, women-only sections of every room. Believe me, I'd rather be here than there." She waved her hand in the direction of the men, many of whom were exchanging long, sincere-looking two-handed handshakes.

The lights dimmed. Ava had to tilt her head to read the huge white screen. The slide title was GOOD GUYS, and it displayed a triple Venn diagram whose sections read YOU, ME, and US. Men appeared to be joining the meeting from across the country, their avatars popping up every few seconds on the screen. Pete F from Naples, Florida. Calvin T from Silver Spring, Maryland. Louis B from Appleton, Wisconsin. Dylan L from Richmond, Virginia. At precisely nine o'clock, a tall, thin man with a fade and a thick red beard sauntered onstage to an eruption of applause from the audience. He casually rested his elbow on the lectern and stood beside it. He seemed to be attempting to make eye contact with every person there, and the applause showed no sign of tapering.

"All right, hey, Good Guys, I'm Lukas, as you know," the man said, motioning with his hands for everyone to settle down.

Someone from the audience shouted, "LUKE! WE LOVE YOU, MAN!"

Lukas chuckled. "And I love you. Any first-timers out there?"

Ava's face grew hot and she kept her hands firmly clasped in her lap. People craned around to look at the dozen or so men whose hands were raised.

"Incredible," Lukas said. "Welcome. We start off each week by taking a moment to align with our mission statement. This is a weekly meeting for guys like us: Good Guys who want to recognize their potential, reconnect with their desires in life, and make a better world, starting with ourselves."

Ava noticed that a couple of the men were mouthing the mission statement as Lukas recited it. "Every week we do the bravest, most radical thing imaginable." He paused, scanning the room. "We make ourselves vulnerable. We take up space. We open up. Think of this like a workout for your integrity. Each meeting we have one speaker who shares the progress he's making with his Personal Flex, and then there's free mic time for anyone to share a story if he feels moved to. This week we have"—he checked his notes—"Mat Putnam. Okay! Let's put it together for our good friend Mat!"

Mat made his way down the aisle, beaming, then hopped

up onstage. The audience erupted, settling down only when Mat motioned for quiet with his hands. He made his way to the lectern and stood in front of the mic. "Hey, guys, I'm Mat, as you know. My Personal Flex this quarter is Personal Truth." The words *Personal Truth* appeared behind him on the big screen, beneath an enormous headshot of Mat, before returning to a slide show of audiences in Seattle, Kalamazoo, and Harrisburg. "I actually brought someone special with me today. My partner, Ava."

Ava froze as several men twisted in their seats to get a good look at her. She had never heard Mat use the word *partner* before and wondered what effect he was going for. Seriousness? Parity? Tolerance? Ella reached over and squeezed her hand. Mat allowed for the moment, smiling down at her. Ava pictured a chain moving smoothly along a gear and looked directly at her lap.

"I've said it here before," Mat continued, "but along with my sponsor, Ella, Ava has been with me on my path for months, helping me become a Good Guy. Just a few hours ago," he continued, "we had a small disagreement that grew out of a misunderstanding. It was about—if you can believe it—an old dog." There was a small wave of laughter. "I know!" Mat said. "I know. But even small stones can make big ripples in the water. I should do a better job of communicating that to her, but that's a Personal Flex for another day."

There were a few friendly, isolated chuckles from the audience. Ava's neck prickled. *Small stones?* Was he pardoning his lie? Was it small? Was it something she would later recollect with a smile?

"I've been struggling somewhat with helping others question their own interpretations of reality," Mat continued. "Even when those interpretations are painful for them. Even when they are shaped by totally unrelated past experiences."

Some men in the audience closed their eyes and nodded their heads.

"But there's a reason patience and empathy are two of our tenets here." He removed the mic from its stand and began pacing the stage with it in hand, reminding Ava of a televangelist. "Because I—just like many of you—once believed my *own* harmful interpretations. And that closed-mindedness, that *certainty* that our perspective is the only perspective? It's like a cancer. It's like rust. It's like a boulder strapped to your back. It will *age* you."

Ava struggled to follow his metaphors. What was he *talking* about?

He took a long, dramatic pause. "So the next time you or I notice someone struggling to hear anything beyond the noise in their head, gently remind that person of what exists *beneath* the noise. In the *now*. That noise isn't *you*. Those embarrassments and grudges and regrets—those aren't you either. I know this because I *know* you—yes, all of you!—and I know *myself*. Because I'm here, right here, right now. And like you, I'm a profoundly good person, as good as the man sitting next to you. *That* is my personal truth. And I'm going to hold tightly to it. Thank you."

He found his way back to his seat as the audience roared with applause. Next to her, Ella had lifted her arms straight into the air and clapped. "I'm so proud of him," she whispered to Ava. "He has really come so far."

Ava felt claustrophobic. She tried to digest Mat's speech as the next presenters came onstage. One man told a story about how he was proud to have confronted his wife for an emotional affair he discovered by reading her text messages. Another man spoke about how he finally convinced his girlfriend to visit his therapist with him to discuss opening the relationship up to polyamory. The final speaker described getting back on his feet after receiving a restraining order. "Being served was my rock bottom," he said. "But you know, like we say here, it was actually the best day of my life, because that's when I realized I needed to take the time and space to reinvent myself."

Ava looked around the room. Men nodded somberly. What had she just seen?

Before she had time to process, Lukas hopped back onto the stage. "Wow. Thanks for an amazing meeting, guys. I'll be carrying each and every one of you with me this week. All right, bring it in, y'all know how we wrap things up here."

They all rose from their seats and cheered in unison: "This! Time! Next! Week!"

"New York, signing off. Be good, guys. Peace!"

Men vanished from the screen, and Luke flipped on the lights. The din in the room increased as men crowded the refreshments table.

Mat had found his way to Ava. He looked ecstatic, as though he'd just safely landed after jumping out of a plane. "Did you want to stick around for a minute?" he said eagerly.

Ava shook her head quickly. "No," she said.

On the walk back to the car, Ava felt unmoored. Mat's meetings had always been a blank spot on his calendar, and she hadn't allowed herself to think much about them. But now she was forced to grapple with the details.

She was aware that Mat was saying something to her, but she couldn't hear him past a rush of thoughts. What had she just experienced? Why did it feel so familiar? All the Mat-isms from the previous several months coursed through her memory. She imagined the entire room of men repeating the expressions in unison. Were there *many* Mat Putnams?

Mat was still talking, apparently unfazed by her silence.

"Wasn't it great, Lamby? Don't you feel better now? Wow, I really feel *energized.*"

He was emphatic almost to the point of drunkenness. He wrapped an arm around her and squeezed her tightly. "Did you like it?" he said. It was a rhetorical question, Ava knew. "Don't you get it now?"

41

"I THINK," AVA SAID, ONCE THEY GOT BACK TO her apartment, "that I want to sleep alone tonight."

It was difficult for her to say it, but necessary, and she watched as Mat dropped his keys dejectedly onto the counter. Behind him the dishes were stacked in the sink and the counter was crowded with spatulas, bowls, a thermometer, a baster, a clogged garlic press, and her Inquisitive Tongs.

"Oh," Mat said softly, "okay," and she immediately wanted to take it back.

"Dinner was so nice," she said, correcting her tone. "I think I just need a little space to think about everything. Emily, the meeting."

"I . . ." Mat said, rubbing the back of his head again. "Okay. I mean, did you have any questions? Because I could probably answer them. I know it's a lot to take in, and questions are only natural."

Ava felt a sting of annoyance that he was wrestling to control the narrative—that in his version of events, it was Ava who needed to do the work of understanding. "No," she said. "I don't have any questions. I just need time to think." She forced a smile. She went to the sink and ran the water until it was warm, then added the dish soap, step one in what she knew would be a full unit and a half of washing. With each dish she scrubbed, her mind turned over a different aspect of the evening: the sponsor seating, the self-congratulatory speeches, the knowing chuckles from the audience.

"I can help you with those," Mat said from her Embracing Armchair.

"That's okay," Ava said. "You cooked."

"Okay," Mat said. "Fair enough."

But it wasn't fair enough, Ava felt as she worked the soapy water into her Benevolent Pan. He *should* be helping her. She had worked all day. She had only refused the help because she felt bad about hurting his feelings. But what had he expected, taking her to that meeting?

While she washed the dishes, Mat crossed his ankle over his knee and began scrolling through his phone, his silence loud and despondent. She had never been less attracted to him. But she remembered what Sofia had said: *Things slow down.*

It had never felt this way with Andie. Was this what it was like to settle into a long-term relationship with a man?

Brutus waited politely for scraps by Ava's feet as she cleaned the dishes, his tail slowly wagging. She slipped her Peaceful Headphones on and found an engineering podcast—not *Thirty-Minute Machine,* which felt in this moment too fraught. She chose *The Feel,* a podcast that rated knobs, cranks, and handles based exclusively on their hand-feel. The podcast soothed her. She was almost able to forget that Mat was in her apartment. She was almost able to forget what she had just witnessed: a room full of men (How many were there, all told?

Thousands?) pulling one another up off the ground, patting each other on the back, spinning their ethically questionable life choices into something that resembled, from a distance, growth and maturity.

She thought of how Mat had twisted his lie about Emily, first into a "white lie" and then into a "misunderstanding," something for a bunch of men to laugh at.

But of course Ava could always make room for self-doubt. Maybe she should have asked more questions about the circumstances surrounding Emily's adoption. Maybe she *wanted* the story to be that Mat had rescued Emily a decade before. Maybe she wanted that because she liked him so much. She thought back to their tour of the Steinway factory, how well he had seemed to understand her then. That day had felt perfect —and maybe she needed Mat to be perfect too. And maybe perfection was too much to ask of someone.

Ava didn't want to turn to look at Mat—didn't want to see his sad, handsome face. What she *did* want to do was check in with her SHRNK, to slowly unwind the evening and come to a new understanding, one in which there was room for Mat to have misled her and for Mat to be good. But she couldn't talk to her SHRNK here, in such close quarters with him. So she focused on the dishes until the work became meditative, mechanical, and numbing. She would work it out with Mat. He *was* a good guy.

She finished drying the last of the Useful Utensils and turned to him. "Want to come with me for a walk with Brutus?"

Mat looked up from his phone. He seemed nervous, as if he were bracing for criticism. "If you'll let me," he said.

"Yes," she said. "Of course. Just . . ."

"What?"

"Just please don't try to talk to me about that meeting," she said. "I just want to walk."

"Deal," Mat said, pushing himself up from the Practical Sofa.

Brutus had sprung into action at the word *walk,* and Ava clipped his Curious Leash into his Curious Collar, and the three of them walked out into the cool, summery night. Ava felt on the verge of something—was it acceptance? She could not condone the lie about Emily, she could not condone the bizarre bro support group, but she could accept Mat for who he was if she tried. She was a problem-solver, and she had a complicated puzzle before her.

They walked quietly around the neighborhood, and she was relieved that Mat didn't try to explain anything. He held her hand and they walked, Brutus trotting alongside her, occasionally lifting a leg at a parking sign. They navigated past groups of people on their stoops, on the sidewalk, leaning against their cars, outside bodegas and bars.

"Hey!" someone shouted. It took Ava a minute to realize that the person was calling to her. "Ava, right?"

She turned and saw a man on a stoop and squinted at him. "Oh god," she said. It was the stoop where she'd met her Kinder date, Amir Cade. It shouldn't have surprised her, then, that it was Amir calling to her. She froze and quickly released her hand from Mat's.

"Who's that?" Mat said.

Amir had stood from the stoop and was now jogging over to them, checking both ways for cars. "I thought that was you!" he said with a smile.

"Yes!" Ava said, a little too frantically. "Yes, well, you were right. Nice to see you."

"I actually tried calling you a few times," Amir said. "I guess I wasn't as big a hit with you as you were with me. Just goes to show."

"I'm sorry I didn't call back," Ava said hastily. "I actually *did* enjoy that dance . . . recital."

Amir's laugh was good-natured, and Ava was relieved.

"Don't worry about it!" he said. "I have obviously found a way forward. And so have you!" He smiled at her and turned to Mat.

"Oh, yes! I'm sorry," Ava said. "I'm a little flustered. This is Mat. My boyfriend." An intrusive memory of the word *partner* went soaring through her.

"Hey, man," Amir said, jutting a hand out. "Nice to meet you."

"Mat," Ava said. "It's Amir. Amir Cade."

Mat looked at her blankly for a moment and released Amir's hand.

"You guys were at Wharton together," Ava said.

"Oh!" Mat said. "Amir! I'm so sorry! I'm a moron. I'm terrible with names and faces. Hey, man!" He clapped Amir on the shoulder.

Amir smiled at Mat and said, "Remind me of your last name?"

"Putnam," Mat said. He squinted at Amir as though getting a better look. "I think we only overlapped a little."

Ava was worried that Mat would bring up Amir's short-lived marriage as some sort of flex.

He rubbed the back of his head. "So you guys, what, went out a couple times?" He pulled Ava closer, squeezing her waist. "Asking for a friend. Ha!"

"You have nothing to worry about, my friend," Amir said, smiling. "She didn't like me very much. Promise." He winked at Ava before turning to Mat. "So what did you end up specializing in?"

"Specializing?" Mat said.

"At Wharton."

"He did their dual program, right, Mat?" Ava said. She felt responsible for clearing the awkwardness from the conversation, because she had created the awkwardness in the first place. She felt like she was encouraging two young children to play a game together. "The marketing-engineering thing," she said.

"Oh, yeah," Mat said, his hand at the back of his head again. "It wasn't really a *program* per se, actually. They just did a trial-run thing with a few of us."

Amir looked at him with a confused smile. "A what? Who was your adviser?"

"Smith," Mat said.

"I don't know a Smith. Wait, we're talking about the same program, right? Wharton MBA?"

Ava's stomach turned over. She turned to face Mat.

"Yeah," Mat said defensively. "That's what I said."

"Word, okay," Amir said, shrugging. "Clearly I had my head buried too far in my books."

"Clearly!" Mat said, too loudly. He was patting the back of his hair with his palm.

"Amir," Ava said, "were you ever married?"

"Married?" he said. "No."

"Ava . . ." Mat said. "I don't think that's really your business."

"Mat," Ava said, "where did you live?"

"What?"

"When you were at Wharton. Where did you live?"

"In an apartment," he said.

"Where?"

"Off-campus."

"Off-campus where? What street?"

Amir stood and looked at them, his mouth slightly open.

"I don't remember!" Mat said. "Stop quizzing me! What is this, a cross-examination?" He looked like a distressed animal —like Brutus refusing a pill.

"Okay, well, nice running into you," Amir said, backing up as if he were avoiding a canvasser. Ava smiled weakly at him and he trotted off with a short wave. "Good luck!" he called behind him, and she wasn't sure which of them he was talking to.

. She turned back to Mat, who was as stiff as a tree. "Who spoke at your commencement?" she said to him, with no intention of stopping there. Brutus whined to turn around.

"Lamby," Mat said, his voice cracking. "Please."

"How many people were in the program? What was the name of a textbook you read? Who would you say was your closest friend?"

42

IN THE WORLD OF OPTIONS THAT LAY BEFORE
Ava—to demand an explanation, to berate him, to end it—
the only thing she wanted to do was to get away from Mat as
quickly as she could.

Brutus heeled closely at her side. Mat yelled after her, jogging to keep up. "Ava? Are you walking home? Where are you
going? Your apartment's in the other direction!"

"Please don't follow me," Ava said, and she could hear his
footsteps slow. She didn't want to give him the satisfaction of
looking over her shoulder, but she couldn't help but imagine
what he would look like if she did. He would be standing there
rubbing the back of his head. He would be criminally charming. His cheeks would be rosy. His hair would be perfectly disheveled. She pulled Brutus ahead, electrified by anger, and
ordered herself a Swyft.

Jaime lived on the third floor of a sturdy Bed-Stuy brownstone whose entrance was crowded by rosebushes that were

fully in bloom. She hadn't been here in years, not since STÄDA's early days, when Jaime and his roommates had hosted *Hotspot* marathons. Having never before watched *Hotspot,* Ava didn't attend the marathons, but when she'd overheard Jaime ask Andie to bring a bottle of wine, she quietly changed her RSVP from a no to a yes.

Now, looking at the pink and white roses, Ava remembered how she'd frozen in place when she'd seen Andie approaching Jaime's apartment from the opposite direction. That night, like this one, had been soft and cool. Andie held a bottle of wine, her work pants streaked with paint, her blond hair lit up by a lamppost. An old man exited the brownstone, and Andie grabbed the door and held it open for Ava. "Coming up?" she said.

"Oh," Ava said. "I . . . I think I'll wait to be buzzed in." She was strung up with nerves. Andie's smile was teasing, but she let the door close, buzzed Jaime's apartment, and waited on the street with Ava. "You're STÄDA's storage wiz, right?"

"Yes," Ava said. Her whole body tightened. What else could she say to elaborate? *Yes, and what are your favorite kinds of boxes?* She was glad it was dark, because she could feel her cheeks glowing.

"Nice," Andie said. "I'm Andie, by the way."

"Ava."

"I know," Andie said.

"You do?"

A knot now pushed against her throat at the memory. She swallowed against it and rang Jaime's doorbell.

"Ava?" he called from his window. "Is that you?"

She felt ridiculous. "Yes," she said, craning her neck. "Can I —can Brutus and I come up?"

The buzzer rang, and she pushed open his heavy wooden door. As Brutus pulled her up the stairs, she prepared for the impending humiliation.

Instead Jaime pulled her into a tight hug. "Come in," he said, shutting the door behind her. "Oh, um, Ava, this is Chas. I don't think you've met."

Chas poked his head out of the kitchen. He reminded Ava of a woodland creature; he was small and fit, and wore jeans and no shirt beneath a Homey Apron that was covered in flour. "Hi!" he said, leaning backward to greet Ava. "Nice to meet you! And you," he said to Brutus, who charged toward him happily.

"Oh no," Ava said, turning to Jaime. "I'm sorry. I crashed your night."

"Not at all. I'm glad you came," Jaime said. "Sit down. Are you okay?"

"I don't know. No."

"Oh, Ava," he said, leading her to his living room with a hand on her shoulder.

His Dignified Sofa was an early STÄDA design reupholstered with floral fabric. Beside it was a pine Very Nice Box, upon which he set an Affable Glass of red wine. That Jaime owned a Very Nice Box touched Ava, and he must have registered the look on her face. "Elegant, simple, useful," he said. "Classic Ava Simon."

Brutus climbed up next to Ava and placed his head heavily in her lap. "I can kick him off," she said.

"Why?" Jaime said. "He's happy there." He poured himself some wine and sat next to her.

"I'm sorry I ruined your date," Ava said. "I feel like a complete mess. Where are your roommates?"

"I really don't think it's possible for you to be a mess," Jaime said. "And I don't know that *date* is really the right word, given that Chas and I have lived together for almost a year now. No more roommates."

"What?" she whispered. "Why didn't I know that?"

"You didn't really ask," he said, shrugging. "You've had a lot going on."

"God, I've been so self-involved," Ava said.

Chas poked his head out of the kitchen again. He'd removed his Homey Apron, revealing faded top-surgery scars. His boxer briefs peeked out from behind the waistband of his jeans. He was pointing a Serious Knife at Jaime and Ava. "Who wants pie?"

"We do," Jaime said.

Ava wasn't sure whether she was hungry, exhausted, wired . . . she barely knew which direction was up. She looked around the living room, which was outfitted with custom shelving, aesthetically pleasing air filters, healthy-looking plants, and photos of Jaime and Chas together. A keyboard sat in the corner of the room.

"That's Chas's," Jaime said.

"He's a musician?"

"A really good one," Jaime said. "He's at Juilliard. I got stood up by my Kinder date and saw him perform, alone. Now I'm very pro getting stood up."

"I can't believe I knew none of this," Ava said. "I'm so sorry I never asked."

"It's okay," Jaime said, topping off her wine. "So. Are you ready to talk about it?"

"I just came from a Good Guys meeting with Mat. Owen Lloyd was there too. You were right about them."

"I *knew* Owen was probably one of them. I can't believe you could even tolerate being in the same room as them. I mean, when I saw them in that footage, I—it's just so scary."

Ava paused. She hadn't opened Jaime's email, and after all she'd endured that evening, she didn't have it in her to follow him on yet another paranoid witch hunt. She tried to imagine what in the footage could possibly be construed as "scary." The weird handshake they did? She felt a deep embarrassment at the thought of anyone else witnessing it, especially Jaime.

Jaime noticed her hesitation. "Please tell me you watched it."

"Yes, I watched it," Ava said. The lie was deeply relieving. "I just don't want to talk about it."

"I don't see what there is to talk about, Ava. I mean, they're criminals! How can you—"

"I said I didn't want to get into it, okay? I'm here now. Can you please just be supportive? I didn't come here to defend myself. I came here for a friend."

Jaime softened. "Of course," he said. "Whenever you're ready to talk, we'll talk. You can stay here as long as you need."

Chas came out of the kitchen and set down two Simple Dessert Plates, each with a wedge of pie and a dollop of cream. "I'm heading out to practice," he said, rubbing Brutus's head. "I'm sorry to run. You know how those practice rooms are. It's like a reality show trying to get one."

"Win the reality show for me," Jaime said.

"I will, baby," Chas said, kissing him on the cheek.

"Can you believe how much I lucked out?" Jaime said, holding Chas's chin.

"All right, all right," Chas said.

"No, really!" Jaime said. "He even makes my lunch every day."

"Wait, those are *your* little sushi rolls?" Ava said.

"Yep," Chas said. "Little sushi rolls for my little tuna."

"Oh god," Jaime said.

"You'd make a good engineer," Ava said. "Those rolls are perfect."

"No," Chas said. "I'm happy keeping a safe distance from all that. Nice to meet you, Ava. Brutus."

Ava turned to Jaime. "Anything else you're hiding from me?" she said as Chas closed the door behind him. "Any children?"

"No!" Jaime laughed.

The pie was so luxuriously tart and sweet that Ava momentarily forgot about her bewildering evening with Mat, who now felt far away, like a distant, unpleasant dream. She closed her eyes as she chewed. "I never want to do anything besides eat this pie. I don't even want to go back to work. I'd be happy if I never looked at cat furniture again."

Jaime poured them each more wine. "Andie probably wouldn't even recognize STÄDA. It's changed so much since she was there."

Ava's head buzzed from the wine, but she still felt the adrenaline course through her at the mention of Andie. "It's true," she said. "Can you imagine her working for Helen Gross?"

"Helen Gross would be working for *Andie*," Jaime said.

Ava stretched across Jaime's Dignified Sofa, pushing Brutus to the far end with her feet. "She was the best," she said.

It was a simple, devastating fact.

Jaime nodded. "She was," he said. "I miss her all the time." He wiped at his cheek with his sleeve.

"Actually, do you want to see what I use my Very Nice Box for?" Jaime said.

"If there's a shrine in there, I'm going to have to leave," Ava said.

"No," Jaime said. "Well, not exactly. Open it."

She did. Inside were Calm Bins holding dozens of clocks and watches. Most of them Ava recognized from Andie's notebooks. Some of them had never made it past the prototype stage. "Do you mind if I . . . ?"

"Of course," Jaime said.

She sorted through the wall clocks first, and then the bedside ones. All of them appeared to be working. She could remember every design clearly, how Andie had poured her focus into each one, never leaving an unfinished design orphaned.

She tried to remember the names of the clocks that never made it to shelves, like the Insightful Desk Clock, which was made of wood. And then the watches, some of which Ava had forgotten about: the Loyal Wristwatch, which glowed in the dark, and the Earnest Wristwatch, which had a bright yellow second hand and no numbers.

"What's this?" she said, pulling a chain from the smallest Calm Bin. At the end of the chain was a pendant.

"Andie made that for me," Jaime said. "I'm so paranoid about somehow losing it that I don't wear it."

From her reclined position on the Dignified Sofa, Ava held the chain up above her face. She saw that the pendant was actually the copper balance wheel of a wristwatch.

"It's from our first prototype of the Straightforward Wristwatch," Jaime said. "Turn it over."

Ava sat up and flipped the balance wheel in her palm. A tiny inscription ran along its circumference: *For JR. With affection.* "How did she even . . ." Ava said.

"It's my favorite thing," Jaime said.

Ava was struck by the realization that there was more to Andie than she had come to know. The thought moved and saddened her. She had been so consumed with her own grief that she hadn't really considered that Jaime was carrying his own around—and that she didn't have to hoard all the pain. It was arrogant to think that was even possible.

"We lost the same person," Jaime said. "We can talk about it, you know."

Ava nodded. She unclasped the chain and fit it around his neck. "One thing I know for sure is that Andie would not have wanted this locked up in a box."

Jaime smiled. "Speaking of what Andie would have wanted for us . . . I know I'm not allowed to ask for details about my nemesis, aka Mat Putnam. But have you had your eye on any-one else?"

The construction site engineer came immediately to mind.

"You have!" Jaime lit up. "Who is it?"

Ava covered her face with her hands. "No one. Okay. Well, I don't know her name. But she's a site engineer for the Vision Tower. She's . . . the hot one?"

Jaime clasped his hands at the confession and Ava could feel the excitement of the crush begin to take shape now that she had named it.

"I know some of those workers! Wait, is that why you've been spending so much time down on Two?"

Ava hid her face in a Supportive Pillow. "No," she said, her voice muffled.

"I *love* it. Tell me everything, starting with—"

Jaime was interrupted by a distressed voice coming from the street. At first Ava thought a fight was unfolding, but by the second wail it became clear that there was only one voice.

"Ava!"

Brutus perked up.

"Is that . . ." Jaime said, looking at her wide-eyed.

Ava was too tipsy to feel afraid. She looked out the window. Mat was three stories down, yelling up at the building. Before she had time to move away, he spotted her.

"Ava! I know you're up there!"

Jaime raised his eyebrows. "How does he even know where I live?"

"He must have followed me," Ava said. "I'm so sorry."

"Ava! Please!" Mat shouted. "I need to talk to you!"

Jaime opened the window and leaned out. "Go away! Liter-ally zero people want you here!"

"What?" Mat yelled back. "Ava!"

Jaime shut the window.

An arrow of panic shot through her. "Shit," she said. "What do I do?"

"Well, I can tell you want *not* to do—"

"*Ava!*"

Mat had begun to ring all the buzzers, and Ava could hear neighbors through the walls, growing irate. Her mouth went dry.

"*AVA!*"

"I have to go down there and calm him down," she said.

"No, you don't," Jaime said. "Stay here. I'll take care of it."

Before she could argue, Jaime had slipped out the door. She could hear a brief, muffled exchange, and then the yelling stopped, and soon he was back inside. "It's resolved," he said, and without another word he fixed Ava a bed on the Dignified Sofa and set a Thoughtful Glass of water on the Very Nice Box. "Get some sleep, Ava," he said.

"Thank you for not saying 'I told you so,'" she said.

"I was *extremely* close, but I restrained myself," Jaime said. He leaned over to hug her, and she let him.

"Thank you," she said into his shoulder.

43

IT WAS DAWN WHEN AVA WOKE ON JAIME'S DIG-nified Sofa with refreshed anxiety: Mat had been lying to her. The run-in with Amir repeated itself in her mind as she folded the Cool Sheets, washed her Thoughtful Glass, and left Jaime a note thanking him. She couldn't make sense of it all, which felt even worse than the lies themselves. She clicked Brutus onto his Curious Leash and closed the door quietly behind her.

In the Swyft home, her head felt heavy, as though it were full of sand. An ache throbbed above her eye. Brutus sat next to her, panting out the open window. She envisioned Mat standing outside her building, waiting for her to come home, but to her relief, he wasn't. "Let's go," she said to Brutus, pulling him out of the car. As she pushed her way inside, it occurred to her that Mat might actually be inside her apartment. He still had a key, after all.

She opened a new chat to her SHRNK. *I think I need your help,* she wrote, climbing the stairs. *Something happened last night.*

An ellipsis appeared. Ava was so focused on the screen that she didn't immediately notice that something had fallen from the crack in her apartment door when she pushed it open.

She picked up what had dropped—a manila envelope—while Brutus whined at her feet. "I know," she said. "I know you're hungry." She filled his Favorite Dog Bowl and sat on her Practical Sofa, turning the envelope over.

A note was scribbled on the front of it, and she recognized Mat's crude handwriting immediately.

Lamby,

You know how I'm paperless? Well, this is the exception.

Inside the envelope was a newspaper clipping. The paper was soft and the edges were worn, and pale crease lines crossed the center. It had been folded and unfolded many times over, and each corner contained a small hole, as though it had once been tacked to a bulletin board.

She read the headline: "Haverford Sanitation Worker Saves Young Man from Dumpster."

The image was of a burly man in polyester safety gear and a hardhat who had his arm around a tall, lanky teenager with long hair, sunken shoulders, and a crumpled, stained suit and tie. The sanitation worker beamed at the camera, but the teenager looked off to the side. Ava read it while Brutus licked his Favorite Dog Bowl clean.

Haverford, PA:

A young man was rescued from a Dumpster outside the Haverford School yesterday by Haverford Township sanitation worker Keith Kowalski, after he was apparently locked inside it by one or multiple classmates. The victim has been identified as eighteen-year-old Mathew Putnam. Mr. Kowalski discovered Mr. Putnam during his routine garbage route.

"Heard banging, heard a voice," Mr. Kowalski said. "Opened it up, there he was. Anyone would have pulled him out. My son gets bullied, so I was especially sensitive to it."

Mr. Putnam demurred when asked about the events leading up to the incident. "Just some guys joking around," he said.

But he was reportedly inside the Dumpster for nearly eight hours. When asked why he was in a suit, Mr. Putnam responded that he had been on his way to an interview at the University of Pennsylvania, where he hoped to enroll. "That interview would have been today," he said. "I missed it."

Mr. Putnam's father, Neil Putnam, offered the following comment: "They can stuff my son in a Dumpster, but I'm getting him into Penn come hell or high water."

Mr. Putnam says he will not press charges and has refused to name any of his peers involved in the incident. This is a developing story.

Ava reread the article, turning it over in case there was more. But no; there was only an ad for a diner in Bryn Mawr. She studied the photograph again. The boy in the photo, the look in his eye, reminded her of the way Brutus would look up at her in the rain: betrayed, hopeless.

She pulled out her phone and saw that her SHRNK had written back. *Of course, Ava. What's going on?*

She closed the window and opened a text to Mat. *You can come over to talk,* she wrote. *I'll be leaving soon.*

I love you, Lamby. On my way.

It wasn't long before he knocked meekly on her door. He looked sheepish and bedraggled, not unlike the photo in the newspaper clipping, aside from the long scraggly hair.

"Where did you sleep?" she said.

"I got a Float-Home," he said. "Can I sit?"

Ava nodded.

"So you read it?" Mat sat next to her on her Practical Sofa.

Ava nodded again. "Mat," she said, "I don't—"

"I know," he said. "But listen. When I was a kid, I wasn't like this." He gestured to himself. "I had no self-confidence. I was tormented at school by these kids whose dads basically owned the school. I wasn't safe anywhere. But my parents paid crazy money for high school, so I didn't want to complain. Some kids rebel, but I decided to work really, really hard. I convinced myself that if I worked hard enough I could get away from the Main Line forever. I was completely focused on getting into Penn, and I wanted it more than anything. That was the dream. Penn, then Wharton."

He was sitting very still, and his gaze was so direct that Ava had to look away.

"The day of my interview, I left school early to give myself plenty of time to get to Penn's admissions office. And who's in the parking lot? Scott fucking McCormack. The *worst.* He was pissed. He'd been trying to intimidate me, to get me to ditch my interview, because he knew Penn would only accept a certain number of applicants from our school, and he was one of them. He knew I was smarter and worked harder. I tried to get in my car, but he was quicker. He punched me in the ribs and shoved me into the Dumpster behind the auditorium. I can still hear the sound of him kicking the metal from the outside. I was in there for what felt like an eternity until a guy came to collect the trash. I missed my interview, and I didn't get in. Penn, Wharton, down the drain. Over. Ava?"

She had closed her eyes and held the bridge of her nose. "But your dad . . ." she said. "Your dad said he'd make sure you got in."

"My dad thought he could bribe his way into anything," Mat said. "Well, not this time. And that quote certainly didn't help." He gazed at her expectantly. "Don't you get it?" he said. "This was my ticket out. And it just, like . . . *evaporated.*"

She did get it. His future had been shattered, and he had tried to restore it. The same urge had chased her after the accident; how many times had she tried to rewrite the facts of it? How many times had she reworked the timing of their departure, the direction of the sun, the speed of the car? How many of her dreams had straightened the crooked parts of her waking life? "I'm sorry," Ava said, "but—"

"No, *I'm* sorry. I just wanted to explain," Mat said. "I don't know why I didn't tell you. I guess part of me was worried you'd judge me."

"It's not an excuse," Ava said. "It's not an excuse for lying to me."

"I wanted to go to Wharton so badly," Mat said. "I was so close." He held up his finger and thumb to illustrate. Ava restrained herself from reminding Mat that the interview he had missed was with Penn, not Wharton, and that anyway it took more than avoiding a Dumpster to get into Penn.

His eyes gleamed with tears. "I'm so sorry, Ava." He put a

hand on Ava's knee as if she were the one who needed comforting. "I lied," Mat said, and his voice shook. "And I am sorry for that. You're right, it's not an excuse. But it's a lie that *should have been true*. I deserved to go to Penn, I deserved to go to Wharton. I would have gotten in. Pretending it was true was the only way I could think of to get over the trauma. I just got so swept up in the lie that I felt like I couldn't undo it, even with you. And I trust you more than anybody."

"So . . ." Ava said, frowning, "you just . . . what? Ate cheesesteaks for six years after high school?"

"Honestly? Kinda," Mat said. "I hit rock bottom. Spiraled out. Major depression. Cheesesteaks were the least of it."

"How . . ." Ava started, staring at her lap. "How am I supposed to trust you?"

She forced herself to meet his eye. The question was not rhetorical. She desperately wanted to know. She wanted to restabilize, to return to the version of herself who believed in him.

"C'mon, Lamby, you know me." He squeezed her knee. "I'm optimistic, I'm driven, I sometimes do stupid things because I'm scared. Tell me that's not what you see in me. You still know me, beyond this whole — this whole situation."

"This *lie*," she corrected.

"Beyond this lie," he repeated. He pulled her into a tight hug.

Ava grappled with the facts as he held her. He had lied, twice. He was part of something adjacent to a men's rights group. He had followed her to Jaime's apartment. And then there was another inconvenient fact: she had been happy with Mat, happier than she had been in years. What would her SHRNK say? *Who could you be if you let yourself be happy?* The answer to the question was simple: she could be in his arms, loving him, his flaws included. After all, she had contributed to the flaws; she had held him to such a high standard that he was doomed to disappoint her. And anyway, their relationship was bound to encounter stress and occasional collapses, the same way new STÄDA designs were pushed to failure.

Yes, that was a good way to think about this. The first run of a new storage cabinet was subject to stress testing, during which giant mechanical arms opened and closed the doors at variable speeds and with variable force, until inevitably a hinge snapped or a handle started to wiggle. Then the team would begin again, this time with better hardware. There were always at least five failures, even with the best, most well-conceived designs. The Very Nice Box had undergone seven. As Mat held her, Ava imagined a screwdriver rotating clockwise, tightening a hinge.

"Okay," she said, releasing herself from his embrace. "Why don't I make us some eggs and toast."

"Scrambled, with a little cheese, the way I like?" Mat said.

As the butter melted on her Eternal Cast-Iron Pan, Ava opened the conversation with her SHRNK. *Never mind,* she wrote. *I'm working it out.*

44

AVA ACCEPTED MAT BACK INTO HER LIFE THE same way she had accepted, after the accident, the screw in her wrist. It was unfamiliar at first, having him back. But after a few days the ease of their reinstated routine overshadowed her doubt. It took energy to be angry, and Ava couldn't resist the comfort of normalcy. Mat went to his Good Guys meetings but never threatened to take Ava along again, or to tell her about his Personal Flex. She was grateful for that. He drove her to work each morning and picked her up. She was grateful for that too. He cooked her dinner, walked Brutus during the day, and worked a handful of freelance jobs on her Practical Sofa. It wasn't long before the Wharton lie was just an asterisk next to the fact of their relationship. Mat had padded his résumé, but he'd been good at the job. He hadn't really hurt anyone, and Ava knew she had overreacted.

Also an asterisk: the site engineer. Ava was embarrassed that she had prematurely disclosed her crush to Jaime. She wished she could strike the admission from the record. But Jaime apparently wanted to do the opposite.

She had successfully dodged his questions by busying herself with this year's Solstice Party, which would be celebrating the Very Nice Box. Ava was quietly proud—its sales surpassed this year's runner-up, the Frank Dresser, by a significant margin.

But now that the day of the party had arrived and her work was done, she met up with Jaime for lunch knowing that she could no longer dodge the subject of the woman in the hardhat or, worse, Mat.

"Okay, which one is she?" Jaime said, peering out the window.

"I don't know what you mean," Ava lied.

"Yes you do," Jaime said. "Tell me!"

"Oh god," Ava said. "It's not even a crush. I just like the way she works, that's all. I admire it."

"Whatever you want to call it," Jaime said. "Which one? Show me."

Ava pointed out the window. "That one. In the red crew shirt and hardhat. But it's not a crush." The woman was directing a large truck as it backed up toward the Vision Tower. She raised her hands for the driver to stop, then hopped on the back of the truck and pulled open its doors.

"Wait, wait, wait," Jaime said. "That's Dev! The first time I saw her was on my Vandals footage, and I asked her for some help tracking down a couple kids who were messing with the construction site. And actually she told me something kind of crazy."

"Crazy how?" Ava said. She watched a crew of men carry planks of wood out of the truck.

"Apparently STÄDA begged her to sign on to the construction project. She told me STÄDA Corporate has cut all sorts of corners with the Vision Tower."

"Like what?"

"Building code violations, environmental codes, all sorts of stuff. Apparently that little steam cloud can't even pass an environmental impact test." He looked smugly at Ava. "Once again I am refraining from saying 'I told you so.' Also, there are apparently huge structural problems because of a glass-bottom lap pool Corporate demanded they build. Dev said she thinks the Department of Buildings was bribed to keep quiet about everything."

"You've just been keeping this to yourself?" Ava said.

"You've been busy with the Solstice Party," Jaime said.

"What a mess," Ava said, squinting out the window.

"More importantly," Jaime said, "she's hot. Let me text her to see if she's single. And the construction site isn't that far away. We could walk over there now, see what she's up to."

"No," Ava said. "Absolutely not. I don't care who it is. I just respect her skill." She felt her cheeks burning and cleared her throat. "Jaime, I—I have to tell you something. You're not going to like it, but I trust you."

Jaime put away his phone, opened his Humble Lunchbox, and began spooning vegetables and tofu into a lettuce cup.

"Are you okay? Did Mat try to get in touch with you? Did you forget to change your locks? Because I told him he better not try to, that you were filing a restraining order."

"You *what*?" Ava said.

"It definitely shut him up."

Ava closed her eyes. "This is what I wanted to talk to you about. I know you hate him and think he's irredeemable, but—"

"Ava . . ."

"But we talked about it—all of it," she said. "And I've come to understand his point of view and why he did what he did."

"What? Ava, how?" Jaime waved a hand in front of her face. "Ava, is that you?"

Ava swatted his hand away. "Don't be condescending. It's complicated."

"No it's not!"

Her neck became hot. "He's actually *not* a fraud. I mean yes, he lied on his résumé and is into weird self-help for boys. Yes. I know." She waved off Jaime, who had begun to interject. "But . . . this horrible thing happened to him." She described the article, and Jaime listened without interrupting, his expression inscrutable, which made Ava feel conscious of every word she spoke. "You can look up the article," she said. "In a strange way, it explains a lot."

"So because he got stuffed into a Dumpster a decade ago, you're just . . . okay with all of it? That's it? He's forgiven? Ava, you saw the footage I sent you. He's dangerous!"

"I would hardly call him *dangerous*," Ava said.

"You're refusing to acknowledge what's right in front of you!"

"Please don't lecture me," Ava said sharply. "Maybe you wouldn't have forgiven him, but I did."

Jaime's expression hardened. He shook his head. "I really don't get you."

"You were supportive the other night," Ava said. "Why can't you be that way now? Why does it always have to be on your terms?"

"I'm trying to be a good friend," Jaime said. "I'm once again trying to protect you. Not that you'd return the favor."

"What is that supposed to mean?"

"Where were you when he reassigned me to that stupid Vandals program? I *liked* my job. I *liked* Engineering. I *liked* working with you. He basically demoted me because I wasn't falling all over him."

"What could I have done?" Ava said. "Judith wouldn't have let you leave."

"You didn't know that, and you didn't even try." Jaime's eyes shone. "You know what, I'm done. I can't waste any more of my energy trying to pull you out of your denial."

Ava shut her Sensible Bento Box. "I need to get back to work," she said.

"Fine," Jaime said, "but don't expect me to pick up the pieces the next time."

She made her way to the elevators and back to her desk, feeling indignant and hurt. That was fine. She could put that energy to work. Helen Gross had asked her for a new scratching post design by the end of the month, and Ava was going to deliver. She was building an Intoxicating Scratching Post, a wall-mounted fixture made of sisal and a base that she would prototype in wood and metal. She could trick herself into caring about it. She focused on the design until all other thoughts disappeared.

She completed a rendering just as a text arrived from Mat: he was around the corner from the Simple Tower. He was going to take her out to dinner before the Solstice Party. Ava knew that she would likely be the one picking up the bill—his job with Praxis hadn't started yet—but she didn't mind. She had the money, and she had learned to consider the time Mat spent with her as a form of currency. After dinner Mat would drop her off at the Simple Tower, where she would make a quick appearance at the Solstice Party, long enough to satisfy the Spirit team. And Mat would be waiting for her in the parking lot, ready to drive her home the moment she wanted to leave.

She made her way down the elevator and to the parking lot just as he pulled up. When she got into his car, he leaned over to kiss her. His lips were warm. "Hey, Lamby," he said. "How was your day?"

"Good, the usual," she said.

Mat put the car in Drive and turned on an episode of

Thirty-Minute-Machine. "I'm a fastidious guy," the caller said. "But I find cat litter all over my apartment. It's in my bedding, on the kitchen counter, you name it. I've tried every litter on the market. They all track. I want a simple, functional litter box that keeps the tracking at bay and goes with my Scandi design taste."

"Well, good luck with *that*," Ava said, though she was already sorting out solutions in her head. A lid with slats or holes? A multilevel box?

"So glad we have a dog," Mat said. A breeze filtered through his open window.

We, Ava thought. She forced away a memory of Emily and listened as the hosts of *Thirty-Minute Machine* began to brainstorm; she was satisfied to hear them float the possibility of slats. "Where are we going for dinner?" she asked.

"I thought you'd never ask!" Mat said. "Recognize the route we're taking?"

"Back to my apartment?"

"Kinda!"

He pointed ahead. NASTY PIZZA.

"Oh my god," Ava said, smiling.

"I *told* you we would go there one day, and I'm a man of my word."

Ava knew not to challenge his proclamation. He parked outside the restaurant, and together they walked inside. It was small and packed, with flickering lighting and tall, circular tables. They ordered at the counter.

"I know this isn't like me," Ava said as the cashier rang them up, "but I am actually looking forward to the Solstice Party. Planning with Spirit was actually fun. They're raffling off all sorts of crazy stuff this year."

"Totally," Mat said, but he sounded bored and scanned the restaurant for an empty table. "I think those people are leaving, so I'll grab their spot if you're okay to pay?" Ava nodded. She wondered whether she should switch this line of conversation; STÄDA had proven to be a fraught topic between them ever since Mat's failed attempt to get his job back.

"Are you sure you want to wait in the parking lot tonight?" she said, joining him at the table. She set a tray of three pepperoni slices in front of him. "Won't that be . . . I don't know, awkward? Boring? I'm sure I could get a ride home from someone."

"Why would it be awkward or boring?" Mat said, dabbing his pizza slices with a napkin. "I can use the STÄDA Wi-Fi to do some freelance work from the car, then drive you home as soon as you're ready. Besides," he said, "it's not like *everyone* at STÄDA hates me. I could probably even make an appearance. I saw the invite. Plus-ones are invited. Wow! This pizza is actually so good!"

"Please don't make an appearance," Ava said. "We know how that went last time."

"True," Mat said, his mouth full. "Can't deny that was pretty rough." He smiled at her while he chewed. For the first time since meeting him, Ava was immune to his charm. She took a small bite of her plain slice and checked her Precise Wristwatch.

After leaving the restaurant, they quickly got stuck in a snarl of traffic. The sun was enormous and lit up every smudge on the windshield. The *Thirty-Minute Machine* episode was nearing its end. Cars crammed together, spilling out into the breakdown lane. Even cyclists were having trouble getting through the knot. They inched forward until they hit a red light. Across from them on the other side of the light, a woman sat in her station wagon, facing them.

As the podcast hosts mused about AstroTurf versus fake grass, Ava saw something that sent her stomach into her throat.

"Lamby, you good?" Mat said, turning the volume down.

But Ava could not speak.

It was the woman on the other side of the red light. She'd squinted and pulled her sun visor down to block a current of light that was beaming directly into her face. Ava tracked the light to its source: the disco ball that swung gently from Mat's rearview mirror.

The hair on her neck stood on end. She felt a familiar chilling dread, a feeling that something was deeply wrong, and it all came flying back to her: the seatbelt catching, the crunch, the squeal, her mother's voice, the searing white light.

She knew it then, the way she knew the ratio of a golden rectangle.

It had been him.

45

SHE KEPT HER VOICE CALM. "I'M FINE," SHE SAID as they inched beyond the traffic light. "Just nervous about the party."

The traffic crawled forward. Ava craned her neck to see what was going on but couldn't make anything out. They were approaching the bottleneck, but not quickly enough. She kept very still. Her mouth was dry.

Mat pulled a mint out of the center console and popped it in his mouth, then offered her one.

"No thank you," Ava said, staring straight ahead. All the blood in her body had traveled to her face.

"Wanna just go home? I'm sure they'd get over it. We could stream a movie, make it a date night. We could watch 7,000 again, for old time's sake! Though I don't know how we're gonna get through this traffic." He opened his window and popped his head out.

"No," Ava said. She struggled to keep her voice steady. She could feel her pulse against her throat. "I told Spirit I'd come to the party, so I will."

"You're the boss," Mat said.

They sat in a horrible silence. The back of Ava's neck prickled. Car horns competed against the occasional siren. She felt as though each of her thoughts were accessible to him. The beam of light. The curtain of hair that she could now match to the photo of him from the newspaper. Her stomach twisted into a new knot. "I'll walk," she said.

"What's the big rush?" Mat said, looking at his watch. "You don't have to be right on time. It's just a party."

"But the party is for the Very Nice Box," Ava said. Her voice sounded far away. She felt for the door handle at the same time that Mat spun the steering wheel, maneuvering around another car. The other driver lay on her horn and screamed at him through her closed window.

"All the more reason to be fashionably late," Mat said, giving the woman the finger. He hit the power lock several times. *Thuck, thuck, thuck.* "It's actually a more confident move to show up to your own functions a little late. Take it from me."

Ava focused on keeping her breath steady. But the focus only made her more aware of her panic. Her throat felt full, as though the breathing tube had slid back down her esophagus. The AC blasted. She was both too cold and too hot. The puzzle of her relationship with Mat Putnam had begun assembling itself in her mind. She thought of the disco ball. *For me it symbolizes my own personal change and growth,* he had said. Right there, hiding in plain sight. A feeling of paralysis prevented her from reaching for her phone. She couldn't risk getting caught texting her SHRNK. She brought her window down. She pictured an angle grinder cutting a clean line. She imagined the feel of a freshly sanded surface. She pictured a compass tracing a circle. She was desperate to leave the car.

"AC's on, Lamby," Mat said.

"Yes," Ava agreed. "Sorry." She brought the window up.

"Looks like there's some sort of commotion near the Vision Tower." He slammed on his horn for no clear reason. "Maybe there was an accident. I guess everyone's racing to celebrate you."

"I'll just get out here," Ava said, smiling at him. "If you don't mind."

"Real nice, leaving me alone to deal with this," Mat said, gesturing at the traffic jam. He was smiling, but Ava felt the edge of a threat. He ran a hand through his hair. "Everyone else is going to be late too, you know. We're not the only ones stuck here." He leaned across the center console and kissed her cheek. "You okay, Lamby?" The coolness from his kiss lingered. She was desperate to wipe it away.

"I just—I'm nervous since it's my design," she said. "And you know me, I hate being late. Even to things that don't matter."

"It's one of the many things I love about you," Mat said, his tone softening. The honking had crescendoed, making its way into the car, into Ava's body, as though the alarms were originating within her. The sweat on the back of her neck chilled her. She checked her Precise Wristwatch.

"I'll get a spot in the lot," Mat said. "Text me when you're ready to leave?"

"Okay," Ava managed, and she forced herself to kiss him on his cheek before pushing the door open.

She navigated through cars, keeping her sight on the Simple Tower. She just had to get there. She just had to get inside, and then she would make a plan. Horns blared. She kept her eyes on the pavement in front of her. The *Thirty-Minute Machine* intro music cycled nonsensically through her head at double speed. She counted every step until she pushed her way inside, through Security, to the elevator bank, whose screens displayed an ad for the Very Nice Box before transitioning to Ava's STÄDA employee photo. *Congratulations to Senior Engineer Ava Simon!* She joined a crowd of Customer Bliss associates and their dates waiting for an elevator. She wished she had a hood and sunglasses.

"Hey, that's her!" someone said, pointing between the screen and Ava.

She quickly stepped into the elevator, where she endured raucous congratulations, pats on the back, and approving nods from her colleagues. "Hell of a design," Owen Lloyd was shouting. "And hell of a campaign, if I do say so myself." He wore this year's Solstice shirt: On the front, an enormous trophy emerged from the Very Nice Box. The back simply read VERY NICE. The Spirit team had ordered the shirts in red, blue, yellow, and green. Ava smiled weakly at Owen, and as soon as the doors opened, she pushed her way through clusters of people to the safest place she could think of: the printer room.

It was dim and cool in there, and smelled like ink. She sat in a dusty Encouraging Desk Chair and put her face in her palms. The sound of her mother's voice looped in her head. *Ira.* She replayed the accident over again, this time with a clear, horrific resolution on the other driver, the mess of hair. Of course it was Mat's; she should have known it the moment she saw the newspaper clipping. Her eyes welled with fury.

She checked her Precise Wristwatch. The party had started in earnest. From where she sat in the printer room, she could see helium balloons shaped like the Very Nice Box, and an enormous piñata, which—if last year's party was any indication—would be full of miniature Very Nice Box–shaped candies. Her heartbeat was everywhere; she looked up and the ceiling pulsed.

What had Jaime seen? She pulled out her phone and

searched her trash folder, scrolling until she found the email: *CONFIRMED: BOTH MAT AND OWEN LLOYD ARE DANGEROUS.* She opened the attachment: a cell-phone video of the Simple Tower parking lot featuring Mat and Owen. The video was shaky and taken at a distance. It zoomed onto Owen, who was keying a row of cars while Mat looked on.

Then the video panned over the cars before stopping on Mat. He stood beside a blue sedan. Her father's car. He pulled a screwdriver out of his pocket and shimmied open the gas flap. He took a handful of something from his pocket and dropped it quickly into the tank through a funnel. He closed the cap, threw the funnel in the garbage, approached the Simple Tower, and disappeared from view.

Jaime's voice sprang back. *I mean, they're criminals!*

She was numb. The volume of the party had increased, and a man's voice erupted through a distant speaker:

When I say Very, *you say* Nice!

Very!

Nice!

I'm gonna need y'all to turn it up, STÄDA! I said, when I say Very, *you say* Nice!

Very!

Nice! The crowd jubilantly obeyed.

Ava texted Jaime. *I need to talk to you. Are you here?*

But she knew he would probably skip the party, given that Ava was being celebrated.

She signed onto S-Chat Mobile to try him again, but his name was grayed out. She sent another text.

Please.

You were right about Mat

Please come

You can gloat all you want

Her mind spun. She rapidly messaged her SHRNK. *I need help.*

The familiar ellipsis appeared. *Are you safe?* her SHRNK wrote. *Where are you?*

In the printer room at STÄDA. I don't know what to do.

Take a deep breath, her SHRNK wrote. *Can you tell me what's going on? I can order emergency services.*

Mat was the driver, Ava wrote.

What driver?

He was driving the other car. From the accident.

Another ellipsis appeared and stuck on the screen. Ava fired off her messages in quick succession.

Don't ask me how I know

I just do

She heard the faint *ping* of a phone down the hallway.

I asked Jaime for help but he isn't responding

Another *ping,* this time a little louder.

I'm alone

Ping! Now the sound was very close.

She looked up from her phone, desperate to see Jaime, but instead there he was. Mat. He loomed over her with a look like something behind his eyes had tilted ever so slightly off-balance.

He slipped his phone into his front pocket. "You're not *alone,* Lamby," he said, using air quotes around the word *alone.* "You have me."

46

THE SAFETY INSTRUCTIONS ON THE BACK OF ALL
STÄDA products listed a series of warnings. Don't substitute
generic hardware for STÄDA hardware or else the Quiet Bedside Table may collapse; don't overtighten the handle of the Di-
vine Drawer or else its face may snap; don't install the drawers
of the Frank Dresser in the wrong order or else it may become
top-heavy. Ava knew this scenario was no different: don't confront a fragile, manipulative man with his own crimes or else
he may kill you.

She spoke quietly. "I know I have you."

But it was too late for him to restabilize, she could see.
Something inside him had ruptured. The image that came to
mind was of STÄDA's stress-tester applying 350 pounds of
force to the Encouraging Desk Chair, just enough weight to
bend its back left leg at a ninety-degree angle.

Ava heard the cheeping sound of rubber sneakers on polished concrete. *Jaime,* she thought. *Please be Jaime.*

It was Owen. "Eyyyy, Mat! Long time no see! What's up, bro? What the hell are you two doing in the printer room?" He waggled his eyebrows. "Or do I not want to know?" He gave Mat the two-handed shake Ava now recognized as the Good Guys greeting.

"Hey, man!" Mat said, his demeanor instantly switching to the Mat Putnam she knew—cordial, fluent, confident. "Actually, man, I'm working on Book Six of the Good Guide."

Owen raised his eyebrows. "Oh, bro, that's important. I didn't mean to interrupt. I'll leave you two alone." He winked and gave Mat a hearty pat on the back.

"Wait," Ava said, but Owen was already walking off.

"Just like we talked about, man!" he called over his shoulder.

Ava recognized the moment as an opportunity to leave, and she took it as quickly as she could, slipping by Mat, into the hallway, skirting past Owen.

"Ava! Wait! I think you're really going to want to hear him out!" Owen called after her. "We've been helping him workshop it!"

She didn't look behind her. Floor 12 glowed with string lights and buzzed with engineers, marketers, Spirit staffers, and technical writers. They drank from Pleasing Water Glasses engraved with the first Very Nice Box prototype sketch. A jumbo screen announced the drink menu for the evening: Very Nice Punch, Very Nice Pils, Very Nice Merlot, Very Nice Pinot.

One of the projector screens played, at super-speed, an endless stream of Very Nice Boxes moving through the warehouse's production line like soldiers. Another displayed Ava's employee photo. A third announced that evening's activities, including a competition to see who could build a Very Nice Box fastest without a manual, and a Pin the Hinge on the Lid station with a stock option for the winner. Ava searched for Jaime. She felt like she was moving through sand.

Book Six of the Good Guide. What was Book Six? Something about forgiveness? Superheroes? Little girls? She didn't have time to ruminate. She saw Mat appear near the elevator bank and quickly shouldered her way through the crowd. She scanned the room, trying to locate the single point that was both farthest from him and closest to the exit.

"Ava! You're like a celebrity!" a Spirit staffer said, blocking her view. It was Lexi, the woman who had first introduced Ava to Mat. She handed Ava a bright blue drink.

"Thanks," Ava said, taking it and searching for a surface on which she could abandon it.

"Can Spirit grab you for a quick interview for the STÄDA newsletter?" Lexi said. "It'll only take two seconds. We could probably do it in the Imagination R—"

"No," Ava said. "I'm sorry, but—"

"Ava!" A hand landed on her shoulder and she spun around. Sofia. "Congratulations," she said. "To both of us." She wore a red jumpsuit with the Very Nice Box screen-printed on it. "Look, I know we've had our disagreements, but let me just say, I'm really proud of us. We're basically a Marketing and Engineering power couple. And from one badass to another, I really think—"

"It's okay," Ava said quickly. "Do you mind taking this?"

She handed Sofia her drink and pushed her way past a throng of Spirit staffers into the Sweet Kitchen, which had been transformed into a full-blown dessert bar, overflowing with Very Nice Box–shaped marshmallow bars, brownies, and cakes, plus colored mints that matched each of the personality types.

Helen Gross stood alone, draining the remains of a Cheerful Pint. "Ava," she said, gently swaying. She had taken her hair out of its usual bushy ponytail. The ringlets looked somehow both greasy and crunchy. A roll of raffle tickets bulged from inside the breast pocket of her brownish green silk shirt. "Do you want a ticket?" she said. "They're free if you agree to do a Spirit survey." She hiccuped once.

"No," Ava said, eyeing Helen's Cheerful Pint. "Walk with me to the elevators? I think I left something in the car." She kept her eye on Mat, who was midconversation with a Marketing rep near the elevators. Beneath Mat's affable expression was the body language of someone being held hostage. If Ava had Helen with her, she could get into an elevator and escape. She was sure of it.

Helen appeared both surprised and elated that Ava wanted to spend any time with her at all. "I would like to try the piñata first," she said, too loudly. "Will you do that with me?"

Ava glanced back at the elevators. Owen and a group of three men in red Solstice T-shirts had joined the conversation. Mat exchanged a Good Guys handshake with each of the men but kept his gaze on Ava. Her stomach lurched. "Oh," she said quickly. "I'm sure there's someone here who could do that with you."

"Just one try," Helen said. She was slurring slightly, and took Ava by the elbow to the center of the room, where the hot-pink Very Nice Box–shaped piñata hung from the ceiling. A line of employees was forming for a chance to hit it.

"VIP coming through!" Helen called, dragging Ava. "Excuse us!"

"Please, no," Ava whispered. She forced herself to smile at the various interns who stepped out of the way as Helen pulled her forward.

Someone handed Ava a blindfold, which Helen took from her hand. "You first!"

"No," Ava said, ducking away from the blindfold. The people in line had begun chanting her name. "Please, no," she rasped.

She could feel Mat watching her from across the room. She could feel the seatbelt cutting into her throat. A piece of glass in her side —

"Don't be shy, Ava!" Helen said, hiccuping again, while someone wrapped a blindfold across Ava's eyes. "It's okay to cut the line when you're the star!"

There was no up, there was no down. Left was right, north was west, across was under. She was suddenly holding a plastic bat. There were hands on her shoulders; someone had begun turning her in circles. "Please," Ava said. But the commotion was too loud; her voice couldn't cut through it. The sound dulled into an unintelligible slur, yielding to something else: the wailing of sirens. Her father's name.

"Swing!" Helen called. Ava swung, hitting nothing.

The crowd reacted. "Not even close!" someone yelled.

Ava felt in the dark for a surface to lean against.

"Try this."

It was Mat's voice. She felt him behind her. His voice was calm. His breath was minty. He placed his hands on top of hers and rotated her in a new direction.

"Don't touch me," she said.

"Just trust me," he said.

She wrestled herself free, tearing off the bandanna.

"I'm trying to *help* you!" he said angrily. He smiled good-naturedly at Helen and the line of interns. "Little disagreement we're working out," he said, running one hand through his hair, the other hand holding the bat.

"Get away from me," Ava said, her head exploding with pain, and in the same moment Lexi from Spirit was back, tapping Ava's shoulder.

"Just thirty seconds with Spirit? I know you don't love to be the center of attention. We're just looking for a quick sound bite and then we'll let you go." She tugged Ava away from the piñata, away from Mat, past a crowd that had gathered to watch Very Nice Box trivia unfold.

A recording of Sofia's voice played over the speakers: *How many prototypes did the Very Nice Box go through before the final design went into production? How many bolts are required to build the Very Nice Box? Which of the following props was* not *used in our marketing campaigns for the Very Nice Box?*

Ava searched the room for Jaime as she followed Lexi past the basketball hoop, through the atrium, past the silent dance floor, where a psychedelic image of the Very Nice Box flashed against the wall.

"Ava! Dance with us!" It was a junior technical writer whom Ava vaguely recognized from her work on the Very Nice Box's user manual. She grabbed Ava's hand.

"She can't," Lexi said impatiently. "I need her for an interview."

"I don't dance," Ava said, pulling her hand free.

"Live a little." This time it was a man's voice. She spun around. Owen held out his hand to her.

"I have to go," she said, stepping out of his way. She nearly crashed into Mat. Her heart stuttered.

"Look who it is," he said. "So *slippery* tonight!" His smile was cold. He pulled Ava close, squeezing her ribs. The more she attempted to free herself from his grip, the more his fingers tightened against her.

"Sorry, but I really need to steal her," Lexi said, her face reddening. "It'll just take a sec and then I'll bring her right back to you!"

Ava could feel her breath pushing against Mat's fingertips. He pulled her closer to him before readjusting his grip. She glanced again at the elevators, which seemed impossibly far.

One of them opened. Jaime stepped out. He rocked onto his toes and peered around.

"Jaime," Ava said, not loud enough.

"What did you say?" Mat said, bending to listen so that his ear was next to Ava's mouth.

Jaime caught her eye.

Ava's heart leapt.

Jaime stared at her—at Mat's arm around her waist, at Mat's head bent to her lips. He narrowed his eyes and turned on his heel.

No, Ava thought. She'd have to catch up to him. She'd have to explain. "I'm getting cold feet," she said to Lexi. "I get stage fright. I'm sorry. I have to go. Let *go* of me," she said to Mat, prying his fingers away.

"Whoa!" Mat said, smiling. "Relax!"

"We'll make everything comfortable for you—" Lexi started, but Ava had already torn herself away, preparing to deliver all the information to Jaime as efficiently as possible. Mat Putnam had been driving the car. Mat Putnam had infiltrated her life. Mat Putnam was not letting her out of his sight. She needed an escape plan.

She cut her way through the Wellness Kitchen, where she had a clear view of the elevators. No sign of Jaime. The lights dimmed and the music blasted. The emcee began announcing a first round of raffle winners. "Looks like *Sofia Alvarez* has a Caribbean adventure in her future!" he boomed.

A crowd of marketers cheered as Sofia shimmied her way up to the emcee.

Ava spun around, searching for Jaime, but he was nowhere. She reached into her pocket for her phone.

"Ava!" It was Mat. He pushed the emcee out of his way.

"Whoops! Sorry about that man," the emcee said into the mic. "Mat Putnam, everyone!"

There was a chorus of cheers. Ava's jaw tightened. She was being stalked in plain sight by a man who was beloved.

She beelined to the elevators and pushed the button repeatedly. "Come on," she whispered. The numbers crawled up from Floor 1. She assembled a plan. She would go directly home in a Swyft, get Brutus, and leave the city on a train. She would figure out where to stay later. Where was the elevator? She hit the button again. It was stuck on Floor 3. When she glanced back at the party, she found herself face-to-face with him.

The burned sugar. The shattered glass.

"Lamby," he said. "Come on. This is silly."

She flung open the door to the stairs.

"Ava!" he hollered from the top of the stairwell. His voice echoed down the chute. She was running now, and so was he, skipping every couple of steps, getting closer, the toes of his boots scuffing the concrete, the sound growing closer.

47

INSTINCTIVELY AVA CUT OUT AT FLOOR 2 AND quickly made her way down the service steps that led to the shipping warehouse. The automated systems she had seen during her tour were in full swing, but the room was empty aside from hundreds of Very Nice Boxes.

Industrial fans spun above the iron rafters. It smelled like sawdust. A labyrinth of conveyor belts connected different stations. On the east side Ava spotted a stack of precut panels in a repeating order: the Very Nice Box's sides and lids. Every few seconds a new piece dropped onto the belt and glided along. At the next station a machine attached hardware to each box at a fast, rhythmic speed. The boxes were fitted and pulled along a belt, out of the warehouse through a wall of thick rubber flaps.

A door opened. She slipped behind the stack of panels. The lid of a Very Nice Box dropped onto the belt beside her.

"Ava?" Mat called, his voice cutting through the din of the machinery.

She held her breath. She imagined a screw tightening. She imagined the ratio of a golden rectangle. She closed her eyes.

"Lamby," he called, "where are you? Are you hiding?" His voice had gotten close, and she opened an eye to find him crouching in front of her. "C'mon, what are we, Tom and Jerry?"

"What do you *want*?" she said, although she did not want to hear the answer.

His towering height, his confidence, his humor: all of it was menacing now. Her coin had flipped, as her SHRNK would say. No, as *Mat* would say. He had reached every corner of her mind. Her insecurities, her fear, her grief, were all his. She felt the beam of light in her face. She was overcome with vertigo.

"Easy!" he said cheerfully. "I want you to come with me, out of this ridiculous warehouse, so I can explain all this to you. I know how it looks, but—"

"No," Ava said. She walked backward, away from him, following the steel belt.

He patted down the hair on the back of his head furiously. "Ava, please," he said, walking toward her. His voice had softened. He sounded purely sad, and even now the sadness tugged at her.

But she knew better, and retreated further into the warehouse, running beside the roller belt that carried the disassembled panels. The sides of the boxes ran under a bridge of machinery that dropped small birch pegs with rounded edges and a soapy finish into the predrilled holes.

Mat was close behind. "All these misunder*standings*," he said, ducking beneath a piece of machinery. He chuckled patiently, as though he were arguing with a toddler.

"You can't rebrand lies, Mat. You don't get to do that."

Ava could see it clearly now: Mat's lies stacked together like Cozy Nesting Tables. Under each layer was a different, darker crime. The scheme was infinite.

She searched the warehouse for an exit. Dead ends crowded her—a concrete wall, two roller belts, and Mat, who would be impossible to slip past. Her heart pounded in her ears.

"All I've done is *help* you."

"You—If it weren't for you, I'd still have my family. I'd still have Andie!"

She ducked under the belt and came up on the other side. Mat's agitation was palpable. Components of the Very Nice Box glided steadily between them.

"It was an accident, Ava," he said, slamming a fist against the belt. "I'm sure you've made mistakes too. I was just a kid, and it took me an entire year to get out of bed and face what I'd done after I saw the news. And I got hurt too, okay?" He pulled up his T-shirt to reveal the scar along his ribs.

"The point guard . . ." Ava said.

"No, not the point guard," Mat said gently. "There was no point guard. You weren't ready back then."

Ava blinked back her rage.

"You see?" Mat said. "You and I are the same."

"No," Ava said.

"Yes. Completely obsessed with the same exact moment in time. Don't you see the beauty there? We were both so busy suffering that we couldn't live. But then I found Good Guys. And I saw that you were still suffering, all these years later."

"How can you even pretend to know how I was feeling?"

"I asked Owen to keep an eye on you before I came here. He confirmed that you had no friends, worked late, only cared about your dog. You were clearly so determined to ignore your own trauma that you had no life. Do you have any idea how hard that was for me? How much guilt that caused me?"

"Owen knew about all of this?" Ava said.

"Good Guys look out for each other," Mat said. "It's a beautiful thing."

"Oh god," Ava said. "Is that how you hacked into my SHRNK account? That SHRNK guy I met? Theo Holloway?"

"I wouldn't call it *hacking*," Mat said gently. "Theo saw my potential as a healing facilitator and allowed me into your account."

Ava spotted a break between the conveyor belts ten feet to her left. If she could get there quickly enough, she might be able to make it out. She prepared herself to run as Mat continued.

"I don't regret it," Mat said. "Listen, Ava, I couldn't handle it. I moved to New York to *help* you! You were so . . . *alone*." He shook his head in a display of sadness. "But Good Guys helped me see that there was still something I could do. That in fact that day on the highway was a gift. To *both* of us." He closed his eyes as though contemplating the beauty of his statement.

Ava knew that a better time to run would not present itself. She bolted, but he was faster, and in an instant he was blocking her only exit.

"I'm taking *accountability*!" He jabbed at his chest as he spit the words. "I can never go back in time and erase what happened to us, but I can help you repair the damage *inside* you. I can help you see that *you* are actually the cause of your own suffering! Not me!" He had backed her against a bright, incomprehensible panel of buttons. "Studies show that forgiveness is healing for victims too, not just for the people who hurt them. It's a *superpower* to be able to forgive. It's a gift I wanted to give you! That's all I wanted! And then along the way I fell in love with you! How beautiful is *that*?"

Fear gave way to a different feeling. Not calmness exactly, but focus. The same focus Ava had relied on for years to figure out a seemingly impossible design challenge in the final hours before a deadline. "I—I hadn't thought of it that way," she said, meeting his eyes. "Maybe you're right. I *was* lonely, and maybe I didn't realize how much I needed help ..." She sighed, forcing the words out. "And it's true that being with you healed me of that loneliness. In a way, I'm grateful for the accident. Because you ... you actually saved my life. *Thank you.*"

Mat regarded her suspiciously, but his agitation appeared to melt away. "Lamby," he said softly, his bright blue eyes fixed on her, "thank you for having the courage to see things clearly."

He reached out to take her hand, and Ava recoiled. He lunged forward and grabbed her arm. His fingers tightened around her like a vice. "You were stuck, Ava, and I saved you from your loneliness."

Ava did not have to tell him that he was wrong. She did not have to argue with him as his guilt and sense of entitlement unraveled him in real time. She did not have to, because a loud mechanical churn from above startled them both and grew louder.

48

IF MAT HAD BOTHERED TO ATTEND STADA'S warehouse safety tour before his transfer, he would have known that he was now standing in the perfectly incorrect spot. Had he attended the training, he would have known that four large mechanical arms were about to emerge from four directions, each carrying a pine face of the Very Nice Box.

Of course assembly was simple; the Very Nice Box, like all of Ava's designs, was straightforward.

"Lower your arms to your side," Ava said, "unless you want to lose one."

"What?"

Mat held his grip, but the mechanical arms kicked into motion, and he quickly obeyed. He let go of Ava and lowered his arms just before the machine clipped him.

She knew he would fit; she was, after all, intimately familiar with the dimensions of both the man and the box. She watched the machinery move around him in a series of purposeful, graceful movements. "Now," she said, "stay completely still."

A look of panic flickered across his face. "You're going to go turn it off, right?"

Was it a whimper Ava heard as two faces of the box converged? She couldn't be sure, given all the ambient sounds of the warehouse. The pegs on sides A and C slipped into the holes on sides B and D, until only Mat's head poked out the top.

"Duck."

"Duck?" he yelled.

"Yes, definitely duck," Ava instructed as a fifth, overhead arm descended smoothly to fasten the final side. Mat ducked. The box was sealed.

Ava couldn't help but think about all the stress-testing her design had endured to reach this stage of production. Kinetic stress, static stress, drop stress. Ten years of damage collapsed into ten minutes. She felt proud to have built something so durable.

"Okay, now let me out! This isn't funny!" The sound of his voice was muffled, as though he were underwater; the pine was impressively sound-absorbent, Ava noted.

"Correct," Ava said.

"Let me out!"

"I unfortunately can't interfere with the machinery at this stage," Ava said, checking her Precise Wristwatch, though she did not feel in any particular rush to be anywhere else. "That would go against STÄDA's safety protocols."

She was determined to enjoy the wave of control that now passed over her. Optimal outcomes rarely landed in her lap; they always required a great deal of testing, fine-tuning, and troubleshooting. The effort was extraordinary and often invisible to her colleagues.

So she would allow herself a moment to enjoy this rare occurrence, when things had fallen into place against all odds. But the moment was interrupted by the sound of footsteps behind her.

She turned to find Jaime. "Ava," he huffed, his cheeks red. "I'm so sorry it took me so long. I ran to get Security after seeing the way Mat was gripping you at the party — you looked so scared, I knew something was wrong. But I couldn't find anyone. I finally tracked you down on the security cameras." He wiped his forehead. "Where is he?"

"Jaime? Is that you?" Mat's voice was muffled. Jaime glanced around the warehouse until his attention settled on the Very Nice Box, from which a dull thudding emanated. Ava could not help but think about the Dumpster. She tilted her head, imagining how the sound would travel differently in a box made from metal or plastic, until Jaime interrupted her thoughts.

"Um . . . Ava?" he said, his eyebrows raised.

"Yes."

"I'm sorry, but . . . is Mat inside that box?"

"YES!" Mat shrieked. "I am! Jaime, please. Thank god. Thank god you're here."

"Jaime," Ava said, "Mat was the hit-and-run driver."

"He what?" Jaime said. He looked between the box and Ava.

"Jaime!" Mat shouted. "If you open this thing up, I can explain it to you — it sounds bad when she says it like that!"

"He's also been posing as my SHRNK," Ava said. "And after chasing me through the warehouse he managed to trap himself inside that box."

"Does he know about the safety release?" Jaime whispered.

"Maybe," Ava said. "If he read the manual."

"What are you guys saying? I can't hear you. Can you speak up? Ava! Please! I was helping *you*!"

Ava studied the box. If Mat had attended the safety training, he would have known what was going to happen next. He would have known that the hydraulic lift he was standing on would rise twenty-three inches to the edge of the steel conveyor belt. He would have known that the lift would then roll twelve inches back, tilting the box horizontally, dropping it facedown on the belt. He would also have known that the mechanized quality assurance line would not stop unless someone pressed the red emergency button against the wall.

"There's gotta be some sort of button!" Mat yelled. "Can you call someone?"

The end of his plea trailed off as the box turned a corner on the conveyor belt, away from them. Ava quickly lost sight of which box contained Mat as others joined the belt. They grew smaller and finally disappeared through the thick plastic flaps.

"What happens on the other end of the belt?" Jaime said.

"The boxes are stacked onto pallets, I think," Ava said. She knew this only partially answered his question, but she had no interest in acknowledging the implications of Mat's predicament. She'd had enough of him.

Jaime glanced between the conveyor belt and Ava. "Do you think we should—"

"What? He's a solutions guy," Ava said.

Jaime failed to hold back a smile. The white noise in the warehouse had subsided and the tinny sound of a voice amplified by a megaphone broke through.

"Now what?" Ava said.

"You didn't see what's going on outside?"

"Some kind of accident?" Ava said. "The traffic was horrible."

"Not an accident, no. Remember how I told you about Dev?"

"Yes," Ava said, blushing.

"Well, she's a whistle-blower. Apparently Corporate tried to bribe her to keep quiet about all the structural and environmental problems with the Vision Tower. They tried to make her falsify wind-test results and lie about that steam cloud."

"And she wouldn't take the money?"

"Look outside, Ava."

She followed Jaime to a window that looked onto the parking lot, where news vans, reporters, and STÄDA employees crowded together in an enormous knot. Ava could hear chanting and commotion but couldn't make out the words. Through the movement of the crowd, she spotted Dev with microphones in her face. In the middle of the interview, two people in neon T-shirts suddenly appeared and hoisted her onto their shoulders, causing a fresh wave of celebration.

"Is that—" Ava said, squinting out the window.

"Ari and Kendra," Jaime said. "It took some persuading, but as soon as I connected them with Dev, they were down to help me get dirt on Mat, which was amazing, because STÄDA's surveillance game had nothing on theirs. They showed me their parking lot footage. If only you'd actually watched it when I told you to."

"I'm so sorry, Jaime," Ava said. "I was desperate for Mat to be good, just to bring back some semblance of normalcy to my life."

"I know," Jaime said. "Speaking of which . . ."

"What?"

"Do you think he's going to, like . . . *die* in there?"

They turned to face the automated assembly line, which continued its beautiful ritual. STÄDA's legal team had given Ava a laundry list of preproduction tests that would be conducted to ensure that the Very Nice box wouldn't harm consumers. Ava knew it wasn't heavy enough to crush a small child and that its oil-based finish was not harmful to pregnant women. But Legal hadn't ordered any tests to measure its oxygen levels. Ava noted this as a good action item for the next large container design. She shrugged.

"If a toddler can figure out the safety latch . . ." Ava started.

"Say no more." Jaime wrapped his arm around her and they watched the commotion from the window. STÄDA employees had emerged from the Solstice Party onto the lot. Some of them were giving interviews. Others exchanged hugs with the twins.

"Is this it for STÄDA?" Ava said. "Is this the end?"

"Probably not," Jaime said. "They'll just stick the Vision Tower somewhere else. And the community garden will stay until some other giant corporation tries to claim it. The twins told me Float-Home is already trying to close in on it for their HQ."

"God, that's dark," Ava said. "I guess I wanted STÄDA to be good, too. I don't really know what my life looks like without it. It's terrifying to think about." Her phone buzzed. "Of course Judith is using S-Chat during the party," she said. "She says she has something for me in her office."

"You are *not* going to leave me alone anywhere near Mat Putnam's trapped body."

"I'm not going to leave you anywhere," Ava said. "Come with me." She took his hand and led him out of the warehouse, into the Simple Tower. In the elevator, she leaned her head against his shoulder. "Thank you, Jaime," she said.

———

Judith's office door was open. She stood at the window that overlooked STÄDA's parking lot and sipped from an Affable Glass engraved with a drawing of the Very Nice Box. Her hair was down, and she wore a green dress patterned with hollow white cubes.

Ava knocked on the open door. "You wanted to see me?"

"As it turns out," Judith said, still looking out the window, "the Very Nice Pinot is actually very average." She turned around. "Oh, you brought a friend."

"I can leave if—"

"No," Judith said. "I'm glad you're here, Jaime."

They joined her by the window. The evening had darkened, the crowd had thinned, and most of the news vans had disappeared.

"They turned eighteen today," Judith said.

"Who?" Ava said.

"Ari and Kendra." She turned to face them. "Eighteen! Can you believe it?"

Ava and Jaime glanced at each other. "Is this . . . good news?" Jaime said.

"Good? It's more than good," Judith said. "You have no idea how long I have been waiting for this day. Much easier to be proud of them when they're not legally my responsibility." She sipped from her glass. "Jaime, I have to thank you for keeping the twins under your wing. I know that was ethically questionable, but their futures were at stake."

"Not a problem," Jaime said.

"I doubt that's true," Judith said. "Which is why I'm especially appreciative. Your transfer to a senior engineering position has been board-approved."

"My . . . ?"

"The only question is the department. I suggested that you would make an excellent senior engineer on the Watches & Clocks team. Would you agree?"

"Really?" Jaime said. "Andie's job? But I thought . . ."

"The position was retired, yes. For a time."

"Are you sure?"

"Do I strike you as someone who would be less than sure about something like this?" She opened the drawer of her desk. "Second," she said, "Karl was looking for you."

"Me?" Ava said.

"No," Judith said, "though he sends his congratulations to you. He was here for about thirty seconds. As soon as the emcee tried to call him up to the stage, he escorted himself from the building. But he did give me this to give to you, Jaime." She took a folded piece of paper from the drawer and handed it to him. "I don't know what it says, but Karl recommends that you consider its contents during a quiet, meditative moment."

Jaime glanced at Ava and stuck the folded note into his shirt pocket.

Judith looked up at her Tranquil Clock. "Now," she said. "It's a Friday night and I have to get going to a real party."

"Real party?" Jaime said.

"Yes. My Portuguese class holds weekly parties that frankly put this one to shame. No offense to you or the Very Nice Box, Ava," she said, "but I find these Solstice Parties tacky."

"No offense taken," Ava said.

"That reminds me. I called you up here for a reason." She pulled a set of keys from the pocket of her dress. "You'll probably need these."

They were Mat's. Ava pinched the key ring with two fingers, as though it was toxic, and studied the keys. His only accessory was a Good Guys key fob.

"Why do you have these?"

"He used the employee valet service, so I had him towed ten blocks away," Judith said. "Between the three of us," she continued, "I personally enjoy getting in the way of people who feel entitled to that which does not belong to them. Ari and Kendra inherited that spirit from one of their parents, and it certainly wasn't their father. Now, I don't know where Mathew is currently, nor do I want to know. Everything about that man makes me want to walk in the opposite direction. But I assume he is up to something unfortunate somewhere in this building. I trust you'll escort him out of here discreetly before he does too much damage."

Ava and Jaime looked at each other.

"Good. Thank you. Now, *tchau e obrigada.*"

49

JAIME LOOKED AROUND AVA'S STUDIO WITH HIS hands shoved in his pockets. They'd left the Solstice Party together in Mat's car, Jaime's bike folded up in the backseat. "Wow," he said. "So many classics." He picked up her Exuberant Alarm Clock and turned it over. "This was one of the first projects Andie let me work on."

"It's one of my favorites," Ava said. She sat on her Practical Sofa with her feet up on her Very Nice Box and watched Jaime take stock of the rest of the apartment while Brutus paced between them. She liked the delicate, thorough way Jaime looked at all her things. He knew which items were discontinued, which ones were first editions, which ones she had worked on, which ones were Andie's.

He pulled two beers from the refrigerator and squinted at the label, which depicted an astronaut dunking a hops bud through a basketball hoop. "Is this that subway beer that's marketed for amateur athletes?"

"Mat," Ava said.

"At least it's organic," Jaime said, cracking open the cans. He joined her on her Practical Sofa and reached an arm around her while they both drank. The beer was surprisingly delicious—cold and rough against her throat. "Which showroom do you think he'll end up in?" Ava said.

"Good question," Jaime said, pulling out his phone. "That's something only someone in Shipping would know. And I don't really know any of the Shipping people. But I bet Dev does. I've seen her eat lunch at the shipping warehouse. How about I call her? I'm sure she'd be happy to stop by and tell us all about the shipping schedule."

"No!" Ava said, wrestling his phone out of his hand.

"All right, all right," Jaime said, holding it out of reach. "I'm texting you her number. Do what you will with it."

Ava leaned her head against Jaime's shoulder. "I'm happy you're here," she said.

"Me too." He reached into his shirt pocket and pulled out the folded note from Karl. "Do you think this counts as a meditative moment?"

As soon as Ava saw Karl's elegant handwriting she felt a pang of nostalgia. She read the note over Jaime's shoulder.

Hello, Jaime.

Do you enjoy the design of this clock? The only STÄDA product I brought with me to the Catskills was your Trusty Egg Timer, which I believe you designed with Andie Sawyer. It is my favorite belonging.

I would like to invite you to work with me. We have converted the next-door barn into a small guest house. I have built a little workshop here and have become fixated on clocks, watches, and timers. It is funny, because time moves very differently up here. We have a vegetable garden and my Siamese cat, Leonard. Your partner would be welcome. I would be pleased to match your salary at STÄDA. You know how to reach me.

Warmly,
Karl

Below the note Karl had penciled a simple clock set inside a wooden block.

"I can't lie," Jaime said, folding up the note and tucking it back into his shirt pocket. "This is an extremely good night for me. Mat Putnam is trapped in a box and I have two amazing job offers."

"How are you going to decide?"

"Are you joking?" Jaime said. "I'm getting the hell out of here! STÄDA is officially the most embarrassing line on my résumé. Plus, have you ever looked up the health benefits of living in nature? If I move there now, I'm adding four or five years to my life at *least*."

"You think Chas will go with you?"

"If I could persuade him to get his aura photographed in Chinatown, nothing is impossible." He sipped from his beer and with his free hand rubbed Brutus's ears. "So I'm on the edge of my seat," he said. "Are you going to break down the whole Mat Putnam scam for me?"

"Well," Ava said, "remember how Mat introduced the partnership with SHRNK?"

"Yes," Jaime said. "Never downloaded it. I'm not telling a government robot my secrets."

"You told *me* to download it!"

"That's different," Jaime said. "You were in desperate need of therapy, even if it was government bot therapy."

"It wasn't a bot," Ava said. "Are you ready for this?"

"I don't know," Jaime said. "Am I?"

Ava told him about SHRNK—how Mat had met the app developer through Good Guys, then posed as a therapist, solely to pry into her deepest insecurities and wishes and then to convince her to choose him so that she would love him enough to absolve him from his guilt of having killed her family in a drunk hit-and-run. Jaime's mouth hung open.

"Insanely," she said, "it worked. At least a little. He made me realize I was still grieving, still alone, still empty, still desperate for connection."

Jaime nodded. "Andie would want that for you. A connection. Your parents would too," he said. "And I would too. Just not . . ."

"Never again," Ava said. "Let us never speak his name aloud."

They clinked their cans and drank.

"Maybe you could come with me to the Catskills," Jaime said hopefully.

Ava imagined the two of them and Karl working together around a long wooden table, like in the early days. Her heart ached for the way things had been, but she knew they'd never be that way again. The thought of starting over with Karl felt like returning to the beginning of a path she'd been stuck traveling on for years. "It's a nice thought," she said. "But I think it's time I . . . I don't know. Expand my world a little. Maybe make some friends. Take an art class. Learn an instrument. I don't even know who I am outside of this job and a car accident that happened years ago. Everything else has been a blur. But," she said, brightening, "I'll give you a Devious Ladder to take to Karl's cat."

"And you'll visit me," Jaime said.

"And I'll visit you," Ava agreed.

"Good."

"Do you feel like staying over tonight?" Ava said.

"I'm not sure," Jaime said. "It depends. Do you have green tea? I need a cup of green tea to begin each day."

"I do."

"Then it's a deal." Jaime set his beer down on her Very Nice Box and pulled out his phone. "I'll let Chas know I have a hot date tonight and not to expect me."

"Good," Ava said. "Because we have hours of *Hotspot* to watch. I'm a year behind."

Her sleep that night was heavy and dreamless, and she woke to the gentle whistle of her Lovable Kettle and the sound of Jaime clicking off the flame. Brutus's nails clicked lightly against the floor. "Good morning," she said, checking her Precise Wristwatch. It was late. They'd spent the night streaming *Hotspot* and musing about which of their colleagues was a Good Guy before falling asleep, Ava in her Principled Bed and Jaime on the folded-out Practical Sofa.

"Good morning," Jaime said brightly over his shoulder. "I made you coffee."

Ava stretched and joined him in the kitchen where he sipped from his Comforting Mug of green tea.

"I don't deserve you," she said, taking her coffee in both hands.

"I won't argue with that," Jaime said, elbowing her in the rib. The coffee was perfect. For a little while they simply stood next to each other, sipping from their mugs, while Brutus lay by their feet. There was nothing else to do or say. The feeling was blissful. Sunlight poured in through her double windows, throwing shadows of leaves against her walls. Birds caucused happily in the maple branches. A breeze pushed its way through her screens. She leaned her head against Jaime's shoulder.

Before biking home, Jaime pulled a sprig of sage from his Studious Backpack and smudged the apartment. "Every measure needs to be taken," he said. He helped her collect all of Mat's single-use kitchen gadgets into a Genuine Storage Box, which they set on the curb. "It's just sort of a shame," Jaime said, unfolding his bike. He stared at the box of Mat's things. "Giving away a perfectly good cardboard box like that." He clicked the straps of his helmet together beneath his chin and smiled.

"I had the same thought," Ava said. "But in the end, it's a small sacrifice."

———

Ava sat behind the steering wheel of Mat's car. She cracked the window, then released the emergency brake and put the car in Drive. She removed the disco ball from the mirror and considered tossing it out the window. She liked the thought of it shattering brightly on the pavement. Instead she placed it in the center console. She would recycle it as soon as she had the chance.

There were so many things to do, she thought as she pulled onto the street. She would give her notice on Monday. She would clear her belongings from her desk. She didn't have much anyway.

She would need to get her mother's Steinway out of storage, and she would give it to Chas. She would work up the courage to call Dev for help with the piano. Maybe she would ask Dev out. Was that too much? Maybe, but for once she allowed herself the fantasy. "Dev," she said aloud as she merged into a new lane. "My name is Ava. I used to be an engineer at STÄDA. I'm wondering if you'd want to get a drink sometime."

But maybe this was too much to consider now; it was important to think about everything in the correct order. First things first.

The route to Underdogs was neither scenic nor efficient, but Ava was fine with that. The car handled easily, as though it had always belonged to her. She was fully in control of its movements, and she felt deeply at peace. She turned on an episode of *Thirty-Minute Machine*. Like every episode, this one was sponsored by STÄDA. Normally she skipped through the ad, but this time she let it play out. She knew it by heart.

What's your favorite STÄDA product? Gloria Cruz says to Roy Stone.

Ummm, are you really gonna make me pick?

Okay, I'll narrow it down. Cozy Nesting Tables or Sturdy Tables?

Cozy Nesting Tables! Roy Stone says. *Okay, okay, the Very Nice Box or Peaceful Headphones?*

You literally can't compare those two things! Gloria shouts.

Yes you can! Roy shouts back. *I'm doing it right now! I'm doing it right now!*

Dude!

Bro!

Then Roy's voiceover: *STÄDA. Simple furniture for your complicated life.*

Ava hadn't bothered calling the shelter first. She knew that Emily would still be there. Nobody wanted an old, ugly, badly behaved dog.

But Ava did. She was very good with dogs, and she loved them all for their trust, loyalty, and company. Even old dogs deserved a good life.

From behind their Plexiglas gates, the dogs looked at her hungrily. Their tails wagged in low, hopeful arcs. They craved an order, a touch, a bed, a home. Ava walked down the narrow concrete corridor slowly enough to peer into each enclosure.

"Let me know if I can help you," a young woman said. Ava recognized her voice from the phone call weeks before.

"You can," Ava said, turning to face her. "I'll take her." She pointed inside the last cell, where Emily was curled up in the corner.

"You sure? You want to take her outside first to see?"

"I'm sure," Ava said.

"One more week and . . . well," the handler said, passing Ava the paperwork. "Let's just say it wouldn't have been a happy ending."

Ava buckled Emily into the backseat of Mat's car and looked at her in the rearview mirror. She remembered Brutus then, how small and curious he had been while Ava had driven with one hand on the wheel, the other on Andie's lap; how he'd sat patiently, quietly, through the entire car ride home, his future a question waiting to be answered.

Acknowledgments

We wrote this novel in the relative dark, with no idea where it would lead us. Thank you to our agent, Faye Bender, who saw the story clearly from the start, and to our editor, Pilar Garcia-Brown, who lit the way forward. Thanks to our wonderful team at HMH: Liz Anderson, Hannah Dirgins, Liz Duvall, Jenny Freilach, Mark Robinson, and Taryn Roeder.

Thank you to Brenna Mork Barringer, Robin Carol, Elana Cogliano, Maddy Court, Molly Dektar, Liz Dickey, Amanda Faraone, Jason Holloway, Julia Kardon, Bo Lewis, Laura Macomber, Ilana Papir, and Lucía Sirota for their invaluable insights and encouragement.

Thank you to the Brooklyn College MFA program and in particular to Helen Phillips, Joshua Henkin, Ellen Tremper, and the Truman Capote Trust.

Thank you to Eliot and Téo, who were very patient; to Anna, who is the best sister; to Laura Fields; to our parents, Badge, Tina, Marie, and Norm; and to Jana La Brasca and Marie Rutkoski, whose love and support is immeasurable.